Slavery in America and Father Abbott

Available from the Simms Initiatives and the University of South Carolina Press

The Army Correspondence of Colonel John Laurens, ed.

As Good as a Comedy and Paddy McGann

Beauchampe

Border Beagles

Carl Werner, 2 vols.

The Cassique of Kiawah

Castle Dismal

Charlemont

The Charleston Book, ed.

Confession

Count Julian

The Damsel of Darien, 2 vols.

Dramas: Norman Maurice, Michael Bonham, and Benedict Arnold

Egeria

Eutaw

The Forayers

The Geography of South Carolina

The Golden Christmas

Guy Rivers

Helen Halsey

Historical and Political Poems (*which includes* Monody, The Vision of Cortes, The Tri-Color, Donna Florida, and Charleston and Her Satirists)

The History of South Carolina

Joscelyn

Katherine Walton

The Letters of William Gilmore Simms, Vol. 1

The Letters of William Gilmore Simms, Vol. 2

The Letters of William Gilmore Simms, Vol. 3

The Letters of William Gilmore Simms, Vol. 4

The Letters of William Gilmore Simms, Vol. 5

The Letters of William Gilmore Simms, Vol. 6 (exp. ed.)

The Life of Captain John Smith

The Life of the Chevalier Bayard

The Life of Francis Marion

The Lily and the Totem

Marie de Berniere

Martin Faber and Other Tales, 2 vols.

Mellichampe

The Partisan

Pelayo, 2 vols.

Poems, Descriptive, Dramatic, Legendary, and Contemplative, 2 vols.

The Remains of Maynard Davis Richardson

Richard Hurdis

Sack and Destruction of the City of Columbia

The Scout

Selections from the Letters and Speeches of the Hon. James H. Hammond, ed.

Simms's Poems Areytos

Social and Political Prose: Slavery in America/Father Abbot

South Carolina in the Revolutionary War

Southward Ho!

Stories and Tales

A Supplement to the Plays of William Shakespeare

Vasconselos

Views and Reviews in American Literature, History and Fiction, 2 vols.

Voltmeier

War Poetry of the South

The Wigwam and the Cabin

Woodcraft

The Yemassee

Slavery in America and Father Abbott

William Gilmore Simms

Critical Introduction by Ehren Foley
With a Biographical Overview by David Moltke-Hansen

The University of South Carolina Press

Pamphlet original of *Slavery in America* published by Thomas W. White, 1838
Paperback original of *Father Abbott* published by Miller & Browne, 1849
Paperback published by the University of South Carolina Press
Columbia, South Carolina 29208

www.sc.edu/uscpress

Manufactured in the United States of America

25 24 23 22 21 20 19 18 17 16
10 9 8 7 6 5 4 3 2 1

ISBN 978-1-61117-618-6 (pbk)

Published in cooperation with the Simms Initiatives, a project of the University of South Carolina Libraries with the generous support of the Watson-Brown Foundation.

William Gilmore Simms: A Biographical Overview

David Moltke-Hansen

Introduction

Harper's Weekly put it succinctly in its July 2, 1870, issue: "In the death of Mr. Simms, on the 11th of June, at Charleston, the country has lost one more of its time-honored band of authors, and the South the most consistent and devoted of her literary sons" (qtd. In Butterworth and Kibler 125–26). Indeed no mid-nineteenth-century writer and editor did more than William Gilmore Simms to frame white southern self-identity and nationalism, shape southern historical consciousness, or foster the South's participation and recognition in the broader American literary culture. No southern writer enjoyed more contemporary esteem and attention, at least after Edgar Allan Poe moved north. Among American romancers (or writers of prose epics), only New Yorker James Fenimore Cooper was as successful by the 1840s. In those same years, Simms was the South's most influential editor of cultural journals. He also was the region's most prolific cultural journalist and poet, publishing an average of one book review and one poem per week for forty-five years.

Before his death Simms saw his national reputation fall along with the Confederacy he had vigorously supported and with the slave regime that many in the North had come to despise. Nevertheless reprints of most of the twenty titles in the selected edition of his works, first published between 1853 and 1860, appeared up until World War I. Thereafter only *The Yemassee*, an early romance about an Indian war in South Carolina, continued in print. The tide began to turn in the 1950s, when five volumes of Simms's letters appeared and a growing number of his works were issued in new editions. Publication in 1992 of the first literary biography, by John C. Guilds, and establishment of the William Gilmore Simms Society and the *Simms Review* the next year at once reflected and fostered this revived interest. Yet not until the 2011 launch of the digital Simms edition of the South Caroliniana Library of the University of South Carolina did scholars of southern, American, and nineteenth-century culture have the prospect of ready access to all of Simms's separately published works. With the University of South Carolina Press's cooperation, readers also will have access to sixty works in paperback editions by the end of 2014. Simms himself never saw nearly so many of his works in print at one time.

Clearly the decline in the critical standing of, and historical attention to, Simms and his oeuvre in the century after his death has reversed in the years since. The last three decades of the twentieth century saw more published on Simms than the previous hundred years (Butterworth and Kibler 126–200; MLA International). The last decade of the twentieth and first decade of the twenty-first centuries saw more dissertations and theses on him (forty-one) than had appeared in all the years before. This is not to say that Simms is yet given the attention directed to some of his contemporaries. For the first decade of the twenty-first century, the Modern Language Association International Bibliography lists roughly four times as many scholarly publications on James Fenimore Cooper, more than ten times as many on Nathaniel Hawthorne, and sixteen times as many on Edgar Allan Poe. Not surprisingly, therefore, Simms is not yet included in most anthologies of American literature, although he is a subject or a source in an expanding and ever more diverse body of scholarship.

To prepare to read Simms, it is important to see his writings in multiple contexts. He rarely wrote about himself outside of his more personal poems and his letters (some fifteen hundred of the many thousands of which survive). Yet he systematically drew on his background, personal experience, and relationships in his work. He also shaped that work through a progressively developed poetics and philosophy of life, history, and art. He did so in the context of his very broad reading of both contemporary and earlier Western literature and in the midst of multiple professional engagements and responsibilities. The richness and variety of these writings and involvements make Simms a key figure for future understanding of the literary culture, issues, and networks in mid-nineteenth-century America.

Background

Simms's family history reflected the dynamics that fueled the spread southward and westward of the populations, plantation economy, and society of the South Atlantic states. Simms's ancestry also reflected the Scots-Irish and English roots of what became identified as southern culture by the 1830s, a generation after the end of most immigration to the region. Two of Simms's grandparents, William and Elisabeth Sims, were Scots-Irish and migrated to South Carolina from Ulster. One, John Singleton, was an American-born son of putatively English immigrants, who had come to South Carolina from Virginia. The fourth, Jane Miller, was daughter of two Scots-Irish and Irish descended people—John Miller, of North and then South Carolina, and Jane Ross. Ross's family also migrated to South Carolina from western Virginia, where members lived cheek by jowl with other Scots-Irish families, who migrated to the Carolinas (White, *Ross*). Simms's father and Uncle James migrated in 1808 from Charleston to Tennessee, then to Mississippi. This was after the bankruptcy of the elder William's business and the deaths of his wife and their other two sons. Following the last of these losses, the elder Simms's hair turned white in a week. To his anguished eyes, Charleston appeared "a place of tombs" (qtd. in Guilds 6, 12).

For the son, however, Charleston was home—so much so that he refused to leave his maternal grandmother and move to Mississippi when his uncle came to get him in 1816. Then the fifth largest and by far the wealthiest city, as well as one of the greatest ports, in America, Charleston was at the peak of its influence (Moltke-Hansen, "Expansion" 25–31; Rogers). Cotton culture on the sea islands to the south, begun in 1790, and rice culture in impounded lowcountry tidal marshes meant that the port was filled not only with sailors of many lands and languages, but also with enslaved people of many African and Creole cultures and speech ways (slaves continued to be imported legally in large numbers until 1808). This street life made vivid the transnational nature of plantation agriculture and the fact that the developing region's dramatically expanding borders "were not just geographic; they also were human, historical, and intellectual" (Moltke-Hansen, "Southern" 19).

Even more important for the future author, the expanding region's borders and nature were taking imaginative shape. The West of the senior William Gilmore Simms and the first Creek War in which he fought, the Revolutionary War of the young Simms's maternal grandfather, the backcountry of many related Scots-Irish settlers, all these became grist for a lonely, energetic boy, who spent as much time with books as he could (Simms, *Letters* 1:161). The possibilities of such settings, incidents, and characters were not confined to history alone. Simms reported that he "used to glow and shiver in turn over 'The Pilgrim's Progress,'" while "Moses' adventures in 'The Vicar of Wakefield' threw [him] into paroxysms of laughter" (Hayne 261–62). Sir Walter Scott's Border and medieval romances and James Fenimore Cooper's Leatherstocking tales also deeply colored his imagination (Simms, *Views* 1:248, and Moltke-Hansen, "Southern" 6–15). As affecting were the ghost stories and Revolutionary War tales of his grandmother and the verses sent, and tales told, by his father.

These diverse tales became reasons to explore—in books, but also on the ground. As a boy, Simms ranged through the city and along the banks of the Ashley River, which fed into Charleston Harbor. He did so in search of scenes of colonial and Revolutionary battles and incidents (*Letters* 1:lxii). He first heard his uncle's and father's many Irish and frontier stories when they visited in Charleston in 1816 and 1818, respectively. He heard more on his trips to Mississippi during the winter of 1824 through the spring of 1825 and again in 1826. The first trip took him through Georgia and Alabama, where he saw elements of the Creek and Cherokee nations. At the time, Simms later reported, he was a boy "cumbered with fragmentary materials of thought, . . . choked by the tangled vines of erroneous speculation, and haunted by passions, which, like so many wolves, lurked, in ready waiting, for their unsuspecting prey" (*Social* 6). When he first got to Mississippi, traveling partly by stage, partly by riverboat, and partly by horse, Simms learned that his father had just come back from "a trip of three hundred miles into the heart of the Indian country" (Trent 15). Later father and son "rode together on horseback to various settlements on the frontier of Alabama and Mississippi" (Guilds 10–11, 17–18). Simms recalled as well "having traveled 150 miles beyond the Mississippi" (Shillingsburg, "Literary Grist" 120). The next year he returned to the Southwest by ship. "During this [second] trip he carried a 'note book.'" There he jotted episodes, encounters, stories heard, characters seen, and descriptions of the landscapes unfolding around him. He also wrote "at least sixteen poems" (Kibler, "First"; Shillingsburg, "Literary Grist" 123).

Simms took a third western trip five years later, writing letters back to the newspaper that by then he was editing (*Letters* 1:10–38). Together these three trips provided materials for his writings over more than forty years. "The first . . . produced mainly short fiction; the second inspired much poetry; . . . the first and third . . . yielded three novels written in the 1830s" (Shillingsburg, "Literary Grist" 119). This was, in part, because of the trips' timing. Sixteen years after the first trip, Simms told students at the University of Alabama that in the interval their world had changed from a howling wilderness into a place of growing civilization (Simms, *Social* 5–6). Had he not gone when he did, he would have been too late to see the frontier. Later travels took him many other places and also provided much grist for his writing. Never again, however, did he experience the frontier firsthand. Furthermore, on these later trips Simms was a practiced professional writer, no longer that boy haunted by passions.

Personal Life

After the ten-year-old boy's momentous refusal to leave Charleston, his grandmother sent Simms for two years to the grammar school taught on the campus and by the faculty of the nearly moribund College of Charleston. By then he already was "versifying the events of the war [of 1812]," just concluded, publishing "doggerel" in the local papers, and learning to read in several languages (*Letters* 1:285). His trip west a decade later helped him decide to pursue both literature and a career in law, but back in Charleston—this despite his father's urging that he stay in Mississippi. Upon his return home, he began to read law and also launched a literary weekly, the *Album*, which ran for a year. He became engaged as well to Anna Malcolm Giles, daughter of a grocer and former state coroner.

A year later the young couple married. This was six months before Simms was admitted to the South Carolina bar, on his twenty-first birthday, not long before he was appointed as a city magistrate. Although living up the Ashley River in the more healthful, less expensive village of Summerville, Simms kept a law office in the city. Shortly after using his maternal inheritance to buy the *City Gazette* at the end of 1829 and moving down to Charleston Neck, just north of the city limits where he had lived as a boy, Simms lost both his father and his maternal grandmother. He also found himself attacked because of his Unionist stance in the Nullification crisis resulting from South Carolina's rejection of a federal tariff. Then, in early 1832, Simms's wife died. Soon after, he took his four-year-old daughter back to Summerville to live and determined to sell his newspaper and leave the state for a literary life in the North.

Fueling his ambition was the correspondence Simms had begun several years earlier with an accountant whom he had published in his *City Gazette* but not yet met—Scots immigrant James Lawson. At the time Lawson, seven years Simms's senior, edited a New York City newspaper and, in addition to writing plays and poetry, was a friend (and, later, informal literary agent) to a wide circle (McHaney, "An Early"). Simms's trip north in the summer of 1832 saw the two begin a lifelong friendship, cemented as they squired ladies about and interacted with Lawson's literary circle. In subsequent years Simms multiplied the number of his friendships, in both the North and the South, making them in some measure a replacement for the family that he had lost. Lawson remained the closest of his northern friends, while James Henry Hammond, a future governor and U.S. senator, became his closest friend in South Carolina.

Late in 1833, after his Summerville house burned, Simms wrote Lawson to say that he was enamored of "a certain fair one" (*Letters* 1:73). Seventeen-year-old Chevillette Eliza Roach was the daughter of "a literary-minded aristocrat of English descent" with two plantations on the banks of the Edisto River in Barnwell District (later County) (Guilds 70). The courtship was protracted, as Simms felt it necessary first to clear debts that friends had bought up on his behalf. He also was determined "to marry no woman" before he was "perfectly independent of her resources, and her friends" (*Letters* 1:78). Therefore he did not propose until the spring of 1836. The nuptials took place seven months later, and as a result, Simms came to call the four thousand acres of Woodlands Plantation, with its seventy slaves, home. It was twenty years, however, before he took over management of the plantation and, then, only in the wake of his father-in-law's final sickness and death. Five years after that, he lost his wife, the mother of fourteen of his fifteen children. Nine of the children Chevillette bore him had already died, devastating Simms repeatedly. Five were still living (three sons and two daughters), as was Simms's daughter by his first marriage, who helped raise the youngest of her siblings. Those remaining children—even Gilly, who fought in the Confederate army—all outlived their father. Gilly and a brother-in-law ran Woodlands after the war, when Simms, though dying of cancer, was earning what he could by writing again for publications in the North and editing one or another South Carolina newspaper.

Career

The trip north in 1832 did not result in Simms moving there. Except during the Civil War, however, he returned almost every year. This was because the contacts he made, and the exposure to literary culture that he enjoyed, helped him define his future as an author. Earlier he had written fiction and criticism as well as journalism, filling the pages of several short-lived cultural journals and his newspaper, but between the ages of nine and twenty-six Simms had focused his literary efforts primarily on poetry. Beginning with his first book of verse in 1825, he had published five small volumes in Charleston. A couple had received positive notice in New York, and in the fall of 1832, J. & J. Harper issued the sixth anonymously from there, *Atalantis: A Story of the Sea.* Coming back the following summer, Simms had in hand for the Harpers a gothic novella, *Martin Faber,* and after his return south, he also would send the manuscript of his first two-volume border romance, *Guy Rivers: A Tale of Georgia.*

The reception of these and the romances and short stories that followed quickly made Simms one of the nation's most successful fictionists. He continued to issue poetry as well—roughly a collection every three years over the thirty-seven years that he worked as a professional author. But this output was dwarfed by the fiction—on average a title every year (counting several serialized works but not counting the many revised editions). Then there were the two dozen separately published orations, histories, and biographies as well as edited collections of documents and dramas and a geography of South Carolina. Add to these the revised editions and the further printings and issues of his own works and it appears that Simms saw a title coming off the presses at the rate of one every three months or so. Making that figure all the more astounding is the fact that, during more than a dozen of those years (the early-to-mid 1840s, the late 1840s-to-early 1850s, and the mid-to-late 1860s), he also was editing a cultural journal or newspaper. Furthermore he contributed reams of reviews and poems, hundreds of op-ed pieces and columns, and dozens of short stories and public addresses, which were never collected and published in volume form.

His career mapped an arc. It ascended meteorically in the 1830s and peaked in the early-to-mid 1840s, before beginning to descend. One reason was the popularity of the historical fiction that Simms began to write. When he left behind the law, his first newspaper, and the Nullification controversy, as well as his sadness, historical fiction was all the rage. Sir Walter Scott had fueled the craze, beginning with the publication of his first Border romance in 1814. He died in September 1832. Seventeen years Simms's senior, James Fenimore Cooper, the closest America had to a Scott at the time, was at the peak of his reputation and success, having started publishing his romances in 1820. Thus the way had been prepared for a writer of Simms's historical imagination and preoccupations. Within five years of his first trip north, moreover, Lawson's (and now his) circle became loosely affiliated with a nationalistic and Democratic group, self-styled Young America, this after Young Italy and similar ethnic, nationalist, European, cultural and political movements (Moltke-Hansen, "Southern"). Edgar Allan Poe and other members gave Simms's first fictions positive, if not uncritical, attention.

By the end of the 1830s, paradoxically, Simms, like Cooper, found his success attracting unauthorized editions of his works because Britain and America did not have an international copyright agreement. Further, in the wake of the panic of 1837, Americans bought fewer books. Simms's response was to diversify his portfolio. He turned to biography and history, including his hugely successful *Life of Francis Marion* (1844). He also returned to the editor's chair, overseeing one and then another cultural journal. These were unlike the ones he had edited in the 1820s: they included contributions by numerous authors, not just those from Charleston, but from the region and also the North. The ambition motivating the journals was to connect and promote Charleston intellectually. Consequently the journals more closely resembled metropolitan quarterly reviews in their offerings.

The mid-1840s saw Simms involved in politics, even serving a term in the South Carolina legislature. By the middle of the Mexican-American War in 1847, he had concluded that the South needed to become an independent nation. Thereafter, although he maintained ties with many in the Young America circle, he no longer promoted his writings as fostering Americanism in literature (*Views*). Instead he increasingly emphasized the ways in which his three romance series—the colonial, the Revolutionary, and the border—were making tangible and meaningful the origins and development of the future southern nation and the sad but inevitable consequences for Native Americans (Watson, *From Nationalism*; compare Nakamura).

Sectional politics colored more and more of Simms's perceptions, speeches, and private communications. The rising tide of abolitionism had him aghast. It also fed his growing sense that his position in American letters was slipping. He returned to editing, and his poetry, which was more often explicitly about the South, became increasingly patriotic in tone. Although his first biographer, William Peterfield Trent, insisted that Simms's declining standing reflected the change in literary fashion from historical romances to realistic novels, Simms in fact wrote more and more as a social realist in the 1850s (Wimsatt, "Realism").

The Civil War consumed Simms. As he wrote Lawson, "Literature, especially poetry, is effectually overwhelmed by the drums, & the cavalry, and the shouting" (*Letters* 4:369–70). He did manage to editorialize often and to rework and finish things long on his desk, including poems, a novel, and a dramatic treatment of Benedict Arnold, the northern traitor in the Revolutionary War. Then, in the wake of the Confederacy's loss and the failure of his vision for the South, he found himself recording the loss in a new newspaper, dealing with the trauma in his poetry, and becoming more existential and psychological in his fictional treatments. Simms's old New York friends tried to help. He did edit and see through publication a volume of Confederate war poetry. Yet it is a measure of his reduced stature that the several new romances he published appeared only in serial form. In part this may have been because he was in a sense competing with himself. Publishers were beginning to reprint volumes out of the selected edition of his writings. Many of Simms's works were available in book form, just not new works.

Associations

As the *Letters* testify, Simms had complex, overlapping networks of friends and colleagues. As a boy and young man, he received the friendship, patronage, and commendation of a variety of well-placed people in Charleston, including Charles Rivers Carroll. It was Carroll with whom he read law, to whom he dedicated his first romance, and after whom he named a son. Both men were Unionists during the Nullification controversy. So were Hugh Swinton Legare (later U.S. attorney general) and the considerably older William Drayton, as well as lawyer and editor Richard Yeadon and Greenville, South Carolina, newspaper editor Benjamin Franklin Perry. Also considerably older was James Wright Simmons, who had joined with Simms to launch the *Southern Literary Gazette* in 1828, when Simms was twenty-two. Through him Simms had direct contact with such British literary figures as Leigh Hunt and Byron (Kibler, *Poetry* 15).

The next group of influential friends and collaborators that Simms acquired were members of the Lawson circle and included such figures as Edwin

Forrest, the Shakespearean actor, and Evert Duyckinck, who published several of Simms's volumes in Wiley and Putnam's series Library of American Books, which he edited. Among the many others were poets and editors William Cullen Bryant and Fitz-Greene Halleck. Simms also made nonliterary friends in New York and Philadelphia, such as John Jacob Bockee and William Hawkins Ferris, the cashier at the U.S. Treasury office in New York who, after the war, helped Simms, Henry Timrod (poet laureate of the Confederacy), and others.

As a Barnwell planter, Simms met a widening circle of South Carolina's leaders and literati. For instance his acquaintance with James Henry Hammond began in the late 1830s and deepened into a friendship in the early 1840s. It was in the early 1840s, too, when he again was editing cultural journals, that Simms became friends with many southern writers. He regarded several of them, including Virginians George Frederick Holmes, Edmund Ruffin, and Nathaniel Beverley Tucker as members, together with Hammond and himself, in a "sacred circle." Uniting the circle were members' devotion to the South and a shared sense of the marginal status and critical importance of the life of the mind in a largely rural and unintellectual region (Faust, *Sacred*). Others of Simms's wide connections in the region did not interact as much with each other, but Simms long corresponded with Maryland novelist and lawyer John Pendleton Kennedy, Irish-born Georgia poet Richard Henry Wilde, Alabama lawyer and writer Alexander Beaufort Meek, and Louisiana historian and assistant attorney general Charles Gayarré, among others. By the 1850s, when Simms once more returned to editing a cultural journal, many of the writers whom he recruited were members of a younger generation. Poets Paul Hamilton Hayne and Henry Timrod were two. Often they and a half dozen others of Simms's and their generations met in John Russell's Charleston Book Shop and adjourned to dinner at Simms's Smith Street home, "dubbed 'The Wigwam'" (*Letters* 1:cxxxvi). Shortly before his death fifteen or so years later, Simms wrote Hayne, "I am rapidly passing from the stage, where you young men are to succeed me" (*Letters* 5:287).

Thought

The welter of Simms's works disguises unities and dynamics of the thought underlying them. From early on Simms was convinced that art ennobles or transforms, as well as gives voice to individuals and societies; therefore it must be cultivated assiduously. Without the potential for high artistic attainment, he insisted, societies are not ready for the independence and regard of free peoples. This is where Simms the historian joined Simms the poet. Societies develop, he argued (using the stadialism of the Scottish historical school), from imitation through self-assertion to achievement and also from savagery through strife to settled agricultural communities and, ultimately, to a hierarchical civilization supporting a rich artistic life. It was the job of the artist to help envision the goal, inspire the pursuit, and inform the process. That process was at once progressive and dialectical. Order, without dynamism, stifled development, as did the obverse—the dominance by ungoverned impulses or uncontrolled license. This was true in the individual, but also in societies as a whole. War was necessary for civilization, but its success was measured in the securities of the home, the center of cultural production and reproduction.

Whether in the public or in the domestic arena, "the true governor, as [Thomas] Carlyle call[ed] him—the king man—" guided rather than impeded the forces of change and progress (Simms, "Guizot's" 122). There were few such men with the capacity to lead. The same was true of nations. Neither all people nor all peoples were equal in either capacity or attainment. That was why Native Americans were overrun and Africans had been enslaved by European peoples in the New World. Indeed, Simms argued, "slavery in all ages has been found the greatest and most admirable agent of Civilization," giving education and examples to less evolved peoples (*Letters* 3:174). The degree to which a people had evolved mattered. That was why, he held, Americans had won independence from the most powerful empire in the world. They had done so through their Revolution, led by an elite that felt correctly its time had come (Simms, "Ellet's" 328). By mid-1847 that also was Simms's judgment for the South: the region had evolved enough to become independent (*Letters* 2:332). The hope inspired and then failed him and the people he sought to lead.

While not all men could rise to the highest rank, they all had the same responsibility at home. There the father was patriarch, protector, and head, while the mother was nurturer, moral instructor, and heart. There, too, children's characters and minds were formed by age twelve ("Ellet's"). Children's upbringing was critical to citizenship, and it was through her sons and the support of her husband, father, and brothers that a woman shaped the public sphere. The culture and character instilled in the child expressed and informed not just the household, but the larger society—the people.

"The history of peoples and their embodiments in institutions, states, and artistic productions—these were the great subjects" in Simms's view (Moltke-Hansen, "Southern" 120). Yet "poets were the only class of philosophers who had recognized" this until his own day, when at last "we now read human histories. We now ask after the affections as well as the ceremonies of society" ("Ellet's" 319–20). Peoples or races—that is, ethnic groups—were not unchanging any more than were their politics and their cultures. They either advanced or were overrun by history. Further, new peoples emerged, and old identities were submerged. The Spanish conquistadors were the creation of centuries of conflict with the Moors: their motivation was the glory of conquest, not the routine of trade or the plow. On the other hand, the English settlements in North America reflected the impulse to transform the wilderness into verdant farms and build society (*Views* 64, 178–85; *Social* 8). The same impulse drove Americans westward in Simms's own day and gave Americans their Manifest Destiny.

To explore these facts of the South's settlement and its place in international conflicts, Simms wrote all together, between 1833 and 1863, two romances set in eighth-century Spain, two set during the Spanish exploration and conquest of the Americas and two during the later English colonization of South Carolina, seven set during the American Revolution, and—depending on how one counts—perhaps eight set on the borders of the nineteenth-century South. After the war he published one more Revolutionary romance and two more that, like it, were set beyond the boundaries of civilization. He also left two unfinished romances, also set beyond society's normal reach. These late works, however, no longer had as their framing justification the cultivation of the South's future and civilization.

White southerners had their independence foreclosed by the war. In his last works, therefore, Simms found himself exploring the psychological, philosophical, and historical impulses that led to the Confederacy's demise and what, in the aftermath, it meant to be a good man and to build for the future, however impoverished. On the first score, he argued that the impulse to idealism behind abolitionism ignored historical realities, becoming inhuman in its consequences. On the latter score, he affirmed responsibility for one's dependents and the virtues of stoicism, as well as a continued commitment to the beauty and truth of art and the impulses to the cultivated life and fields. Therefore, in the face of the burning of his Woodlands home and library in February 1865—during Sherman's march and in the midst of desperate circumstances—he insisted that home, or the ideals and past characterizing its potential, still was at the center of true civilization, but only if elevated by art (*Sense* 8, 17). It was wrong to measure civilization by the getting, spending, and mad dashing, or material progress and utilitarianism, characteristic of both a capitalistic North and also many southerners. These traits he often had attacked even before the war, insisting that "the work of the Imagination, which is the Genius of a race, is only begun when its material progress is supposed to be complete" (*Poetry* 12).

Writings

Simms expressed many of his ideas most personally in letters and most cogently in essays, speeches, and occasional introductions to his books. But he illustrated them most fully in his fiction and poetry. By the time he arrived in New

York in 1832, he had formed many of the core ideals and beliefs that would shape his work. His application of them, however, modified his understanding over time. Growing as a writer and growing in knowledge and experience, he also grew as a thinker.

In his hierarchy of values, poetry came first. It was a prophetic calling as well as evocative of the deeply felt (or, sometimes, the fleeting) and thus testimony to the perdurance and transcendence of the beautiful and the human spirit. Yet, as Simms often ruefully reflected, prose spoke to many more people. That was a principal reason why he turned to writing prose epics or romances. He gave his most concerted consideration of poetry's value and roles in three lectures in Charleston in 1854. Over the prior three years he had given portions of them in Augusta, Georgia, Washington, D.C., and Richmond and Petersburg, Virginia. Entitled *Poetry and the Practical,* they did not see print until 1996, as Simms never found the time to expand them as he wanted. On the other hand, his last address on the same themes, *The Sense of the Beautiful,* was issued soon after he delivered it, also in Charleston.

Many of his important reviews have not yet been gathered, but Simms collected some in 1845–46, and *Views and Reviews in American Literature, History and Fiction* came out in 1846 and 1847 in two "series." Beginning with a consideration of "Americanism" in literature, the first series explored the themes and periods of American history for treatment by the novelist. Simms argued there, and in forewords to several of his romances, that fiction rendered the past more truthfully, interestingly, and tellingly than histories and biographies could because fiction—like poetry—required imagination to look beyond what is not known or expressed. The second series examined additional American writers and what distinguished them, for instance, in their humor.

Despite their early success, Simms's romances, novellas, and stories provoked mixed reviews. Poe eventually concluded that Simms had become "the best novelist which this country has, on the whole, produced" but also insisted that "he should never have written 'The Partisan,' nor 'The Yemassee.'" This was in a review of *Confession.* That novel, like the gothic *Martin Faber,* demonstrated, Poe contended, that Simms's "genius [did] not lie in the outward so much as in the inner world." Yet he nevertheless wrote of Simms's short-story collection *The Wigwam and the Cabin* that "in invention, in vigor, in movement, in the power of exciting interest, and in the artistical management of his themes, he has surpassed, we think, any of his countrymen." Other critics, especially in the genteel and Whiggish Knickerbocker circle, joined Poe in condemning what they considered to be the excessively graphic and vulgar qualities of many characters and scenes, and Simms's prolixity and sententiousness, in his romances (Butterworth and Kibler 64, 50).

The violent realism and earthiness of the romances did not result in realistic novels. Although Simms received early praise for his characterizations (particularly of women), he used the romance formula, with its stereotypic heroes and heroines, predictable themes, and conventional polarities. People were on quests or had lost their way or were fighting long odds or were carrying forward the banner of (and modeling) civilization or were mired in the slough of despond or were resisting all the claims of civilized society and behavior or were pursuing love interests. Deceitfulness, selfishness, and greed opposed honor, high-mindedness, and honesty against the backdrop of the South's development from the earliest days of Spanish exploration to the westward movement in Simms's own youth.

It was only gradually that Simms married the psychological acuity of some of his portraits of the interior struggles of his gothic characters and fiction to the historical romance. Helping him think through how to do so were the biographies he wrote in the mid-1840s, but also the incidents on which he focused particular fictions, such as the murder in *Beauchampe; or, The Kentucky Tragedy* (1842). However incomplete the blending of realism and romanticism or of stereotypical and socially individuated renderings through the 1840s, by the 1850s Simms fundamentally had made the transition to social realism in such works as *Woodcraft* and *The Cassique of Kiawah.* Indeed some scholars have considered *Woodcraft* the first realistic novel in America (Bakker; Wimsatt, "Realism").

In some sense disguising the transition is the fact that Simms also increasingly wrote as a humorist and, in so doing, often rendered his late narratives fabulistically, when not writing social comedy or stories of manners. This dimension of Simms's work was largely hidden, however, until the 1974 publication of *Stories and Tales,* volume 5 in the Centennial Simms edition. There, for the first time, readers had access in print to "Bald-Head Bill Bauldy." There, too, for the first time one could read together that story, "Legend of the Hunter's Camp," and "How Sharp Snaffles Got His Capital and Wife," which was published posthumously in *Harper's Magazine* in October 1870. These and other stories and tales made it clear that Simms was a fecund contributor to southern and American humor.

Humor let Simms take up issues that he could not otherwise address in print and still expect to be well received. He did so both during and after the war. The war also pushed Simms past the emerging fashion of social realism. Having destroyed the familiar, the preoccupation of much realistic fiction, the war made the liminal central (Shillingsburg, "Cub"). While his romances and tales had often explored life on the edge or in extreme circumstances, whether in war or on the frontier or on the verge of madness or in fanciful realms, it had done so against a backdrop of, and with the goal of affirming, social norms and development. In the war's wake that goal seemed absurd. Mythologized memories of a healthy past might nurture a sense of the beautiful but could not help one deal with the present. Thus Simms's conclusion, in a March 1869 letter to Paul Hamilton Hayne: "Let us bury the Past lest it buries us!" (*Letters* 5:214). Fifteen months later he lay dead in the 13 Society Street, Charleston, home of his oldest daughter, with the shell holes in the walls of the bedroom he had shared with several children.

Posthumous Reputation

The twenty years after Simms's death saw him often respectfully treated, first in obituaries, later in memoirs and columns, and also in literary dictionaries and encyclopedias. Yet Charles Richardson's 1887 *American Literature: 1607–1885* proved a harbinger of a shift: Simms, Richardson observed, was "more respected than read," having "won considerable note because he was so sectional" and then having "lost it because he was not sectional enough," although he showed "silly contempt for his Northern betters" (qtd. in Butterworth and Kibler 130). Five years later Trent's biography of Simms appeared. It was the first full-length, scholarly treatment. Its central thesis was that Simms's environment frustrated his abilities: the South was inimical to art and the life of the mind, and Charleston high society's hauteur marginalized Simms despite his talent and character. Trent's second thesis was that Simms's commitment to the romance and his romanticism meant that his works had become largely unreadable in an age of literary realism. Although Vernon Parrington and later scholars recognized Simms's impulses to realism, the two theses long shaped Simms criticism and, indeed, also helped frame study of antebellum southern literature and intellectual life (Parrington 119–30).

A Virginian born in 1862, Trent was a progressive who wanted a New South radically different from the old. He saw his pioneering study of Simms as an opportunity to criticize what the Civil War had made untenable. From his perspective the Old South was not the expanding and rapidly developing environment, with a deep history, that Simms portrayed, but a place where slavery stultified and stunted the growth and progress displayed by the North. Southern—especially South Carolinian—writers occasionally challenged Trent's agenda and conclusions, but those critiques had little impact. Not until after publication of the Simms letters in the 1950s did scholars begin to consider the author in the historical and contemporary contexts that he had rendered in his poetry and fiction. And not until after the centennial of his death did a growing number of scholars, having concluded that southern intellectual history was not an oxymoron, begin to study in detail the culture in which Simms participated and to which he contributed so voluminously and variously.

Some of these scholars also have had agendas: they have wanted to see Simms included in the American literary canon, for instance, or they have wanted to defend the heritage that in their view Trent, and so many others, inappropriately belittled or ignorantly dismissed. More fruitfully, other scholars have begun to reframe the understanding of nineteenth-century American intellectual life by stripping away preconceptions that characterized earlier evaluations of Simms and his contemporaries. They are closely examining the historical record and transatlantic and other contemporary contexts and developments in the process. Although the pursuit of canonical status in a post-canonical age seems quixotic at this point, the explosion of the canon is leading to more varied fare being offered and may, therefore, mean that Simms, once his work is widely available, will be more often anthologized as well as studied. Defensiveness about Simms and the antebellum South may warm the hearts of like-minded people, just as critics of the Old South have been encouraged by shared presuppositions and disdain. Yet dueling cultural ideologies do not advance comity and may only reinforce mutual incomprehensions. Continued, deep research in original sources and the theoretical reframing that Atlantic history, the history of the book, and other perspectives offer—these approaches promise most for further study of Simms, his works, and his world.

Works Cited

For amplified readings by and on Simms and on his world, go to http://simms.library.sc.edu/bibliography.php.

Bakker, Jan. "Simms on the Literary Frontier; or, So Long Miss Ravenel and Hello Captain Porgy: *Woodcraft* Is the First 'Realistic' Novel in America." In *William Gilmore Simms and the American Frontier,* edited by John Caldwell Guilds and Caroline Collins, 64–78. Athens: University of Georgia Press, 1997.

Butterworth, Keen, and James E. Kibler Jr. *William Gilmore Simms: A Definitive Guide.* Boston: G. K. Hall, 1980.

Faust, Drew Gilpin. *A Sacred Circle: The Dilemma of the Intellectual in the Old South, 1840–1860.* Baltimore: Johns Hopkins University Press, 1977.

Guilds, John C. *Simms: A Literary Life.* Fayetteville: University of Arkansas Press, 1992.

Hayne, Paul Hamilton. "Ante-Bellum Charleston." *Southern Bivouac* 1 (October 1885): 257–68.

Kibler, James E. "The First Simms Letters: 'Letters from the West' (1826)." *Southern Literary Journal* 19 (Spring 1987): 81–91.

———. *The Poetry of William Gilmore Simms: An Introduction and Bibliography.* Columbia: Southern Studies Program, University of South Carolina, 1979.

McHaney, Thomas L. "An Early 19th-Century Literary Agent: James Lawson of New York." *Publications of the Bibliographical Society of America* 64 (Spring 1970): 177–92.

Moltke-Hansen, David. "The Expansion of Intellectual Life: A Prospectus." In *Intellectual Life in Antebellum Charleston,* edited by Michael O'Brien and David Moltke-Hansen, 3–44. Knoxville: University of Tennessee Press, 1986.

———. "Southern Literary Horizons in Young America: Imaginative Development of a Regional Geography." *Studies in the Literary Imagination* 42, no. 1 (2009): 1–31.

Nakamura, Masahiro. *Visions of Order in William Gilmore Simms: Southern Conservatism and the Other American Romance.* Columbia: University of South Carolina Press, 2009.

Parrington, Vernon L. *The Romantic Revolution in America, 1800–1860.* Vol. 2 of *Main Currents in American Thought.* New York: Harcourt, Brace and Company, 1927.

Rogers, George C., Jr. *Charleston in the Age of the Pinckneys.* Columbia: University South Carolina Press, 1980.

Shillingsburg, Miriam J. "The Cub of the Panther: A New Frontier." In *William Gilmore Simms and the American Frontier,* edited by John Caldwell Guilds and Caroline Collins, 221–36. Athens: University of Georgia Press, 1997.

———. "Literary Grist: Simms's Trips to Mississippi." *Southern Quarterly* 41, no. 2 (2003): 119–34.

Simms, William Gilmore. *Atalantis: A Story of the Sea: In Three Parts.* New York: J. & J. Harper, 1832.

———. *Beauchampe; or, The Kentucky Tragedy.* 2 vols. Philadelphia: Lea and Blanchard, 1842.

———. *The Cassique of Kiawah: A Colonial Romance.* New York: Redfield, 1859.

———. *Confession; or, The Blind Heart. A Domestic Story.* 2 vols. Philadelphia: Lea and Blanchard, 1841.

———. "Ellet's 'Women of the Revolution.'" *Southern Quarterly Review,* n.s. 1 (July 1850): 314–54.

———. "Guizot's Democracy in France." *Southern Quarterly Review* 15, no.29 (1849): 114–65.

———. *Guy Rivers: A Tale of Georgia.* 2 vols. New York: Harper & Brothers, 1834.

———. *The Letters of William Gilmore Simms.* Edited by Mary C. Simms Oliphant, Alfred Taylor Odell, and T. C. Duncan. 6 vols. Columbia: University of South Carolina Press, 1952–82.

———. *The Life of Francis Marion.* New York: Henry G. Langley, 1844.

———. *Martin Faber, the Story of a Criminal; and Other Tales.* 2 vols. New York: Harper & Brothers, 1837.

———. *Poetry and the Practical.* Edited by James E. Kibler. Fayetteville: University of Arkansas Press, 1996.

———. *The Sense of the Beautiful: An Address . . . before the Charleston County Agricultural and Horticultural Association, May 3, 1870.* Charleston: Charleston County Agricultural and Horticultural Association, 1870.

———. *The Social Principle: The Source of National Permanence. An Oration, Delivered before the Erosophic Society of the University of Alabama . . . December 13, 1842*. Tuscaloosa: Erosophic Society, University of Alabama, 1843.

———. *Stories and Tales*. Vol. 5 of *The Writings of William Gilmore Simms*. Centennial edition; introductions, explanatory notes, and texts established by John Caldwell Guilds. Columbia: University of South Carolina Press, 1974.

———. *Views and Reviews in American Literature, History and Fiction*. 2 vols. New York: Wiley and Putnam, 1845 (1846).

———. *The Wigwam and the Cabin*. 2 vols. New York: Wiley and Putnam, 1845–46.

———. *Woodcraft, or Hawks about the Dovecote: A Story of the South, at the Close of the Revolution*. New York: Redfield, 1854.

Trent, William Peterfield. *William Gilmore Simms*. Boston: Houghton, Mifflin, 1892.

Wakelyn, Jon L. *The Politics of a Literary Man: William Gilmore Simms*. Westport, Conn.: Greenwood Press, 1973.

Watson, Charles S. *From Nationalism to Secessionism: The Changing Fiction of William Gilmore Simms*. Westport, Conn.: Greenwood Press, 1993.

White, William B., Jr. *The Ross-Chesnut-Sutton Family of South Carolina*. Franklin, N.C.: Privately printed, 2002.

Wimsatt, Mary Ann. "Realism and Romance in Simms's Midcentury Fiction." *Southern Literary Journal* 12, no. 2 (1980): 29–48.

Critical Introduction

SLAVERY IN AMERICA & FATHER ABBOT

Ehren Foley

In 1833 William Gilmore Simms found himself an erstwhile Unionist newspaper editor who had sunk his own personal funds into trying to save the moribund Charleston *City Gazette.* As a champion of free expression and opponent of nullification, he had placed himself in opposition to two powerful political forces within South Carolina, H.L. Pinckney's Charleston *Mercury* and John C. Calhoun. Throughout the heated political debates, Simms and Pinckney would exchange increasingly vicious editorials, with Pinckney, especially, moving beyond the political and engaging in personal attacks against Simms's character. Simms would emerge from the Nullification debates badly bruised, both personally and politically, and as his *City Gazette* fell into oblivion, he retreated from the overtly political world of newspaper editing and instead focused his attention towards his work as a novelist, poet, and social critic (Wakelyn 19-40).

It was in the service of these more literary pursuits that Simms began editing *The Cosmopolitan,* a short-lived journal published in Charleston, in the spring of 1833.[1] In the first number he engaged in a dialogue about the value of historical romances to the creation of a national literature. His argument was that authors should focus their attention on those regions and places with which they were most familiar. On that basis he lamented that James Fenimore Cooper, in his most recent productions, had allowed himself to stray far away from the sketches of the people and landscapes of upstate New York (*Cosmopolitan* 22-24; Wakelyn 54). This emphasis on the importance of local and regional literature to the creation of a truly American literature would become a powerful focus for Simms as he entered the next stage of his career as an author and editor.

For the next fifteen years or so, Simms, along with a cohort of American authors and artists — Edgar Allan Poe, Nathaniel Hawthorne, Herman Melville, Evert Duyckinck, and Thomas Cole among them — would pursue this cultural agenda with vigor. They were all members of the loosely affiliated movement that became known as "Young America," and they tended to be Democratic in their politics and nationalist in their cultural outlook.[2] Simms would champion this quest for an American literature through a number of literary outlets, from his historical romances, to his poetry, to his short fiction, and even through his voluminous writings as a review essayist. The present volume reproduces and offers examples of two of these genres: the review essay and serialized short fiction. What unites these two seemingly distinct works —the first, *Slavery in America*, an extended review essay critiquing Harriet Martineau's *Society in America* (1837), and the second, *Father Abbot*, a series of dialogues between the fictional Father Abbot and his disciples — is their attempt to describe, explain, and defend the society and culture of Simms's region, the American South. They both, in their own way, were part of the broader cultural agenda that Simms had pursued since at least the early 1830s, though they also hint at how his thinking would evolve by the eve of the Compromise of 1850. By the time he penned *Father Abbot* in the fall of 1849, his nationalism had transitioned into a commitment to sectionalism. In a letter to Virginian Nathaniel Beverly Tucker in January 1850 Simms made the point plainly. "The idea grows upon us rapidly, and we are pleased to think upon the Southern people," he wrote, "I have long since regarded the separation as a now inevitable necessity" (*Letters* 3: 8).

Intellectually the transition was significant, but, for Simms, it was not especially abrupt. Instead, the move was subtle, at least in his writing, as evidenced by the two works reproduced in this volume. He had always believed that sectional literature was the gateway to national literature and wrote in the dedication to the Redfield edition of *The Wigwam and the Cabin* (1845; 1856), "No one mind can fully or fairly illustrate the characteristics of any great country; and he who shall depict *one section* faithfully, has made his proper and sufficient contribution to the great work of *national* illustration" (4). But the politics of the late 1840s, especially the tensions arising from the war with Mexico and the battles over the slavery question in the territories acquired as a result, had led Simms to believe that the nation as presently constituted could not long endure. These same tensions had also caused "Young America" to crumble under the weight of the sectional crisis. This disintegration was particularly evident in that more idealistic strain of the movement that was focused on the production of cultural nationalism through literature and the arts during the 1830s and 1840s, and that Simms had done so much to foster.[3] By the late 1840s Simms had effectively transitioned from a writer who believed that by writing sectional literature he, along with others, could produce an American nation, to one who remained committed to writing sectional literature, but who now did so in the service of what he hoped would become a unified southern nation.

Slavery in America

Simms's commitment to writing sectional literature — first in service to the American nation and later in service to a southern one — had, almost of necessity, included a willingness to interject the proslavery argument into his themes. In *The Yemassee* (1835), for instance, the character Hector, a slave, refuses to accept freedom when it is offered to him, explaining that he was unfit for it and incapable of handling it. This theme of the civilizing force of slavery and the potential dangers of unbounded freedom had become a centerpiece of the proslavery argument as articulated by southern intellectuals, Simms among them. The argument rejected the more radical contentions about human equality that were finding increasing voice at least along the fringes of northern free labor society, most especially by those caught up in the various idealist revolutions then underway — be they revivalist, socialist, transcendentalist, or abolitionist. Increasingly, though, southern intellectuals offered a critique of these emerging ideologies and developed an alternate worldview, one that celebrated individualism and human difference, and, of course, defended the perpetuation of human bondage.

Simms's most notable and sustained defense of southern society and southern slavery, at least in a work of non-fiction, came in 1837 when he was offered the opportunity to review *Society in America* (1837), written by the English social theorist Harriet Martineau, for the Richmond-based *Southern Literary Messenger*. His essay quickly gained wide circulation and newspaper articles throughout the South quoted from Simms's review (Wakelyn 65). Its popularity convinced the publisher of the *Messenger*, Thomas W. White, to issue a significantly expanded version of the review in pamphlet form, which he did in 1839. It is that pamphlet version that is reproduced here. Like the original review, the pamphlet, released under the title *Slavery in America; Being a Brief Review of Miss Martineau on that Subject*, received warm notice. Two New York papers, both with a strong literary persuasion, the New York *Mirror* —where southerner Edgar Allan Poe served as a literary critic — and the New York *Evening Post* — where noted poet and Simms friend William Cullen Bryant was editor-in-chief — each noticed Simms's *Slavery in America* and offered favorable reviews (Butterworth and Kibler 43). Later, it was also included in the 1852 collection, *The Pro-Slavery Argument*, issued first by Walker, Richards, and Co. of Charleston and then, in 1853, by Lippincott, Grambo, and Co. of Philadelphia. That five-hundred page tome included essays by leading lights in southern society and politics, including William Harper, James Henry Hammond, Thomas Roderick Dew, and, of course, Simms. The essay's success, and extended relevance to southern thought, served to divorce it somewhat from the occasion of its original production, which was the review of Martineau's book. Indeed, it may represent that exceptionally rare instance where a review essay proves more significant, or at least more enduring, than the work it treats.

Harriet Martineau had travelled to the United States in 1834, and for two years she toured the country recording her observations, which she published in two volumes. *Society in America* was wide-ranging and discussed a number of topics, from government to agriculture to manufacturing, but in his review Simms focused special attention upon Martineau's chapter entitled "Morals of Economy," and more specifically upon the section touching upon the "Morals of Slavery." While Martineau began her chapter by recounting two extraordinary examples of slaveholders who went to great personal sacrifice to protect their bondpeople — one in South Carolina who personally nursed his slaves during a cholera outbreak and another who sold his slaves rather than have them abused by his young wife — the thrust of her chapter was the hypocrisy and degradation inherent within the system, which, she argued, infected all participants, both white and black (Martineau II: 312-52). Her position as an outsider within both American and southern society gave her a unique perspective and one that remains worthy of perusal. For Simms, though, Martineau's foreignness utterly disqualified her to comment upon the southern social order. To contend otherwise would have run counter to his long-standing belief that to truly know a nation or a people, an individual needed to be of that place. That was, after all, the rationale that led him to write, when not treating literature, almost exclusively about southern and western themes, and to argue that other writers should also explore the intricacies of their own regions. Simms's attack on Martineau's understanding of southern society, however, did not end with her foreignness. In fact, his arguments ranged far beyond Martineau's text itself, and he used the review essay instead as a vehicle for exploring and articulating his own views about proper social order, civilization, and race. It is this expansive quality of the essay that makes it worthy of study today.

For Simms, slavery was merely one facet of a properly ordered society, one built upon organic hierarchy and the interconnectedness of labor and capital. It was this organic whole that Simms envisioned when he viewed southern slave society and that was threatened by the various -isms and -ologies then being spawned in Europe and the American North. The very basis of this organic society, however, was inequality, and Simms made clear his break with Jefferson's dictum that all men were created equal. Of course that was a fallacy, he argued, as even a cursory study of either nature or human society would reveal. Interrogating this notion of fundamental equality, he wrote:

> The stars are lovely in their inequalities, the hills, the trees, the rivers and the seas; and it is from their very inequalities that their harmonies arise. Were it otherwise, the eye would be pained by the monotony of the pro-

spect everywhere. As it is, we love to look abroad upon nature, and it is with a pleasure no less sensible than that of the savage, that we learn 'how to name the bigger light and how the less.' They have their names only as they are unlike and unequal. It is because these shine *in their places*, however inferior to other orbs, that they are lovely. (*Slavery in America* 62)

It was the organic hierarchy offered by slavery, Simms argued, that was the key to a properly ordered society and that provided the remedy for the social fissures that had prepared the way for the downfall of older nations and empires. By uniting the interests of labor and capital, slavery protected against the urban riots and social upheavals that invariably led to the imposition of dictatorships and the destruction of republican liberty. Even more than that, a hierarchical society recognized something fundamental within nature: that each individual within a society had different capacities and abilities. Or, to reverse another Jefferson quotation, some were, in fact, born booted and spurred and others born with saddles on their backs. Obviously this construction appealed to members of the master class, but perhaps just as much, it also appealed to southern intellectuals like Simms. Not only did the logic justify holding some men in bondage, but it also suggested the superiority of a man of letters within a society that too often neglected his talents.[4] In the era of the "common man" and the expansion of political democracy within the nation, the proslavery argument served not only to defend black bondage, it also served as a full-throated defense of social hierarchy more generally at a time when that notion seemed under attack.

The point was an important one for Simms and others who contended that the founders "were democrats, not levellers." To properly understand the founders' republic, and to establish proper social harmony, it was necessary to recognize that:

Democracy is not leveling – it is, properly defined, the harmony of the moral world. It insists upon inequalities, as its law declares, that all men should hold the place to which they are properly entitled. The definition of true liberty, is the undisturbed possession of that place in society to which our moral and intellectual merits entitle us. *He is a freeman, whatever his condition, who fills his proper place. He is a slave only, who is forced into a position in society below the claims of his intellect.* (*Slavery in America* 65, original emphasis)

It was this logic that allowed Simms to conclude at the end of *Slavery in America* that it was improper to apply the appellation of slave to the servile in the South. "He is under no despotic power," Simms argued, "There are laws which protect him, *in his place*, as inflexible as those which his proprietor is required to obey, *in his place. Providence has placed him in our hands, for his good, and has paid us from his labor for our guardianship*" (82-83, original emphasis). Every man in his place, each fulfilling his divine sanction, this was the true definition of liberty for Simms. It was the social order described by Hector in *The Yemassee* when he refused his freedom, and it was a social vision outlined in countless other of Simms's writings. Unbounded individualism was a path to chaos and disorder. It threatened to rend asunder the Great Chain of Being and destroy the God-inspired social order that southern intellectuals identified within their own society.

These divergent visions of the relation of the individual to society lay at the heart of the emerging conflict between pro- and antislavery thought. It was an area where intellectually, and even religiously, the North was beginning to divide from the South. The evangelical fervor that swept through places like upstate New York, carried by charismatic purveyors such as Charles Grandison Finney and that spawned countless religious movements, including Joseph Smith's Latter Day Saints, tended to carry with it a more optimistic vision of human nature, one that celebrated the possibility for individual and social perfectibility. It was the spiritual and intellectual fuel behind so many of the social reform and social utopian movements that Simms identified as threatening the very fabric of society. Like many other southerners, even under the influence of the Second Great Awakening, he tended to subscribe to a more orthodox Christianity. These southerners retained a belief in the innate sinfulness of man and averred that only through a social order that imposed proper discipline could man truly thrive and achieve his proper station in life. They worried about, and wrote withering critiques, as Simms did in *Slavery in America*, of a social order that accepted the exploitation of laborers without the guidance of a ruling class that would provide material aid and spiritual guidance. Slavery, Simms and other southern intellectuals argued, offered a different path. It protected labor under the guiding hand of the master. It was a patronizing view of slaves, one grounded firmly in a deeply held paternalistic worldview, and it also offered a skeptical view of human nature. But it was at the same time a worldview grounded in a particular understanding of Christian morality (Fox-Genovese and Genovese, "Divine Sanction" 211-33).[5]

Because of the centrality of Christianity in the development and articulation of the slaveholders' worldview, and of the proslavery argument, it is worth paying special attention to Simms's use of religion in both of the following texts. It is implicit throughout *Slavery in America* through Simms's continual insistence upon the civilizing effect of enslavement. Throughout the text he made the argument that many races had passed under a period of enslavement on their path towards civilization and lamented those instances where slavery was not employed and civilization lagged as a result, most notably through his discussion of Native Americans. In several instances he made the connection more explicitly, pointing towards the end of the pamphlet to the direct Biblical sanction of slavery, noting that if the historical examples he had offered "were not enough, for the purposes of authority, God himself, we are given to understand, actually in two remarkable instances, placed a favorite people in foreign slavery" (71). He continued, just a few pages later, to make the connection to his narrative of progress and civilization, arguing that "our native North American savage ... needed nothing by an Egyptian bondage of four hundred years to have been saved for the future, and lifted into a greatness to which Grecian and Roman celebrity would have been a faint and failing music" (73). The implication, of course, is that lacking that period of bondage Native American societies lagged far behind their Euro-American counterparts, but Simms at least held out that possibility for progress. It is a possibility that he extended also to African American slaves, writing, "The time will come, I doubt not, when the negro slave of Carolina will be raised to a condition which will enable him to go forth out of bondage. When that time comes, it may be, that we, like Pharaoh, will be loth to give him up," though he concluded, "that time is very far remote" (78). Here again, Simms turned to Biblical allusion to justify and defend racial slavery. But orthodox Christianity was not simply a crutch used by cynical slaveholders to defend their peculiar institution. It represented a deeply and sincerely held component of their broader worldview, a fact that is evidenced through Simms's deployment of religious elements in his collected series of dialogues between the titular Father Abbot and his group of followers. It was no coincidence that Simms chose a religious figure to serve as the main character in his series of essays that would extol the virtues of southern society.

Father Abbot

Father Abbot originally appeared as a series of newspaper columns, entitled "The Home Tourist," published in the Charleston *Mercury* between mid-September and early November 1849.[6] In very short order Simms, working with publisher Miller & Browne, collected and published the columns in a pocket-sized edition that sold for twenty-five cents a copy. Despite the hurried nature of its publication, the collection generally received warm reviews, both in the Charleston papers and by former Charlestonian J.D.B. DeBow, whose *Review* said that the imagery brought the reviewer back to "the banks of the Ashley and the Cooper" where they could "hear the waves beating up against the beach of old Sullivan's" (Butterworth and Kibler 77, 79; "Editor's Department" 312). A review in the *Literary World,* a publication edited by Simms's friend and fellow Young America booster E.A. Duyckinck, was more mixed. While the reviewer lamented that Simms seemed to dilute his literary prowess by issuing such a vast amount of material, some of which they judged unworthy of publication, they also noted that, though segments of *Father Abbot* bore evidence "of a hurried communication to the newspapers," others remained "as clear, strong, and highly-finished as anything we know of in the language" ("Simms's *Father Abbot*" 80-81).

Interestingly, none of these contemporary reviews made note of the political dimensions of the work, yet the primary reason for its hurried publication seems to have been Simms's belief that the collection might advance his electoral prospects in South Carolina. He admitted as much in an 1849 letter to his friend and former South Carolina governor James Henry Hammond, writing , "The articles to the *Mercury* had an object beyond what was apparent on the surface," and suggesting, "they contributed to the nomination to Congress" (*Letters* 2: 563). Simms, though, ultimately would decline that nomination and never would win a seat in the U.S. Legislature. Still, the late 1840s marked the most politically active period of Simms's career and *Father Abbot* was part of that political engagement.

Following his experience during the Nullification Crisis, Simms had turned to literature and cultural criticism as a way to shape, indirectly, the course of southern politics. By the late 1840s, however, he attempted once again to interject himself more directly into formal politics. In 1848 he served as a campaign organizer for Zachary Taylor, hoping both to hasten a political realignment that would generate a united southern party and also to elect a president who would be sympathetic to the expansion of slavery into the territory acquired as a result of the recently concluded war with Mexico. Following Taylor's victory, Simms thought he would be in line for an ambassadorial post and turned down an appointment as South Carolina's Lieutenant Governor so that he could accept a foreign posting, but the ambassadorship never materialized (Wakelyn 137-49). It would not be the last time that Taylor would disappoint Simms. Like other southern expansionists, Simms became disillusioned by Taylor's presidency, especially when his behind-the-scenes attempts to admit California as a free state became public (Levine 190-92). Simms then turned his attention back towards his previous attempts to develop a unified southern party. He supported, and sought election to, the Nashville Convention that was held during the summer of 1850 for the purposes of generating southern unity. While his support for the convention was unwavering, here again his electoral ambitions resulted only in frustration ("Southern Convention"; *Letters* 2: 574-77; *Letters* 3: 8-13).

It was amidst this political fervor that Simms penned *Father Abbot*. Despite the political motivations behind its production, however, it is not entirely surprising that many of the contemporary reviewers failed to appreciate its political dimensions. While *Father Abbot* does contain policy statements, they are embedded within a much richer narrative and remain subordinate to the dominant themes of place and progress. It is for this reason that *Father Abbot* rises above simple campaign propaganda and has enduring value beyond its original position as campaign ephemera.

"The Home Tourist," which was the title of the column in the *Mercury* from which *Father Abbot* emerged, also served as the subtitle for the pamphlet, and this is significant. It gets right to the core of Simms's mission, which was to display for his readers the virtues of their region and home place. Simms's own loyalty to place had shaped so much of his literary and political career, and *Father Abbot* represented another attempt to write a regional literature that vividly described his local environs. The character of Father Abbot leads his followers, and Simms's readers, on a journey to Sullivan's Island, a place so near at hand that they had for too long taken it for granted. Father Abbot laments that southerners, even Charlestonians, have ignored the virtues of their home and instead "plodded annually to that vulgarest of all social places, Saratoga"; he hopes that soon they might "begin to discover that Sullivan's is a much more famous place" (58). In the heated political environment surrounding the debates over the fate of the territories acquired from Mexico, what was at stake was more than just the capture of revenue from tourists; it was a matter of civilization's survival. By promoting Sullivan's Island as a destination that might hold southerners at home rather than having them travel to New York, Simms was again beating the drum for southern unity in the face of increasing sectional tension.

Another area where Simms melded immediate policy concerns with broader philosophical arguments is during his discussion of the hotel under construction on Sullivan's Island. That discussion dominates the narrative, and it likely references the Moultrie House, a hotel designed by the Charleston architect Edward C. Jones, which was completed in 1850.[7] The immediate utility of the building was obvious: it would house the tourists whom Simms envisioned coming to Sullivan's Island. But for Simms, the hotel represented something more than a utilitarian structure. It was, he said through the person of Father Abbot:

> one more step to our emancipation. It is a gain upon our former condition. It will do something towards curing us of that self-disparaging weakness, that of *absenteeism*. It is the infirmity of a provincial people that they have

> no faith in home. But the Hotel proves something more. ... Now, when you show me Carolina going into her own manufactures, sending her own ships upon the sea, and providing for her own people home places for refuge, you show me the first three steps taken towards an indefinite progress. (203-04)

It was nationalism, which by this time Simms was voicing as a sectional idea, expressed through architecture. This project extended further, though, as when Father Abbot describes the *tableaux vivants* that might be staged at the hotel, drawing inspiration from a "series of studies, from Southern History and tradition," rather than "the stale repetitions of Dukes and Marquisses; Macbeths and Hamlets; Queens and Shepherdesses; Turks and Banditti" (197). Here the character of Father Abbot is essentially endorsing the program of cultural nationalism that Simms had pursued over the course of his literary career, and that he was continuing to develop in the present volume. His celebration of local themes and local artists also extended to his endorsement of the amateur Charleston painter Auguste Paul Trouche, who is mentioned several times in the text and who, one imagines, might have produced artwork that would hang on the hotel walls, at least if Father Abbot had his druthers.

This discussion of art and architecture was important for Simms and it was no coincidence that included among the fellow-travelers who accompany Father Abbot to Sullivan's are Pictor, the painter, and Beauclerk, the poet, because Simms was throughout the text making the argument that literature and the arts are of central importance to the project of creating national identity. They were all necessary figures for illuminating to their fellow citizens what Simms called "The Home Secret" — only these artists could demonstrate to their people the virtues of their home place. They were the ones who would "discover what a people are, what they need, and what they may become," and without whom "the race, after a certain period of gestation must die out" (*Father Abbot* 17). Here Simms was emphasizing the connection between loyalty to place and societal survival. It was a theme that he had explored in numerous other writings and that he extended in *Father Abbot*. Simms was also, of course, making the case for his own significance within his society and within the life of the nation. For the nation, he proposed, could not survive, indeed, could never come into being, without the man of letters.

But *Father Abbot* was not simply a celebration of the Carolina shoreline. Simms also included social criticism within his text. He lamented, especially, the lack of industry that he saw within his home state. "Enthusiasm," he wrote, "has been crushed out of us by frivolity," making "life a mere drowse in the lap of vanity" (145). Sloth and vanity were precursors to social decay and Simms, through Father Abbot, instead advocated a mission of commercial development and a future where domestic manufacturing, commerce, and agriculture could all exist in harmony. Yet he was not just imagining the New South that would be endorsed, decades later, by boosters like Henry Grady. His social vision, as outlined in *Father Abbot,* was more subtle. He did not want Charleston to become another Lowell or Waltham; he instead hoped to braid elements of progress and modernity with the conservatism and order that he so valued in southern society. While he admitted that "[c]ommerce is, perhaps, the greatest of civilizers," he also warned that "no man must seek to revenge himself upon society for its seeming neglects, by abandoning his soul to Mammon. This is to sacrifice the substance for the shadow; the soul for the purse" (185). Here was the great dilemma for the southerner and slaveholder living in the era of the Market Revolution. How could he maintain the social order and organic hierarchy that he believed preserved society and at the same time stay competitive with modern, industrial, free labor societies?

The answer for Simms, as it was for other southern intellectuals who grappled with these problems, was measured progress that came on their own terms and that was devoid of the democratizing and, from their perspective, deleterious, effects of free labor. It was a progress that brought industry, but retained agriculture; that incorporated elements of modernity, but maintained organic hierarchy. So Father Abbot, towards the conclusion of the text, advocates experimentation and innovation in agriculture, but does so by looking back to antiquity and referencing Edward Gibbon's chapter on Roman economy in his *Decline and Fall of the Roman Empire* (218). The juxtaposition is significant. Innovation is vital to survival, but so is a proper appreciation of the past and a veneration of tradition.[8]

Conclusion

This tension between innovation and veneration marks the chief linkage between *Slavery in America* and *Father Abbot,* the two works reprinted in this volume. For southern intellectuals like Simms, it was slavery, and more specifically proper Christian slavery, that pointed the way through their dilemma. Slaveholding became the means of slowing down the processes of social change that accompanied modernity. It allowed southerners, they argued, a way to escape from the social decline and chaos that plagued free labor societies. They studied Ricardian theories of rent and diminishing returns on agriculture, as well as Malthusian predictions that population would outstrip society's ability to provide for it, and they saw in them predictions of the destruction of free labor societies. Working classes exposed to these privations would rise in revolt and topple society, leading either to anarchy or despotism.

In either case it would mean the destruction of freedom and republican liberty. Men like Simms watched world events closely and in the European revolutions of 1848 they saw these predicted outcomes coming to fruition.[9] It was only a matter of time, they believed, before the American North would suffer the same fate. But Christian slavery offered a way out of this cycle of destruction. By protecting and providing for the working class, and thus avoiding the inevitable working class revolutions, slavery not only made measured progress possible, it also protected freedom for those individuals capable of handling it.[10] It made possible the melding of industry with agriculture and southern society's participation in a modern world economy, as Simms advocated at the conclusion of *Father Abbot.* It did so, however, without sacrificing their social values or social order.

Of course it was easier to articulate this worldview from a plantation office then from the slave-quarter and it was also deeply self-serving, but ideologies, especially those articulated by a ruling class, oftentimes are. One need not, though, deny the enormity of slavery to appreciate the intellectual work that was required to defend that social order. Both *Slavery in America* and *Father Abbot* represent, in different ways, bricks in that intellectual edifice and are important and sophisticated elaborations upon the worldview that was articulated by southern intellectuals in the generation preceding the American Civil War. That Simms mentioned slavery only once in *Father Abbot* — towards the beginning of the text when he suggested that slavery is a seemingly necessary condition for making a nomadic people stationary and inculcating in them "The Home Secret" — suggests also that the defense of southern society was not merely a cynical defense of a profitable labor system.

Southern intellectuals like Simms believed they were engaged in an epochal clash of civilizations and that at stake was nothing less than the survival of American society and republican liberty. If they failed they predicted a decline into social decay and anarchical chaos. If they prevailed they might escape from this fate and secure a future marked by social harmony and ordered progress that would endure for a millennium. Doing so would require a recognition of the peculiar advantages of the southern political economy and also the creation of political unity within the region, two missions that Simms sought to achieve through his writing and editing work, including the production of the two texts reproduced herein.

A close reading of these texts reveals the intricacies of this intellectual project, one to which Simms would devote ever more time over the course of the following decade. While he was continually frustrated by his efforts to gain entrance into formal politics, Simms would continue to use the power of the pen as a way to create national identity. It was a role that he had advanced first as a member of Young America, writing in service of the American nation, but it was one that he would continue, and which is evidenced in the writings below, as a moral philosopher of southern nationalism. He did not work alone in that project, but he remained the most significant southern man of letters in the years of growing sectional tension that would finally explode in April 1861, fittingly, just off the coast of Sullivan's Island, where Simms's alter-ego, Father Abbot, had extolled the virtues of southern climate and southern society – in service of creating a southern nation – just over a decade before.

Notes

1. For the best discussion of Simms's engagement with the *Cosmopolitan* see Guilds, "Simms and the *Cosmopolitan*."

2. For more of the Young America Movement see Widmer, Lause, and Eyal.

3. See especially Widmer.

4. Drew Gilpin Faust most fully articulated this interpretation of the connection between the proslavery argument and the alienation of southern intellectuals in *A Sacred Circle*. See, too, her edited collection *The Ideology of Slavery*.

5. Historians Elizabeth Fox-Genovese and Eugene D. Genovese collected, synthesized, and most fully articulated their interpretations of the worldview of the southern master class, with special attention on the role played by their reading of both history and religion, in *The Mind of the Master Class*.

6. The dates of publication were September 18-22, 27, 29; October 1, 3, 6, 10, 13, 16, 23, 27; November 3, 5 (*Letters* 2: 565n).

7. Simms was familiar with the Moultrie House, attending a ball there on 29 August 1850, and it also appeared in a novella, *Flirtation at the Moultrie House* (1850), that John C. Guilds has attributed to Simms (*Letters* 3: 60n; Guilds, ed., *Stories and Tales* 780).

8. For discussion of slaveholder's attempts to grapple with modernity and progress see Moltke-Hansen "Ordered Progress," Genovese *Slaveholders' Dilemma*, and Smith *Mastered by the Clock*.

9. See, for instance, William Gilmore Simms, "Guizot's Democracy in France."

10. The argument about the slaveholders' dilemma derives from Genovese, *The Slaveholders' Dilemma*, which is a characteristically erudite, complex, and concise statement on this tension in antebellum southern thought.

Works Cited

Butterworth, Keen, and James E. Kibler, Jr. *William Gilmore Simms: A Reference Guide*. Boston: G.K. Hall & Co., 1980.

"Editor's Department," *DeBow's Review* 8 (March 1850): 312.

Eyal, Yonatan. *The Young America Movement and the Transformation of the Democratic Party, 1828-1861*. Cambridge: Cambridge UP, 2007.

Faust, Drew Gilpin, ed. *The Ideology of Slavery: Proslavery Thought in the Antebellum South, 1830-1860.* Baton Rouge: Louisiana State UP, 1981.

———. *A Sacred Circle: The Dilemma of the Intellectual in the Old South, 1840-1860.* Baltimore: Johns Hopkins UP, 1977.

Fox-Genovese, Elizabeth and Eugene D. Genovese. "The Divine Sanction of Social Order: Religious Foundations of the Southern Slaveholders' World View. *Journal of the American Academy of Religion* 55.2 (Summer 1987): 211-33.

———. *The Mind of the Master Class: History and Faith in the Southern Slaveholders' Worldview.* Cambridge: Cambridge UP, 2005.

Genovese, Eugene D. *The Slaveholders' Dilemma: Freedom and Progress in Southern Conservative Thought, 1820-1860.* Columbia: U of South Carolina P, 1992.

Guilds, John C. "William Gilmore Simms and the *Cosmopolitan,*" *Georgia Historical Quarterly* 41 (1957): 31-41.

———, ed. *The Writings of William Gilmore Simms.* Vol. 5, *Stories and Tales.* Columbia: U of South Carolina P, 1974.

Lause, Mark A. *Young America: Land, Labor, and the Republican Community.* Champaign: U of Illinois P, 1995.

Levine, Bruce. *Half Slave and Half Free: The Roots of Civil War,* rev. ed. New York: Hill and Wang, 2005.

Martineau, Harriet. *Society in America,* 2 vols. London: Saunders and Otley, 1837.

Moltke-Hansen, David. "Ordered Progress: The Historical Philosophy of William Gilmore Simms." In *"Long Years of Neglect": The Work and Reputation of William Gilmore Simms,* edited by John C. Guilds, 126-47. Fayatteville: U of Arkansas P, 1988.

The Proslavery Argument: As Maintained by the Most Distinguished Writers of the Southern States. Charleston: Walker, Richards, and Co., 1852.

Simms, William Gilmore, ed. *The Cosmopolitan: An Occasional,* No. 1. Charleston: Wm. Estill, 1833.

———. *Father Abbot, or, The Home Tourist; A Medley.* Charleston: Miller & Browne, 1849.

———. "Guizot's Democracy in France." *Southern Quarterly Review* 15.29 (1849): 114-65.

———. *The Letters of William Gilmore Simms.* 6 vols. Ed. Mary C. Simms Oliphant *et al.* Columbia: U of South Carolina P, 1952-2012.

———. *Slavery in America; Being a Brief Review of Miss Martineau on that Subject.* Richmond: Thomas W. White, 1838.

———. "The Southern Convention." *Southern Quarterly Review* 2.2 (1850): 191-232.

———. *The Wigwam and the Cabin.* New York: Redfield, 1856.

"Simms's *Father Abbot, &c.*" *The Literary World* 6.156 (26 January 1850): 80-81.

Smith, Mark M. *Mastered by the Clock: Time, Slavery, and Freedom in the American South.* Chapel Hill: U of North Carolina P, 1997.

Wakelyn, Jon L. *The Politics of a Literary Man: William Gilmore Simms.* Contributions in American Studies, No. 5. Westport, Ct: Greenwood P, 1973.

Widmer, Edward L. *Young America: The Flowering of Democracy in New York City.* New York: Oxford UP: 1999.

SLAVERY IN AMERICA,

BEING

A BRIEF REVIEW OF MISS MARTINEAU

ON THAT SUBJECT.

BY A SOUTH CAROLINIAN.

[William Gilmore Simms]

RICHMOND:

Printed and Published by Thomas W. White.

1838.

To the Hon. the Delegates from South Carolina,

in the Congress of the United States.

GENTLEMEN:

If I did not regard you as representatives, not less of the interests of the slave of Carolina, than of the rights of his owner, I should not trouble you with this inscription, nor the press with the publication of this little essay. Originally put forth in one of our southern periodicals, it has been so far honored by the approbation of its readers, as to make it desirable, in the estimation of many, that it should have a more extended circulation. This, it should not have, if I could bring myself for an instant to believe, that I was moved to its preparation by any motive but a sincere desire for the truth;—or, if I could doubt that it contains principles which no sophistry can subvert, and no misapplied ingenuity, whether of cunning or of self-blinding philanthropy, could keep from the ultimate reception of mankind. The argument, indeed, is chiefly drawn from what would seem to be the inevitable sense of mankind upon the subject of which it treats, as that sense is illustrated and shown by the practices and the necessities of men throughout the world, and through all its successive ages, from its known beginning. I will not seek, therefore, to fortify my views by the accumulation of authorities which he who runs may read. In my humble notion the whole world of human experience is tributary to their maintenance; and I would as soon doubt that it is truth which I profess, as doubt of the final triumph of these opinions upon which the practice of all nations has invariably settled down. I speak now, only as I deem it desirable that we should facilitate the advent of truth, and not because I have doubts of her final coming. We should labor in her assistance, not so much because she may need our service, as because our feeble race stands so grievously in need of hers. This we can best do, not by persuasive and specious doctrines, and fine flexible sayings, but simply by a firm adherence to what we know, and to what we think we have already gained. As yet, we have, confessedly, but partial glimmerings of her divine presence,—her fixed and all sufficing light!—we must treasure up these gleams and glimpses, few and feeble though they be, until to our more familiar eyes, star by star, she unfolds her perfect form, and, with the loveliness and the light of heaven, irradiates the dim cloud that now hangs between her and the earth. That we shall pray long and vainly, for this ideal of the moral world—that we shall look for it, with but little hope, whether in your day or in mine,—is not a matter of difficult prediction while there are so many, and so bold, prophets that proclaim themselves aloud throughout the land. But, that the continued and cheering presence of this blessed hope in the hearts of the few, will at length achieve what they so earnestly desire and sometimes die to realize, may be predicted with not less confidence. Let us, at least, labor that we may verify our own wishes; and find renewed impulse to our labors as we behold the industry of those who toil against us and it. We may neither of us do much in this holy cause, but, if we gather, each, but a single shell from the great ocean of truth—to employ the fancy of one whose constant thought was the best philanthropy—we shall at least diminish the toils of those who shall follow in our footsteps along the shores of the same solitary and unknown regions.

With profound respect, I am, gentlemen,

Your fellow citizen and friend,

THE AUTHOR

PREFACE.

Frequent applications having been made for the "Review of Miss Martineau upon the subject of Slavery," which originally appeared as a contribution to the Southern Literary Messenger, the publisher has determined to issue it in pamphlet form, in which some few typographical errors have been corrected. The errors into which Miss M. has been led by a pre-existing prejudice and a partial acquaintance with the facts, induced the able author of the "review" to present to the public a faithful criticism of the glaring misrepresentations and absurdities contained in her "Society in America." If the object of the author,—viz., to impart accurate information in relation to one of the most interesting and important domestic institutions of the south, and thereby remove an unfounded prejudice, now extensively existing,—can be obtained by the republication of the "review," the most ample remuneration will be secured to

THE PUBLISHER.

REVIEW.

A friend, with whom I travelled last summer, reading the late work of Miss Martineau, entitled 'Society in America,' drew my attention to certain portions of her remarks upon South Carolina. As I have the honor to be a native of that state, and the fortune to have been, for the better part of my life, a resident within it, he referred to me as one likely to know how far she was correct in her facts;—her deductions from them,—we were mutually agreed,—were after matters. I complied with his desire, so far as I was able, and we looked over the volumes together. In this hasty manner, I notched with my pencil, here and there, a few passages, as we turned the pages, which I noted, either for general incorrectness in the premises, or for an unfair and erroneous conclusion from them. When I had done this, and dwelt somewhat at length upon the various incidental topics which the matter necessarily suggested, he observed, that it might be well, if in every state through which the lady travelled, and upon which she has elaborated notes equally partial and unjust, some citizen who knew better, would come forward and correct her. By this means, the public, as well at home as abroad, for which the book was prepared, would not only be better able to determine upon its own accuracy, but would be materially assisted in arriving at a knowledge—which at this day seems so difficult, yet so very necessary—of a region so barbarous as ours. In ordinary cases, a colony is very apt to resemble in most of its habits, customs, achievements and pursuits, the people from which it was sent out; but America would seem to be held an exception, in the estimation of the modern English, to this general rule; and their travellers come to write of, and to survey us, as if we were literally the natives of some new-found-land—some Polynesia, or Australasia—that fifth portion of the world, for which we are only now providing fine names, and probably foul destinies. It does not seem to be thought, for an instant, that we can at all resemble the worthy progenitors from whom we came; or that, in adopting a new government, we should yet wear the same old faces; but the law of Caliban is to be forced upon us whether we will or no; and in getting new masters, we are required, at the same time, to become thoroughly new men—a change, not so easy of execution in the sight of those who know anything of the difficulty of bringing new truth into the world at any time; or of effecting any material alteration in the habits and modes of thinking, which prevail among the great masses of mankind. Upon this hint I have spoken. Adopting the suggestions of my friend, I procured the volumes in question, and proceeded to examine their contents more at my leisure. The result of this examination is the somewhat desultory remarks which follow.

When Miss Martineau, after acknowledging the peculiar disadvantage under which she labors as a traveller, in being deaf, proceeds to look up and to dwell upon some of the advantages of such an infirmity;—and, with an ingenuity which deserves credit, (and in New England might have found it, had she withheld her remarks upon that region,) dilates upon the winning power which her trumpet exercises in tête-à-tête—we, at once, discover the sort of person with whom we have to deal. Had she written volumes with the design of illustrating the peculiar properties of her own mind, she could have said nothing which better conveys the idea of the adroit casuist, ready and able to make the best case from the worst;—to raise hypotheses,—to suggest means of fight and defence,—to plan sorties and escapes; and, whatever might be the fate of the conflict, if she did not 'change sides'—at least 'still continue to dispute.' The passage of her preface, in which this singular stretch of self-deception (if we may so style it) occurs, is truly an amusing one. Her accuracy of information, she insists, is not diminished in consequence of her deafness, for her trumpet is one of 'singular fidelity,' and she "gains more in *tête-à-tête*, than is given to people who hear general conversation." This is one of those passages, with which the volume is abundantly provided, which most admirably illustrate the perfect assurance of the author. What deaf person beside herself would undertake to say so much? Here she assumes cognizance of a subject which she is physically incapable of considering; and, without thought—for the reflection of a single instant, would have saved her from the absurdity—proceeds to determine upon a point utterly beyond her capacity. Satisfied herself with the "charm of her trumpet," and fully persuaded as she seems to be, of the truth of what she has said, she is yet dubious that there will be some unwisely skeptical whom it is yet necessary to convince; and the reason which she gives for the faith that is in her, may amuse many whom it will certainly fail to satisfy. "*Its charm* (the charm of chatting through a trumpet with a deaf damsel of a 'certain age'!) consists in the new feeling which it imparts, of ease and privacy!" It does not seem to strike her for an instant that, among a people, like the Americans, who are rather shy and shrinking in society, there would be nothing half so awkward as to be subjected to this charming *tête-à-tête*. Yet such is the case. We have heard of many intelligent persons who declined to make the lady's acquaintance while in this country, simply on account of her trumpet, and the awkwardness of such a chat in company, who, otherwise, would have been very well pleased to know her, and who might have afforded her some very useful information. This latter opinion, she, perhaps, will not so readily believe; since she tells us, in brief, that during her travels of nearly two years among the Americans, seldom more than two weeks in any one place, and thus dividing her time among fifteen or eighteen millions of persons, she made the acquaintance of nearly all of the distinguished people, and believes that she "heard every argument that can possibly be adduced in vindication or palliation of slavery!" In a note, only a few pages apart from this precious sample of assurance, she gives a little anecdote which will answer all the purposes of a commentary upon it. She says:—"A fact regarding Mr. Gallatin, shows what the obscurity of country life in the United States may be. His estate was originally in Virginia. By a new division it was thrown into the back part of Pennsylvania. He ceased to be heard of for some years. . . . . During this time an advertisement appeared in a newspaper, asking for tidings of 'one Albert Gallatin,' and adding, that if he were still living, he might, on making a certain application, hear of something to his advantage." So much for the story, which may be true or not. It is highly probable. And yet, it will be remembered—that the hardihood of our traveller may be the better understood—that Mr. Albert Gallatin has the reputation of being one of our most celebrated economists. It was left for Miss Martineau, in spite of the "obscurity of country life in the United States,"—which is peculiarly the nation of great distances,—to find out all the distinguished men, and to hear all the arguments that were worth hearing. The "charm" of her trumpet, however, being taken into consideration, the greatness of her achievement will not be so highly estimated.

A little proem taken from a paper in the Edinburgh Review, furnishes the text for a portion of her preface. This text dilates, though summarily, upon the folly and impertinence of any traveller assuming, by a brief race through a neighboring country, to generalize, for the people thereof, from his own partial and hasty observations. Miss Martineau, with an air of no little humility at first, acknowledges the force of this paragraph; and is almost resolved, as she felt the reasonableness of its suggestions, to say nothing "in print on the condition of society in the United States." But she does not keep in this mind long. Indeed, how could she? To quote the paragraph, was only to serve its suggestions, as she does so many conversational ninepins which she sets up, here and there, throughout her two volumes, simply to show how well she can knock them down. This is her obvious purpose in her quotation of it; and she concludes not to mind its arguments but to print and generalize for good or for evil; contenting herself with saying, most illogically, in defence of her resolve, that "men will never arrive at a knowledge of each other, if those who have the power of foreign observation refuse to relate what they think they have learned; or even to lay before others the materials from which they themselves hesitate to construct a theory, or draw large conclusions."* No wonder error should breed so fast, and attain a growth so vigorous, when this sort of morals is to be inculcated. "I am not sure," says Miss Martineau, "that

* This reasoning might do well enough in relation to a country of which nothing could be otherwise known. But to apply it to such a country as the United States, of which England has it in her power to know so much—of which so much is known—and the knowledge of which is extending daily, in accordance with the extension of joint or corresponsive interests, is not less silly than unfriendly. The traveller who goes among an utterly new people may be allowed, in the absence of any better opportunities of information, to tell what he sees. But even then he should confine himself to the simple relation of facts, and leave his speculations to his more unbiassed and deliberate reader.

what I tell you is the truth, but never mind, it looks like the truth, and better that than nothing. If we scrupled to say what we conjectured, we should know nothing of one another, and therefore I give you what I have gathered. Be thankful, with Sancho, 'and look not the gift horse i' the mouth.'" This is the amount of her argument. It does not not seem to enter her thoughts for an instant, that it is far better to be ignorant of the subject entirely, than only to learn that which is erroneous in respect to it. Better be compelled to learn everything anew, than be required, before we can know anything truly, to go through that painful and most tedious process of all, of first unlearning error. Such, however, is her mode of education.

From the same preface, we learn that Miss Martineau "went with a mind, *she* believes, as nearly as possible unprejudiced about America, with a strong disposition to admire democratic institutions, but an entire ignorance how far the people of the United States lived up to or fell below, their own theory. *She* had read whatever *she* could lay hold of that had been written about them; but was unable to satisfy *her*self that, after all, *she* understood anything whatever of their condition. As to knowledge of them, *her* mind was nearly a blank; as to opinion of their state, *she* did not carry the germ of one."

If this be true, Miss Martineau was capable of far more forbearance on the subject of the United States, than is usual with her upon most other subjects. She is one of those strong-minded, bold, disputatious persons, who are never satisfied until they have formed a leading notion upon every topic to which their thoughts may be addressed;—and the consequence is, that she has formed—along with a habit of speculating as she goes, upon whatever meets her glance—a much less valuable habit of declaiming her notions aloud as fast as they arise. Nothing escapes her tongue;—no subject is too great—none too little for her analysis. The shallows and the deeps alike form her elements, and to those who simply glance at the titles to her chapters, her sections and her subdivisions, the wonder at her universality will be unqualified.* While other travellers are usually satisfied to relate what they see, and only now and then dilate upon some single topic, with which they assume to be particularly acquainted, our author, with a surprising capacity, and a boldness rather remarkable than attractive, theorizes upon all. 'Politics,' 'Parties,' 'the Apparatus of Government,' 'the Morals of Politics,' 'Public and Private Economy,' 'Agriculture,' 'Internal Improvements,' 'Manufactures,' 'Commerce,' 'Morals of Economy,' 'Civilization,' 'Honor,' 'Woman,' 'Children,' 'Sufferers,' 'Utterance,' 'Religion,'—'its science, its spirit, and its administration'—these are the heads under which come up a thousand specifications and subdivisions, upon all of which she is equally elaborate, bold, and singularly dogmatical. How far she may have been ignorant of the United States before she

* The distich forced itself upon me:

—— "Still the wonder grew
How one small head could carry all *she* knew."

came to this country, and how utterly opinionless she was thereon,—though reading every book she could lay hold of which treated of the subject,—we will not pretend to determine; but, certain it is, she has been anything but slow in forming opinions since her visit, although we can readily believe in the limited degree of her knowledge upon many of her topics even now. But we are not willing to believe in this alleged mental passiveness on the part of our author. We doubt not that she deceived herself on the subject of her dispassionateness, as English travellers invariably do, before going abroad. Hall, Hamilton, Mrs. Trollope, *et id omne genus*, all allege the same grateful impartiality; and, like Miss Martineau, the greater number of them insist, with no little earnestness, upon their democratic tendencies at first, the better to effect their object in the end. Miss Martineau was, indeed, we well know, something more than a democrat in England. There she was a decided leveller. She was opposed to the policy of her own government in many respects, and consequently pleased with ours in all those particulars, in which, departing from that which she hourly assailed, it seemed to approach more nearly to her theories. But she could neither have been ignorant of our people, our institutions, nor of our society; and that she had opinions previously formed in respect to them, is everywhere obvious throughout her volumes. It is, indeed, from these previous opinions that many of her errors have arisen. Her notions of democracy, for example, lead her frequently to overlook the fact, that, as a nation, we have a limited and restraining charter, which is continually conflicting, in its operations, with the cherished idea in her mind.* On the subject of American slavery, her detestation is avowed as being entertained long before entering the slave states; and so cordial is this detestation, that it is fed and fattened by everything which she sees, and in sundry cases, we are sorry to add, at the expense of truth. I do not mean to say that she has wilfully related falsehoods. Not so;—I think the book of Miss Martineau written in good faith throughout. But she was biassed and bigoted on this subject to the last degree; and could neither believe the truth when it spoke in behalf of the slaveholder; nor doubt the falsehood, however gross, when it told in favor, or fell from the lips of the abolitionist. Thus, for example, in proof, not less of this unhappy bias, than of the dogmatism of the writer, we are told that the abolitionists sent no incendiary tracts among the slaves, and that they use no direct means towards promoting their objects in the slave states. "It is wholly untrue that they insinuate their publications into the south." Such is her bold assertion; yet, "Mr. Madison made the charge, so did Mr. Clay, so did every slaveholder and merchant with whom I conversed. I chose afterwards to hear the other side of the whole question; and I found, to my amazement, that this charge was wholly groundless." Here the lady undertakes to decide a question of veracity

* Of course, in all such cases, the charters are defective and anomalous. The ideal of Miss M. is the genuine standard.

with singular composure, in favor of her friends, and at the expense of the first names in our country.

"Nor did it occur to me," she writes, "that as slaves cannot read," &c. This is one of her facts, which is notoriously false, and which may be proved to be so, in every southern city. Thousands of slaves do read; and, if this were wanting to their information, the slaveholders assert,—though the abolitionists may deny,—that gross prints are employed in these abolition newspapers to help the understanding where it may lack, and that these prints are sometimes put upon manufactured cottons, such as are employed entirely for negroes, and insinuated here and there, at decent intervals, among the bales intended for the southern market. Such bales were discovered in a merchant's collection in Charleston, to the knowledge of the writer, but a few years ago. "*Slavery of a very mild kind*, has been abolished in the northern parts of the union," &c. Another of Miss Martineau's facts, which may call for a remark. What knowledge had Miss M., except from parties interested, that this slavery was of a mild kind;—and did she ask whether the slavery was abolished from principle, or because it was more profitable to work the slaves in a richer soil than that of New-England? Did she inquire how long a time was granted to slaveholders to dispose of their slaves to the south, before the act of abolition went into operation; and did she farther inquire, from what colonies the vessels and crews were fitted out which brought the African to America, and sold him to the south? A little more inquiry might have resulted in her hearing,—to her surprise, no doubt,—that the province of Carolina was the very first from which a prayer ever arose to the British government, that this trade should be abolished, and no more slaves be permitted to enter within its territories.* But, to proceed.

In order to prove the insecurity of the whites in the slave states, and their dread of the black population, we have a number of little anecdotes, some ludicrous enough, and others merely vicious or foolish without being ludicrous. We quote a single paragraph, and will analyze it, by way of showing how small a surface of truth is necessary to this lady when she has a favorite theory to sustain. In doing this, it will be seen how singularly obtuse the mind may become, even of one so generally acute as Miss Martineau, when inveterate in the pursuit of a given object, and yielded up entirely to the one controlling prejudice.

"At Charleston, when a fire breaks out, the gentlemen all go home on the ringing of the alarm bell; the ladies rise and dress themselves and their children. It may be the signal of insurrection: and the fire burns on, for any help the citizens give, till a battalion of soldiers marches down to put it out."

Now, we take it, that in any city in the world, slave or free, the gentleman who happens to be absent from his family when the fire-bell rings, will be apt to hurry home to see that all is safe, and to quiet the alarm of his wife and children—particularly, indeed, in a large city, where it

* Vide Hewatt, and public documents.

is so very difficult to determine at all times where the fire is. There is nothing remarkable in such a fact, nor is it peculiar to Charleston. But, in a city that is chiefly built of wood, such as Charleston, and where a fire extends with amazing rapidity, it becomes doubly necessary that the gentleman should not only hurry home, but that the lady should get her children and her jewels ready for flight. This would seem natural enough; but the rest of the paragraph commits a *felo-de-se*, which a moment's reflection would have prompted the author quietly to avoid. "The fire burns on for any help the citizens give, till a battalion of soldiers marches down to put it out." Now, who are the soldiers, but the citizens,—and how can soldiers extinguish a fire? By guns and bayonets? These questions, had she put them to herself, would have saved her from the publication of this absurdity. We have none but a citizen soldiery in Charleston, and by an arrangement, which would be of great advantage if adopted in other cities, a detachment of these is required to appear at all fires for the protection of rescued property, and for preserving public order, which is always liable to be disturbed at such a period. So little is the popular apprehension of the negroes, that of fifteen or twenty fire-engines owned by the city, one half of the number is entirely worked by slaves; and they are generally the most uproarious and noisy on such occasions.*

* The "Fire System" is particularly complete in Charleston. In addition to the ordinary engine, hose and axe companies, there is a detachment of citizen soldiery, consisting of three companies or

In the chapter devoted to Revenue and Expenditure, we are told in an extraneous sentence, which is closed with a note of exclamation, that in "South Carolina there is a tax on free people of color!" Had it not been that Miss Martineau was too well satisfied with the surface of the fact, she would have inquired farther; in the New England states she certainly would have done so; but it was quite enough to show, that in Carolina a special poll tax was levied upon the unhappy free negro. Let us complete the fact, and probably do away with the mystery and injustice, by stating that the same free person of color enjoys an exemp-

more—say two hundred men—always on what is called alarm duty. This feature of the fire system in Charleston may have deceived our author, and in obedience to her prevailing prejudice, she ascribed it to that one cause which, in her mind, is the source of all evil in America. These soldiers are relieved by others every three months. Their duty, as stated in the text, is chiefly to receive and protect the rescued goods, and to preserve order; since fires are most commonly the work of incendiaries, who avail themselves of the public alarm to plunder. Nor is this the only respect in which the fire police in Charleston is superior. There is a salaried officer,—an engineer—who, with certain assistants is required to appear at every fire, properly provided with powder made up into certain forms, and with the necessary *chevaux-de-frise*, for blowing up houses, in order to the more summary arresting of the conflagration by making a vacuum. Had these two departments been connected with the ordinary fire department of New York, the destructive fires of that city would be greatly curtailed—since the presence of the military would defeat the aim of the incendiary, and the timely blowing up of a house would arrest the flame when an engine could not.

tion from militia, from patrol, from fire and jury duty—for which exemption, the white mechanic and laborer would be very glad to pay ten times the amount paid by the free negro as a capitation tax.

In her remarks upon the policy and institutions of Carolina, to which I chiefly confine myself, there are sundry little errors of fact and inference like the preceding—which it is not worth our while to pursue—into which she has fallen from the single cause to which these have been ascribed,—namely, her bias upon the subject of slavery. This bias has been of so tyrannical a sort, as not to permit to her the free exercise of a correct judgment or true observation in any matter with which this topic is connected, however remotely or incidentally. To those who think for themselves, and examine the subject honestly, these errors will, in the greater number of cases, carry their own refutation along with them. They are the errors of a mind solicitous to obtain a support for its theory at all hazards, and consist accordingly of a very hotchpot collection. She records the vague apprehensions of women, the partial rumors received in cities, of doings upon the borders;—stories which have a narrow base of fact, upon which wanton conjecture and wide-mouthed declamation are always prompt to raise the most towering superstructures. All the crimes committed in the south, of whatever kind, and among whatever class, are studiously ascribed to slavery. Of the rapes, and hangings, and burnings upon the frontiers, she has an ample collection, and records many, of which the good people of the south themselves never heard. She makes no inquiry into these matters at the north; she does not seem to have asked about the offences of New York and Philadelphia, or the quality and color of the offenders in those cities.*

* And yet what daily atrocities reach our ears from the north. How many women are cruelly murdered in the cities—sometimes by priests, sometimes by merchants and merchants' clerks. What a volume of depravity was unfolded in the trial of Robinson; and there was the case of Avery. Of course the offender escapes, if he be not poor. If he be poor, he goes to the gallows or the state prison. The finding of the jury, declaring that the supposed murderer is not guilty, does not do away with the fact that the poor woman is murdered—nor does it diminish the aggravation that she is invariably murdered with impunity. The newspapers frequently record forgeries by priests, by priests' sons, and by the founders of splendid cities; and while they wonder passingly that such good people should be so bad, their chief regrets are, the loss of such enterprising citizens to the fine cities which they did so much for. Alleged rapes, by negroes upon white girls, are frequently stated by northern journalists, and one of these was tried, to the writer's knowledge, but a few years ago in Connecticut. We refer to Mr. Tappan for such particulars as resulted from the examination of the Commissioners of the Magdalen Asylum into the morals of New York; and we regret that Miss Martineau had not looked more closely into the negro quarters, and into the various police trials of negro offenders in the different cities of the free states. Had she done this, she would have spared us the entire chapter on the morals of slavery. Indeed, had she as narrowly examined the brothels and the stews and the alleys and sinks of London, with as keen a nostril as she has thrust into the southern country, she would have paused before taking ship for the new world; and, as a good chris-

If she hears that a slave poisons an owner in Carolina, though this event may occur once in an hundred years,* she declaims upon it lustily; but the crimes of free negroes at the north, with whose condition alone the comparison of the southern slave should be made, entirely escape her attention. Her ear is open to all that may be said against slavery; all that is said in its defence, she dismisses as not worth hearing. This partiality affects her general sense of justice towards slaveholders on other subjects. At page 44, vol. 1, she says—"In the senate, the people's right of petition is invaded. Last session, it was ordained that all petitions and memorials relating to a particular subject,—slavery in the district of Columbia—should be laid on the table unread, and never recurred to. Of course the people will not long submit to this." Mark how her tone changes when it is your bull that has gored my ox! At page 70, of the same volume, we find a similar proceeding of congress dismissed with a complacency quite remarkable, when compared with the evident indignation of the preceding

tian, would have set to work for the reformation of her own home. It is a modern British statistician who tells us, that, in London alone there are five thousand persons who will cut your throat for a shilling. No wonder our country should be tainted, when we have not only the provision, but the reformation, of all these rascals, thrust upon our hands.

* The very instance which she records was given to her as a remarkable one. She infers it to be a common occurrence, in spite of its notorious isolation.

paragraph. She is speaking of Carolina nullification. "Congress went on legislating about the tariff without regard to this opposition; and the protests of certain states against their proceedings *were quietly laid on the table as impertinences.*"

Speaking of the great spread of abolition doctrines, which it is her object to prove in advance beyond all calculation, she asserts the "absolute abolition strength in the house of representatives to be forty-seven," and draws this inference from the vote taken on the question, whether their petitions should be received or not; though she very well knew that many persons voted to receive the petitions who were yet hostile to their prayer.

She dwells upon the hatred entertained by the white towards the colored population. "Lafayette," she says, in illustrating her remarks on this point, "on his last visit to the United States, expressed his astonishment at the increase of the prejudice against color. He remembered, he said, how the black soldiers used to mess with the whites in the revolutionary war." Had Miss Martineau asked the reason of this change, which she should have done, she would have found that it was a change which was altogether confined to those regions where slavery had been done away with! The black soldiers of whom Lafayette spoke *were slaves*, and were satisfied with their condition of inferiority. By emancipation, the coarse and uneducated negro became lifted into a condition to which his intellect did not entitle him, and to which his manners were unequal—he became presumptuous accordingly, and consequently offensive;—and the whites who had regarded him with favor in his inferior and proper place, could not easily endure him as a tyrant, for such always is one lifted into a condition beyond his merits. The case is very different in the south, where slavery exists. There the negro is not hated. Far from it. He is there regarded as filling his true place, and as occupying his just position; and while he does so, he does not offend, but meets with favor and indulgence. It is only in the northern regions, where he contends for an equality with a people to whom he is morally and physically inferior, that he provokes hatred, and lives in a state of continual personal insecurity.* The hatred which Miss M. has seen in

* I need not refer to the frequent demolition of the houses and the property of the negroes, which take place at the north. This the abolitionists will ascribe to the slaveholders They already ascribe an influence to the slaveholders over the most noble communities of the north (as Miss Martineau does in her account of the friendly relations of Boston and Charleston,) which is not less insulting and degrading to those communities, than it is complimentary to the minds and characters of those supposed so to influence them. But this is ridiculous. The south,—Miss Martineau tells us in the very next breath,—is teaching disunion, because she has no influence. She then treats us with frequent anecdotes of the envy and hatred of the latter to the north. The true reason for the hostility of the whites to the blacks in the free states, is that given in the text. The latter become presumptuous, and their habits of idleness increase their presumption. The complaint of the white citizens of the northern cities is constantly to this effect. The blacks do not labor on the same terms with the whites. In fact they will not generally labor at all if they can help it. They will do light work—they will

the eyes of the clergymen, and the ladies, while speaking of this subject, (see p. 382, vol. 1,) was only seen through the medium of her heated and extreme prejudice. She looks, as "through a glass darkly." Her eyes are jaundiced—they are not healthy. They need the operation of that great oculist, Truth—and even he will not be able to operate upon her with success, until she has first had them well washed by that gentle handmaid, whom moralists call Humility. As yet, she is too talkative to listen, and too dogmatical to learn, even from Truth himself. We proceed with Miss Martineau. "When to all this is added that tremendous curse, the possession of irresponsible power over slaves," &c. There is no such irresponsibility in America. The laws protect the slave as a being of an inferior caste, it is true; but they do protect him. He is secured from murder as effectually as the white man, and from all wanton or aggravated punishments. That there are instances in which he suffers wrong, brutality and loss of life, is unquestionable; but these risks are not peculiar to the slave.

Here is a passage which should not have been published except on the most unquestionable proof: "A planter

job, brush boots, go on errands, sweep, tinker, and thieve; but they avoid the most manly and honorable toils, which the laboring whites boldly undertake and resolutely perform. The black seeks for the menial situation, and will always be considered—as he must be—an inferior, until he grapples with the most difficult and the greatest undertakings of the community.

stated to a sugar-refiner in New York that it was found the best economy to work off the stock of negroes once in seven years." Truly, the credulity of Miss Martineau on the subject of slave cruelty is perfectly English. It would be difficult to point to this Louisiana planter; and, we venture to say, that the sugar-refiner might not be so readily forthcoming to support the indictment. If he is, he should come forth, like an honest man, and denounce by name the heartless wretch by whom the speech was uttered.

We have been apt to think and say, in the south, that there were few people so very happy, hearty, and well satisfied with their condition, as the southern negro. Such, indeed, has been the general admission of the traveller; but the testimony of Miss Martineau is far otherwise. She never saw "in any brute an expression of countenance so low, so lost, as in the most degraded class of negroes. There is some life and intelligence in the countenance of every animal; even in that of the silly sheep, nothing so dead as the vacant, unheeding look of the depressed slave is to be seen."* But that it was necessary to the opinions of Miss M. that such a depression of countenance and such brutality should result from slavery, we think it probable

* It is the testimony of most English travellers, Miss Martineau among them, that the American countenance (that of the white man) was that of one careworn, and prematurely old. This is true of the commercial community. Touching the negroes, we may quote a dozen passages from Miss Martineau herself, which do not consist with the preceding.

that such would not have been her observation. But it is curious, not to say amusing, to remark how singularly indulgent our senses become to the prevailing moods and desires of our minds. An instance of this lately met my eye in the travels of a very pleasant writer and amiable citizen of our country, Mr. Hoffman of New York. On his arrival in Kentucky or Virginia, (I forget which, and the volume is not by me,) he sees, for the first time, one of those sights which remind him painfully that he is in a slave state. What is that sight? A stout, able-bodied white man is sitting or lying at his ease in his piazza, while an old negro is at work in the fields without. Now this is what we see hourly in the streets of New York. We continually encounter the nabob riding in his chariot, or sitting at his palace windows, while the aged laborer plies his heavy task of paving the streets, or piling wood or bricks, or doing a thousand things far more laborious than the task of any slave in the south. The one proves the existence of slavery no more than the other. They both simply testify to the universal inequalities of fortune in all parts of the world.

"There is an obligation by law to keep an overseer, to obviate insurrection." This is said of Alabama. We are not aware of the obligation by law to keep an overseer, and we believe there is none in Carolina; but it strikes us as sufficient authority for doing so, that the profits of the plantation would be sadly diminished without one; and in Carolina, as in New England, the interest of the proprietor is a paramount motive. We know, indeed, of no part of the world, where, if the subordinates be numerous, the overseer can well be dispensed with. They are employed, if not necessary, in all the factories in the free states. According to Miss Martineau the purpose of the overseer is to prevent that which it would be equally his policy, as a white man, to prevent if not one. He is in the same ship with the employer, and the storm which would destroy the one, would never spare the other.

"For any responsible service," says Miss Martineau, "slaves are quite unfit." This is not true; but allowing it to be so, Miss M. infers that it is because they are slaves that they are thus irresponsible; and yet we all know how superior is the Virginia and Carolina negro not only to the people from whom they came, but to the aboriginal North Americans, who invariably defer to them; and, in many cases, as in that of Micanopy and Abraham,* make them the "sense-keepers" or "sense bearers," that is, counsellors and advisers of the nation. On this point the notes of Miss Martineau are full of contradictions. In one place we are told, that the slaves prove themselves susceptible of education in numberless instances, (that they are susceptible of continual improvement there

* Perhaps, it may be safe to assert, that a treaty made with the negro Abraham would have been found more binding than that with his indian master. A moderate *douceur* would have bought over the sense-keeper, and he would have sold the entire Seminole nation for a few barrels of whiskey.

is no sensible slaveholder who will not assert, and that they have improved and are improving in their bondage, there is no honest observer who will venture to deny:) in another, they are denied the ability even to cut out the most common garments. The book is full of these contradictions, and in either case the assertion is made to prove the odiousness of slavery. If the negro is alleged to have improved, she insists that it is an improvement in spite of his bondage, not in consequence of it, and that his improvement would have been far greater had he been left to himself—if he be incapable, it is only because he has been degraded by slavery into fatuity. We may add, that some of the best tailors and mantuamakers in the southern states are slaves. In the cities, all of the hair-dressers and barbers, many of the butchers, and sundry of the tavern-keepers, are slaves or free negroes.

Miss Martineau not unfrequently takes the position of the slaveholder, and argues his case for him, simply to show the weakness of his cause. The defence is usually pitiful enough. To show our own inequality to the argument, she records all our angry speeches; and the disputant whom on another subject she would scorn to notice, is honored with a heedful ear, and a chronicled remembrance, when he utters himself on a topic which is at all times apt to provoke us. "We have our slaves and mean to keep them," was never uttered by any southern gentleman, by way of argument on the subject of slavery; but simply in answer to a party seeking to exercise a power in the councils of the government, in relation to a subject upon which the jurisdiction of government is expressly denied by the southron. She asserts that the Southampton insurrection took place "before the abolition movement began." Before it was generally detected,* she should say, for incendiary pamphlets, tracts, papers, and preachers, had been, according to the assertion of the slaveholders, common enough among the slaves before. But this she will probably deny as a gross slander upon the abolitionists themselves, from whom she has a different account.

The failure of christian preaching among slaves, in making them any better, is insisted upon as the result of the institution. "The testimony of slaveholders was explicit as to no moral improvement having taken place in consequence of the introduction of religion. There was less singing and dancing; but as much lying, drinking, and

* Speaking of the Southampton insurrection, Miss Martineau says, "It happened before the abolition movement began; for it is remarkable that no insurrections have taken place since the friends of the slave have been busy afar off." "Whereas rebellions broke out as often as once a month before, there have been none since." The effect is here mistaken for a cause. The insurrection ceased the moment that the labors of the abolitionists were discovered, and when they were compelled to "be busy afar off." The fact is a remarkable one. The moment that the south grew angry at the abolitionists and drove their laborers away, and burned their pamphlets and papers, the insurrections, which had "broke out as often as once a month before," entirely ceased. Miss Martineau should get glass eyes.

stealing as ever." It is to be feared that this failure of the teachers is not confined merely to the slaves—and the budget of horrors, brutalities and miscellaneous vices, which the book of Miss M. unfolds, as of occurrence among the free people of the country, should have taught her to hesitate ere she ascribed the evil to slavery. The very abolition of singing and dancing, as the result of the religion, must sufficiently show the sort of religion which was busy; and should certainly have produced some doubt in the mind of one so subtle on most subjects as the writer, whether the religion itself which, at the outset, subverted the innocent and natural recreations of a people, was not likely to produce even greater evils than it professed to cure. The philosophical mind has long since been anxiously watchful of the fearful progress of a gloomy bigotry throughout the land.*

* Miss Martineau should have remembered, while ascribing to slavery the defeat and failure of the professors of religion to make any impression upon the slaves, what she has herself said of their progress among the indians, who are freed from all the restraints which she deems so pernicious to the slaves. The gloomy and ascetic doctrines of our teachers have resulted only in the greater depravation of the savage; while the French catholics, who taught an easier faith, and indulgent laws of exercise and recreation, have been eminently successful in improving them. "Near Little Traverse, in the northwest part of Michigan," says Miss Martineau, "there is an indian village full of orderly and industrious inhabitants, employed chiefly in agriculture. The English and Americans have never succeeded with the aborigines so well as the French; *and it may be doubted whether the clergy have been a much greater blessing than the traders.*"

There is one passage in Miss Martineau's book which calls for the serious attention of the philosopher. We quote the passage entire. She is describing the state asylum for lunatics, in Columbia, South Carolina. "I observed that no people of color were visible in any part of the establishment. I inquired whether negroes were as subject to insanity as whites. Probably; but no means were known to have been taken to ascertain the fact. From the violence of their passions, there could be no doubt that insanity must exist among them. Were such insane negroes ever seen? No one present had ever seen any. Where were they then? It was some time before I could get a clear answer to this: but my friend the physician said, at length, that he had no doubt they were kept in outhouses, chained to logs, to prevent their doing mischief."

The fact above stated—not the conjecture of the physician—is a curious one, and well deserves the consideration of the public. It is singular, indeed, that we should find so very few insane persons among the blacks. The restraints of labor, tending to the subjection of those brutal passions of which Miss Martineau speaks, and which are not in consequence so active, I am inclined to think, in the negro as in the white man, must greatly abridge the tendency to insanity; and it may be that, the generally inferior activity of their minds, is one cause of their freedom from this dreadful malady. Certain it is, that we have few or no madmen among the negroes. The idea that they are chained in outhouses to logs, is idle enough; since, in that condition, they would require the constant attention of one or more able slaves, which a master would not be willing to afford; and would be, in other respects, a monstrous annoyance. Were insanity at all common among them, "it would be," in Miss Martineau's own language, "the interest of masters to provide for their useless or mischievous negroes;"—and this—were there sufficient occasion—would have been the case. But, in truth, there is little or no madness in South Carolina, whether among black or white. The lunatic asylum, which originated with the late William Crafts, of Charleston, and was pushed through the legislature mainly by his efforts, is not a popular institution in the state—as it is known to be unprofitable, and was believed to be unnecessary. The patients are usually few—not enough to support the establishment—and these, in half the number of instances, are drawn from other states. The few cases of madness known in the state, prior to the establishment of the asylum, were kept in a small building devoted to the purpose, in Charleston, connected with the poor establishment of that city. Among the inmates there were one or two negroes, both women—I do not think that there were more. The number was greater during the revolution, when the building appropriated to their confinement stood in the same neighborhood with the fabric more recently put to their use, and both within a short distance of the place of arms—or arsenal—which, when Charleston fell into the possession of the British, was assigned as the depôt for the reception of the weapons of the defenders. A melancholy fate attended the maniacs in consequence of this propinquity. The American prisoners, ordered to deposit their arms in the arsenal, under the feelings of mortified pride and shame, which naturally enough followed the surrender of their city, threw the weapons and ammunition confusedly together into the hall designed for them, without any regard to the danger of such carelessness. The consequences were dreadful. The building was blown up—the guard of British soldiers, fifty in number, destroyed—and the contiguous houses, the poor-house and mad-house, destroyed also, with the greater number of their unhappy inmates.

But to return to our author.—Miss Martineau does not let this opportunity slip, of conveying an imputation of inhumanity at the expense of the slaveholders. "No member of society is charged with the duty of investigating cases of disease and suffering among slaves, who cannot make their own state known. They are wholly at the mercy of their owners." We had almost called these wilful misstatements. The grand juries of the country are bound to take cognizance of all such matters, and frequently do so. The slaves, themselves, will always contrive to make their sufferings known, and have few scruples in complaining, whether they have cause or not. A brutal master is sometimes punished, and always known, and his offences against law and humanity in the treatment of his slaves, are quite as often the subject of public inquiry and prosecution, as in any other cases over which juries possess jurisdiction. But it is not often that he offends by their ill-treatment. His interest in the life and health of his slave, obviates the necessity of any particular supervision of the subject by the public authorities. No better security has ever yet been devised by man for the safety of man, and the proper observance of humane laws by the citizen, than that given by the southern slaveholder, in the continual presence of their leading interests. It would be fortunate for the country if the securities of the abolitionist were half so good. As for the chaining in the outhouse, the notion is ridiculous. A case of temporary necessity like this may have occurred, but nothing more. A madman chained in an outhouse, would be a sufficient source of disquiet to all the country round; and the neighborhood would soon rise *en masse*, and compel his removal to a place of safekeeping.

There is one painful chapter in these two volumes, under the head of "Morals of Slavery." It is painful, because it is full of truth. It is devoted to the abuses among slaveholders of the institution of slavery; and it gives a collection of statements, which, I fear, are in too many cases founded upon fact, of the illicit and foul conduct of many among us, who make their slaves the victims and the instruments alike of the most licentious passions. Regarding our slaves as a dependant and inferior people, we are their natural and only guardians; and to treat them brutally, whether by wanton physical injuries, by a neglect, or perversion of their morals, is not more impolitic than it is dishonorable. We cannot blame Miss

Martineau for this chapter. The truth—though it is not all truth—is quite enough to sustain her and it; and we trust that its utterance may have that beneficial effect upon the relations of master and slave in our country, which the truth is at all times most likely to have every where. Still we are not satisfied with the spirit with which Miss M. records the grossness which fills this chapter:—she has exhibited a zest in searching into the secrets of our prison-house in the slave states, which she does not seem to have shown in any other quarter. The female prostitution of the south, is studiously looked after, as if it were the peculiar result of slavery—she makes no corresponding inquiry into the prostitution of the north. She picks up no tales of vice in that quarter—no rapes—no murders—no robberies—no poisoning—no stabbing. She has addressed her whole mind to the search after these things in the slave states; and with a strange singleness of vision, she has entirely forborne the haunts of the negro at the north, and the degraded classes in the free states. She says nothing whatsoever about them. Had she demanded of Mr. Tappan a copy of the report of the commissioners of the Magdalen asylum of New York, of which he was the president and one of the founders, she would have been told by that publication that, in the city of New York alone, not including blacks, there are ten thousand professional prostitutes. We do not answer for the truth of this assertion; but as Miss M. has given elsewhere a most lavish eulogy upon the veracity and general good character of the abolitionists, and as Mr. Tappan has been heretofore regarded as the very Coryphœus of that fraternity, she will be able to determine for herself the degree of confidence which she should yield to this statement. The fact is, that in the southern states the prostitutes of the communities are usually slaves, unless they are imported from the free states. The negro and the colored woman in the south, supply the place, which at the north is usually filled with factory and serving girls. The evil is a dreadful one in both regions, but having its good more particularly in the south. The result of illicit intercourse between the differing races, is the production of a fine specimen of physical manhood, and of a better mental organization, in the mulatto; and, in the progress of a few generations, that, which might otherwise forever prove a separating wall between the white and the black,—the color of the latter,—will be effectually removed. When the eye ceases to be offended, the mind of the white will no longer be jealous, and that of the colored person will gradually approximate to the general capacity, the inflexible courage, and directness of purpose, which, at present constitute the moral difference between the two people.—But let us turn from this unpleasant subject.

Perhaps it may be safe to say, that two-thirds of Miss Martineau's book are more or less given to the slave institutions of the south, either in the shape of metaphysical speculation, the statement of supposed facts, or her declamation upon them. Setting forth with a resolution to uproot and utterly destroy an institution which she has previously resolved to be evil, she sees no aspect of it which is not so. The kindness of the master to the slave, is likened to the kindness which he has for his dog—the affection of the slave, and his respect for one whom he looks up to as greatly superior, is ascribed to the fear of punishment, or the utter fatuity of his intellect. Every anecdote of cruelty which she hears is religiously written down, and honestly believed;—and even the jealous apprehensions of a jaundiced wife, who fears that her husband is no better than he should be, are chronicled with a sad solemnity, which is amusing, as the fruit of slavery. The outrages of the borderers—the frontier law of "regulation," or "lynching," which is common to new countries all over the world, are ascribed to slavery. Miss M., along with too many others, seems to think that none but well-bred, quiet, peaceable men, should tame the wilderness. All her stories of great crime, of burning, and hanging, and stabbing, which she has raked up with such exquisite care, are stories of the borders. They belong to that period in the history of society, when civilization sends forth her pioneer to tame the wilderness. Your well-bred city gentleman is no pioneer—he belongs to a better condition of things and to after times. It is the bold, reckless adventurer—the dissolute outcast—the exile from crime, or from necessities of one sort or another—who goes forth to contend with the wild beasts, the stubborn forests, and the savage tribes who prowl among them. These people naturally enough become as wild almost as those whom they conquer; but they have their uses. They are the lower limbs of civilization, and the links which connect the wilderness with the city. They prepare the way for civilization, if uncivilized themselves; and however much we may deplore the crimes which they sometimes commit, we must content ourselves with the knowledge that these crimes seem to be unavoidable under the circumstances, and will continue, as they have been, to be committed, by the same class of men, whenever in a new country the presence of such adventurers becomes necessary. Still there have been crimes and outrages which are without their excuse, and I do not seek to excuse them. I look upon all violence and all injustice as brutal, whether it be the burning of the convent, the assault upon the trembling nuns, and their subsequent denial of justice—the frequent murders of women in places professing to be civilized, and where they are pleased to declaim very much about the outrages upon the borders,—or the cruel "lynchings" at the south of the sturdy incendiary. These atrocities in the settled communities of our country, may, most generally, be ascribed to the constant appeals which are made to what is called "public opinion;" an appeal to a something—a power beyond the laws—which is expected to take the form of an equitable jurisdiction, and remedy their supposed deficiencies. This I take to be one of the great causes of so much mobbing and lynching in modern periods among us. "Public opinion," so called, is very apt to become public action; and the mob, whom an editor invokes to ridicule the militia law, will not hesitate long to tar and feather the colonel, who is something of a martinet, and desires to sustain it. But it is not public opinion which is thus invoked—it is popular passion and a vain insolence which is cherished and brought into activity by such appeals, and which then becomes a tyranny, being out of its place. Public opinion is of very slow, very temperate, and very judicious formation. It is the aggregate of small truths, and the experience of successive days and years, which, heaped together, form a general principle, which is of instant conviction in every bosom. It only requires to receive a name in order to become a law; and a law which is precipitately imposed upon a people, in advance of the formation of this sort of public opinion, will soon be openly abolished, or become obsolete in the progress of events. For my own part, I am satisfied with the existing laws, until the convictions of the majority, and the progress of experience, shall call for their improvement. I have no respect for those who set themselves up for makers of public opinion; and as for the "hell-broth" so compounded, I know not any draught which would not be more wholesome than that which makes the body politic a body plethoric, and leaves no remedy to the physician but the cautery and the knife.

A goodly portion of the two volumes of Miss Martineau, is made up of the conversations and opinions of

Americans, who are nameless, and of her examination of these conversations. She sets up these argumentative nine-pins with the utmost gravity, and bowls them down with great rapidity and wonderful adroitness. Many of her arguments are carried on with women; and as there are very few women so "cunning of fence" on her own ground as this professional disputant, it is easy to see not only that she obtained no great victory, but that she derived no increase of knowledge from the controversy. Her own estimate of the mental pretensions of the American women, should have saved her from a misplaced confidence either in their evidence or judgment. Indeed, she only confides in their opinions when it answers her purpose to do so. She describes them as little above fatuity. The three chapters devoted to this subject, under the general head of "Woman," is a singular and contradictory compound of truth and error—which nothing but a rabid desire for publication could have suffered her to put forth. Their minds, according to her estimate, with few exceptions, are little else than a blank. They have little or no practical philosophy—no thought;—and they confound learning with wisdom. Wherever she heard of a woman having a local celebrity, she was sure to find her a mere linguist; and she winds up her generally contemptuous estimate of the sex, by ascribing drunkenness to the more enlightened among them—a vice, perhaps, more utterly foreign to the native female American, than to the woman of any other country on the face of the globe. "It is no secret on the spot, that the habit of intemperance is not unfrequent among women of station and education in the most enlightened parts of the country. I witnessed some instances and heard of more. It does not seem to me to be regarded with all the dismay which such a symptom ought to excite." The wonder is that with such an estimate of the sex, she should have drawn most of her authorities from them. This she does commonly on the subject of slavery. Her dialogues are mostly had with them; and these are silly enough, in most cases, to support her estimate. Fortunately, since the days of Lady Blessington's protracted conversations with Lord Byron, men are not satisfied with reports of this description, unless they have proof that the stenographer has been by and busy.

Another source of authority with Miss Martineau, is the public men of our country—the members of congress of both parties; and those, seemingly, among the most violent. It does appear to me that she could not have erred more strikingly than in this particular, since the furious partizan, whether in England or America, is usually the last person in the world from whom the unprejudiced and ungarbled truth can be derived. That she should not have given the most implicit confidence to their statements, is the legitimate conclusion from her own report of them. She tells us that they strove to make a partizan of her,—sought to secure her favorable opinions,—and, on all occasions, exhibited no less earnestness in making proselytes to the party, than they would have done in securing them for the cause of truth. It is true, she is, here and there, annoyed with something in their conduct that seems to startle her with the semblance of an inconsistency; but she does not, even then, doubt the good faith of the speaker. She suspects the judgment first—ay, always—with a self-confidence in her own, which is thoroughly English—the weakness—anything but the prejudice and the interest of party. The politicians of Carolina give heed, and bow ready assent to her anti-slavery propositions; and when she believes that she has them all snugly within the hem of her garment, she is thunderstruck to hear them vote aloud in approbation of Governor McDuffie's thoroughgoing, yet only half-elaborated, opinions in behalf of slavery. To this day she does not suspect that a polite southern gentleman, in a ball room, would infinitely prefer bowing assent to all her propositions, than gravely undertake to refute them through the medium of her "charming" trumpet.

"It was necessary to purchase Florida, because it was a retreat for runaways." This was one reason, perhaps; but Miss M. seems to have been imperfectly acquainted with the history of Florida. It may be well to inform her, that one of the best reasons for the purchase of that country, is kindred to that reason which prompts the United States and Great Britain to maintain so jealous a watch upon the island of Cuba, in order to prevent it from falling into the possession of any great maritime power. From the first, Florida, under the Spaniards, has been the scourge of the southern states. As colonies and states, they were subjected to the continual incursions of the savages under Spanish influence; and the wars of the borders between the two people, were among the most sanguinary of those that ever took place in America. St. Augustine was emphatically styled by the early English settlements in the south, the "Sallee of America." In later days a more urgent necessity arose for the acquisition of this territory; as it furnished a foothold during the war of 1812 to our affectionate mother, England, to plant her standard upon it, and summon her red brethren to pile up the scalps of her banished children beneath it. Had Miss Martineau read this history, she might have found stronger reasons for the acquisition of this territory by the United States, than the recovery of its fugitive slaves; though that is reason quite enough in our estimation to justify the purchase.—Of the Texian invasion, upon which her eloquence is purely invective, I do not propose to say any thing, except that I, for one, among thousands in the south, apprehend more injury, from its competition with the southern Atlantic states, in their domestic interests, than I ever hope benefit from its additional votes in the national assembly.* It

* Yet our reluctance to receive Texas into the union, would have the effect of delaying only, and not defeating the settlement of that country by North Americans. The safety, perhaps, of the south-west demands its conquest, and the restless character of our southern population—indeed of our whole people—will ensure it. Nor can

may be added, however, that the Texians tell a different story from Miss Martineau, respecting the settlement of their country. Certainly, one tribute of applause cannot be withheld from them. If they have usurped the possession of a territory not their own, they have exhibited the most singular and noble forbearance as victors towards their captives—a forbearance the more wonderful, indeed, as it was so utterly undeserved by the merciless and false-hearted savages, whom it was their good fortune to overcome.*

Miss Martineau insists upon the greater dependance of the south upon the union, than of any other portion, and ascribes to the slave system the weakness from which this

they stop there—nor stop at all until they are within the walls of Mexico, unless, with a greater degree of wisdom than they have hitherto shown, the Mexicans shall not only recognise their independence, but form a treaty of alliance with them. It will be the death-knell of Mexican power, if they provoke these fearless adventurers to lay down the plough and resume the rifle. As for the interference of England, she will have work enough to do to shake off her present colonies, which are greater bonds to her than to them, and to carry through her domestic war with the levellers, Miss Martineau at their head,—or wherever else she pleases.

* Miss Martineau styles the victory of the Texians over Santa Anna, in which he was made prisoner, "the unfortunate defeat of the Mexicans." She has not a word to spare touching the massacre of the "Alamo;" and yet she looks upon the taking of life as crime; to say nothing of the criminality of a violation of faith to those who surrender upon a solemn pledge of safety.

dependance is supposed to spring. "In case of war, they might be only too happy if their slaves did run away, instead of rising up against them at home." I must again remind her of a period, the history of which she has possibly never read, or possibly forgotten. The slave population of Carolina was quite equal in number to its white population in 1776, and, with the exception of two small corps of cavalry, which the British incorporated with their arms, and uniformed with their scarlet,* the entire mass of them adhered, with unshaken fidelity, to the fortunes of their masters—never deserting them either in trial, or danger, or privation, and exhibiting amidst every reverse of fortune that respect, that propriety of place, which did not presume in adversity, and took no license from the disorders of the times; and this decorum was exhibited, we may add, at a time, when, to the danger of invasion from a foreign power, was added the greater curse of a reckless and unsparing civil war at home. Perhaps the whole world cannot exhibit an instance, so singular and so worthy of grateful remembrance, as that of the conduct of the serviles of Carolina, during the seven years' war of the revolution.

Of the causes of the Seminole war, she gives the following account: "According to the laws of the slave states,

* A little more domestic history for this British lady. The negroes so incorporated with the troops of England—such as survived at least—together with several thousand beside, whom they could steal but not incorporate, were carried off to the West Indies and sold to slavery by the captors.

the children of the slaves follow the fortunes of the *mother*. It will be seen, at a glance, what consequences follow from this; how it operates as a premium upon licentiousness among white men; how it prevents any but mock-marriages among slaves; and, also, what effect it must have upon any indians, with whom slave women have taken refuge. The late Seminole war arose out of this law. The escaped slaves had intermarried with the indians. The masters claimed the children. The Seminole fathers would not deliver them up. Force was used to tear the children from their parents' arms, and the indians began their desperate, but very natural war of extermination." Such is the story of Miss Martineau. Without doubt it came from the mint of the abolitionists—the people of such veracity. This version is entirely new in the south. It is a budget of errors, one growing out of the other. The laws of Florida do not prevail over the indians. The children of slaves only follow the condition of the mother, where the laws prevail. If a runaway woman is recovered from the indian territory, her child will, of course, follow her condition under the laws of the state whence she escapes; and there may have been an instance where the child of an indian father is thus recovered with the slave mother, and carried back into bondage, but I am disposed to doubt even this. The occurrence is rare, if it ever does or did take place. The Seminoles own slaves, which are either brought from the island of Cuba, or are stolen from the whites at remote periods. They are only transferred from one kind of slavery to another; since they are held by the indians without any restraints of law whatsoever, and are liable to all their caprices of sudden rage, drunkenness, gloomy ferocity, and a malice which seems natural to them. Under these influences the slave is frequently murdered, and his murderer is unpunished. It is only such philanthropists as modern abolition provides, who esteem it better for the negro to be the slave to the savage, than to the civilized man. The indians do not often have intercourse with their slaves. They are a cold and sterile people, as is the case with most of the wandering tribes. Fecundity is one of the fruits of a settled and stationary population. The marriages among the negro slaves of the whites are much more formal, and quite as rigidly observed, as among the indians, who are polygamists or anything. They are creatures of impulse, having nothing but the mood of the moment for their laws. The rule, that the child shall follow the condition of the mother, is not a stimulant to licentiousness among the whites, and we almost wonder to find Miss Martineau meditating such a matter. She certainly knows but little of human passion, if she supposes that in matters of this nature, the mercenary desire of gain will prompt the white man to such excesses, other provocatives being wanting. So far from this being the motive, it may be stated here with perfect safety, that the greater number of the southern mulattoes have been made free in consequence of their relationship to their owners. Of late dates some arbitrary laws have been passed in Carolina, which forbid the citizens to free their slaves. I do not approve of these laws myself, but they have their advocates among the majority; and reasons of state policy are given in their behalf, which are imposing enough, if not altogether sound.* The war in Florida arose from other and more natural causes, which the philosophical mind of Miss Martineau would have soon enough ferreted out, if the demon of abolition had not possessed her brain, and too entirely darkened her vision. The hunting grounds of the indians were too much circumscribed by the gradual gathering of the whites around them, to permit them to procure sustenance after their customary habits. The game had become scarce, and, as they had not yet been taught the first lesson of christianity, as it is the first decree of God—namely, the necessity of labor—they were half the time in a state of starvation. Their contact with the civilized must always result—as such contact has everywhere resulted—either in their subjection as inferiors, or their extermination. Their only safety will be found in their enslavement, or in their removal to a region where the hunting grounds are open and uncircumscribed. They must perish or remove; unless they conform to the

* I am persuaded that it would be a wholesome policy to revoke these laws. It would, in the first place, prevent their frequent evasion. A more important consideration is, that it would give to the owner a power now denied, of doing full justice to the claims of the faithful and the intellectual, without compelling him to banish them from their native homes while bestowing upon them their own mastery.

established usages of the states in which they linger, and fall into the customs of the superior people. The government of the United States has aimed at their removal for many years; but this removal has been resisted in various quarters, and chiefly by the instrumentality of those universal philanthropists, who are now known as abolitionists. They were strenuous in opposing it, and did not confine their opposition to the councils of our own nation. They preached resistance to the indians themselves, and encouraged them to stay where they were and starve. Their eloquence in these exhortations overlooked the absolute necessities of the indian, and was chiefly devoted to the imaginary privations consequent upon his removal. They dwelt pathetically upon the loss of his homes, and his banishment from his forefathers' graves; and in dilating upon privations such as these, they entirely forgot all the more serious evils arising from the state of sufferance in which he dwelt, in an abridged territory, and under a government whose regulations, his necessities and his ignorance, alike, drove him momently to violate. In the poverty of the indians, they must either beg, steal or starve. In seeking to avoid the latter, the commission of crime is frequent. They become embroiled with the whites, whom they despoil of their hogs and cattle, and whatever else they can lay their hands on—they refuse obedience to the authorities they offend—they fly from the officers of justice, and seek for shelter in their wild recesses—their swamps and everglades. They are pursued, and from their refractoriness, are treated, naturally enough, as outlaws by their pursuers. The numbers on both sides accumulate, and blood is shed, and can only cease to be shed in the utter extermination of the inferior class. To avoid this dreadful necessity, the government has been laboring to remove them to other homes and a wider extent of country, where they may follow, without let or hinderance, the customs which they like. And this removal is but a small and partial evil, in comparison with the many evils which must follow upon their stay. Our homes depend for their comfort, not so much upon the associations of our childhood, as upon their fitness for our mental and moral condition. Men—civilized men, whose sensibilities upon such matters are duly educated, and made fine and susceptible by the institutions of society—daily dispose of their dwellings and depart into strange lands; and while we doubt not that all men must feel a sense of regret at parting from the homes of infancy and youth, we should be paying but a sorry tribute to their manliness and proper nature, in regarding this as a sore and overwhelming evil. The indian, too, of all people in the world, is the last to feel much, if any regret, at such a necessity. It is no great sacrifice for him. From the moment that his eyes opened upon the light, he has been a wanderer. He has never known a fixed abode, until the appearance and settlement of the whites formed a point of attraction, to which, with all the consciousness of his inferiority, he tacitly inclined. His fathers before him were wanderers, and according to their histories, their whole lives have been passed in bearing their stakes from the wilderness to the seaside, and from the seaside to the wilderness again. The habitations of the indians prove all this.* During the space of three hundred years—the time of our acquaintance with them—they have made no improvements—they have built no house of sufficient comfort or importance to be occupied by two successive generations. Their habitations have been such only as they could readily remove, or leave, without loss, to the use of some succeeding occupant. Their towns—if the collections of filthy wigwams in which they fester and breed vermin, may be called towns—are few, far between, and the men seldom in them. Their women have ever been their drudges, in the most degrading slavery—brutes without indulgence, and slaves to the most vicious caprices of their masters, without restraint or redress, unless it comes

* The account which the aborigines gave of themselves to the first discoverers, represented them to be the invaders of a people far superior to themselves in civilization, which their greater numbers and savage ferocity destroyed. This was the boast of the indian to the white man. The antique remains of works, fortifications, temples, and other fabrics, which are dispersed all over the country, confirm this intelligence; without regarding the obvious fact that these were remains utterly beyond the ability of the indians to erect. This history, we may add, is the history of the world, as we read it everywhere. The moment that civilization pauses in her conquests, she is overrun by the savage. She cannot rest in her conquests. She must conquer, not only to improve the savage, but to save herself. Let her pause, with an inferior tribe beside her, not acknowledging her sway, and she is overthrown.

in the sudden vengeance of some irritable relation. Such people have no idea of home. That is their best home which gives them elbow room, and full forests in which to hunt. The Florida war has sprung entirely from the want of such freedom; and we may add, that most of our indian wars have arisen from the same single cause. The philanthropists who would keep them in a region in which they have no resources of life, are those only to whom such wars are to be ascribed. Still, we do not deny the wanton injustice, and the occasional cruelty of the base white borderer. It would be wonderful, indeed, if such people did forbear the commission of injustice. Their labors are not of such a sort as would lead us to hope for their forbearance; and the necessities of the savage give them but too frequent provocation for the exercise of their unrestrained and brutal propensities. The true evil is in the condition of things which keeps the two races in contact, yet not in connection. The inferior people must fly from the presence, or perish before the march of approaching civilization.

I have now gone through most of the points which concern or affect South Carolina in these two volumes. I have confined myself to that state—simply, in order that my answer should be comprised within the limits of a magazine paper; and as I felt myself more at home in that region.*

* It would have been easy to show many errors in these books, extending from Maine to Mexico, arising only from the too ready disposition of Miss Martineau to theorize upon the slightest surfaces

There are sundry little anecdotes, however, which are given by Miss M. which are opposed to the general truth, but which, it is likely enough, are in themselves true. She has picked up anecdotes in all quarters that tell against slavery, *per se*, though not always reconcilcable with each other. Occasional opinions of discontented wives, morose husbands and disappointed politicians, are caught up by the "faithful trumpet," and now rise in retribution upon their utterers, to their own discomfiture no doubt, as they are to the discredit of their country. We do not object to these, and care not to pursue them. They involve no general principle, and, in many cases, are so decidedly inconsistent with other relations in the same pages, that the observing reader will readily detect and contrast them for himself. They will do no harm, and, indeed, the work itself will do no harm. On the contrary, I am disposed to think it will be of some considerable service. Like the book of Mrs. Trollope, it tells us some home truths, north and south, in spite of its errors and erroneous assumptions. We sincerely hope that

of fact: but this is a labor which will no doubt find a pen more able than mine in the several regions which she has wrongded. A work like that of this lady, who seems to think, and certainly tries to do so, as well as her hurry, and the variety of her topics will permit—is the proper one for dissection. To point out her errors may be of excellent use in England, where they know so little about their own descendants, and count so confidently upon their universal degeneracy; though, with a strange inconsistency, admitting them in some wonderful instances of moral and mental achievement, to have gone, at times, so far beyond all the rest of the nations.

it will be read with that unprejudiced attention, which will enable the reader to see and estimate the occasional truth which gleams up amidst the wilderness of words in which it is enveloped.

Miss Martineau is a monstrous proser. She is probably one of those persons who never believe that they have been talking all the while. She declaims constantly, and is forever searching after exceptions. She scruples at no game—fears no opponent—and whether the meat be washed or unwashed—hawk or heron—it is all the same to her. She discusses the rights of man, and—heaven save the mark!—the rights of women too, with her chambermaid, when she cannot corner a senator. Smart exceedingly—well practised in the minor economies of society, and having at her tongue's end all the standards of value in the grain, cotton, beef and butter markets, she does not scruple to apply them to the more mysterious involutions of the mental and moral organization of tribes and nations. It is but too evident that with all her cleverness, she lacks that more advantageous wisdom which begins with humility. She is too dogmatical ever to be wise. She comes to teach, not to learn. She gets nothing from her hearer, for she does not hear him. If she listens, it is simply because she is confident that her answer is ready. That she has never listened while in America, is evident from these volumes; though I doubt not that a great many words have gone through her trumpet.

Miss Martineau came to America with two or three

texts in her memory, which she assumed to be the standards by which our institutions and our people were to be tried. These texts were arbitrarily in her memory—not in her mind. She has taken them upon trust, and has not condescended to analyze them. One of these is the doctrine of majorities. These she insists will be right—right in the end. This arbitrary law applied to sundry cases in her mind, to which it is not common to apply it in America, alarms her by the annoying inconsistency which follows; and hence her wild chapter about the rights of women—their exclusion from the offices, the suffrage, and the authorities of state. Certainly, if mere numbers are to be considered the sources of power in a state, the inference is necessary that women are to be considered parties to the government; but the fact that they are not, in a country professing to be ruled by a majority, should have prompted Miss Martineau to an inquiry into the rights of the majority, and the definition of this phrase in its received political sense. Now, the truth is, the doctrine of majorities is simply the doctrine of physical power, determinable by an abstract standard, which obviates the necessity of the application of brute force. The majority tells us where the brute force lies, and we submit to it in most cases where the authority brings with it no greater hardships than would follow our resistance to it. When the injustice of a majority passes beyond the ordinary bounds of patience, it is resisted; and the *ultima ratio* is resorted to by the minority, either in hope or desperation. There is no abstract charm, in mere numbers, to compel the obedience of those who are wronged, and who think themselves so. But when it is known that votes represent men—able-bodied and armed men—the case is different. We at once see the enemy with which we have to contend, and the superior capacities which he possesses of coercion. The doctrine of majorities is in truth no new doctrine. It is as old as the hills. The only difference between times past and times present consists, simply, in the superior facilities, which, in modern times, we enjoy, of determining where the power lies, without any resort to blows. It is more easy, now-a-days, to compute the strength of the opposition, than it was in the distant periods when war was almost invariably the result of ignorance on both hands—and never was the doctrine more clearly illustrated than in the wars of Napoleon Bonaparte, whose many successes were the sheer result of his attention to this fact. His mode of concentrating his force at a given point, in advance of his enemy, was the true secret of his wonderful victories. Minorities would never submit to the frequent injustice of majorities, but that they well know that the court of dernier resort is one just as little likely to give them redress, as the power which robs them of their rights by a mere resort to the numeration table.

Her other texts are also drawn from the governing principles of our society. Her deductions from these principles, sometimes at variance with those practically drawn from them in the United States, are the occasion of much complaint and fault-finding. One of these, "that all men are created equal," is a subject of some disputation among philosophers in every country; and the dispute is not likely to be settled soon. Our forefathers, when they declared this truth to be self-evident, were not in the best mood to be philosophers, however well calculated they may have been to become patriots. They were rather angry in the days of the declaration, and hence it is that what they alleged to be "self-evident" then, is a source of very great doubt at present, when we are comparatively cool. But the truth is, that neither they nor we can well determine this subject. Nobody now-a-days is born naked. We are none of us in a state of nature. The artifices of life are around us, and we receive them with the light. But, not to gainsay our fathers, for whom we have every possible respect, let us endeavor to support their proposition. We must regard their assertion in a limited sense, for they evidently were not thinking of the *accouchement* of a lady, but of a nation. Their work was limited entirely to the claims of the citizen, *each in his place*, upon the government which he was required to sustain, for the protection,—while he obeyed its laws and performed his duties—of his life, his liberty, his pursuits, and his possessions. That God has not created the physical man, or the mental man, alike and equal, is not less true, than it is in perfect harmony with all his creations. Nothing, indeed, can be more remarkable or more delightful to the mind and eye, in the examination of the works of the Deity, than the endless varieties and the boundless inequalities of his creations. Whether we survey the globe which we inhabit, the sky which canopies, the seas which surround us, or the systems which give us light and loveliness, we are perpetually called upon to admire that infinite variety of the Creator, which nothing seems to stale. The stars are lovely in their inequalities, the hills, the trees, the rivers and the seas; and it is from their very inequalities that their harmonies arise. Were it otherwise, the eye would be pained by the monotony of the prospect everywhere. As it is, we love to look abroad upon nature, and it is with a pleasure no less sensible than that of the savage, that we learn "how to name the bigger light and how the less." They have their names only as they are unlike and unequal. It is because these shine *in their places*, however inferior to other orbs, that they are lovely. They are all unequal, but each keeps its place; and the beauty which they possess and yield us, results entirely from their doing so. A greater philosopher than Thomas Jefferson—and we may add, after a long interval—Jeremy Bentham and Miss Martineau, has given us a noble passage devoted to this subject, which is no less philosophical than poetical—indeed, it is the true poet alone, who is the perfect and universal philosopher. Let us hear William Shakspeare. I quote from "Troilus and Cressida." The speech is made by Ulysses at the close of the seventh year of the siege of Troy, when the Greeks, emulous of each other, each striving for sway, begin to despair of success in the continued disappointments of the war. After a prefatory passage, he says:

"Degree being vizarded,
The unworthiest shows as fairly in the mask.
The heavens themselves, the planets, and this centre,
Observe degree, priority and place,
Insisture, course, proportion, season, form,
Office and custom, in all line of order:
And therefore is the glorious planet, Sol,
In noble eminence enthroned and sphered
Amidst the other; whose med'cinable eye
Corrects the ill aspects of planets evil,
And posts, like the commandment of a king,
Sans check, to good and bad: *But when the planets,*
In evil mixture to disorder wander,
What plagues, and what portents? What mutiny?
What raging of the sea? shaking of earth?
Commotion in the winds?—frights, changes, horrors,
Divert and crack, rend and deracinate
*The unity and married calm of states**
Quite from their fixture? Oh, when degree is shak'd,
Which is the ladder of all high designs,
The enterprise is sick! How could communities,
Degrees in schools, and brotherhoods in cities,
Peaceful commerce from dividable shores,
The primogenitive and due of birth,
Prerogative of age, crowns, sceptres, laurels,

* This line would be an admirable application, in the shape of a motto, to what should be the feeling, and the communion of our confederacy. With the sense of the whole passage, as our rule of action, it might be so yet.

But by degree, stand in authentic place?
Take but degree away, untune that string,
And hark! what discord follows! Each thing meets
In mere oppugnancy: The bounded waters
Should lift their bosoms higher than the shores,
And make a sop of all this solid globe:
Strength should be lord of imbecility,
And the rude son should strike his father dead:
Force should be right; or, rather right and wrong
(Between whose endless jars justice resides)
Should lose their names and so should justice too.
Then everything includes itself in power,
Power into will, will into appetite;
And appetite, an universal wolf,
So doubly seconded with will and power,
Must make perforce an universal prey,
And last, eat up himself. Great Agamemnon,
This chaos, when degree is suffocate,
Follows the choking."*

* Pope, too, not to speak of an hundred others, has like authority.

"Order is Heaven's first law, and this confest,
Some are and must be greater than the rest."

The laws of society are not intended to disturb the natural degrees of humanity; but to reconcile them—to make them consistent with and dependent upon one another—not to make the butcher a judge, or the baker a president; but to protect them, according to their claims as butcher and baker. Let us illustrate these distinctions by some well known cases. In a claim for maintenance the jury will inquire what have been the habits, what is the education, the tastes, sensibilities, &c. of the wife—in an action for damages, in slander, the words being the same, the jury will adjudge the amount of damages according to the profession, the moral and intellectual stand-

This noble passage is full of meaning and truth. Degree, or things in their proper places, is well insisted upon. All harmonies, whether in the moral or physical worlds—arise, entirely, from the inequality of the tones; and all things, in art, nature, moral and political systems, would give discord or monotony, but for this very inequality. The equality insisted upon by the levellers, would result in the necessary forfeiture of names to things, and all barriers of present distinction would be broken down. This, too, would be against the very nature of man, whose perpetual effort is to rise above his fellows. This was not in the contemplation of the fathers of our country. They were democrats, not levellers. Democracy is not levelling—it is, properly defined, the harmony of the moral world. It insists upon inequalities, as its law declares, that all men should hold the place to which they are properly entitled. The definition of true liberty, is the undisturbed possession of that place in society to which our moral and intellectual merits entitle us. *He is a freeman, whatever his condition, who fills his proper place. He is a slave only, who is forced into a position in society below the claims of his intellect. He cannot but be a tyrant who is found in a position for which his mind is unprepared, and to which it is inferior.* That such

ing of the slandered person, and this too, without reflecting, that it is wholly in defiance of this doctrine of universal equality. Yet the trial by jury is, perhaps, even beyond that of representation—nay it is representation—the very bulwark of the equal-rights principle.

were the definitions of democracy in the days of the declaration, is fairly inferrible from the fact, that they left the condition of their social world precisely as they found it. They might, indeed, have held as an abstract notion, that in a state of nature, men were born equal; but they certainly never held that they must of right continue so, nor is this a fair conclusion from what they say. The birthright of man may be alienated in a thousand ways, and it never was an unqualified one.

The next subject is the *inalienable rights of man.* "All men are created equal; they are endowed by their Creator with certain inalienable rights; among these are life, liberty, and the pursuit of happiness," &c. Now, is it true that life, liberty, and the pursuit of happiness are inalienable under the practice of our governments? Do we not alienate them every day? Men are hung for rapes, for treason, for murder, for forgery, for burglary, and many other offences. We cast them into prisons and deprive them of their liberty; we sue them in the courts, and take from them their property. On what pretence, if these rights of man be inalienable, do we deprive him of them? There is some mystery in all this, not to be explained by a resort to the ordinary mode of argumentation; and those who insist, as Miss Martineau does, upon the unlimited and unqualified meaning of these natural laws—for, natural rights are natural laws—will certainly be at a loss to reconcile a difficulty like this.

There must be a qualified acceptation of these principles and phrases, or they are nothing. *The truth is, that our rights depend entirely upon the degree of obedience which we pay to the laws of our creation. All our rights, whether from nature or from society*—and these are the only two sources of right known to us—*result from the performance of our duties.* Unless we perform our duties, we have no rights; or they are alienable in consequence of our *lâchse.* The man has no rights by nature, unless by a compliance with the laws of nature; as he would have no rights from society, unless by a compliance with its laws. *These laws, in a state of nature, require from the man the application of his mental and physical energies, to the improvement of the passive world around him.* It was given to him for this single purpose. The indian, who finds himself upon a hillock, has no more right to it, by nature, than the hog which burrows along its borders, until he proves his right by the exhibition of faculties superior to those which the hog possesses. He is no more a man than the hog, until he complies with the natural laws of his being. This, he does, when he builds himself a cabin from the woods around him—when he bends the branches into a bower overhead, and covers the roof with leaves, and strews the floor with rushes; and thus protects himself against the elements;—when he gathers fuel, and by rubbing two dried sticks together, builds himself a fire, and warms himself against the cold;—when he plants his maize and beans, and provides against future hunger. These prove his superiority to the brute, and maintain for him the proper rights which his superior powers have fairly established to be in him. He literally obeys the first decree of God to the expatriated man, and by tilling the earth, obtains his bread in the sweat of his brow.* As he proceeds, labor, which, alone, is but a blind Polyphemus at the best, receives a divine assistant from heaven in the shape of art. She gives life and animation to his toils, cheers him with her smiles and her songs; and when his work is ended, with a plastic hand smoothes down its roughnesses, and from the rude block commands the upspringing presence of beauty. In the progress of time, nature supplies him, from his own bosom, with another ally, of whom he had no previous knowledge, in the shape of science. This ally is many-winged and many-handed, and makes all the elements subservient to his purposes. He shows labor where to place his shoulder, and the mountain is heaved from its base. He tells where he shall strike, and the crag is cleft by his stroke. He hews down the high trees of the forest at his bidding, and guides his dwelling place upon the waters. These gifts prepare man properly for life. The crowning and last gift, which is spiritual religion, prepares him for death. But the inevitable law must be first obeyed, or he gains none of these blessings. He must first *labor*. This is the destiny from which he is forever

* And this is one of the first elements of religion, as it is the prime element of human prosperity. Genesis is studied in vain, unless this be the conclusion of the student.

seeking to escape.* It is only by a compliance with this, the first law of his creation, that he can hope to be secure in life, successful in his pursuits, benefited by society, and made happy by religion. It is the key-stone of religion itself; and the missionary who seeks to teach the mysteries of christianity to the wandering savage, can never hope to be successful, so long as he neglects to inform him of the first duty consequent upon his creation.

The result of labor to the man is property. The possession of property is the first cause which brings about the formation of society: numbers become necessary to defend it from the barbarians, who do not labor, and who have none. As society improves and increases, and it must inevitably do so, while it continues to comply with its natural and obvious laws, it extends its dominion and controls the surrounding tribes for its own safety. These succumb, are enslaved, and as they improve in intellectual respects, are lifted by regular degrees, into the bosom of

* The desire to escape this destiny, is one of the true causes of the present distress of our country. We are all toiling to avoid toil; and we cog, lie, swindle, speculate—do any thing but delve and dig. We import our labor—the most useful and necessary arm of our population—from a foreign country; and a long train of miseries must ensue in consequence, which the narrow mind will always be unwilling to trace back to this seemingly unimportant origin. But it is so. It is a moral disgrace to a nation such as ours, not less than a political and social evil, when we are compelled to import from foreign lands our grain, our bread stuffs, and the forage for our cattle. Land was given us for cultivation, not for sale.

that society which has first enslaved them.* The superior people which conquers, also educates the inferior; and their reward for this good service, is derived from the labor of the latter, which, being in all moral respects, the inferior people, can yield no other recompense. Unless the civilized and superior nation does this, it will inevitably fall a victim to the barbarous tribes which gather around it—forever poor, desperate and daring—having no possessions to lose, and from their bestial improvidence, compelled, in all inclement seasons, to resort to war with their neighbors, to avoid starvation. It is no less the duty, than the necessity, therefore, of civilization, to overcome these tribes; to force the tasks of life upon them—to compel their labor—to teach them the arts of economy and providence; and with a guiding hand and unyielding sway, conduct them to the moral Pisgah, from whence they may behold the lovely and inviting Canaan of a higher and holier condition, spread out before them, and praying them to come. When civilization ceases to extend her conquests, she falls, like Rome, the victim to the savage. She must conquer, or she must perish. The war is as endless between her and her foe, as between any two diametrically opposite principles in the same moral circle; and as

* This is a natural and therefore an inevitable result. Without referring to the moral law to this effect, the southern slaveholder finds it his interest to lift the more intelligent slave into stations of higher responsibility and more honorable trust, than are commonly yielded to his fellows.

her sway is the more gentle, and as she conquers only to improve, while the savage only conquers to destroy, it follows, inevitably, that hers is the only legitimate conquest, and every other is but tyranny.

Every primitive nation, of which we have any knowledge, in the whole world's history, has been subjected to long periods of bondage. They have all been elevated and improved by its tasks and labors; and a positive sanction for the use of slavery, and a proof of its necessity, are fairly to be inferred from this inevitable consequence;—but, as if this were not enough, for the purposes of authority, God himself, we are given to understand, actually in two remarkable instances, placed a favorite people in foreign slavery, making them hewers of wood and drawers of water in the land of the stranger; as, from their refusal to comply with the laws of their creation, they had shown themselves unfitted even for the very comparative degree of social liberty allotted to men at these periods—requiring them thus, through that ordeal, which is improperly called slavery, but which is simply a process of preparation for an improved and improving condition, to work out their own moral deliverance. For, truly is it, that we shall not only gain our bread by the sweat of our brow, but thus subdue those barbarous appetites, and degrading brutal propensities, without the removal of which our minds could never have that due play and exercise, which can alone fit them for social dependance, and the friendly restraints of a guardian government. The nature of man is one of continual conflicts, and those chiefly with himself; and the proverb which inculcates the victory over himself, as the most glorious of all victories, is one strictly and philosophically growing out of a just knowledge of his own attributes and the difficulties which oppose their exercise.

Our general views, in modern times, on the subject of slaves and slavery, are distressingly narrow. Our forefathers were less precipitate, but more certain in their philosophy. They did not scruple to go forward, but they were first sure that they were right in doing so. We do not resemble them in this. We are too ready to follow multitudes to do evil. Having commenced our political career, by a grand innovation upon the existing condition of things, we would still innovate; and like any other good principle suffering abuse, the zeal which released us from a foreign yoke, would also release us from our allegiance to higher influences than kings. We are losing our veneration fast. The cry is "on," and we do not yet see the beginning of the end. Never was fanaticism more mad than on this subject of slavery, which was a very good thing enough when "England and the north" sold slaves, and the south bought them; and it is a good thing now, if we would only reason rightly, and find out what slavery is. We make no distinction between those restraints which impose labor upon the body,—improving its health, bringing out its symmetry and strength, and fulfilling a destiny, which, the analogies of all histories, not less than the faith which we profess, teach us is the decree of the universal parent;—and that bondage of the mind and denial of its exercise, which are always the aim of tyrannies, and which, as in the case of some of the *unlaboring* people of Europe, must result in the utter enervation, sluggishness, and shame of body and mind alike. Pity it is, that the lousy and lounging lazzaroni of Italy, could not be made to labor in the fields, under the whip of a severe task-master—they would then be a much freer—certainly a much nobler animal—than we can possibly esteem them now;—and far better had it been for our native North American savage, could he have been reduced to servitude, and by a labor imposed upon him within his strength, and moderately accommodated to his habits, have been preserved from that painful and eating decay, which has left but a raw and naked skeleton of what was once a numerous and various people—a people, that needed nothing but an Egyptian bondage of four hundred years to have been saved for the future, and lifted into a greatness to which Grecian and Roman celebrity would have been a faint and failing music.*

* I will be referred to the experiment of this nature, made by the Spaniards in the island of Cuba, in which the poor savages were utterly destroyed. But this is no parallel case to the proposition in the text. The reason why the Spaniards failed, and the indians perished under the *repartimiento* system, arose from the fact, that the masters had only a temporary and not a permanent interest in their services. The Spanish governors were compelled to arrive at sudden

This clamor about liberty and slavery, is, after all, unless we get some certain definitions to begin with, the most arrant nonsense. "License they mean when they cry liberty," and we may add, "license they mean when they cry slavery!" The extremes are near kindred, and in all these clamors they are sure to meet. The Russian boor is called a slave, and the German subject of Austria is called a slave, and the Italian is called a slave, and the negro in the southern states is called a slave,—and yet, how unlike to one another is the condition of all these slaves! The right of ruling themselves is that which is assumed to be the test of freedom. The native African has that right, and what is the rule of Africa? A sufficient commentary upon it will be found in the naked, unmarked outlines, hanging upon the walls of our houses, and dignified with the title of a map of Africa. Murder awaits the missionary and the traveller who penetrates the country; and civilization seems to be as far remote as ever from their attainment. They cannot improve until they learn to labor,—they will not learn to labor until they become sta-

wealth, or not at all; and they worked the savages to death in order to obtain it. Had the indians been allotted to them, not according to geographical, but numerical divisions, those results would not have followed. They should have had a limited number of slaves, and in these they should have had a life interest. Their policy, then, must have been to economise that labor, of which, under the existing circumstances, they were inhumanly profligate. The fate of the indians, under such rule, might have been predicted.

tionary; and the wandering savage has seldom yet become stationary, unless by the coercion of a superior people.* But the right to govern themselves requires first a capacity for such government. The right can only result from a compliance with the laws of their creation; and the capacity requires long ages of preparation, of great trial, hardship, severe labor and perilous enterprise. The responsibilities and the duties of self-government, demand a wonderful and wide-spread knowledge and practice of morals, before such a capacity can arise; and it would be an awkward and difficult inquiry at this moment to discover any two of the leading nations of the globe where such a capacity exists. *I will not even believe it to exist in the United States, until I see the people willing to tax themselves directly for their own protection. I will not believe it, so long as they need to be deceived by indirect and circuitous taxation, into the expenditures which are necessary for their own good. They are not yet willing to look in the face the cost of their own liberties.* The practice of the English government denies the existence of

* For the sake of the African world, it is to be regretted that, instead of abolishing the slave trade, the nations had not contented themselves with regulating it. Vessels should have been licensed for this trade, of particular burden and construction, and carrying limited numbers; by which means the disgusting and dreadful horrors which resulted from the compression of the unhappy captives, in great numbers, into fœtid and narrow dungeons, would have been avoided, with all of the evils consequent upon their change of condition; leaving them only to the thousand benefits, which make the American slave so superior an animal to the African freeman.

any such capacity among its people;* and France!—what have all her bloody days, through successive ages, effected for her liberties, but cries for more blood, an increasing discontent, and the fever and the phrensy which continually

* Great Britain has freed her slaves, yet denies equality to a large portion of her own people—yea, denies them equal liberties of conscience. But why has she freed the blacks? If they had an unqualified right of freedom, by what right has she limited their freedom, in making them apprentices for a term of years? Their rights, if absolute, demanded, on her part, an absolute release of them. While I write, I am reminded of a paragraph in the Table Talk of Coleridge. It is kindred to our notions, and we give it accordingly. He says: "You are always talking of the *rights* of the negroes. As a rhetorical mode of stimulating the people of England *here*, I do not object; but I utterly condemn your frantic practice of declaiming about their rights to the blacks themselves. They ought to be forcibly reminded of the state in which their brethren in Africa still are, and taught to be thankful for the providence which has placed them within the means of grace. *I know no right except such as flows from righteousness;* and as every christian believes his righteousness to be imputed, so must his right be an imputed right too. *It must flow out of a duty,* and it is under that name that the process of humanization ought to begin and to be conducted throughout." In another paragraph devoted more distinctly to the proceedings of the British parliament, Mr. Coleridge speaks thus: "Have you been able to discover any principle in this emancipation bill for the slaves, except a principle of fear of the abolition party struggling with a fear of causing some monstrous calamity to the empire at large? *Well! I will not prophesy; and God grant that this tremendous and unprecedented act of positive enactment may not do the harm to the cause of humanity and freedom which I cannot but fear!*"

defies and defeats her own laws, in the appetite which calls for fresher uproar? Perhaps, the very homogeneousness of a people is adverse to the most wholesome forms of liberty. It may make of a selfish people (which has succeeded by the aid of other nations in the attainment of a certain degree of moral enlargement,) a successful people; but it can never make them, morally, a great one.* For that most perfect form of liberty, which prompts us to love justice for its own sake, it requires strange admixtures of differing races—the combination and comparison of the knowledge which each has separately arrived at—the long trials and conflicts which precede their coming together; and their perfect union in the end, after that subjection on the part of the inferior class, which compels them to a knowledge of what is possessed by the superior. This was the history of the Saxon boors under the Norman conquest—a combination, which has resulted in the production of one of the most perfect specimens of physical and moral organization

* The moment that a people boasts of its homogeneousness, we may begin to doubt its farther improvement, particularly if the community be a small one. The homogeneousness of the jews is, probably, the true reason of their national inferiority. They are a people, without a nation. All insulated communities degenerate; until, in time, they cease even to have issue. The intermarriages of islanders, villagers and other homogeneous people, should be forbidden by law; and so should the intermarriages among cousins. *Perhaps, it would be well, if our men in America always chose their wives from other states and sections, than their own.*

which the world has ever known. And where this amalgamation cannot be effected, as in the case of the Israelites—who are too homogeneous for commixture or even communion with other people,—the slave, in the progress of events, acquires the knowledge of the master. When Moses could emulate the Egyptian priesthood, he was able to embody and to represent his people, and to lead them forth from bondage; for then they had acquired all the knowledge which was possessed by the Egyptian. The time will come, I doubt not, when the negro slave of Carolina will be raised to a condition which will enable him to go forth out of bondage. When that time comes, it may be, that we, like Pharaoh, will be loth to give him up. But that that time is very far remote, is sufficiently evident from the condition of the free negroes in the northern states. Without restraints of any kind, they have yet founded no city to themselves, raised no community of their own; but are willing to remain the boot-cleaners and the bottle-washers of the whites, in a state of degrading inferiority, which they are too obtuse to feel; and are only made conscious of their degradation by the occasional kicks and cuffs which they are made to endure, at the humor of the whites, and without any prospect of redress. They have not that moral courage—the true source of independence—which would prompt them, like the poor white pioneer, to sally forth into the wilderness, hew out their homes, and earn their rights by a compliance with their duties. They feel their inferiority to the whites, even when nominally freemen, and sink into the condition of serviles, in compliance with their natural dependance and unquestionable moral deficiencies.

The circumstance which, more than anything beside, prepared the Anglo-American for the comparative condition of freedom which he enjoys, was the desperate adventure, the trying necessity, and the thousand toils through which he had to go, in contending with the sterility of an unfriendly soil, and the continual and thwarting hostility of surrounding and savage men. The very sterility of New England, by imposing upon all classes the necessity of labor, gave strength and energy to her sons, and stability to her institutions. Her severe austerity arose even more from her own toils and trials, than from her puritan ancestry; and bating the bigotry and miserable exclusiveness which, among the vast majority of her people, can find no greatness and little worth beyond her own borders, she confessedly stands among the highest of any people on the face of the earth. The fertility of the soil in the south, by readily yielding to the hands of labor is, without any paradox, the true source of our enervation, and of the doubtful prosperity of our country—as a country merely. Individuals are successful and prosperous, but not the face of the country; and however much this may be the subject of regret on the one hand, like the trumpet of Miss Martineau, it is not without its advantages. It results, we may state, in individuality of character among its people; who never, in consequence, devolve upon societies, combinations, and their neighbors, their several duties of charity, hospitality and friendship; and who sufficiently esteem their own morals, their sense of honor and humanity, to think they can do justice to the claims of their dependants, without the interference or tuition of any gratuitous philanthropy.

The chapter which Miss Martineau devotes to the "Morals of Slavery," should rather be styled the morals of the community. The excesses to which she refers, and in some respects particularizes, are excesses not confined to the slave states, and which do not, in any state, result from slavery. We contend for the morality of slavery among us, as we assert that the institution has brought, and still continues to bring about the improvement of the negro himself; and we confidently challenge a comparison between the slave of Carolina, and the natives of the region from which his ancestors have been brought. No other comparison, with any other people, can properly be made. We challenge comparison between the negro slave in the streets of Charleston, and the negro freeman—so called—in the streets of New York. Compare either of these with the native indian, and so far as the civilized arts, and the ideas of civilization are involved in the comparison, you will find that the negro who has been taught by the white man, is always deferred to, in matters of counsel, by his own indian master. The negro slave of a Muscoghee warrior, to my knowledge, in frequent instances is commonly his best counsellor; and the primitive savage follows the direction of him who, having been forced to obey the laws of his creation, has become wiser in consequence, than the creature who wilfully refuses.* This subjection to the superior mind is the process through which every inferior nation has gone, and the price which the inferior people must always pay for that knowledge of, and obedience to, their duties, which alone can bring them to the possession of their rights, and to the due attainment of their liberties—these liberties always growing in value and number with the improving tastes and capacities for their appreciation. Show me any people, which, complying with this inevitable condition, has not improved! Show me one, refusing to comply, which has not perished!

* "The indian," says Miss Martineau, "looks with silent wonder upon the settler, who becomes visibly a capitalist in nine months, on the same spot, where the red man has remained equally poor all his life." Elsewhere and everywhere she describes the negro slaves of the indians as looking better than their masters. She attributes this to the milder form of their slavery to that of the whites; though the obvious inference should have been, the greater advantages of white slavery in so educating the inferior African, as to lift him into a mental condition vastly superior to that of the red man, who, in a state of nature, is decidedly more intellectual than the black in a like state. She says, speaking of the religious education of the indian—"I fear that the common process has here been gone through, of taking from the savage the venerable and true which he possessed, and to force upon him something else which is neither venerable nor true." This is one of those vague phrases and seeming philosophies with which the book abounds. The fact is, that the only "venerable and true," which is necessary, for the improvement of the indian, is to compel him to labor—the venerable and true which he never yet has been taught, and is not now very likely to acquire.

Look at the history of man throughout the world, with the eye of a calm, unselfish, deliberate judgment, and say if this be not so. Regard the slave of Carolina, with a proper reference to the condition of the cannibal African from whom he has been rescued, and say if his bondage has not increased his value to himself, not less than to his master. We contend that it found him a cannibal, destined in his own country to eat his fellow, or to be eaten by him;—that it brought him to a land in which he suffers no risk of life or limb, other than that to which his owner is equally subjected;—that it increases his fecundity infinitely beyond that of the people from which he has been taken—that it increases his health and strength, improves his physical symmetry and animal organization—that it elevates his mind and morals—that it extends his term of life—that it gives him better and more certain food, better clothing, and more kind and valuable attendance when he is sick. These clearly establish the morality of the slave institutions in the south; and, though they may not prove them to be as perfect as they may be made, as clearly maintain their propriety and the necessity of preserving them. Indeed, the slaveholders of the south, having the moral and animal guardianship of an ignorant and irresponsible people under their control, are the great moral conservators, in one powerful interest, of the entire world. Assuming slavery to be a denial of justice to the negro, there is no sort of propriety in the application of the name of slave to the servile of the south. He is under no despotic power. There are laws which protect him, *in his place*, as inflexible as those which his proprietor is required to obey, *in his place.* ***Providence has placed him in our hands, for his good, and has paid us from his labor for our guardianship.*** * The question with us is, simply as to the manner in which we have fulfilled our trust. How have we employed the talents which were given us—how have we discharged the duties of our guardianship? What is the condition of the dependant? Have we been careful to graduate his labors to his capacities? Have we bestowed upon him a fair proportion of the fruits of his industry? Have we sought to improve his mind in correspondence with his condition? Have we raised his condition to the level of his improved mind? Have we duly taught him his moral duties—his duties to God and man? And have we, in obedience to a scrutinizing conscience, been careful to punish only in compliance with his deserts, and never in brutality or wantonness? These are the grand questions for the tribunal of each slaveholder's conscience. He must answer them to his God. These are the only questions, and they apply equally to all his

* The slaveholder has no right to free his slave—unless he is perfectly assured of a mental and moral capacity in the slave, sufficiently strong and fixed, to enable him not only to maintain his elevation, but to improve it. Having done so, let him appear before God, if he dare, and account for the trust committed to his hands. The moral and mental worth of the slave, can, alone, give us the right to discharge him from his dependance.

other relations in society. Let him carefully put them to himself, and shape his conduct as a just man, in compliance with what he should consider a sacred duty, undertaken to God and man alike.

FATHER ABBOT,

OR,

THE HOME TOURIST;

A MEDLEY.

By W. GILMORE SIMMS, Esq.

CHARLESTON, S. C.
PRINTED BY MILLER & BROWNE,
No. 5 Broad-street.
1849.

ADVERTISEMENT.

The papers which follow appeared during the last summer, in the columns of the *Charleston Mercury*. Frequent applications to the writer, have persuaded him to consent to their republication in the present form. They may be allowed to speak for themselves without preface. I beg leave to inscribe them to the Hopeful, the Believing, and the Working Spirits among us, as designed, in part, to inculcate a faith in *place*, as necessary to a just performance of appointed duties.

The Author.

THE

HOME TOURIST.

I.

The members of the Monastery—our merry Monks of the Moon—had accomplished a third rubber of whist, when it was perceptible that a general cloud of gravity—it would be irreverent to call it dulness—had fallen upon the assembly. Our excellent Father Abbot himself was detected in a most expansive yawn, showing an extremity of condition such as had never befallen him before. We had our Jester, but he failed, in a laboured effort, to provoke the merriment of the order at the expense of our venerable head; and we were fast sinking into that state of collapse, which betokens dissolution and departure in social as in human bodies, when our excellent Father Abbot startled the brotherhood into sudden vitality, by an exclamation as unnatural in his case as it was uncongenial with the faith professed by the fraternity.

Abbot.—I am weary of this life, my brethren, weary of this life!

The Editor.—Does our Reverend Father design to commit suicide?

Abbot.—Get thee behind me, Sathanas!—Would'st thou make a wanton paragraph? Do thy wits wander? Do'st thou deem me a fool, an absolute ninny, to suppose me capable of thinking that one may fling off the consciousness of life as if it were a garment—a thing of wool or linen—such as thou wearest in the vulgar form of the sack—a habit, which I take leave to say, is as unbecoming to thy person as it is ungracious in my eyes? Life is not to be flung off, or its consciousness. It is a thing to last forever. Change of condition is not death, whether wrought by the inevitable will, or by the rash and ridiculous madness of the poor and imbecile discontent. Of this I had no notion. I was meditating upon the unprofitableness and weariness of the present life we lead; of the lack of variety in our enjoyments; of the eternal same faces, and of the vexing monotony of thy newspapers, of which the shame and reproach are particularly at thy doors; lending thyself and press to this disgusting scramble after loaves and fishes, on the part of those who only fill their mouths with patriotism in the hope of filling them with bread.

Editor.—Verily, Father, thou art right. Our papers have been but too much filled with this politician brawling.

Abbot.—To loathing, sir—to utter sickness of heart and stomach! Thou hast thy lesson, let it be amended hereafter. With the cares of heat upon us—the apprehensions of disease—the pestiferous perseverance of mosquitoes—the newspapers should be filled only with soothing and grateful matters. It is then, especially, the duty of the

Editor to put forth all his strength, summon all his recruits to his assistance, and win the thoughts of men from present cares and troubles by the magic play of wit—the summer flashes of a joyous lightning that illumines the cloud without shattering the house top.

Editor.—Ah! would our holy Father but assist us in this goodly performance.

Abbot.—Hath he ever withheld himself from those who were in the condition to need and to receive his service? But, with the city deafened by the eternal and intolerable clang of contending factions, each of which cries with a tongue, the roots of which are in his abdomen, shall the singing birds of poesy or philosophy be heard? Preposterous! Purge ye of that. Let there be a calm, and smooth waters, that the dove may go forth on her mission, and proclaim the greenness and the beauty in that land which ye have but too much labored to defile.

Editor.—We repent, Father. We have already made the confession of our sins. *Assolvi; assolvi!*

Abbot.—If thy repentance be sincere, thy sin is forgiven thee! But for the future, our future as well as thine, beware how thou offendest after this fashion. The press is a trust confided to thy hands. It is not merely that thou should'st furnish intelligence of passing events, and advertise the wants of customers. It is for thee to exercise an overruling control even of the advertisements tendered thee, so that neither vice nor error shall expose itself for traffic in thy columns. Thou shalt even make grammar of thy advertisements, no less than of thy paragraphs, and suffer no scaramouch to play his antics in thy pages, unconscious of his own sootiness of aspect, to the annoyance of more modest neighbors. *Verb. sat!* And now for more personal matters. As I have said, this life hath become passing tedious. Even the Monastery lacks of its usual attractions.

Beauclerk.—Alas! it is even so!

Abbot.—It takes its aspect from the city, and from the depressed humors of the system, which are humbled by these excessive heats. The heart longs for change. Change is the life of nature. We must vary the prospect. Many a sick man dies from the monotonous aspects of his chamber. Give him another room, show him gleams of green and sunshine from any quarter of the heavens and the earth, and you give him hope—hope, sir, which lives ever on the refreshing resources of change. We must seek this change for ourselves. We are all sick;—thou no less than the rest. There is a greenness about thine eyes which tends to jaundice mine. The tongues of the Club are drowsy. *Thou* hast written no pleasant paragraph for a week or more, and Pictor has abandoned his easel. I mark ye, all, that ye drink more deeply of your claret, and your voices and brains seem to thicken accordingly. We must go abroad: we must wander—all who may—that our winter evenings may be made pleasant by draughts upon the grateful memory of our summer rambles.

Pictor.—But whither, father?

Abbot.—Ah! Pictor, already thy fancy rises; thy imagination begins to spread her wings. Thou art thinking of the mountains of Saluda, of the Apalachian ranges, of the stupendous glories of the Tzelica, which the vulgar persist in calling the French Broad, because of the rude hunter, French, who, looking after "Bear and other varmint," crossed the great back bone of the country, and stumbled upon its surpassing waters. Thou would'st fly, now, to Cæsar's Head, and to the Hickory Nut Gap; to tbe Table Mountain; to Tallulah, and to Toccoah! "Season thy patience for awhile," my son. Thou shalt visit these favorite realms of sun and shadow, of temple and devotion, at the proper opportunity, but our present purpose contemplates not the interior. I would conduct thee to views along the great plain of ocean, rather than the wild ranges of rock and mountain. I would conduct ye to the finest watering place in all America—to one of the most glorious beach-drives that we may boast; where thou may'st daily behold the worshipping waters of the Atlantic, either subdued and sleeping at thy feet, or rising, rolling, revelling, or raging, in the wildest antics, for the surprise of thy fancy, or the excitement of thy imagination.

All.—Where? Holy Father! Where is the delicious spot from whence we may behold these things? Long Island, Rockaway, Nahant!

Abbot.—Pshaw! Yankee Humbugs, all!—with which our poor nincompoops, who find nothing good or beautiful but the foreign, have been deluding themselves for the last hundred years. Something nearer home, my children; more easy of access—more worthy, as well of our love, as our admiration. There, with the ocean opening its wide gates of foam, for a thousand leagues before us on the one hand, shall we turn upon the other to behold green islets, whose grassy slopes and wooded crests stoop to the brink of the sunny billows. We shall see smiling villages crowning the modest heights, the smooth waters of a bay scarcely less lovely than any we may name, its entrance strongly watched by frowning fortresses, which lie grimly waiting for the enemy, in a vigilance which never shuts the eye; and, beyond, a gay city with her daily rising spires, which seem to spring out from the ample bosom of the great sea itself. What would you more? Is not this a subject for your pencil, Pictor? Is not this a theme better fitted for your columns, Master Editor, than the cry of young and old ravens, equally clamorous with the chorus of the daughter of the horse leech—"Give! Give!

Beauclerk.—But whither, Father; where is this scene of which you speak? Where do you mean to take us?

Abbot.—Ah! you are all agog with curiosity. The charm works. The drowsiness hath left your eyelids, and the claret remains untasted in the goblets of Pictor and Beauclerk. Drink, children, that ye may have strength for the revelation. It will surprise you yet more. *Io so che avete sete, perciò bevete!* You will feel better after it.

All.—We obey—and now.

Abbot.—Can you not guess?

All.—We have tried: No.

Abbot, (solemnly.)—My children, such of ye as may, will leave with me in the last boat to-morrow afternoon for Sullivan's Island.

II.

Omnes.—To Sull--Sulli--Sullivan's Island, Father?

Abbot.—Ye seem confounded, my children!

Beauclerk.—And well we may be, Father. Who, till now, ever heard that Sullivan's Island was a place of so many attractions? Here have we been living, man and boy, for a matter of near two hundred years, and it is now, for the first time, that we hear the place spoken of as one possessing such superlative beauties.

Abbot.—You mistake, Beauclerk! When we were a people of simple pursuits, and of a more manly and less dependent nature, it was greatly valued because of these very beauties. The grant which confers upon every citizen the right to build his wigwam upon Sullivan's Island, free of charge for land, was based upon its notorious attractions to the City, to which, indeed, it was conceived a place of prime necessity.

Beauclerk.—For health, I grant you.

Abbot.—"Dost grant me, hedgehog?" Well, and what is health, but the great essential of happiness; and upon what plea do our people fly northward with the summer, but that they seek for the securities of health? But the enjoyment of health necessarily implies comfort, though I am not satisfied to base my argument in behalf of Sullivan's Island upon its salubrity alone. I repeat the challenge, that ye will name to me a nobler beach, a broader empire of sea prospect, upon which the eye may wander, sweeter, cooler, or more cherishing breezes, or a prospect within the harbor, of more becoming loveliness?

Editor.—But, Father, the unmitigated heat, the blazing sun at noon-day—no trees, no shade!

Abbot.—It is because ye live like vegetables rather than like men, when ye get there, that ye suffer from the heat! Do ye feel the sun when fishing, under an ample awning, with your anchor dropt just on the edge of Drunken Dick, and the billows lifting your bark, with a swell of breezes that come all the way from Cuba to fan your cheeks?

Pictor.—Warmed moderately, and gratefully perfumed, with the sighs of the Cuban damsels.

Abbot.—Precisely! The imagination of Pictor begins to glow. But, in truth, it is the stagnation, and not the heat, from which you suffer on Sullivan's Island. The heat is not a whit greater there than I have found it at noon-day, in the same season, at Saratoga and Long-Island; and the evenings are far lovelier and more refreshing. But, remember, I am not now speaking of what art has done, or may do, to make Sullivan's Island perfect as a place of summer resort. The houses are calculated rather against sudden tempest, than with regard to human comfort. Their plans, if indeed they ever were planned, are as wretchedly unsuited to the scene and situation, as if they had been tumbled out of rolling clouds. We should borrow for such a situation, the plans of the people of Bagdad. The oriental style of courts, should be coupled with our verandahs, securing us shade always. Light moresco wings should enclose a central space, where we may rear shade and shrub trees, and find fragrance and shelter from the same sources. There is some talk of a fine hotel for the Island. Make it as fine as you please, but, above all, let it be suitable to the place and the season. Give it a noble court. Cover with it three sides of an open square, with a colonnade compassing the entire front, and a basement which would be cool always, spanned by ample arches. The buildings within the Fort are somewhat on this plan:—let the architect improve upon them.

Editor.—All this is very good, Reverend Father; and no one doubts that art can so perform its offices, with nature, as to supply many of her defects. But I confess to a surprise, with the rest of the brotherhood, that, all on a sudden, our Island should be discovered to be a place of such admirable natural superiority. Now, I may claim to be tolerably familiar with it.

Abbot.—Pshaw!—shooting curlews when you had nothing but the birds in eye and mind; or going down to a dinner party, when the great essential object of thought was C——'s wit, and C——'s champagne! On such occasions, let me tell you, men never look out for the beauties of a region. In fact, no man looks to make a discovery, unless first satisfied that a discovery is to be made. We undertake the search after neither a truth nor a beauty, unless first assured that they are in existence. This is a law of nature, requiring that the medium of search should first be in the mind, before the object ever grows up before the eye. Now, the very fact that you have never heard of the resources of Sullivan's Island, except as a place of health, is conclusive with you that it possesses none. It is thus that a man too frequently lives only in his great grandmother, and if she died without having known the virtues in a melon, he will be apt to grow up in the perfect conviction that a melon is nothing better than a squash.

EDITOR.—Your zeal, Father, may make you eloquent, but not conclusive. Your sarcasm applies too generally, to fall with force upon any. Unhappily, the opinions which I have expressed, are universal with the brotherhood.

ABBOT.—Why not add—with the whole City?

EDITOR.—And so I may!

ABBOT.—Ay, and so you may, and with propriety. A people who have done nothing but look abroad, and live abroad, all their lives, will be the last people to see anything worth looking at in their own provinces. Indeed, their justification for absenteeism depends entirely upon their assertion touching the deficiencies of home. What Irish nobleman or landowner, living in Italy, will admit any attractions in Ireland, except his rents? But, in arguing from our previous refusal to acknowledge the *home* attractions, in point of place and climate, you must go further. We happen not only to refuse our faith to the place, but to the persons. We do not believe in one another, my children.

PICTOR.—Fie, Father! Has our brotherhood done nothing to repair this evil? Was not our blessed and beloved order, the "Monks of the

Moon," created especially to teach this faith in one another.

ABBOT.—And what if we have done something towards it? Does this make against my argument? Enough, that the want of faith in the virtues of the race, *was* the pregnant deficiency of the community. It is still so to a most lamentable degree; and your questioning in regard to what has been alleged in behalf of the attractions of our Island, is simply illustrative of our pernicious local habit in every respect. You all persist in refusing to see the thing as it is. You refer me perpetually to the past. When I say, look at the loveliness of this harborage—look at at the green shores which gird it in—behold the proud fortresses which dignify and defend it—see the noble City, with its spires, rising, almost like another Venice, from the bosom of the deep; and see, where, at the very entrance to this beautiful region, lies an Islet by the sea, its broad, hard, sandy beach, glittering in the moonlight, and the glad waters subsiding to a musical rest upon its gently sloping shores:—when I have said and shown all this, what do you answer? Why—that your grandmothers lived here a thousand years, and never, in all that time, thought these things worth looking at.

BEAUCLERK.—Ahem! Father, my grandmother was an honest woman.

ABBOT.—God bless her! Let her rest! We have not summoned her. Be not offended, my children. Ye are still in the shadows and depths of the valley of ignorance—ye are still steeped to the lips in the waters of prejudice and a narrow vanity—ye labor still under certain infirmities common to our city. Let us cure these infirmities if we can—let us couch this blindness if it be possible—and let us first begin, by dismissing from our lips those stereotyped laws of a very dull and purposeless convention, which have been ruling us too long. Our infirmity has grown out of too rapidly acquired affluence, under circumstance which can scarcely happen again, unless perhaps, in California. It may be, that, sixty years from the present time, there shall be on the waters of the Gila, a pet community. These shall constitute what will be called there the aristocracy. They will dine from plates of gold—they will revel in halls of marble—they will marry only among one another; and they will be acknowledged as the lords of the land. Your grandson will probably discover, among these people, the grandchildren of persons, who, in the old States, were not held worthy to unloose the latchets of your shoes. Yet, on the Gila, what airs will they take on! How they will swagger! They will realise a common history; they will despise the region where their fathers made their fortunes, and from which they still draw their resources: they will curse it by absenteeism; they will see nothing of its attractions; and will turn up their puppy noses at every argument which goes to show the treasures of their own homes. My children, we cannot well cure this disease in persons who are far gone with it. But, if possible, let us keep these people, the younger generations, from being inoculated. Now, I give you too propositions to chew upon. They involve the horns of a dilemma. A region will always represent its race: they will take their tone and coloring from its elemental aspects; they will be fashioned morally and mentally by its climate and its necessities; they will suit no other half so well. The other is like unto it. No individual is superior to his race. He is, perhaps, never more distinguished than when he represents the highest condition of its character and intellect. Very few do this. He, therefore, who believes neither in his place, nor in his race, is the worst of infidels—a besotted one—an ass that never sees his own ears—which I take to be the worst sign in the condition of such a beast. But is Pictor asleep?

PICTOR.—Only absorbed, father!

> ———" *Qual ne' tuoi dètti*
> *Magia s'asconde.*"

ABBOT.—No blarney, Belial! Enough, that we both know who talks well. Why need we advertise unnecessary knowledge?

EDITOR, *(suddenly waking.)*—Advertise, did you say? Eh! Ah! Proceed, good Father, I hear—I listen.

ABBOT.—What a heathen Greek it is! But I will not be confounded. I will proceed; for, in truth, I have something more to say.

BEAUCLERK, *(aside.)*—When had he not?

ABBOT.—And now, my children, let me remind you of what the Germans tell us of "the open secret." It is that secret which lies at the feet of every man; but which, by reason of his own blind follies, vanities, or prejudices, he can never be made to see. The bounty of God leaves no man without his treasure, would he only stoop to pick it up. Every land, in turn, has its own resources of wealth and beauty; nay, of enchantments; fairy climes, weird wonders, and spoils of magic, precisely as it hath resources of soil and fruitage. These, indeed, are its moral fruitage, which a race possesses only in degree with the exercise of its faith and courage. In the resources of the race, there is no stint of the individual. There is a wealth for each, in turn; but it can belong to him only who seeks to find it. The successful search naturally depends upon the conviction that we feel that the thing sought for *is in existence.* To him who searches with this proper faith, there are discoveries at every footstep. Hills that seem barren on the outside, have wondrous metals and minerals within. Rocks that frown in granitic grandeur, but strike them with the right hand and hammer, and they open straightway, and reveal beneath, the wondrous loveliness of articulate and living marble. Trees that bear no fruit to the eye, have yet strange, sweet singing birds, that harbor in their branches; and the dull clod, the seemingly unconscious plain of prairie, under the proper stroke of the wand, discovers the secret currents of pure and refreshing waters. But there must be a divining rod for the revelation of these treasures. They belong only to those whom the *slaves* of the *lamp and ring* declare themselves willing to obey.—These find avenues among the hills, paths through the interminable thickets, forms of beauty in the cavernous rocks, and voices of rare melody in otherwise silent birds. These are your magicians. They possess what we may call, "The Home Secret." These are the Genii of Art and Labor, who consecrate themselves to *place;* and unless these discover "The Home Secret" for a people, the race, after a certain period of gestation, must die out, failing their mission, like herbage that never reaches seed time. Such men constitute the genius of the nation. They are the first to discover what a people are, what they need, and what they may become. In short, they lay hands upon and develope the secrets of a country;—and every country has certain secrets peculiar to itself. For them, only, does Isis, the great Mother of Mysteries, remove her veil, and without falsifying the inscription on her shrine. They are *not* mortal. They sound the fathomless, they trace the pathless, they gather from all systems the blessings and the light, and preserve them for the benefit of one. And all this, my children, *only because they look at home!* It is in the very humbleness of their seach that they make their discoveries. Tell the vulgar man of morbid self-esteem, of some great wonder passing before him, and he elevates his eyes, and pitches his vision to the farthest possible point within his horizon; and all the while the great spectacle is passing at his very feet. The difference between the great and the little man is in nothing more remarkable than this. The former makes himself the master of his provinces; the latter seeks for servitude in the provinces of other masters. The mental forage of the one, can only be furnished in foreign pastures. He turns up his nose, with a nice antipathy, at the thing which grows beside his own doors. It is the noble duty of the other, which springs from an unselfish love—perhaps, in some degree, from an inevitable destiny—to labor ever in its proper cultivation. It is his pleasure to draw the novel from the familiar, the precious from the cheap, the rare from the common, the ideal from the actual. And these, by the way, are the greatest of all studies—the studies of the great in every age.

Editor.—How little does the common mind understand this, particularly in the development of home treasures. Mere egotism and vanity, certainly, never find anything at home but themselves. How often have I heard the small author, in America, disparaging native art.

Pictor.—Ay, and how often have I heard the native artist aver that he could never tolerate an American book.

Abbot.—This is the weakness of persons, who, having acquired some position themselves, respectively, in their professions, presume in judgment, and claim a right to preside, as oracles, before they have earned the right, which sympathy alone can impart, to ask an audience. Their self-esteem blinds them to the fact, that such avowals of opinion are fatal to none more than to themselves. If the race is competent in one department, why not in another? If wanting in a literature or an art, why not in all? If not unendowed in one, demanding the same requisites of taste, fancy, imagination and thought, why should they be wanting in any province, which demands the exercise of these agents? But the notion is an impertinence, as surely as it is an absurdity. The Providence of God leaves no nation utterly without the means, not only of its extrication and deliverance, but of its high moral and intellectual triumphs. The seeds of glory as well as life, are thickset in every land. There might have been poets, and artists, and philosophers, among the savage tribes of Apalachy and the Rocky Mountains, great as ever were produced among the fairest of the Caucasian tribes, had they taken the first step in the discovery of "The Home Secret." But here was their difficulty, at their very threshhold—they had no homes. The history of a national progress to civilization may be comprised in few words. The first step is to make a people *stationary*. Slavery seems to be the only process for effecting this.—To be stationary, labor becomes inevitable, as the habitual law of life. Labor begets thought, training, method, morality and art, finally. These, in turn, beget the spiritual tendencies. From these come all the higher aims of the intellectual and religious nature.

Editor.—Ah! but that first step! What a courage is implied in the voluntary assumption of the tasks of labor. One would think it necessary that a race should first be favored with an inspired man—a prophet as well as a master.

Abbot.—And such is the master. The master of the Lamp and Ring, is endowed, no doubt, for his mission, if he be not false, like Balaam, to his duty. He must show to the nation what is lying at its feet, declare the uses of its own hands, un-scale the domestic vision. There is a moral, no less than a physical near-sightedness, which is one of the prime sources of a national genius. There is nothing so sectional, so exclusive, as genius.—How Homer subjected the possessions of the world, to illustrate and make glorious his own tribes of island fishermen. How Shakspeare makes English every thing that he touches! What tributes have Burns and Scott drawn from the surrounding nations, with which to crown with verdure the bald, bleak hills of their own petty domain! And how natural that this should be so! Our affections and sympathies are of little use, scattered over all the dominions of mankind. We better prove our sympathies with the rest, when we attach ourselves to one of its sections, and expend our strength, our art, our affection upon that. Let the *Genius Loci* do thus always, and what region will remain without its tutelary god and crowning altars! It is in this very moral near-sightedness that we find the seeds of all true patriotism; all other is counterfeit and hollow. Without the representative genius which possesses it, and which asserts the right of a people to position, one race is simply the shadow of another. It is servile because purposeless—the creature of a foreign enemy, feeble with all it numbers, and flinging its misdirected arms in air, while its head is down, muffled, beneath the arms of a superior.

Pictor.—Beauclerk sleeps, Father.

Abbot.—Ah! I see! You have my benediction! Remember, we depart to-morrow by the last boat. *Au revoir!*

III.

Omnes.—Welcome, Father, you are just in season. It is the last bell which you hear.

Abbot.—As it should be, my children. I am never late, but love not to be too soon. Ha! who is this? our Poet, our Lopez de Vega? Whence come you, my son? Whither have you been?

Poet.—To Georgia, Father.

Abbot.—What, Rowland Springs?

Poet.—No, indeed! I remembered too well your favorite maxim, never to go where all the world goes; in particular, to those places where we see little besides our own people. I have been on a visit to the wild places—the mountains, the rocks, the waterfalls, the Currahee, Tallulah, Toccoah.

Abbot.—Ah, dog! But there rests against your name, in the records of the Monastery, a fine of a dozen of Champagne. You went without leave, after your usual fashion: without beat of drum; selfishly seeking pleasures which you were not disposed to share with your brethren. For my part, I can enjoy no pleasure unless I share it. I see but a small part of the beauties of the landscape, unless some dear one is nigh to partake my delight.

Poet.—And it was with this very feeling, Father, that I went alone. I shall report their beauties and delights hereafter. Too much company spoils for me the charms of the prospect. There will be always some blockhead to cry aloud, at the moment when you are bathing in rapture—"What a glorious prospect!" Such people distress and sicken me. I seek to feed, and in silence—to feed the soul through the medium of the eye—and, at such periods, I care not to listen to the buz of human voices. I would hear no sounds save those which are properly kindred with the scene: the voice of the torrent, or perhaps of some grey eagle or lordly vulture, as he sweeps in mighty circles, and screams in unison with the hoarse roar of shrieking waters. Feeding thus alone, my digestion is always good.—The thoughts and fancies which I then enjoy are taken into the system, and become *fused*, as it were, with all the natural faculties. In after days they find utterance as a part, not simply of the scenery, but of myself. It is thus, and then, that I share all my delights with my brethren. I give them no crude exclamations. I give them the symmetrical conception—the full conclusion---the perfect wholeness of the prospect—with enough of *myself*, to enable them to determine to whom they should be grateful. To have them with me when I am studying my picture, is to endanger its propriety and symmetry. Their exclamations at such moments are as ungracious and intrusive as the interruptions, by the vulgar and pretending, of the favorite strain of music, breaking the symmetry of its finest parts, under the impudent plea of declaring their delight, and applauding the performer.

ABBOT.—You are ingenious and subtle, as usual contriving to rebuke your neighbor in defending yourself. But do you class your fellows of the Monastery with the vulgar who are guilty of such monstrosities as those you describe? Do you hold us to be people of that order, who perpetually demand your opinions of what you see, and challenge your admiration of the things they affect to admire? Do we not all know what a fine and unusual prospect demands? Do we not know that nothing is more gradual in growth than the capacity for judging of the new and unfamiliar? Who sees all the charms of a picture, where the picture has anything in it, at a first glance? We must wait until our standards grow, as they do always if we give them time, from the survey of the scene itself; and nothing is more vexing or impertinent than the vulgar challenge: "Is'nt that beautiful?" from people who can scarcely tell an eagle from a cow, and know no more of poetry than a donkey. Verily, my son, your offence is great, if you confound the children of our beloved order with such miserable cattle.

Poet.—It were a great sin, Father, were I guilty of this offence. I spoke in generals only. I have had the brotherhood gratefully in mind, during all my journey. It was to prepare the way for them, to make myself familiar with the *terra incognita*, that I might be useful in their guidance, that I went first alone. It was the first suggestion to our Brother, the Editor, upon my return last evening, that we should all visit together, the scenes which I have been compassing; for verily, Father, they well deserve the regards of our blessed order. In particular, Father, they appeal to *thee!* They will refresh thy fancies, they will stimulate thy imagination, they will fill thy mouth with good things, and thy youth will be renewed like that of an eagle, when he has bathed his pinions in the fountains of the Sun!

Abbot.—Thou amendest thy error, child! We will think of this tour of survey which thou counsellest. It may meetly follow after our return from Sullivan's. They tell me much of these wild regions of our sister State. They speak of Tallulah as being a scene of great magnificence.

Poet.—Equal, in most respects, to Niagara, Father.

Abbot.—Ha!

Poet.—More various and wild, full of beauties which Niagara does not possess, and of a grandeur little short of the awful glory, which is the charm and wonder of that great world-cataract.

Abbot.—Toccoah?

Poet.—Beautiful as a virgin's first dream of love. Beautiful as a nymph gazing into the maternal fountain.

Abbot.—Son, we shall go thither on our return. But our boat is underweigh. Let us get to the bows. I like ever the forward prospect.

Editor.—We owe much, Father, to Master Hillard, by whose enterprise frequent boats ply between the city, the island, and other places. He hath opened the way to Haddrell's Point.

Abbot.—Drop the Point, I prithee! Why cumber the language unnecessarily? The place should be called "Haddrell" only. It is a good name,—sounding, without being affected or petty, and needs no addition. We have a most atrocious habit of finding bad names for good places, and spoiling them when they are excellent. We must clap on a *ville* or a *ton*, when there is no sort of necessity for it. How much do we improve Rutherford, as the name of a village, or Clinton, by mounting it with a rider? I abominate these terminations! How much better were Charleston, as Ashley, and Georgetown, as Winyah, instead of perpetuating clumsily, the memory of a Scotch-French profligate, or a Dutch-English-Hottentot! Hereafter, say Haddrell—the Point will be understood.

EDITOR.—*Ita lex.*

BEAUCLERK.—Certainly, for such a pretty city, Charleston should have a more appropriate uame.

ABBOT.—It *is* a pretty City! With a thousand deficiencies, it has yet a thousand attractions. Our egotism has led us to insist upon our *moral* qualities only; our graces of society, our frank hospitality; the elegance of our women, the high character of our gentlemen. These are things, certainly, of which we may be proud. But we have regarded these too exclusively, and have accorded nothing, or but little, to the physical beauties of our home. Certainly, no city could have been more happily seated. Two tributary rivers enclose her in their ample embrace. The ocean sweeps up to her very doors, making a grateful murmur at her portals, and bringing her the odors from a thousand islets of the deep. If she lacks a back ground. such as high mountains alone can bestow, she has a compensative beauty, thus rising nymph-like, from the very bosom of the waters. Had our architecture corresponded more with our situation, there would have been few cities along our Atlantic border to surpass, or even equal her, in beauty to the eye. But our buildings are generally very wretchedly conceived. Our architecture has been *sui generis.* It has borne no likeness to anything in heaven or in earth, or in the waters that surround the earth.

Editor.—There is an improvement, Father.

Abbot.—So there is! We have now some clever native architects, and they have done something already, and will do yet more. But a great deal is yet necessary. There is one important preliminary to be taught and *felt,* before we can do any thing successfully in this department,—namely, that every climate has its own requisites for building, and its necessities must determine the character of its structures. Now, instead of looking to Venice for our models in Charleston, we have been going back to the Greeks. The Yankees first fell foul of the Greeks, and made sad havoc of their mighty fabrics. A retired shopkeeper in Manhattan will build his kitchen after the plan of the temple at Icomium, and the model of the temple of Theseus, is the humblest that he could choose after which to plan the little structure at the extremity of his half acre lot, which, considering its uses, need not be seen at all. The passion for Greek models, for a season, spread here and there, and every where among us. And it was all a monstrous absurdity. We can admire the glorious fabric of Minerva, kissing the clouds from a lofty elevation of a thousand feet above the sea; but the same building, squatting down in the streets of a squat city like Philadelphia, is a manifest absurdity. These ambitious imitators overlooked the fact, that the Greeks planned their buildings for mountain elevations. They were made low and bulky accordingly, the mountain being, in fact, a great foundation pile for the edifice. To relieve the weight of the buildings they were surrounded by colonnades. If these colonnades were necessary to the relief of a building when on a mountain, how much more necessary on a plain? Yet, among us, the side columns, which were thus employed for the purpose of lightness and relief, have been knocked away entirely, and the density and dulness of the structure have been correspondingly increased. Our models should be found among the old states and cities, the sites and climates of which have some correspondence with our own. As I have already said, some good ideas might be got from the architecture of Venice—we might look also among the Byzantines,—and something quite as good might be gleaned from the abandoned stores of the Moors of Grenada—an elegant people; the atmosphere of their region resembling that of Charleston, if the scenery does not. I have no doubt that our best models would be found among the Saracens of the time of Abderrahman. They were a people accustomed to warm climates, of exquisite tastes, and a rare appreciation of all the luxuries of life. How they would have adorned that Battery!—What glorious courts, what delicately wrought columns, what umbrageous verandahs, what minarets and porches, with what a happy distribution of light and shadow, sparkling fountains and Mosaic avenues and pavements, to say nothing of the green relief from vines and festooning shrubberies would they have made to crown that promontory, so beautifully placed at once for ostentation and enjoyment. There is a corner lot, one of the best, still remaining at the point of the Battery. I know not who owns it, or whether it remains in the hands of the city or not. If it does, let them sell it at any price, to some man of equal taste and wealth. Let him employ one of our excellent young architects, and let the space be crowned with a couple of light Moorish towers, connected with a court of columns opening on the south. The towers should be quite lofty. Indeed, to be light, they must be so. The basement should be sufficiently high to enable the architect to begin the real building at a point sufficiently above the line of the Battery, as to be distinguished—base no less than apex—from the sea. It was a sad error in those who built, having any part of the building *below* this line. This basement, given up to the offices, to kitchen, and even carriage house, would leave the lot, otherwise a small one, large enough for all purposes. Such a structure, judiciously adapted, would give that *finish* to the Battery, which is at present its great deficiency. There is a new Custom House to be built. What a glorious chance here for a fine structure, looking loftily out upon the sea! And a model adapted from the architecture of the Saracens, would be of the very best sort, inasmuch as their style is susceptible of the most various application. Every requisite vault, office, court, or chamber, essential to such a building could be had ; while the structure at the same time, would accord with and relieve the flatness of the sight, and could be adapted to soothe and disarm the oppressive languors of the climate.

EDITOR.—We are passing Castle Pinckney. Do you remember, Father, whether that Fort existed in the Revolution ?

ABBOT.—It did not. It was simply a marsh-flat, with very little soil, such as you see its unoccupied extremity now. I believe that its chief uses were as a place of execution. Remind me to ask our venerable friend, Dr. Johnson, if it was not there that Tweed and Groundwater were hung. It was there, certainly, ór at White Point. I believe that many of the Pirates, by whom our coast was haunted in ante-revolutionary periods, were *justified* at the spot now covered by the Castle.— What a pity that Government does not enclose and build upon the *whole* of this flat, making an ample Citadel, which, even if Charleston were in the hands of an enemy, could, if well provisioned, be held by five hundred men.

EDITOR.—But its health is said to be doubtful.

ABBOT.—Would not enclosure, with a wall of stone, and filling up, render it healthy ? Would it not have the effect also of contributing to deepen the channel and the harbor, by circumscribing the river, and preventing the wash from the shoals? Fort Johnson in the Revolution, was then employed to do the duty of Castle Pinckney; but it answered the purpose very imperfectly. Its guns failed to cover the ships of the British lying in Rebellion Roads.

IV.

Abbot.—You spoke justly when you bestowed a passing compliment upon Master Hillard, to whom our public owes much in the way of improvements. His "Line" is a good and useful one. The boats are sufficiently large, and, under existing circumstances, run sufficiently often, with a single exception, to the Island. There should be a night boat from the Island to the City, leaving at ten, and running while the weather is fine, and on moonlight evenings. The sweetest period of our day is from the approach of sunset, until the small hours of the night. Those who take a prolonged siesta, before or after dinner, will always remain bright and vigorous till midnight. Let me counsel this improvement, which must be equally grateful to monks, as to "maids who love the moon."

Editor.—He shall hear of it.

Abbot.—Master Hillard hath done other things which deserve our countenance. He hath erred only in stopping just at the point where his greater exertions should have begun. I have no sort of question that Haddrell, with its groves opened fairly, and proper pathways smoothed along the sea, with ample grounds for exercise and sport, would, in these gloomy and perilous days, when cant and cholera assail us every where at the North, become quite as attractive and grateful to our people, as any of the thousand watering places which they rush abroad to visit. But money must be spent, and largely too, before the scene can be made what it should be. At the North, nobody thinks that nature can prove the sole attraction, without the help of art. They furnish her with all manner of assistants, and we must do the same, if we hope to rival the Yankees. It is enough if nature gives us the *susceptibilities;* we must do the rest. Our people have been spoiled with luxuries. They require easy carriages, fine steamboats, pleasant lounges, rich parlors, gay pictures, and the best of feeding. See how the small wits, who set out for our interior, professedly to see nature in her fastnesses, complain of their landlords, and the excess of lard in their gravies! We must provide for all this sort of people. To make Haddrell what it should to be, requires money. But I am free to say that, with money properly laid out, there would be few places better calculated to persuade the summer wanderer. Certainly it might be made a sort of Hoboken for us; a place where, of an afternoon, you might see hundreds from the city, young and old, taking the air along the shores, and sheltered from the sun, at the same time, by overhanging forests.

EDITOR.—For an afternoon's exercise, or even for a day, the thing might answer. But there would be no stopping there at night. The Village of Mount Pleasant is healthy enough; but even at Shell Hall the case is very doubtful.

ABBOT.—I have heard so; but these statements rest generally on tradition. All newly opened placés, in the low latitudes, are of doubtful health *at first.* But drainage, and free ventilage, by opening avenues through the forests, and clearing up the undergrowth, repairs the evil; and the children of the soil are as healthy as any others. We are too well disposed to believe these traditions in regard to the dreadful sickliness of places among us, which should be fostered rather than deserted, since this belief furnishes us with an excuse, which we desire, to get away. We find very poor people, who cannot leave the swamp neighborhoods, enjoying comparatively good health,—while their children flourish and fatten in spite of malaria. Charleston, itself, now one of the healthiest seaports in the Union, was, at one period, known as the American Batavia! What has wrought the change? What but drainage, ventilage, and a denser population, sufficiently numerous to work these improvements? So of many of our country villages. Orangeburg, for example, one of our oldest country towns, had the worst of reputations for its unhealthiness. It is now known as a summer retreat, equally healthful and agreeable. Haddrell is so situated that, with proper clearing and drainage, it cannot but be healthful. There are few influences from which malaria should arise. The winds, in summer, prevail generally from the South and Southwest; and all the places that are open as this is to the breezes from these quarters, are usually the healthiest among us. These winds sweep towards it from the open bay. The soil is little more than sand; the vegetation no where in the neighborhood, seems to acquire much rankness; and, all things considered, I fancy the tradition of its sickliness rests upon very doubtful authority. At all events, a little pains-taking ought to render it unequivocally safe and salubrious. What glorious bathing regions might be had all along these shores—

Beauclerk.—But for the sharks!

Abbot.—Confound the sharks! Do I tell you to rush into their jaws? I say *might* be had. Pillars made of our Charleston Cement, (Bowman's Concrete,) with stakes driven between, might be made to take in a vast extent of level beach. From this line of pillars and stakes, which effectually shuts out the sea attorney, you have only to stretch out awnings or tents of canvass: each family might have its own; and here Beauty might take her bath, in the embrace of Neptune, without even the eye of Apollo to disturb her security or compel her blushes.

Editor.—Are you aware, Reverend Father, that you have been somewhat anticipated in your cogitations, touching the susceptibility of Haddrell as a place of afternoon resort for the goodly people of the City?

Abbot.—Most likely! Great wits jump together you know. But what have you on this subject?

Editor.—Some one of our hundred City Poets has touched upon the theme in one of the newspapers. I happened upon a fragment in an old sheet the other day. The writer describes the drives of some heroine, of whom the scrap which I happened upon could afford me no other information. But that need not affect us. The portions in point are these. You will see that the Poet has caught your idea with the most perfect accuracy.

ABBOT.—By anticipation. Proceed!

EDITOR.—(Reads.)

"She made the round of the Battery, twice or thrice,
In this triumphant manner;—gazed about,
And thought James' Island look'd exceeding nice,
With its great crown of pines, so tall and stout;
And wonder'd why we had no such device
In Charleston, for its people to go out,
In summer,—seeking still such pleasant places
As Gotham keeps to cheer her mingling races.

"There were the sister-islands, just at hand,
Over that arm of Ashley and the bay;
The drives are excellent along each strand,
And sweet the beach where rolling breakers play;
Between, are groves by ocean breezes fanned;
Beyond, it must be very sweet to stray,
To fields Elysian,—such as in New Jersey,
Invite alike the folk in cloth and kersey.

"We too might have—I speak it without joking—
As sweet retreats for summer as the best;
We might command our Brooklyn and Hoboken,
Though no Wehawken crowns the Ashley's breast;
Yet nature has for us some joys bespoken.
Bright flowers, and forest shades our clime have bless'd,
Deep Groves invite us, which, with little trimming,
We might make precious for our babes and women.

"There's Haddrell, for example! Some slight clearing,
The underwood removed from the old trees,
And you might ramble onward, nothing fearing;
Still looking out from Sullivan's to the seas;
While birds above, and boats beneath you, steering,
The languid spirits cheer, the fancies please;
And, wanting rocks, instead of sybil cavern,
Some Druid grot might answer for a tavern.

"There Hillard might provide you with your ices,
As well as Marion and Petit;—and there,
He might contrive the prettiest of devices
For tempting languid folks to take the air;
Swings for the children—games at moderate prices,
To keep the young from ill, the old from care;
And show our Southern folks they need not wander,
Northward, their joys to seek, their sixpences to squander."

ABBOT.—Well read, Mr. Editor, a good song and well sung. The unknown rhymester hath anticipated all my philosophy. May our mutual counsels find their way to the thoughts of men of action, and persuade Mr. Hillard to do the thing handsomely. I am satisfied it will be done in process of time. Perhaps not many years will elapse, when we shall behold all these headlands, these green skirts of shore, crowned with beautiful villas, smiling through noble avenues of oaks, or decorated with drooping willows and redolent of myrtle and orange. It needs but an increase of manufacturing establishments near the city, and a large body of operatives who require to live free of the heavy burdens of city taxation, to make all these favored spots of nature flourish under the auspices of art;—and how lovely will be the *coup d'œil* when these shores are all handsomely studded with nice white boxes, with green blinds, and fancy pailings, even down to where the billows kiss the beach. Look about you, and behold! The *tout ensemble*, even now, is, to my eye, singularly beautiful. The expanse of bay is admitted to be a magnificent one. Before you lies the smaller space, crowned, on the one hand, by Castle Pinckney, on the other by Mount Pleasant; while, beyond, like a fairy empire, rises up Sullivan Island, sweeping round like a crescent, and circumscribing the area of water in its rear, so that it seems fitted, by its snugness and security, to be the proper abode of some such Lady of the Lake as beguiled the King of Scotland into the lowlier garments of the Knight Fitz James. To the right, as you gaze, how beautifully does the scene expand, smooth and blue, to the white beaches of James and Morris islands, upon which you behold, soft and slightly curling, a lengthened line of foam. The fortresses, Pinckney and Sumter, relieve the expanse of water of all monotony; and as the eye passes beyond, it rests with a sense of pleasure, natural to every such scene of quiet and delicacy, upon the lowly rising, but conspicuous cottages upon James Island, nor turns away dissatisfied from the undulating sand-hills that stretch outward to the sea. Back, you see where the Ashley opens—rounding the Battery, and sentinelled in its progress by that crest of pines directly opposite, which forms a peculiar feature of the scene. There the eye rests for awhile, reverting finally to the city, over which—her spires, smitten by the soft flush of a glorious sunset, beauty seems to hang, hushed and happy in the arms of peace. Turn we now to Cooper River, the Etiwan of the aboriginal possessors---what a sweet and prolonged avenue of water, girdled by greenest slopes, by gentle headlands, its great trees stooping to the stream, and following all its sinuosities, as if guarding the shores with suspicious care against all intrusion. But we need not travel in this direction. Is it not all written in the Book of Irving ?*

Poet.—It seems strange to me, venerable Father, that you have omitted to notice one peculiar and very pleasing feature in this landscape: I allude to the skirts of green marsh which relieve the eye on almost every hand, which contrast most lovelily with the waters, and soften, with the most delicate effect, the otherwise too bright glare of the sands beyond. There is an islet with a single oak, a mere hillock, rising from yonder bed of marsh. How pretty and pleasing the appearance. Follow the creek, now opening beneath the eye, and see where a troop of cranes are fishing in the shallows, their tall white forms showing brilliantly amidst their spaaious empire of waving green. We, perhaps, disparage the effect produced by these tracts of marsh, in consequence of ideas that belong to their supposed agency in promoting disease. I am satisfied that their noxious influences are much exaggerated. At all events, they add greatly to the picture—they seem absolutely necessary to its beauty, relieving its uniformity, and making it picturesque by the exquisite delicacy of the contrast.

Abbot.—It is true that I had forborne the subject, but I had not overlooked it. It occurs to me

* A Day on Cooper River.

as it does to you. You have so well expressed the thoughts proper to the additional effect, as to spare me the necessity of further remark. Something, however, in this connection, might be urged in regard to our low country scenery generally. But here we are at Haddrell. Do you know anything of the tavern kept here?

Editor.—I spent a day not long ago at Shell Hall. It is kept by a worthy German, whose name I forget. He gave me an excellent dinner, very well dressed and served, and his demand was moderate. What with books and billiards, and delightful breezes, I spent the day most delightfully.

Abbot.—We will visit him hereafter.

Poet.—You were about to speak of low country scenery. It is the common practice to disparage it.

Abbot.—Unjustly. Every thing in the prospect depends upon the mind of him who surveys it. The mind, and the sort of preparation and training through which it has gone, is the usual medium for making the survey. To the eye that looks only for its attractions in *form*, our scenery must always be unimpressive. But it is full of character, requires nice observation, and will reward close study. It depends for its effect upon the exquisite gradations of shade and color, the nice blending of tints, the harmony of its transitions, and, if I may so phrase it, a certain delicate intensity of life. It does not impose upon you, at a glance, like the scenery of the North, or our own back country. Its great deficiency is *in form*.—

There are no stupendous eminences—no frowning heights, that, rising up like giants, stretch themselves with their grey heads into the clouds, compelling the admiration of men, and seeming to challenge that of the gods. Our rivers run not through ledges of bald rock, that threaten momently to tumble headlong upon the hissing steamboat as it glides beneath. Our hills do not cluster together, bald and desolate looking groups, as if seeking alliance against the assaults of winter. Our outlines are neither startling nor imposing, but they are persuasive and grateful. They do not strike you at a glance, but it will please you in time to study them. Nay, they will reward study, when the object which depends for its effect upon mere outline, will provoke none. After all, your vast rocky or mountain pictures are very cold and cheerless. They strike you with awe, but they invite no sympathies. They demand your wonder, but they yield and expect no love. You see all their possessions at a glance—you feel that there is nothing in reserve. Beyond the grand, bold outline, they have no treasures. They move you at the first sight, but seldom reward a second; and the mind at length becomes discouraged and becomes discouraged and sad in their contemplation, and turns from them to the crowded city, as if seeking human association and relief. But the effect is far otherwise of our Southern slopes, our woods and waters. They do not strike you at first, and seldom startle, but, at the same time, they never offend. They rather woo and invite you by their soft attractions. You wander among their groves as you would among the enchanted bowers of an Armida. They tempt you to look out for enchantments. The brightness of their green, the wondrous luxuriance of their growth, the rich glow and glory of their flowers, the songs in profusion, and of every note, of their profligate birds—arouse the fancy, until the spiritual nature feels a flush of expectation, which gradually peoples the scene with fairy and imaginative creations. You are won away, unconsciously, into thoughts and musings which give a strange and sweet vitality to all that you behold. A thousand delightful meditations inform the mind, and you wander onward, soothed and satisfied with attractive fancies that give you the most appropriate companionship.—Nor is it the soft and gentle alone that is awakened in your nature by these scenes. They can impress with equal awe and solemnity. What more imposing spectacle than the dense pine forest, stretching away for leagues, a monotonous waste, like that of sea or desert, of unvarying forms—a realm of equal shadow and silence, gloom and deep, in which all the dwellers are crowned sovereigns—sovereigns without subjects,—voiceless, hopeless, heirless—without speech, without communion—waving to and fro their inexpressive heads, with one unbroken swing of solemn idiocy! What more wondrous and awful, than the very waste fertility of our mighty swamps—shrined in flowers, wrapped in beauty, gorgeous in natural wealth, rich in all shapes and colors, wondrous in vine, and wreath, and jewel—terrible in the startling beauty of their reptiles, in the scream of their mighty birds, in the awful majesty of their deep recesses? Their buds press your cheek as you go forward—their vines stretch forward with a thousand fingers to wind you in their grasp—your footsteps crush perfume from their leaves—your fingers are crimsoned with the delicious juices of the wild grape—and life, in forms the most magical—and loveliness, in gleams the most musical—are ever rising to the senses, as if to persuade the faith into those ancient fancies, which never left such regions without their elves and fairies. The deep impenetrable thickets skirting the narrow river or oozy lake, seem the very regions of ambush and surprise; and you look momently to see the feather-cinctured warrior darting out from the shad, in all the panoply of forest warfare. A gloom, which is not painful, gives a mysterious tone and character to this peculiar realm of loveliness and life, and the very droplets of sunlight that fall and trickle through the tree tops and shrubbery upon the earth below, seem so many wandering shadows—shapes of spiritual life—that come only to declare that, however little sought or beloved by man, the region is not yet utterly abandoned of Heaven.

Editor.—Take my arm, Father: we are at the Island.

V.

ABBOT.—My children, the day is over, and all things are quiet now. The Island sleeps—the people—all but ourselves. Bring your chairs out upon the beach. We will sit upon the solid gray sands, at the very edge of the waters. Let us have a table, and bring out a bottle of Champagne, that our spirits may be refreshed.

EDITOR.—But, Father, what will people say?

ABBOT.—Let them say! So long as we offend none of God's ordinances, and violate none of the laws of the land, let the fool's tongue wag as it pleases. It is one of the curses of the community that we perpetually ask what our neighbors think of us. Vanity forever asks the question, and, in doing so, shackles human freedom. Commend yourselves to your own consciences, my children, and be at peace. It is surely something wonderfully distressing to our little world, that we, the Children of the Moon, venture to pitch our tents upon the beach, and sit beneath the blue arch of Heaven, instead of the rude rafters of Mrs. Cheney or Mrs. Stevens.

EDITOR.—Not that exactly, Father; though that is something new in this region. But the Champagne!

ABBOT.—My son, drink you none of the beverage if you fear it, or your neighbors. It is a proper prudence that children should not play with edged tools. But we who know the uses and the virtues of the thing, need not be so scrupulous.

Editor.—But your example, Father.

Abbot.—Would be bad, perhaps, if we drank more than a bottle, or more than our heads could bear. But such is not the case. If men never trespassed beyond our limits, there would be no sorrow from intemperance in the land. At my age, with the habits perfectly formed—and these are among the best securities of character—I may surely be presumed to be safe in my indulgencies.

Editor.—But the world will doubt. They will suspect us of excesses. They will know nothing of our limits.

Abbot.—Then is the world a transgressor. The good Christian is bound to presume favorably of the practices of men, when he knows nothing against them. If he does not, his Christianity is at fault.

Editor.—Public opinion, Father.

Abbot.—Is too frequently insolent, under the pretext of virtue. Be at ease, my son; or if thy doubts trouble thee, retire to the dwelling and refresh thee, by way of quieting them, by drinking a few goblets of cool ice water. Meanwhile, thou shalt have our prayers. I tell thee, my children, there is something petty and peevish in the habits of this little community of ours, whenever it comes to sit in judgment upon its neighbors. Every departure from the beaten track, receives its condemnation from some upstart fool, no matter whether the innovation be a virtue or a vice. We are such miserable slaves of convention, that we crush all individuality as a crime; though, in the exercise of this very individuality, we find the source of all great virtues. What are great heroism, great self-sacrifice, world-blessing charity, but departures from the common practices? We have got into a world of humdrum here in Charleston, from the uniform monotony of our habits. You cannot change the style of your dress in any respect, but you see stupid wonder opening its great eyes, and silly conceit stretching wide its broad grinning jaws, as if something enormous had taken place. The old gentlemen begin to fancy some revolution at hand, as did the Usher in the time of Louis the Fourteenth, when he saw a nobleman enter the royal presence with strings instead of buckles to his shoes. A summer ago, I went into one of the manufacturing establishments of the North, and groped through a great collection of hats. I desired one, which should be light and soft—which should not bind the head, or be burdensome to the brain. I got me something which answered my purpose exactly. It was fashioned somewhat like the old Cavalier's hat, of the time of the Stuarts, high crowned and slouch brimmed. But you have seen the hat, my children.

BEAUCLERK.—Did not the brotherhood adopt it, Father?

ABBOT.—Well, what was the consequence? All Charleston was aghast when they beheld it.—'What!' said one of our *habitues* to me, the day after my arrival, 'do you expect to force such a hat upon the people of Charleston?' I fear me that I answered somewhat irreverently, with regard to the good people of Charleston. 'Let them wear what they please,' was my answer, 'but pray you suffer me to do the same.' It is, perhaps, the most striking symptom of feebleness, a regard for petty objects only, and an incapacity to rise to the consideration of more important concerns, that people should waste breath upon costume at all. I can respect the Turk who has a national dress, which, once established, and suited to his climate and his occupations, becomes a thing unchangeable by fashion, and is no longer a subject of speculation. When Mahmoud, in his blind zeal for reformation among his people, beginning at the tail, rather than the head, proceeded to clothe his troops after the manner of the Franks, I was prepared to believe that he was not the man to effect any good for his people. And he did not. His whole labors were a miserable failure. My sons, I pledge you in this generous beverage. It commands itself gratefully to the veins of an old man.

Beauclerk.—An old man, Father.

Abbot.—Seventy, at least, my son.

Beauclerk.—Impossible!

Abbot.—To those who count life by years, my children, quite impossible. But you will not have forgotten the line of our gentle Latin poet—'*Actis ævum implet, non segnibus annis!* Change the deeds to events, and the reading is admissible, and the application is correct. A man lives in his experiences. If to have seen, in a single year, most of the sorrows that range through a life of seventy; if to have broken all the ties that bind to friends and kindred, in that short space of time; if to have seen one's graves growing around him—the graves of several generations at once—while he is yet in the green of life, and ere his sinews have well hardened into manhood; if, in addition to this, to have seen the wreck of all one's earthly fortunes, almost of his hopes;—be the usual experience of seventy years, why should I not count mine at this number? For such has been my experience.

Editor.—But scarcely one among us, Father, wears more the aspect of youth than yourself.

Abbot.—Many a great oak waves a massive coronet of green, my children, into whose core the worm has eaten, and upon which it preys ever more, without ceasing. It is pride—possibly, a nobler feeling—that stifles the pain of its secret hurts, and makes no outward confession of its malady. But some one walks along the breakwater. He stops, as if to muse upon the prospect. He drinks in its beauty, in loneliness. There is a something in the scene which is refreshing to the soul, and most men who think, need to refer often to the refreshing influences of nature. There are some men who have pleasure in no other communion. I often meet with such men. I have one in my mind's eye at this moment. You must all have seen the man. He is known to us for large and various endowments, classical acquirements, excellent taste, and a spirited and glowing style in composition; but you meet him nowhere in society. When you see him he generally walks alone, and then not often in the public thoroughfares. He goes abroad towards nightfall, and his eyes are cast upon the ground as he walks, or his vision pierces into space; but he looks not about him for his fellow, and he asks no man's communion. What is the secret sorrow of this man: what his troubled dream; what his defrauded hope? Who shall tell? Is it a peculiar nature, an idiosyncracy, that wraps itself up in loneliness, as in a garment, brooding upon its own heart, and not attuned for the communion of any other; or is it the result of a life-disappointment, the overthrow of a great and generous ambition, which makes him feel, possessed as he is of the best treasures of literature and of a world-sufficing mind, scornful of the very possessions which are the envy of other men? My children, most men who seek for solitude have great sorrows which they are doomed to nurse in secret. Yonder stranger may be one of this description. But for this doubt, we should ask him here among us.

ABBOT.—And such is not our custom, Father.

ABBOT.—Here again starts up the shadow of that conceited convention, which chills humanity and denies sympathy to our neighbor. It has always struck me as a delightful characteristic on the Continent of Europe, particularly among the Germans, that, sitting beneath their shade trees, dancing at evening, or quaffing the generous juices of their grape, they entreat the passing stranger to their festivities, and make him one of them at once. What should they fear?

BEAUCLERK.—The contact with the vulgar.

ABBOT.—True superiority has no such fears. Vulgarity never shows itself on such occasions. The rude man takes his tone from the social circle which admits him, and adopts his new standard with a wonderful instinct. He is charmed by the complacency of the superior, and he never trespasses upon the proprieties, which stand like so many guardian watchers around the happy company. We gain nothing by our coldness. We may lose much by our reserves. In this way, we are told, by the highest authority, that the host has frequently entertained an angel. For my part, travelling as I have done, among the wildest regions of the South and West, at periods when they were a thousand times wilder than now, I have never encountered anything but kindness and hospitality. I seldom took with me any other weapon than that which best suits the traveller—good humor. I have met roughness which springs from ignorance, and not from ill-nature; simplicity, but that which never vexed either a taste or a judgment, regulated by a just sense of the circumstance or the situaiton; and a frankness that requires only to be met with a corresponding spirit, to become a lasting and pleasant, if not a profitable, friendship. Yet, ordinarily, the city-bred gentleman, full of his conventional laws, and not able to overcome old habits, or perhaps not capable of perceiving their unsuitableness to his present condition, seldom succeeds in winning the confidence and sympathy of the forest-bred inhabitant, or the rugged mountaineer. He will cherish his old strut, and his new waistcoat, and be at particular pains, always to remind the peasant, that he *is* a citizen; the very thing he should avoid.

POET.—Father, the City makes a very lovely picture now. The moon touches those steeples with the prettiest frost-work; and the metallic shaft of the new Church in Wentworth-street, flashes out at intervals with the happiest effect.

Abbot.—Yes, there are subjects all around us for the pencil of Pictor. He is meditating some of them now. Fort Sumter, by moonlight, would make a conspicuous object; with the foreground spreading from the beach at our feet, while in the background sweet fairy-like glimpses might be had of the village on James Island; a point further west might enable him to bring into a corner of the picture the crest of pines of which we have spoken already, and of which Trouche made an excellent portrait. His error was in reducing the extent of water stretching from the Battery to the Island. A glimpse of the Battery might also be included in a wing of such a landscape. I confess that I nowhere have seen prospects more lovely than such as are afforded from the spot where we sit, in a moonlight view. Mind you, I do not say grand or even impressive, though in a storm the same prospect would have its grandeur. But sweetness, the charm of delicate repose, a fairy-like vale of shining sands, green glimpses and shores, that seem to steal upon you, relieved by occasional objects, such as Fort Sumter and Castle Pinckney—these are all present, and actively appeal to the fancy for the moral adjuncts. Besides, there is the aid of ship and steamer, now looming up white with bellying canvass, or lazily rocking at anchor, as if lulled into repose by the seductive calm of winds and ocean.

Poet.—What a glorious spectacle in a storm must these seas present—the great billows rolling in upon the beach, threatening destruction—sworn, as it would seem, to overwhelm the crouching, shuddering houses, yet subsiding, smoothing down their haughty crests, as they encounter with the steadfast sands.

Abbot.—I have witnessed just such a spectacle. It was in the summer of 18—, I forget the year. I can never remember dates. The Island was fairly flooded. People fled to the upper stories of their dwellings, or to the Fort, for shelter. I had my fears; for winds and seas seemed both to have conspired for our destruction. The Gulf appeared to have risen in fierce hostility, and was pouring in upon us with its thousand squadrons of blue and foam. Never did I behold such great and threatening billows. As you beheld them rolling forward, you involuntarily crouched, expecting them upon you. Mountain after mountain, far higher than any dwelling upon the Island, came tumbling headlong forward; and just when it seemed inevitable that we were to be engulfed, they would encounter with the shoal, and with a hoarse groan would part, scatter, subside, and roll upward upon the shore, covering it with their waters, but no longer embodied in mighty and overwhelming masses. The change of wind only saved us. Terrible was the evening and the night of that fearful day. I shall never forget the spectacle, which a painful sort of fascination made me eagerly contemplate, in spite of all my apprehensions.

Poet.—I remember to have heard just such a description. There were lives lost on that occasion, Father. One fair creature.

ABBOT.—Yes! Yes! The event haunted me for long seasons after. It troubled my dreams, and furnished the materials of one of them, which so impressed my imagination that, for a moment, I ventured to usurp your lyre, my son, and shape the oppressive fancies into verse.

POET.—Let us have it, Father.

ABBOT.—Surely! I have no affectations; and there is something classical, you know, in declaiming by the shores of the sea to the music of the billows. Homer, on the Chian Strand, must have experienced a joy in doing so, apart from his audience, in hearing the murmur of the waters which he could not see.

EDITOR.—And Demosthenes.

ABBOT.—I doubt if Demosthenes felt any of the poetry of the situation. Softness, or the sense of beauty, was not his province. But we need not these or any examples to justify us here. If there were any scruples, it might be that a diseased self-esteem, trembling at your conventional usages, might suggest that some of the lodgers at Cheney's are awake. In their charity, they would suppose us mad, or drunk, to hear our recitations. They certainly would never be liberal enough to suspect that the spirit of Homer or Demosthenes had been the source of our inspiration. And now, children, remember that these are boyish verses, written twenty years ago.

POET.—We listen, Father.

ABBOT—(Recites.)

I dream'd that I was walking by the sea,
Whose billows, forced by winds of Mexico,
Brought in the dark blue waters of the Gulf
Close to my feet. The breaking surges dash'd
In white foam round me; and a solemn song
Rose from the gathering ocean, which, at hand,
Hung threat'ning, as if challenging for prey,
The shores on which I stood. A narrow ledge—
A low frail barrier 'gainst a foe so strong—
Its own bright tribute, from the heaving deep,
Laid at the city's foot—as if to check,
The wild, free progress of its reckless mood,—
Offer'd but feeble foothold, to the crowd,
Now crouching in their terrors. Soon, the waves
Come rushing upward; while the shores grew faint,
And buried their gray heads. A bird of wo,
Scream'd overhead in warning,—then flew off,
In dread,—and, with example, counsell'd me
To my own safety. On each hand, the seas
Rear'd their green crests, and, backward as I fled,
Their tongues pursued me with a gushing hiss
That threaten'd fiercer speed. The summer homes
Of the affrighted Islanders were gain'd,
And the wild waters, rushing in with roar,
Drove them to upper chambers, or the sands,
That sunk beneath them. Death was in the wrath
Of those wild torrents! Death upon the winds,
That gave the torrent wings;—and sights, and sounds—
If sight were in the blackness of that night,
Or sounds in that one thunder of the wave—
Spoke only, and spoke equally, for death!
Thus seem'd his empire certain—and we fled,
A mixed despairing multitude! The weak,
Shrieking, unnoted, in the ocean's roar,
Vainly, for succor from that human strength,
Which then was strength no more!

There was a pile,
A stern, strong fortress, that, beside the deep,
Stood guardian of the City. It had borne
The storm of iron in the perilous hour,
Rearing its brows in conquest, and with pride,

When the long day was ended. Thither, then,
We fled in safety.

We had fled in vain,
But for the victim! There was one, devote
That hour, to destiny!—and the wild seas
Rush'd still insatiate on, with outstretch'd jaws,
And had not been appeased—we had been lost—
But quickly, from the crowd, a sheeted form,
Sprang out to ocean! Suddenly, a light,
Flash'd from the sated Heavens—and we beheld
Each feature of the victim. Young and fair—
A maiden in her budding. Pale, but bright,
Her cheeks were whiter than the drifting foam
That broke around us. In her lovely eyes
The light seem'd holy, and bestow'd on all
A delicate lustre. But a moment more,
Its lambent beauty cheer'd us, while she sprang,
Tossing in air her slender and white arms,
That soon embraced the billows. Down she sank;
And there was from the shore and from the seas,
A mutual cry—the one of a deep wo,
The one of triumph!

And the storm was hush'd
In that same instant! Sullen from the shores
The waves went backward with a murmuring song,
And slept upon the deep. The ravenous sea,
Having its prey, grew calm; and all was peace,
Where all awhile was fright. But in my dreams
I yet behold that maiden, with her arms
So white and slender, tossing in the waves,
That sucked her down forever in their gulfs.

And now, my children, shall we walk? Leave chairs and table, they are safe, and let us take the beach till twelve.

VI.

Abbot.—Here we are at the beginning, the present terminous rather, of the Breakwater. The rocks afford us a pleasant range of seats. The point is a good one for affording grateful glimpses of the prospect. Behind us lies the fortress, Moultrie, in still and beautiful repose. Before us rises Fort Sumter, looming us gracefully in the moonlight. To the left you behold the uniform revolutions of our Light House Star, shining, like the smile of Hope, to the lonely wanderer, over the multitudinous waters. The South line is beautifully bounded by the shores of James's Island, and the eye, bending upon the West, loses itself happily among the infrequent lights of the distant City. Let us sit, my children, and enjoy the delicious charm of a prospect, which unites sweetness with solitude, and the breathing hush of nature with her tenderest beauties.

Editor.—The Breakwater seems to have admirably answered the purpose for which it was designed. For this part of the Island it has certainly done wonders. Our beach had been nearly swept away in this quarter. I have seen the billows breaking against Fort Moultrie itself; and, it is said that a portion of the wall was undermined by the ocean. Yet now, what a wide interval stretches between the fortress and the sea, and the sands are hourly accumulating. The old line of rocks, laid down originally from the Fort, when the effort was first made to arrest the ravages of the sea, is now nearly obliterated by the sands; and the beach, from this point at least, to the extremity of the Island, is, it strikes me, even increased in breadth, infinitely beyond what it was twenty years ago, when I remember the drives along the whole front of the Island, as in admirable perfection.

ABBOT.—Such is my impression also. The loss is on the inner quarter of the southern exposure. Is this loss final? The breakwater precludes the hope of again enjoying a beach drive in this direction; yet is it so certain that the deposits from the sea will not form a new beach *without* the breakwater? Is not the shoal increasing at the point of junction between the back beach and the front, and will it not continue to accumulate when the stone work is completed? The channel seems to me to be destined to be circumscribed in width, while it gains in depth. The mole on which Fort Sumter is raised, will tend necessarily to throw from it the press of water, on the one hand; while, on the other, the stone line, stretching from Fort Moultrie along the southern shore of the Island, to its extremity, must serve, in like manner, to break and defeat the action of the billows on the opposite side. The agitated waters will leave their deposits, which must gradually accumulate against the breakwater, and, in process of time, the beach may be renewed along the entire southern front of the Island.

BEAUCLERK.—It is doubtful, Father, whether this will be desirable. The result might be productive of other consequences, not the most agreeable. The formation of a new beach *without* the breakwater, might prove an obstruction to the departure of the waters which now accumulate *within.* These now afford the most admirable bathing places to the inhabitants. Nothing, indeed, could be more admirable. The ground floor of the bathing place is the most natural slope in the world. You pass, inch by inch, from a depth not over the latchet of your shoe, to your armpits. The child of two years old may bathe in security, while the athletic swimmer may wanton in the most vigorous wrestlings with the billows. The effect of any accumulation of the sands *without,* would, probably, turn this inner body of water into a lake, which might become a marsh. It is a question what contribution of its sands is made by the higher portions of the Island towards filling up this basin; and whether this filling up *within,* will keep pace with the accumulations *without.*

Abbot.—Sufficient for the day is the evil thereof. The progress of events must be watched, and openings made in the stone at proper intervals, for the free intercourse of the fresh billows with the waters which remain within. It may be necessary, a hundred years hence, to carry the breakwater out a hundred yards farther. In that event, my son, the subject is one which we may commend safely to the consideration of our great-grandchildren.

Editor.—I could have wished that the plan of the breakwater had contemplated the enclosure of the shoal at the Point. An obtuse angle, thrown out, and returning, at this quarter, would have given a good finish to the work; would have increased the territory somewhat; and the proprietor at the Point might have thrown above the stone reservoirs, thus created, some such light and graceful specimen of Moresco architecture, in the shape of a bathing house, as you have previously described. If Sullivan's Island is to continue to increase in popularity and population, as it has done—bringing from the interior, with each returning summer, the *elite* of our Middle and Up-Country Planters and Professors—we shall need all the bathing places we can find. These must be *covered* also, since it will be impossible to enjoy the tides during the day without such exposure to the sun and eye, as few persons, properly educated, are willing to incur. Besides, sea bathing in perfection should be taken *in puris naturalibus*. We should strip to it as to any other pleasure. This bathing in the obstructions of breeches and petticoat, shroud and wrapper, is not only a very *unnatural*, but a very uncomfortable way of doing the business.

Beauclerk.—I like the idea of tents for each family pitched within the breakwater.

Editor.—Why not neat, light, graceful fabrics of wood, with ornamental roofs, Saracen or Chinese.

Beauclerk.—Pagoda fashion?

Editor.—Yes! Just showing above the line of stone, like so many nice little turrets.

Abbot.—No doubt something will be done to meet the wants of the community, and satisfy the requisitions of propriety and taste. The subject,

I am told, is in good *working* hands. A working man is almost inevitably an improving one. The erection of this Hotel is the first step; and a first step is usually half the journey, as a first blow is half the battle. Let the virtues of the Island be once made known to the interior, and you will find that they will be acknowledged by our own citizens. Men who plodded annually to that vulgarest of all social places, Saratoga—whither every poor devil was sure to go, who could raise a couple of hundred dollars—will then begin to discover that Sullivan's is a much more famous place than Saratoga. That it is a thousand times finer place, any one who is capable of judging must readily acknowledge. Besides, it has advantages of a much higher social tone than is to be found at any of the summering places at the North, unless perhaps Newport; whither our Southern gentlemen have been so much in the habit of going, as, necessarily, to have carried with them the delicacies and refinements of good society. Here, the intercourse with a large city is hourly—the voyage short between the two places—the expense of transit a trifle, which, with competition—which I am told is threatened—and an increase of population on the Island,—must be made still lower. There are the markets of the city at your service; all the resources of the city—books, society, amusements; and you may even see, in process of time, the theatrical entertainments of the city, during the winter, transferred to a summer theatre upon the Island. In brief, you may command all the pleasures and advantages of a large city, with all the quiet, repose and health of a country seat, and place of summer refuge. You shall escape the cares of the town—its anxieties, heat and dust, without forfeiting any of its pleasures.

Beauclerk.—What is the length of the Island?

Editor.—From three to four miles. The width seldom quite half a mile, and frequently little more than a quarter. The beach drive is estimated at two miles and a half in length, and, in width, at low water, from fifty to an hundred yards. As you see, from the Fort to the end of the Island, it is such a beach as you find nowhere surpassed on the whole Atlantic coast.

Beauclerk.—Shall we walk it to-night, Father?

Abbot.—I think not, my son. We may try it to-morrow. For the present, I prefer that we should meditate, rather than explore. We may drink in pleasure enough from the scene, by simply unfolding ourselves to it. You see our Poet and Painter, as they lie there, stretched out on the very brink of the breakwater. The ocean breaks beneath them, sending the cool spray, glittering like diamond dust in the moonlight, on their cheeks and bosoms. Yet they heed it not. They seem to feel it not. They are brooding, almost unconscious, it would seem, in emotions which they cannot now express. Some of these days, it may be a year hence, you will see a painting, or hearken to a poem, which will bring all this scene before your eyes.

Beauclerk.—Certainly, Father, there is much that is strangely beautiful in the scene, but much that is cheerless also. Those heavy white hills of sand have the ghostliest appearance, and there is something saddening to my sight, even in the grouped palmettoes which stand up, knee deep, in the great grey hillocks.

Abbot.—What would you have, my son? Would you have the season always winter, or always spring; the scene always green with grass and shrubbery, and crowded with forest trees! This is only one of the thousand aspects of the various Nature. She puts on new forms and features, accommodating herself to all the tastes, and all the necessities of men. Here, you behold her, in one of the earliest processes by which she shapes a habitation for the race. Where we stand, was once the empire of ocean. She hath plucked this lovely place from his domain; she hath reared it above his head, as a barrier to more valuable empires; and thus roling his billows, forever restless, against its modest shores, he seems to assert his possessions, and to seek their rescue from the usurper. You must look upon this scene with feelings accommodated to the season of the year, the temperature, the circumstances of the city, your own exhaustion in its daily toils, and the desire which you feel to escape to places of refuge in the enjoyment of novelties. The Island is sterile, but who comes here to plant? It is treeless, but cool nevertheless. These breezes, and such nights, compensate for all deficiences of shade and forest. The music of these solemn sounding billows, the beauty of this silent and spell-imploring spectacle of sky and sea, and this verdureless domain of sand, furnish the sensibilities and the imagination with an empire no less grateful than unique. One sleeps with a rare sense of pleasure, having in his ears, in the last moment of consciousness, the rolling murmur of these waters breaking heavily upon the shore.

Editor.—But it is a mistake to speak of the Island as verdureless. There are farms and gardens above, which show equally the taste and skill of the cultivator, and the susceptibilities of the soil. Clumps of cedar, of oak, and of laurel, gay shrubs and fragrant myrtles, rise up among the sand hills, giving you the *oase* amidst the desert, and affording, on a small scale, some idea of that which is so gateful to the traveller in the mighty empires of the desert in the East. Truesdell, of oyster excellence and memory, has acquired high renown as an island farmer. He makes sea and shore equally tributary to his objects. One foot he plants in a field of okra, another in a field of oysters. The ocean breaks between his legs without disturbing his securities. He looks on the right hand and on the left, and feels that he is monarch of all he surveys. He has been a patriarch to the oyster family. It is wonderful how they have flourished under his auspices. He has shown the wonderful powers of education, for the development of dormant faculties. He has taken the unsophisticated muscle from his native bed, where he crouched and lived, rather than grew and flourished, and has given him a knowledge of the world. His *proteges*, under his benignant care, have grown to enormous sizes. That he should require that they should yield of their annual growth for the reward of their benefactor, is but a reasonable appeal to their gratitude. How little do the gourmands at Columbia, during the Legislative session, conjecture the toil, the care, the watchful anxiety with which he has reared these young and artless creatures, that they may minister to the delights and appetites of the Statesman and the Politician, exhausted by the toils of office and the constant draughts, upon their wisdom and patience, of a not easily satisfied constituency. Truesdell deserves well of the Legislature, Father.

ABBOT.—They tell me his Oyster Beds are no more safe than those of New Jersey. Report says that he has had to watch them nightly, at low water, with a loaded blunderbuss.

EDITOR.—Very probably. It is difficult to teach a negro that a property can be had in an oyster before he is gathered; and, assuming that Truesdell planted his oysters, benevolently, and with no other object than the good of the oyster itself, Sambo and others of his tribe, conceived that his sole object was reached when the young creature had attained a marketable size. It cost the excellent proprietor, I am told, a matter of ninety dollars in advertisements against trespassers—announcing and setting forth his rights; sixty in blunderbusses and pistols, and some thirty more in shot and powder—to say nothing of the anxiety and loss of rest—in keeping his *proteges* from abduction. Statutes have not saved him always.

ABBOT.—Truesdell is a benefactor my brethren. If the man may be considered so who makes two blades of grass occupy the spot which originally could rear but one, he certainly deserves as much who can convert a racoon oyster into a Blue Pointer, or a Shrewsbury. We owe something of gratitude to Truesdell. Something is due also to the oysters. They have done the State some service. Monuments have been built to thousands whom we could have much more readily spared, and who have been far less gratefully swallowed.

Beauclerk.—Talking of monuments, Father, reminds me to ask whether the name of the man from whom the Island takes its name was not O'Sullivan.

Abbot.—It was—Captain Florence O'Sullivan. He seems to have been for a time a sort of Alexander Selkirk. His title to the Island must have come from simple occupancy. The first account of him, given in the history, is that which occurs in Hewat. It appears that, during the administration of Sir John Yeamans (who succeeded to Sayle, the first Governor,) the colonists were on the eve of civil war. The Government was feeble, and the colonists quite unequal to their own defence against the Indians. Their supplies from Europe had failed them, and they became seditious. The settlement at Charleston was about to be involved in bloodshed. At this juncture, it appears that Florence O'Sullivan had charge of a post upon the Island which mounted a single gun. This was probably mounted in a block house rather than a Fort; and the block house was probably framed of Palmetto logs, affording the suggestion, in after times, for the construction of the fort, made famous by the battle with the British fleet. It may have occupied the self-same spot. Capt. O'Sullivan's command may have consisted of half a dozen or a dozen men. He was stationed here, rather to give notice to the town of the approach of suspicious vessels, than expected to offer any very serious defence. At this period, it must be remembered, that the coasts were covered with the pirate craft of all European countries. Capt. O'Sullivan became impatient of the inferior duties which had been assigned him. He shared in the discontents of the people; and, being, as we infer from the name, a son of Green Erin, he was not to be kept from the fun when a fray was in progress. He deserted his post upon the Island, hurried up to the town, and took the command and direction of the insurgents. But O'Sullivan was premature. The fruit was not quite ripe. The Governor maintained his ascendancy, and the worthy Captain was arrested on a charge of sedition, and compelled to give security for his future good behaviour. The history tells us no more of Florence O'Sullivan. Our provincial records might supply the deficiency, and we recommend to some of our young lawyers, who have not yet found the business of an approaching term too oppressive, to look through the documents of the State Department. I confess to only a vague notion of the tenure by which he conveyed the Island to the good people of Charleston.

Editor.—The inquiry deserves to be made. We owe something to O'Sullivan, which we have doubtfully acknowledged by stripping his name of its Hibernian prefix. Still it is doubtful if we could well avoid it. Something is due to euphony, and the "O!" would scarcely help the name at present.

I wish we could restore the aboriginal name of the Island. What will they call the new Hotel, I wonder? It will not do to say "Sullivan's Island Hotel." nor is it altogether complimentary to a hero to call a Hotel after him. Besides, the Fort already bears the name of Moultrie.

ABBOT.—The subject is a nice one.

BEAUCLERK.—"What's in a name?"

ABBOT.—Much: in spite of Shakspeare, names are things. The christening is one calculated to give trouble, and leave some parties still dissatisfied. I could wish to see the old Indian names restored. They were eminently musical and suitable; and if their meanings are not so obvious at this day, they would certainly labor under no worse disadvantage than attends half the names that we employ. For the settlements here, the names of Moultrie and Pinckney have been appropriately chosen. They are words of meaning in association with the scenes which they honored by their valor. I could also wish that the name of Col. Thomson, who had charge of the defences at the eastern end of the Island, on the famous 28th of June, could be also, in some way, distinguished by a local appropriation. But I abominate the absurdity which persists in tagging the names of Moultrie and Pinckney with the French *ville*. What use? Why not simply Moultrie and Pinckney? the village is understood. Should another village spring up in this wide waste tract between the two villages, I trust that our Colonel from St. Mathews and his sharp-shooters, will be remembered, and the new settlement be called St. Mathews or Saint Thomson.

VII.

Editor.—It is mentioned, Father, that the present Fort does not occupy the site of that of Revolutionary memory.

Abbot.—I suppose not. It is understood to be recessed; probably in consequence of that gradual gain of the sea upon the land, which, of late days, grew so imminent a danger. How many fortresses preceded the present, it is scarcely possible to say. I myself have seen the *debris* of an older structure, of brick, which we know did not constitute the material of the original fort which Moultrie defended. It is probable that, when the successful defence was made in 1775, the fort rose greatly in public opinion, and money was expended upon it. It was finished, and possibly enlarged in plan, and improved in other respects. When, in 1780, the Island fell into the possession of the British, it is not unlikely that they attached sufficient importance to it, to add still farther to the strength of the works. These opinions must rest wholly upon conjecture. No details have been preserved. As a place of summer resort, I have my doubts whether the British made much use of it, while they were in possession of the State. It may have been used as a sort of Lazaretto or Hospital, or Quarantine refuge, as was Haddrell's—perhaps, like Haddrell's, as a deposit for prisoners;—but being in possession of a good Cavalry, their favorite places of evening resort, ride, and recreation, were "Up the Road"—the "Quarter

House," below Izard's camp, being the usual *terminus* of their wanderings. It was rather unsafe to venture beyond this point, and even here, towards the conclusion of the war, they were frequently picked up by the Partizans.

EDITOR.—Have you ever been within the present structure, Father?

ABBOT.—A thousand times, my son, while under different commands. Recently, I had much pleasure in mounting the ramparts, and looking abroad upon the glorious prospect.

EDITOR.—The place is admirably kept, Father.

ABBOT.—It is; the Garrison orderly, civil, and wearing those looks of brightness and intelligence, which show great subordination, without despotism. This is highly creditable to their officers, none of whom have I the pleasure to know.

EDITOR—You should know, them, Father.—They are all fine gentlemen—intelligent and graceful; soldiers who have served honorably in Mexico, and wear their laurels modestly at home.

ABBOT.—The school is a good one, my son, for social as well as soldier-training. A military man, where the service is an honorable one, must always be a gentleman. The *prestige* of the service compels it, and society recognizes him. Where the great body of a people are fighting men—valor being the common property, and cowardice the melancholy exception—high refinement, the result of intelligence and polish, must inevitably belong to the officer, since, otherwise, there would be nothing to elevate or distinguish him above his men. He who does not feel this and act upon it, becomes rapidly degraded, and passes out of sight, if not out of the service. The day is gone by, when a rough and surly monster—a drinking, swearing, strutting animal, who had nothing but brute courage and his epaulettes to mark him as a soldier—could pass muster in society. We undoubtedly owe a great deal to the Military School at West Point. I am free to say that the South should have such an institution also. I would plant it somewhere, looking down at once on the Gulf and Atlantic, among the mountain ranges of North Carolina or Tennessee.

Beauclerk.—I can conceive of no greater injustice, Father, than that which, in our popular histories, gives so much credit to Charles Lee, for his share in the action of Fort Moultrie.

Abbot.—There could be no greater. Lee's share in the defence was really none at all; or what there was, was discreditable to his judgment, if not his manhood. The credit is due to John Rutledge, William Moultrie, and his brave companions—the sons of the soil all of them—who took their stations at the guns with but one feeling—the conviction that they had to fight. Lee was not willing to fight, steadily opposed the defence, and, being an Englishman, with the most perfect faith in a British fleet, swore bloody oaths, that the fortress was a mere slaughter pen, which the British broadsides would 'knock about the heads of the garrison in half an hour. He would have abandoned it had the Governor permitted. Rutledge swore, that before he would write such an order, his right hand should be stricken from his body.

Moultrie's temper, on the occasion, was not a whit more yielding: "If they knock the Fort about our ears, we can still fight them behind the ruins," was his language. Subsequently he said: "I never imagined that the enemy could force the post. I always considered myself able to defend it."

EDITOR.—And he did!

ABBOT.—Admirably; it was one of the greatest actions of the war, and preceded the Declaration of Independence, which was made six days afterwards. We do not know the fact, but where was the impossibility of having the news of this event expressed in five or six days to Philadelphia? If the fact was known by Congress, it doubtless contributed to the firmness of that body on that memorable anniversary. We know that the express, bringing the news of the battle of Lexington, took a much longer time in compassing the same distance; but, at that period, no previous arrangements had been made for expressing intelligence. Routes had not been opened, nor emisaries employed before hand; and these were the most substantial difficulties in such a performance. But we have no reason to suppose that, with the whole seaboard anxious in regard to events in daily progress, the public authorities would have neglected the necessary organization of expresses. Besides, it was known that a powerful British fleet had left New-York, as it was supposed, for South-Carolina or Georgia. How natural that the American Congress should employ all its agencies to ascertain its destination and the result. I repeat, it is not impossible that something of the battle of Fort Moultrie was known in Philadelphia on the 4th July ensuing; and the effect must have been sensibly felt. It was, in truth, a most bloody battle. It has been shown that, for the number of troops which they had engaged, the British loss was greater, by far, than it was in the terrible victory at Trafalgar.

Editor.—Yet how the account of this affair is slurred over in our Northern histories.

Abbot.—How every thing *Southern* is slurred over in Northern histories. We hear, for example, in never ending declamations, of the Tea which was emptied into the harbor of Boston. It is scarcely known, even to our own people, that the same thing was done in the harbor of Charleston. New England claims to have done every thing, first to last, in the Revolution! yet she did very little. Her writers may well begrudge us the great battles fought within our borders. Recently, a most impudent attempt has been made to show that these battles were fought by New England troops; but the absurdity of the claim defeats itself; and, fortunately, they have not been able to destroy the records. It is curious that, even before the Revolution, this tendency of New England to usurpation (a characteristic always of the Puritans) was emphatically dwelt upon by persons in Carolina, to discourage the progress to union of the several colonies against the mother country. They distinctly predicted the pretensions of our Yankee brethren. Josiah Quincy, who was sent from Boston to Charleston, as an emisary to foment the occasion for quarrel, states that one of a dinner party, at the residence of Miles Brewton, urged that "the Massachusetts were aiming at sovereignty over the other provinces; that they now took the lead; were assuming dictatorial authority, &c." To this Mr. Josiah Quincy put in a modest disclaimer, as a matter of course. The other replied, however: "You may depend upon it, if the Colonies shake themselves free of Britain, you will have your Governor from Boston. When it comes to the test, Boston will give the other provinces the shell and the shadow, and keep the substance. Take away the power and superintendence of Britain, and the Colonies must submit to the next power." If New England did not succeed in this desire, or design, it was not because of the infirmity of her ambition. She got the better part of the Major Generals and Brigadiers at the beginning of the war, and cursed the military of the country with a most incompetent crew of Captains, Deacons, and others fit only to be Deacons. How much of the prediction might have been verified, subsequently, had not New-York been more favorably situated, not simply for commerce, but for connection with the South? Let the South once set up for herself, and where will be New-York?

EDITOR.—I heard it stated some time ago, Father, that, when the battle was actually in progress at Fort Moultrie, the Priest at St. Michael's prayed for the success of the assailants, to the wives and daughters of the garrison; who left the Church in a body, accordingly.

ABBOT.—The story, I suppose, is true. I have not only heard it repeatedly, from old persons, but I have seen it somewhere in print. I don't know but what you may find it in Dalcho, together with the name of the officiating minister. It must not be forgotten, however, that the Church was a State establishment, under the control of the Church of England, and most of the Divines of that period were sent to us from abroad. These matters deserve the attention of our antiquaries. I wish we could persuade some of them into giving us a series of walks about Charleston. I do not know any city in the Union, which might be found more abundantly rich in antiquities. How many trials by storm and fire hath she undergone—by siege and battle! how many adventurous enterprises hath she undertaken! Her people were always military. She carried her arms to the banks of the Mississippi, and fought the French in their own colonies. Her troops traversed the waters of the St. John's, and the Mauvilla, (Mobile) and her harbor has been penetrated by French, Spanish, and piratical assailants. Thrice has she been besieged, and in no instance hath she been dishonored, even when overthrown.

EDITOR.—The chronicle is a beautiful and extensive one, which records the patriotism of our women of Charleston. There is one item, however, Father, which comes from good authority—that of one of the oldest inhabitants—which has never been in print. When Charleston was in possession of the British, the women of the place would frequently procure passes to go to their farms or plantations in the country. They seized these occasions for carrying forth supplies of cloth, linen, and even gunpowder and shot, to their countrymen in the Brigade of Marion. These commodities were concealed beneath their garments; and, in preparation for their departure, the dimensions of the good women were observed sensibly to increase. At length it was noticed by the officers on guard, that the lady, who, when she left the city, was of enormous bulk—of absolute dropsical *physique*—would return reduced to a shadow. Strange suspicions naturally ran in their heads as to the causes of a change so surprising; and these suspicions were not always creditable to the fair fame of the lady. But other notions, less unfavorable to her virtue, began to prevail, and at the expense of her safety; and it was arranged accordingly to subject the emigrating parties, hereafter, to a test, which should infallibly exhibit the nature of a disease which had such curious results. Accordingly a jury of spinsters was provided, and the fat ladies were taken into custody. The discovery was awful in the last degree—bales of blue broadcloth were unrolled from about the slenderists waists; and swan and duck shot, and gunpowder and ball, rolls of duck and cotton flannels, and Heaven knows what besides, appeared from beneath the ample petticoats, attesting the patriotism of the sex. This put a stop to their growth, as well as their peregrinations.

ABBOT.—No doubt a world of anecdote is yet forthcoming, My venerable friend, Dr. Johnson, has a great variety of stores of this sort, which should make their way to the public. A Stranger's Guide Book through the city—and this might include the Parishes—which, at that period were in singular and close connection with the city—would be as full of interest as a popular novel. The habits, manners, customs, sports, trials, troubles, adventures, anecdotes of life in peculiar forms, and society under the most various circumstances, are still to be gathered and described, in regard to Charleston, if the subject is seized upon now, and before the present generation passes. Another race will know nothing of these things.

EDITOR.—Such a book would need be published by subscription, otherwise it would scarcely pay.

ABBOT.—True, we are exceedingly patriotic, but don't like to pay for it. True patriotism would say, that such a volume—every volume, indeed, which illustrates the deeds and virtues of our people—should be a *family book*. It should be in every library; and yet —— but the subject is an ungracious one.

EDITOR.—Will it ever be any better?

ABBOT.—Yes, when our individuality stops short of mere *egötism*, and, in the development of a peculiar nature, is yet modest enough to remember all its debt of gratitude—equally to the past and the present. Hearken, my son. We have been discoursing of Moultrie and his public services. His is one of those names by which we swear. He constitutes a portion of that sectional capital of character, of which we may boast to our neighbors, and to foreign nations. He is *ours*, and, therefore, we boast. Now, listen. It is now fully a year, since I read in the columns of the Charleston Mercury, a communication, from an anonymous source, which pointed out to our public the fact, that this same Moultrie was reported, annually to the Legislature, as a bankrupt debtor to the State, to the amount of some five hundred dollars! The writer of the article proffered to join with others in a subscription to efface this offensive and ungracious record from the books!—In vain! I am glad the suggestion was not adopted. It is an act which the Legislature itself should perform, for its own credit, and to save the State from shame. As it is, the only monument to Moultrie's memory, which we keep in repair, is one to his reproach and shame! Moultrie was poor, and died so. His virtues and honesty have never been impeached. Let our people boast no more of the memory of this man, until the State shall have written against his name, in the language of Loredano, "*L'ha pagata!*" He has more than paid her. Something will be always due to him, which the future can only acknowledge!

BEAUCLERK.—Our Poet and Painter seem asleep, Father.

ABBOT.—Not they! I never rouse them when they dream. I know that we shall get the benefit of all their dreaming hereafter.

EDITOR.—See, they bestir themselves.

ABBOT.—We will join them. Ho! Son of Apollo, arouse you! We are in our moment of *exstase*, and you have doubtless passed through yours.—

Give us the fruits of your inspirations. I see that the Muse has been with you. You would else have never been so quiet. Come, my son, the Poem. Let us taste the quality of your fruits.

BEAUCLERK.—A sentence! a sentence!

POET.—But, Father! extemporaneous verse, as you well know ——

ABBOT.—Is no verse at all, you would say. No matter. We are indulgent. "Leave off your damnable faces and begin." Is this a time for affectations? Speak, sir, the Poem! It is a decree of the Brotherhood.

POET.—I obey. (Recites.)

Soft is the veil of moonlight o'er the waters,
Softly the swell, upon the shore, of billows,
Soft in the distance, the great city's spires,
And soft the breeze.

Peace is upon the land and on the ocean,
Peaceful the slumbers of this ocean hamlet,
And the blue concave, by a cloud unshadow'd,
Speaks still for peace!

Before us sleeps a mound, whose solemn shadow,
Beseems the red man's tumulus of ages,
As keeping in its deep and vaulted chambers,
A realm of dead.

With gentle light, the moon stoops down to hallow,
The deep repose that wakes not to sweet voices.
She leaves her smiles, where sad, in seasons' vanish'd,
Man left but tears.

No sleepless bird disturbs, with cry or music,
Unsuited to the quiet, deep and sacred,
Where silence, in her own primeval temple,
Still rules supreme.

Who that beholds that ocean wrapt in brightness,
Who, that enjoys embrace with these soft zephyrs,
That feels the beauty and the calm about him—
Would dream of strife?

Would dream of tempests raging o'er this ocean,
Clouds in that azure vault, its charm effacing,
And for this breeze, so meek, yet full of fondness,
Would look for storm!

Yet will the tempest, with a wild transition,
Stifle these gentle breathings of the zephr,
While great tornados sweep the face of Heaven,
With all its charms!

Yet will the seas, in beauty now reposing,
Boil up in madness, and o'erthrow their barriers,
Defacing lawny shore and verdant meadow,
Now blest with peace.

Thus, in a moment, let the foe but threaten,
That silent mound becomes a fiery fortress,
Whose flashing death-bolts, hurtling o'er the waters,
Ring out his doom!

Such awful change, of old, this shore hath witness'd,
When first our young Republic, bold but feeble,
Claim'd, though at peril of all wreck of fortune,
Her place of pride.

Thus calm the seas, when o'er the waters raging,
Rush'd, swollen with wrath, the giant form of Britain,
Her thunders hurling on our peaceful hamlets,
With hate of hell!

Thus silent lay our bulwarks of Palmetto,
Behind them, little groups of youthful heroes,
Waiting the signal, when, with answering thunders,
To meet her wrath.

How patient was their watch beneath that banner,
The slight blue streamer, lighted by one crescent,
That show'd the modest hope that warm'd their courage,
In that dark hour.

How doubtful, yet how fearless of the struggle,
When, in the strength assured, of thousand battles,
Britain, in armour, 'gainst the youthful shepherd,
Came fiercely on!

Doubtful our young men stood, but undespairing,
Not blind to all the fearful odds against them,
But sworn, in faith, that finds it better falling
In fight, than fear!

How beautiful—as serpents fang'd with venom,
Glided the swans of battle to the conflict,
Their streamers flaunting with Britannia's Lion,
Rampant in red!

How silently they moor'd beneath our fortress,
Unmuzzled their grim ministers of vengeance,
And waited but the signal, to send terror
Among our sons.

One awful pause preceded the wild tempest,
Then roar'd the storm, and fell the hail of battle,
A thonsand fires were lighted, in a moment,
At Moloch's shrine!

One look of yearning to the distant city,
Where hung in tears and fondness, wives and mothers,
Forms of most fond delight, and dear devotion,
Weeping in prayer!

And then, the brave hearts of our youthful warriors,
Nerved with new courage by those sweet spectators,
Conscious what hopes and eyes were set upon them,
Rush'd to the strife.

Thunder for thunder, and defiant voices,
Bore witness to the love that faced that conflict—
How the brave spirits, battling for their homesteads,
Defied the Fates!

Through the long day of summer, still unshaken,
They stood beside their cannon, while each broadside,
Shook their frail rugged bastions of Palmetto,
But shook no hearts.

There Moultrie coolly stands, the scene surveying,
Ranging his muzzles on each mighty frigate,
Speeding each fearful missile on its mission
Of blood and wreck!

There Marion ministers, his young Lieutenant,
Wheels the swift piece, and sights the flaming cannon—
Or, when the bullet rends the reeling vessel,
Shouts loud with cheer!

There, stout McDonald, slain upon the rampart,
The first brave martyr in the fearful battle,
Shrieks, as he falls: "I die, my gallant comrades,
But not our cause!"

Down sinks the crescent streamer of the fortress,
While o'er the city sudden darkness lower'd,
As if a star, the only one in Heaven,
Had sunk in night.

But, lo! it rises from the cloud, and waving,
Reveals the lithe and active form of Jasper—
He plucks it from the beach, and rears it proudly
Through all the storm!

If then one heart had trembled in its terror,
It gathers hope and pride from that glad omen,
And hears the whisper'd cry from each fond mother,
"Be strong, my son!"

And they were strong, as for the rock, the eagle,
Who hears the cry of young ones in his eyrie,
Assail'd by subtlest foes; and bends his pinion
To guard his nest.

Day wanes, and night hangs out her starry banner,
Blue spread the curtains of the sky for slumber,
Peace soars aloft, as if in pray'r imploring,
For peace below!

But still the cannon thundered with its mission,
Still spoke fierce music to the hearts of valor,
Still shouted high the brave, and shriek'd the dying,
'Till midnight fell!

The Lion-banner sunk, at length, in darkness;
The crescent soar'd, in every eye triumphant;
While in the distant city rose the shoutings
From hearts made glad.

With dawn, the shatter'd hulks to sea were drifting;
Upon the shores the gentle waves were breaking;
And, with the triumph of our virgin valor,
Came peace once more!

VIII.

Editor.—*(rapping at the Abbot's window)*—Father, you bade me call you at daylight. It is now dawning, and the tide is pouring in magnificently.

Abbot.—Son, I will be with you in an instant. I have but to slip into my drawers, since I understand that bathing here is conducted *selon les regles.*

EDITOR.—I fancy you need not be so scrupulous. It is so early that objects are scarcely visible at any distance. You see but the vast spread of the waters; and the breakwater, though contrasted with them, seems but a remote and indefinite line upon the horizon. Beauclerk has presumed upon the doubtful light, and is in that primitive condition which suggested to Eve the uses of the fig leaf.

ABBOT.—The irreverent dog! But I will not follow his example. I am ready: and now, my son, remember that you have more than Cæsar's fortunes to take care of. I have been modestly reluctant, all my life, to venture out of my depth. Should you see me floundering confusedly, kicking away with amazing rapidity, and yawing about like a vessel in the hands of a tipsy helmsman, remember to come to the rescue. I fancy I am one of the few Charleston boys that cannot swim. I tried it when a boy, but could never work the vessel and keep her afloat at the same time. My head had always a leaden-like proclivity downwards, and I could never learn. I believe that some men are denied the faculty altogether. You are aware that this is the case with some horses, who will rather lie down in the water, or wade along upon the bottom, than make the attempt. No practice, no frequency of experiment, ever changes the result. The vulgar superstition in the country is, that all *May colts* have this disposition to lie down in the water, though it is not said that all May colts refuse to swim. I was once nearly drowned crossing an arm of Pearl River, in Mississippi, by the mulish tendency of my steed in this matter. The stream though a frequent ford, was swollen beyond its bounds. The atrocious beast went down and down, the waters rising higher and higher at each moment. They were soon at the saddle skirts; soon over *my own* skirts; and, finally, I was nearly lifted off by the current. I had only to stick to the animal, to thrust my legs down, and cling to his sides, taking it *coolly* (as you may suppose,) while I saw the beast's head fairly go under. It was but a moment, however, and in the next he scrambled up a bank. Powerful and precious was the long breath which we both drew in the same instant, though from different emotions.

EDITOR—A narrow escape, Father. But here you are in no danger. The water deepens gradually, and at no ordinary tide is it above the head within the breakwater. But I am with you, and all the rest of us swim like ducks.

ABBOT.—Or tadpoles! Beauclerk, I see, is already in. What a floundering and plunging he keeps. I can see his white form as he leaps and wantons in the glorious element. What a delightful faculty. What pride to realize the painted picture of Shakspeare:

> "To beat the surges under you,
> To ride upon their backs; to tread the water,
> And fling aside its enmity; still breasting
> The surge most swollen, that meets you—your bold head
> 'Bove the contentious waves still kept, and oaring
> Yourself, with your good arms in lusty stroke!"

This is, indeed, a power and a grace to be desired—to be toiled after; and I envy few accomplishments to my neighbors so much as that of being an adroit and skilful swimmer.

Editor.—It seems strange, Father, that, with such feelings, you never acquired the art.

Abbot.—Perhaps it is not so strange. My education in all things was greatly neglected in my childhood. I need not say that most physical acquisitions, to be well made, must be made in early youth. Riding, for example, running, boxing, and even shooting. Now, it so happens, that I was a sickly child. My infancy was marvellously feeble. I was half the time in the hands of the doctor, drugged and dieted. I lived in spite of him, but my opportunities were lost; for years I remained feeble, and timid accordingly. I shared not in their exercises with the athletes of the school; and books, from my close confinement, soon superseded field and water sports, and studies; and now, it is too late to learn, my son. I now see that swimming should form a part of one's education, as becoming as dancing, and far more necessary. What a place here for a swimming school. I trust that our new Hotel will keep this matter in mind, and keep a competent person always, and convenient places assigned, in which "to tëach the youthful athlete how to swim." The practice is common in England. The art is taught like boxing.

Editor.—A good suggestion. Franklin's counsels may be well enough; but *physical* accomplishments are not to be learned from essays or books. Practice is the only school; and the first experiments in swimming ought always to carry the urchin beyond his depth: always taking care that succor is at hand. This throws him upon his resources, and brings out all his energies. It is thus that he acquires confidence and courage. Now, these are the first essentials, and these acquired, all the rest is easy. A good swimmer is the most audacious being in the world when in the element he loves. The billows seem to be as conscious when they have to deal with one who fears them, as the horse, when crossed by a timid rider. Horse and water equally take advantage of such persons. They must equally be taught to feel, that he who rides, is their master, and is determined to remain so. Let him learn to slap saucily the billow on the chops, and clap fearless spurs to the steed, and the empire is his own.

Abbot.—A truth! The moral of the steed is in the spur of the rider! I have heard with some surprise that large numbers of sailors are ignorant of the art of swimming. It is said that some of them have refused to acquire it, and have given as a reason that swimming is of no service at sea, but a real misfortune; that it frequently prompts the courage to experiments of extreme recklessness; that in the event of danger, the good swimmer is usually despatched on the perilous performance—made to swim on shore with a rope, for example—and if he falls overboard, at sea, the possession of the faculty would only prolong his tortures and his dangers. He prefers to sink outright rather than protract a struggle, which will most probably be useless—since few are saved who fall overboard at sea—and be exposed to the agony of a piecemeal death in the jaws of the ravening shark. There would seem to be some reasoning in the argument, though it is difficult to persuade ourselves that the acquisition of any power, by which we increase our manhood, should be at any time an evil.

Editor.—The sailor who argues thus, argues rather to excuse his deficiencies, I fancy, than to prove their advantages. He probably belongs to that class who swim stone-fashion, as you described yourself to do. He has found the acquisition difficult or impossible.

Abbot.—But why take to the sea?

Editor.—From necessity—the world's ill usage, vice, fugitive moods, and a thousand other occasional impulses. I suspect that most of those who go to sea, from erratic desires, are good swimmers. Boating and swimming are likely to have prompted their choice of vocation. Are you fairly in, Father?

Abbot.—Up to the middle.

Editor.—Good! Let us wade some ten yards further now, throw your hands *thus*, above your head, and bury yourself in the waters.

Abbot.—It is done!

Editor.—That first shock reconciles you to a bath of twenty minutes: only keep moving. It may be well to make an effort, old as you are, to float and swim. Use equal movements of arms and feet, at the same time, occupying as much surface as you can.

Abbot.—That is, spreading myself out?

Editor.—That will keep you afloat; and to do this will not be difficult, if you will only be cool—

be not impatient—be not flurried. Be deliberate; and this ought to be easy, when you remember that you are within your depth, and may, at any moment, lift your head above the waters. Timid persons find their difficulty in this. They do not give themselves time, get flurried, and having swallowed a pint of sea-water, lose all stomach for the experiment. There! that will do! I see you understand me.

ABBOT.—I certainly contrive to float. How delicious is the temperature! How refreshing! The morning, just after sleep, is always the best time for the bath, from head to foot. The system is relaxed from sleep. The nerves need the restoration of tone. The whole body demands the refreshing influences of water, precisely as the face and hands. But for the languor induced by our habits, quite as much as our climate, such would be the common practice.

EDITOR.—Look at Beauclerk, Father.

ABBOT.—How the dog rollicks! What antics does he play with the billows! He frolics like a young colt, just escaped from the stables to the common. What's he after now? Whither does he go?

EDITOR.—Towards the stone wall. He is after a dive, I fancy. Yes, there he clambers up. Our Poet is there before him. Do you see their forms together on the breakwater? They mean to dive together. Both swim well, and I suppose they design a match for the shore. You see them?

ABBOT.—Yes, by Saint Jupiter, and both naked as innocence. They are off. The plunge was a fine one; but, between us, Mr. Editor, there is a little too much light, methinks, for such bold experiments. The day thickens. Those bright grey streaks, "the sudden arrows from the eastern bow," give us warning to depart.

EDITOR.—Not so, Father! Our Islanders are reluctant risers. They will keep their pillows for an hour yet.

ABBOT.—I hope so: for, in truth, though no swimmer, I find the bath a rare luxury. What a generous glow! The sea is a buoyant couch. It sustains me, though not its master. How sadly sweet is the mysterious chiding of the waves against that barrier of stone; and how softly, with what velvet steps, did the tide creep in this morning. I rose and looked forth some time before you knocked at the window. In the dim light of stars, I could discern the breakwater, and the flashing billows beyond it. But within the basin there was no sign of water. All was dull grey sands, and that seemed only an hour ago. How noiselessly it stole upward to the very porches of the dwelling. What a wondrous and beautiful mystery in the decree that moves these glorious elements, in an order so matchless and unerring, and all, as it would seem, in a service tributary to the tastes and the fancies, no less than the common wants of man! See you, in the east, where a little drift of white clouds, a sort of rippled muslin, puts on a delicate carnation tinge. The day is making progress. The sun will not be slow to follow. We must hurry our bath.

Editor.—Not yet, Father; not yet! How I wish that you could swim. I must take my plunge from the breakwater also. I am half tempted to do it on the outside. There can surely be no sharks at this early hour. There is no proof that the sharks rise with the fowls.

Abbot.—If fowls were their common diet, I should presume that there could be no question of their habits; but unless you can show that the fish, which are their food, retire with the sun, and keep *perdu* until he re-appears again, it is mere madness to risk anything upon the habits of the sea-wolf. No! no! my son, *veto!* I forego none of the functions of the Father Abbot, even though "half seas over;" and I positively forbid you trying any foolish experiment.

Editor.—I submit, Father. Yet you little dream of the delights of breasting the more vigorous billows. It is then that the swimmer feels himself, and exults in his possessions. You remember the line of Pollock, describing Byron's passion for the sea. They seem, to me, among the noblest and smothest of our heroic blank:

> "He laid his hand upon old ocean's mane,
> And play'd familiar with his hoary locks."

Abbot.—They are fine, but borrowed from Byron himself, who borrowed, in turn, from the Bible:

> "Once more upon the waters—yet once more,
> And the waves bound beneath me, as a steed,
> That knows his rider."

Pollock, I am half disposed to think, has improved upon the original. But, turn your eyes from the sea, my son. Look back upon our ocean hamlet, as *our* poet properly calls it. How sweetly does it sleep in the cold light of the dawn. The outline of the settlement seen in the imperfect light, actually looms up nobly and picturesquely. The rudeness of the exterior is not perceptible; and one might fancy that a proper architecture had been at work to address the most elaborate appeals to the eye. But, hark! What is that? It sounds like a regular war whoop!

EDITOR.—It is, and it is from the throat of Pictor. He learned the war whoop among the Choctaws.

ABBOT.—But why does he gives it to us now. It is surely a signal. It must mean something. Where is he?

EDITOR.—Down, close under the shadow of the breakwater.

ABBOT.—I see! and hark, again! Look! he waves his hand toward the shore. What can he mean?

EDITOR.—By Jove, Father, we are not alone. There is another party within the basin. They do not see us. Should they be ladies now.

ABBOT.—I see! Three tall forms, muffled up like the witches in Macbeth. They wave their hands also. "Thrice to thine!"

EDITOR.—"And thrice to mine!"

ABBOT.—"And thrice again to make up nine." Can they be women? Or only of that breed, *Desinit in piscem, mulier formosa superne?*" Should they be women, that fellow Beauclerk is in a pretty fix.

EDITOR.—They may be mermaids, in sooth. They are too tall for women.

ABBOT.----They only seem tall in this light, and standing up, as they do, in shallow water. They are women, I am certain!—and there go Beauclerk and the Poet, in full plunge, toward them. In their trial of skill and speed, they see nothing but one another. See what tremendous *splurges* that fellow, Beauclerk, makes. Little does he dream who sees his antics. How wantonly he darts, and skims, and wallows—half the time out of water:—and, now, only look at the blind, the utterly besotted, mortals. They have actually begun to splash away, like overgrown urchins, at each other's faces, making every thing foam about them.

EDITOR.—Beauclerk is beaten, and the Poet pursues him.

ABBOT.—And there they rush, by all that's gracious, directly among the strangers. We shall soon see whether they are women or not. Ha! We have it! what a shriek! Push for the shore, my son. Keep within the shadow of the breakwater, and let us make away toward the Point House. We may yet escape unseen. Pictor is ahead of us, moving in the same direction. See, how the strangers scamper. They tumble headlong, one over the other, toward the beach; while our naked athletes push, equally headlong, in the opposite quarter.

EDITOR.—The Poet has his drawers on, Father.

ABBOT.—A fig for his drawers! He might as well be as naked as a Pict. His drawers stick to him like a pitch plaister, shewing the beauties of his form in all its absolute perfection. Ho! there, you runagates! What a mischief have you done!

BEAUCLERK.—All your fault, Father.

ABBOT.—My fault, monster!

BEAUCLERK.—Yes, Father, the ambition to show off before you, led us into this misfortune.

ABBOT.—Hence, infidel! To the house with all despatch, and into your breeches. We shall steal away, and take our breakfast at .the East end of the island. There is a friend who keeps good cheer in that quarter, who will gladly welcome us. The storm will blow ever in our absence. In flight alone is safety. '*Sauve qui pent,*' is the cry.

EDITOR.—We breakfast then with ———?

ABBOT.—Yes! And see his farm and dairy. His cows, his calves, his pigs, his poultry, his ox, his ass, and every thing that is his. He affords a happy instance of a man, brought up to business cares in a city, who has a taste for nature, and whose humanity has never been corrupted by a selfish occupation.

BEAUCLERK.—Do we ride, Father?

ABBOT.—Get yourself into your garments! Ask no questions! Join us on the back-beach. We walk! It will help digestion. A long walk after the bath, and a good breakfast after that, and a wise man is a happy one for the day. He is then more apt to realize that condition of sound mind in sound body—*mens sana in corpore sano*—which is the

F5

very perfection of humanity—in its capacity for enjoyment, at least.

EDITOR.—Beauclerk, you should never have gone in without your drawers and shirt.

ABBOT.—A grave truth, just one hour too late. But we must enforce and make the caution a permanent one in his mind by a proper penalty. Let the decree be registered against him;—a basket of champagne.

BEAUCLERK.—A hard case, Father. But is it understood that we invite our mermaids to sup with us?

ABBOT.—Out Polyphemus, out! before I couch thy sight for thee with a staff as potent as that of Ulysses. Away, Centaur, and get thyself clad.

EDITOR.—This is a mischance, Father.

[*Ex. Beauclerk, &c.*]

ABBOT.—Yes, if it chance that there shall have been a miss among these strangers; but between us, son, you may make your mind easy. These are no women, but our own brethren, Beaurevoir, Bienami, and Beauregard, who came down in a sail boat late last night, and came to my chamber as I was about to retire. I wished to give Beauclerk a scare, in order to curb his tendency to excess. The thing was arranged with our brethren who will join us, on the way to breakfast.

EDITOR.—I breathe, Father. I am relieved. Had they been women!

ABBOT.—Pshaw!—had they been *ladies*, the affair would have been a little annoying, but nothing more. To the pure, all things are pure, and keeping in mind the phrase of the King in regard to the Countess—of whom, by the way, nothing need be said---we must, in all such cases, find our security in the motto,----"*Honi soit qui mal y pense.*" But let us away, and leave the boys to follow.

IX.

Abbot.—There comes the sun! He is just struggling above the waters. How like a struggle it appears! The effect, at this moment, conducts irresistibly to this impression. The waves seem to rise about him, laboring to keep him down.—They have lashed themselves into foam in the endeavor, and though they fail in their object, yet it would seem that his victory has not been won without loss. His wounds seem to have dyed the torrents with his blood. The crimson and the white foam mingle together; and we fancy that were we near enough to hear, we should be stunned by the howls of disappointment on the one hand, and the shouts of victory on the other. We hear the murmur of billows even here; and it seems to be allied to the conflict, and to have been occasioned by it. The clouds have shared somewhat in the affair. They wear the hues of blood also. One great and reptured mass hangs directly above the head of the conqueror. It is the smoke reeking up from the field of fight, rising above, and forming its appropriate canopy. The sun employs it as a trophy. It becomes his banner; and its torn and tattered edges are spread out, and rise with him, as if borne aloft by the tallest of his angel legions—some Azazel of the imperial host! Other banners now appear along the horizon, as if rising with him from the deep; forming a grand procession to accompany his onward march. And see, those pale white groups of cloud, flitting fast away, right and left, as remotely as possible from his line, of march—a wild and capricious disarray. May we not suppose them to be the scattered camps of some auxiliary host, flying confusedly to escape destruction or captivity. The whole broad expanse of heaven exhibits as many contrasts and varieties of shape and shadow, in the advance of the morning splendor, as any field of various conflict, or any country under the march of a dreaded conqueror. It would seem as if the hosts of night and ocean, assembled under the cover of darkness for the conquest of the earth, had been dispersed by a single glance from some glorious messenger of heaven.

Editor.—You make quite a picture, Father.

Abbot.—It makes itself. This is one of those spectacles that convert all men, more or less, into painters. The mind catches from the prospect, a thousand suggestions for the fancy, and the eye looks forth for pictures. But the sunrise is not simply a spectacle. It is a moral emblem. We see the great invisible work of creation performed anew with the return of every day. We see the results of the Almighty working, as at the dawn of all mortal being, though the process is wholly hidden from our eyes. We see in the glorious spectacle the moral that is designed to excite our emulation. The day of man is a march in light. It is a constant progress forward. It rises in night, to have its setting in other regions, which it is to enliven and illumine also. We pass on from world to world; with an active duty assigned to us in each. He only is the true Christian, who goes on working and marching to the close. In this way only can he unfold his possessions, and bless other eyes with that *trust of light*, which is conferred upon him for this very purpose.—Happy he who obeys the law of his nature as implicitly as the sun! Who rises regularly to his duties, and, heedless of storm, and strife, and temporary obscuration by cloud, vapor, and interposing and envious bodies, still keeps in his old path, "the ordered course pursuing."

Editor.—Is not that last member a quotation, Father? I think I have heard the phrase before.

Abbot.---Doubtlessly. It is a quotation from a version which I made twenty years ago of Goethe's famous Hymn of the Archangels, at the opening of the Faust. It suits the scene, and you shall have it all.

HYMN OF THE ARCHANGELS.

RAPHAEL.

And still the sun as ever,
Chimes with his brother spheres,
His order'd path pursuing,
With the thunder's solemn roll—
Though him we may not fathom,
He yet gives strength to us—
Glorious, oh! mighty Father,
Thy works, as at the first!

GABRIEL.

And with a mighty fleetness,
The pomp of earth revolves;
The glorious blaze of Heaven,
Now chang'd for fearful night;
The broad waves of the ocean
Foam up against the rocks,
While whirling on, both rock and sea
Chime with the ever rolling spheres.

MICHAEL.

And roaring as in rivalry,
From sea to land, from land to sea,
The storms erect around a chain
Of deepest elemental rage;
And flashing desolation there
Glares in the thunder's rushing path—
But, Lord! thy messengers revere
The milder goings of thy day.

THE THREE.

Though Thee we may not fathom,
Thy look gives strength to us—
Glorious, oh! mighty Father,
Thy works, as at the first!

Editor.—I wished you had rhymed it, Father.

Abbot.—So do I. I shall rhyme it some day when I am in the mood, and have the leisure; but there are some subjects for verse which rhyme does not seem to improve. Sacred poetry, for example, always appears to me to lose something of dignity and solemnity, by the petty tagging of the rhyme. To pursue our moral analogies: it matters not to man, keeping his natural symbols in his sight, that his light may sometimes, nay, frequently, fail to be seen, by those for whom it is designed, and who are supposed to look for it. Enough that he can reply with the magician in the mysterious cave of the Visigoth: "*I do mine office!*" It is quite sufficient that he wilfully withholds no portion of his precious beams. It is the misfortune and the error of those who wilfully refuse to see.

Editor.—Yet unless they see, Father, where is his recompense; where their acknowledgments?

Abbot.—His ample recompense lies in his own exercise, if his ambition be the right one: looking to the only proper source of reward. Shall man look ever and only to his brother; and what shall be the virtue in his charity, if he is perpetually groaning for the *quid pro quo?* Genius is the world's great benefactor. Shall it cease to be genius because the world is ungrateful; and shall the benefactor look to the pauper for his pay. What is it to the noble----which is always the giving and the performing mind----that his petty puling race, each cursing himself and his neighbor with his miserable little two-and-sixpence vanities, his small conceit of place and position, and the strut which is always laboring, not to be high, but to seem high----stubbornly refuses to acknowledge the benefits of the benefactor----in the powerful phrase of Milton, "crams and blasphemes the feeder," and decries the claim, which it feels that it can never satisfy? Nay, what were the real value of the tribute of acknowledgment, were the world to make free and full confession of the benefits received? Would that be sufficiently compensative for the performance, which still strives, and serves, and saves? It is not intended that it should be! *The essence of compensation to man, for good and great works upon earth, is to be found in the performance itself.* This is the principle of vitality in the moral system. It is in the feeling that he does, is doing, and has done, that the worker finds his reward, in all moral and intellectual labors. This, indeed, constitutes the secret of his dignity. He is the master of a world-wide charity. The sense of a gratified obedience, in the heart of man, is the source, not only of the *mens conscia recti*, but of the higher rewards of a justifiable ambition. Milton alludes to this, when he says in Lycidas:

> " '*But not the praise*,'
> Phœbus replied, and touch'd my trembling ear;
> 'Fame is no plant that grows in mortal soil.' "

No! we fulfil a destiny, my son. The duty must be performed; and it is not to man that we are to look ever, for the reward of the worker. The sense of duty done, and grief endured, without complaint and in a cheerful, sanguine spirit, naturally directs the eye of the laborer to the great Giver of all endowments, and assures him of ultimate acknowledgment, in the shape of continued and higher employment hereafter. In other words, though the Prophet toils for man, he toils in the employ of God. To which ought he to look for reward?

EDITOR.—What new and hopeful prospects does such a view open to those who seem to toil in vain.

How it unfolds the vista of hope to labor and art.

ABBOT.—Necessarily! Man belongs to a system, even as the sun, the moon and stars. With greater discretion allowed him, he is subject to laws which are quite as exacting in degree. *His simple duty is obedience.* In obedience lies the whole secret of his usefulness; and usefulness, understood in its enlarged and proper sense, covers the entire tract of Christian obligation.

EDITOR.—Is there not some danger, Father, from such a doctrine? Does it not tend greatly to narrow the province of humanity? What will become of our friends, Poet and Painter, if we establish the utilitarian principle on such an eminence?

ABBOT.—You do not give due value to the words I use. I am not arguing for the *vulgar* doctrine of utilitarianism. I said *usefulness*, in its enlarged and *proper* sense, in which the Poet, in all probability, occupies the highest position as a social benefactor. He is the father of the profoundest philosophy. He speaks for our noblest nature. His very language belongs to a condition which humanity may understand and feel, but cannot ordinarily use. As one of the tribe has described it—"is the large utterance of the early gods!" It is a divine speech, worthy of prophecy and inspiration—in which true inspiration has usually—nay always—spoken.

EDITOR.—But all the studies and labors of the great body of mankind, will fail to endow them with this utterance—*Poeta nascitur non fit!* What then becomes of its usefulness?

ABBOT.—It lies partly in this very particular. It is at once desirable and unattainable. It is not intended that the world at large should speak this language. It is enough if the world is content to hear and take it to their hearts. If men were all poets and prophets there would be no men. Humanity would be advanced, at a bound, to one of those higher conditions, which it may be supposed to be designed to reach, only through long ages of probation—toils ceaseless, and humiliations that purge pride of all its grossnesses. We are permitted to hear and comprehend this language of the poet, and this is all. Enough if we acknowledge its diviner impulses; if, freeing our souls, at moments, from the miserable toils and vulgar anxieties which form the clogs to the soul's progress upon earth, we occasionally give ear to the pure harmonies of the poet, while he soothes the stormy ocean around us, and subdues to repose the vexed and vexing billows of passion in our hearts. Our merit will be quite sufficient, if we incline our ears to the poet without seeking to emulate his song; enough if we comprehend the divine utterance which we cannot hope to imitate. Still we may yearn to employ this speech. It is desirable that we should. It is desirable as a motive to honorable ambition—

> "Fame is the spur which the clear spirit doth raise
> To scorn delights,"

that we should seek to speak this language; and, for another reason—that, as it is unattainable by the unendowed, it should leave us always discontents.

Editor.--And is discontent, Father, a desirable condition for humanity?

Abbot.----The most desirable of all! The very condition which constitutes the lot of man on earth. It is through this condition only that he finds the usual stimulus to performance. Were it not for this he would *do* nothing and *be* nothing. We prattle a great deal very absurdly about content; and what is hope itself but a happy sort of discontent? It tells us of unattained objects and conditions, and so paints their attractions to our mind, that we naturally yearn and strive for their acquisition; and hence our best performances. Man, as an inhabitant of earth--as man—was never meant to be satisfied with his condition. He is still evermore afflicted with aspirations after the possible—the vague—the, perhaps, unattainable! In this yearning he establishes his ideal; and the pursuit of his ideal affords the clue to his existence. It is thus that he works out his deliverance. It is thus that he finds out and exercises his powers; and shows what are his highest conceptions of the Deity, as well as of his own nature. The Mahometan's dream of Heaven, for example, is one of sensual delights and physical repose. He dreams that he shall sleep in Heaven, on couches of amaranth, tended by houri's—beings of celestial origin, but meant as ministers to the faithful among the sons of earth. He is not tasked with cares, nor required to serve. He does not even engage in hosannas to a common sovereign. All his being lapses away in dream and reverie, and the gratification of simply voluptuous fancies, without physical effort. At most, he amuses himself with archery, which the Prophet seems to have exulted in as a practice of delight almost too good for earth! But, with the Christian philosopher, the future is a world for struggle and conquest, the same as this; for exercise and continual achievement, for which the present is a mere ordeal and preparation. I say Christian *philosopher*, mark you, and not Christian simply. I am afraid that too many professing Christians look forward to a Heaven, in which, if the delights be not sensual exactly, they are yet designed to minister to the desire of ease, and repose from struggles, which always made them groan and grumble under their fardels, throughout the preliminary state, as a very much ill-used people. This was certainly the Puritan philosophy, with a difference. They were too much given to insist upon themselves as the suffering Saints, having title to, if not tenure of, the Lord's possessions upon the earth, to forego, at any time, the free use of its fruits in their season. We all seek our ideals, and, in so doing, declare the degree of elevation in our thoughts and sensibilities. The world knows no higher ideals than those of the poet. If we give him our ear, he invariably conducts us out of the present. That is something. He lifts us from the earth. That is something more. He thus weans us from the pleasures of the sense, and raises us up from the wallow into which the brutal parts of our nature would constantly conduct us. In this lies *one* secret, and not the largest of his usefulness. This is enough for us; and, in the employment of this influence the poet shares with us his nature and his gifts. The natural tendency, struggling as we do, with petty daily necessities, and against special social vanities, is continually downward. The fine arts, of which poetry is the most supreme, are perpetually interposing to arrest or to modify this tendency. In this office they are potent handmaids of religion, which has at heart this object only; and even when serving us simply through the tastes, they operate wonderful results in behalf of the higher objects of the soul. You are passing now two of the churches upon the Island. Is religion aided in her objects, think you, when the passer by smiles, or sneers, at the dwelling to which we implore the presence of Jehovah? Our tastes should no more be allowed to contemn, in religious matters, than our philosophy. We can understand why a temple of God, in a small community like this, need not be a massive, or of immense structure. But surely, society should not allow itself to be in possession of any arts superior to those with which she builds to her Creator. If you lack the material for building, the money, or the architect, why, then, the excuse for a wretched temple is legitimate. But where you possess the means, and where you have the necessary arts, such structures as these are not only discreditable to our tastes, but to our religion. In other words, we employ a superior art in the erection of a stable or a kitchen, to that which we summon to our service in rearing the temples of the Lord. You require *Him* to occupy a dwelling in which you would not deign to reside yourself. I have alluded to the expense of a good structure. I need not to have done so. It is just as cheap to build a good, as a bad structure. The same money which has been expended on these buildings, with the usual expense of repairs upon them, for ten years past, would have put up pleasing and graceful edifices, to which the eye of taste would incline, as well as religion. To build symmetrically, and according to the laws of art, is not necessarily to build expensively. To make a *fine* house, seldom costs more than to make an *atrocious one!* This is the secret of art! She builds *economically because she wastes nothing. She builds securely and durably, because she builds symmetrically.* The secret of strength is quite as much in the *symmetry* of the structure as in its materials. It is to this that we owe the wonderful preservation of so many monuments of ancient art, which have been preyed upon by storm, siege, fire —the wilful assaults of man, and the corroding and sapping influences of time. The building gains nothing in strength, from the enormous bulk of the mass. A well sprung arch will tie the granite together in bonds which neither storm nor fire can rend asunder, but it must be the hands of art which must forge the bolts for their union.—We have been accustomed to leave these matters to the mechanic. But the mechanic seldom aims, or pretends to be an architect. He has quite enough to do in carrying out the plans of the architect. We have buildings among us—churches—which contain unnecessary brick enough to wall the city! Some of our towers were made so massive with brick, as to split and crack, and sink, and cave in, and yawn—leaving the proprietors doubtful whether the foundation would endure its own weight, to say nothing of that of the spire which it was designed to sustain! It was very easy to respect such a doubt, and to forbear all further experiments, when it was found that the money, raised for the steeple, was all consumed in the foundation. You perhaps recall the doggrel which sang of a

> "Christian people,
> Who built a Church in Meeting-street,
> But could'nt raise the steeple."

The Church alluded to, has, of late years, repaired its short comings. But we still see others about the city—crude, unfinished monstrosities of architecture—discrediting equally taste and religion—without plan or purpose—symmetry or strength—great barn-like fabrics, with porches and pediments that seemed to have been fashioned after an awkward squad of revolutionary officers, six portly legs and pursy bodies, with one great sharp cock'd hat upon the heads of the entire line. I repeat, it is just as *easy* and *cheap* to build a fine fabric, in good style, according to proper laws of taste, as to build a mean one; and that the secret of durableness consists much more in the symmetry and just proportions of the structure, than in the materials which you employ. A house, for example, of soft and inferior brick, well planned, well covered, with ample eaves and cornice, and plaistered or stuccoed, will last just as long as the same building made of the best brick, and finished in the same manner. Nay, it will last much longer, indeed, if while the proportions of the former be in accordance with the laws of art, the latter issues from the hands of a hodman in the business.

EDITOR.—I am curious, Father, about the new Hotel on the Island. I confess to great anxiety as to its establishment.

ABBOT.—Be at ease on the subject. It will be built. It will be done effectually, and in proper manner. I have enjoyed an hour of *prevision*, my son—a peculiar faculty, you are aware, which I possess—which enables me to satisfy all your doubts, and to soothe all your anxieties. I can give you the whole particulars relating to the Island House, though nothing has yet been resolved upon. But all will happen as I tell you. We will wait till our scape-graces come up—I see them now approaching—when you shall have the full history of the Hotel, its site, its style, its extent, and all that belongs to the subject. In the meantime, before I forget, let me remind you of something which was said in a previous conversation, in regard to the tenure by which lots are held on the Island. It was then assumed that the grant was from O'Sullivan. This may be so; yet, in the absence of proof, it is well to know what old Jack Drayton says on the subject. You will find at page 206 of his "View," a paragraph which states that the first settlement of Moultrieville "was about the year 1791, when the Legislature passed a resolution permitting people to build there on half acre lots; subject, however, to the condition of being removed whenever demanded by the Governor or Commander-in-Chief. Of course, this contemplates nothing more than the exigencies which might follow from invasion; when it might be necessary to convert the whole island into a fortress. The eastern extremity, which was threatened when Sir Peter Parker assailed Fort Moultrie, should certainly have its defences also.—Drayton mentions further, that the island was at one time well wooded, and continued so till the year 1700, when, by an act of Assembly, the trees were cut down; a few prominent ones excepted, which were left standing as marks for pilots.—What motive could have prompted this proceeding, seemingly so barbarous, is not said. Drayton refers to Trott's Laws, p. 81, where probably the preamble of the act affords the motive. Invasions from French and Spaniards were common about that period, and Pirates frequently made the coast, its inlets, creeks, and marshes, their secret places of resort. They might well have sheltered the masts and spars of their little crafts, behind a clump of forest trees, invisible from the city, whence, were there presence suspected, they might have been pursued, or signals given to the unsuspecting merchantmen, approaching the shore, for whom they lay in wait. The commerce of Charleston suffered dreadfully from these marauders, whom, under irresponsible administrations, her people had rather encouraged. You are aware, perhaps, that the Pirates walked the streets of that good city with impunity, not only tolerated, but in favor with the people.

Editor.—Is it possible?

Abbot.—The secret was this. The Pirates were good Britons. They preyed only on the Spanish galleons, and filled their beakers only from the wines of the French Islands. They were, therefore, our natural allies. The French and Spaniards were, in that day, our natural enemies. Charleston encouraged the pirates, as Queen Elizabeth did; and for the same reason. Her mariners held the doctrine, that there was no peace beyond the Line; and the cavaliers of Carolina esteemed this doctrine to be not a bad one, in a period when an English Monarch knighted Morgan, the Buccaneer. Subsequently, however, when the British Government, threatened equally by France and Spain, was compelled to frown down the piracies practised in her name in the seas of America, South-Carolina was made to pay the penalty of the eccentricities in morals of the mother country. The Pirates who were denied to enter the port which once received them graciously, became its bitter assailants—watched its entrances day and night, carried off its rich merchandizes, and more than once laid the city itself under contribution. Remind me at a moment of greater leisure of this matter, and I will tell you some curious pirate traditions of these very islands.

X.

MINE HOST.—Venerable Father, and you, Reverend Brethren, I pray ye consider yourselves at home. Hold me as a serving brother only, and command accordingly. These fish are the very best that swim—at least to my notion. They are the Cavalli. Here is butter, fresh from my own poor dairy; and these eggs were laid, according to instructions, the moment I heard of your coming. My hens have had their training. I find them as docile as my neighbor, Truesdell, finds his oysters. Here, also, are some cream cheeses, the receipt for preparing which is peculiar. I procured it from a traveller who brought it from Bagdad. It had there the traditional reputation of having been the favorite dish of the famous Caliph, Haroun Al-Raschid. Of course, I have not omitted hominy. That dish I hold to be the *sine quâ non* in a Carolina breakfast. But this is prepared of no common corn. It is from a peculiar grain called the silver eye. I beg that you will say nothing of it to John Michel, or h'll be for crossing and improving it. Now, I have a weakness in regard to this grain. I do not wish its virtues perilled by any experiments. It may undergo change, indeed, and that change may be improvement; but my taste is now so admirably accommodated to the commodity, as it is, that I fear I should suffer some loss of appetite, were I conscious of any variation in its flavor. These rice waffles I can commend to you, and the flappers and griddle cakes. Estifania, my housekeeper, has a rare capacity in breadstuffs. She is the very flower of my household.

ABBOT.—Blessed is the woman that hath the approbation of her master! Such a being is not to be carved out of common wood. I can believe all her merits. My nostrils agreeably confirm all the impressions of mine eyes. You have made princely provision for us, Mine Host, and you have our blessings. The gods keep your larder always full, your fowls always prolific, and your wine always ripe, cool, and abundant. Receive from my paternal hands the badge of our order.

MINE HOST.—Holy Father! This is too much. It is overwhelming! I had never dreamed of such proud distinction.

ABBOT—Modesty is the jewel of youth. Look up, my son, and take heart. It is well to feel humility, but not to sink under it. Henceforth, be known to the order as Brother Bonhommie! Our tenets and faith shall be opened to you at the first solemn chapter which we hold hereafter. For the present, Brother, do thine office. The Cavalli, if you please. You do no less than justice to this hominy, which you are right in assuming to be the essential on a Southern breakfast table. Maize is one of the noblest of the breadstuffs. We owe something to the red men for that which we inherit from them. That you have improved upon it, by judicious culture and selection, is to your own honor. It is the curse of too many of our planters, of the Low Country, that they do not attend to their own farmsteads. What can the overseer know where the master knows nothing? This absenteeism—this wandering off into distant and ungrateful States—wasting profligately, in foreign expenditure, the substance drawn ruthlessly from the bowels of our own—is a crime no less than a folly! Our misfortunes are almost wholly due to this single cause; for the practice not only involves us in a waste of substance, but a waste of time, which is more valuable still. The waste of time involves all sorts of wastes, not the least of which is the waste of intellect. No man's mind can possibly improve, who has no habitual occupation. All progress fails in the community, or with the class which devolves its duties wholly on subordinates.

Editor.—But, Father, the climate of our Low Country,—so fatal to the white race.

Abbot.—I have not lost sight of this matter, my son. There is something in it, but not every thing. Many need not leave their homesteads at all; and many need not go far. Settlements are to be found within ten miles of almost every rice plantation in the Low Country, where the summer might be passed in healthy security. But look at those who come to Charleston—and the Island. Need they be idle because they leave their plantations? Could they not do as has been done here, by our worthy brother, Bonhommie? Surely, there is nothing in the native character of *this* soil, but sterility; yet, what has art and industry already achieved for this isolated spot! Here has he snatched from the desert a pretty little cantle. He hath made the wilderness to blossom as the rose. With honest pride, and parental pleasure, doth he behold his pigs and his poultry. See how his peafowls, and his turkies, his ducks and his chickens throng about his footsteps as he approaches. Even those chickens, which, in the earliest stages of their growth, exhibit but downy and unfeathered extremities, they have a chirp of welcome and affection for the hand that scatters forth the pea and grist to them at night, and noon, and morning. Verily, Brother Bonhommie hath reason to be happy. He is a benefactor to the inferior. But his boast is larger still, when he casts his eye over his little territory and sees its increase. With what pride doth he behold his fields smiling in green and grain—his mammoth pumpkins, of a rich golden yellow, rolling about among his hillocks, like so many great turtles on the beach, turned over by the captors, and showing their yellow bellies to the sun. See him, as we did this morning on our arrival, thrusting his fingers into his potato beds, to assure himself of the dimensions of his yams! Hear him discourse of the cabbage and cauliflower, in his own domain, as of treasures which, some day, should emulate those of Dr. Bachman and Captain Paine; and while he points out his cornfield, his eye glistens with the secret hope which inspires him to persevere in the laudable ambition to rivel Michel, in making his hundred and five bushels of flint to the acre!

BONHOMMIE.—Oh! Father, such praise!

ABBOT.—Nay, blush not, my son. Thou hast done much in thy day and generation. Thy brethren will be careful of thy fame—it is a common property. Suppose, now, that our worthy planters, who have left their plantations on the plea of *malaria*, had gotten themselves little farmsteads on the Neck, or in St. Andrew's, to which they could have gone daily, and there perfected themselves in the knowledge of their vocation by daily and diligent toils and studies, trying all manner of easy experiments under the guidance of thought and science, how different would have been their fortunes, and how much more beautiful and prosperous the country! Look at the scene now between Line-street and the Four Mile House: what a garden has it become within the last ten years. Twenty years ago the greater part of it was a common, the farms mostly abandoned as worn out and exhausted. What blathering stupidity is in such a phrase. It is not possible for us to exhaust the earth's resources, even should we try. It is true, that a culture the most wretched, and a system the most wasteful and improvident, did all that could be done towards this unhappy consummation. But the thing was impossible. The earth cannot fail us. To the industrious man it was given for an eternal heritage. It has sustained a thousand generations which have gone before him—it will sustain thousands of generations which are to follow after him. The long tract of ages, countless and unfathomable, behind and before us, dazzles the imagination and defeats the judgment. We are bewildered with the vain attempt to enumerate the various races which have risen from and sunk into that almighty bosom; which have fed at its exhaustless granaries, and which will continue to find ample provision upon its surface to the very crack of doom. There is no such thing as exhausting the earth. You may impoverish it by barbarous cultivation, and profligate waste; but leave it to itself, fly from it, surrender it once more to its Creator, and lo! the event of a single season. The grass comes forth from the eternal principle of germination which is everywhere intact and indestructible. The trees re-appear, and cover and beautify its surface. The work of decay which goes on annually among their leaves, suffices to refresh and reinvigorate the soil upon which they perish; and the new forest which once more protects it from the sun, proves the munificence of God, which thus wondrously repairs the wastefulness of man. These few truths prove every thing. It is enough for us that they prove one thing: *that he will reap who sows, and reap only as he sows; that labor, governed by thought, will effectually keep the earth from exhaustion; and that cultivation, so far from impoverishing, if judiciously managed, must always improve the soil.*

Bonhommie.—I believe it: I *know* it, Father. See to the mountain of sedge which I have gathered for manure. The late gale brought me in, to the very edge of my enclosure, as much as I can haul and gather in the next six weeks. I feel sure that a man who makes manure of good quality, in abundance, may make a soil what he pleases, and raise every thing upon it.

Abbot.—No doubt of it, my son; and the process is comparatively an easy one. In fact, I regard agriculture as really the simplest and most obvious of all arts—as really teaching its own processes, inevitably—if the heart of the cultivator goes with his occupation, as it should in every business. There was surely nothing either very mysterious or very intricate, in the labors which were required by the Deity at the hands of man. In the sweat of his brow—such was the simple form of that decree which was to be the elementary law of his existence—he was to earn his bread. Whether easy of compliance, or not, no law could have been more obvious and simple ; and even now, perverted by evil counsellors, and misled, as we have been, by false lights and vitiating habits, it appears to me that a prompt return to its provisions will bring back the fertility to our fields, and prosperity to our homesteads. No books are needed for the tuition of those who obey this law. No recondite sciences need to be explored. That degree of observation and thought, which are the inevitable fruit of industry, will bring us more knowledge in a single season, than can be gleaned from all the heavy volumes ever yet written by grave and scholastic self-sufficiency. "Experience," says the Roman poet, whose moral maxims for the agriculturist should be got by heart by every planter,—

"Experience best forelearns
Where best to sow, where best to reap, discerns."

In the earth itself, the teacher and the treasure lie buried together. The ancients did not vainly fable, when they proclaimed Plutus to be the god of the subterranean regions. There, in truth, he sits, enthroned amid the equal splendors of his metalic, his mineral and his vegetable worlds. *We have only to dig for his possessions.*

Editor.—But, Father, you would not exclude book learning in agriculture?

Abbot.—I exclude no *learning* in *anything*, where learning would be useful. But first assure me that it *is* learning, and not the vain speculations of those who do all their planting in their writings, and never in their fields;—who undertake to teach others, without being successful themselves. I say to the planter, as I say to all the arts and professions—get knowledge wherever you can find it. But how much knowledge, of a truly valuable kind, can you get by the common course among us of asking questions. You concur with a man who complains of hard times and an unprofitable staple, and he straightway calls upon you to tell him what he shall do. How unmanly and unbecoming it is that people should be running hither and thither from their fields, asking counsel, in their own professions, from those who are no older than themselves. A man who has been brought up a planter, should know his own business surely. Let him put his questions honestly and manfully to the soil itself, and I guarantee that he will never want an answer long. It is not denied that a good farmer may occasionally receive information from his neighbor; but a good farmer is one who will seldom need to inquire; and the principle which we would inculcate, is the one equally broad and simple, that a devout and undivided attention to one's own interests, will be the best mode of learning how to conduct them. It is so, not in planting, simply; but in every thing—in all the trades, professions and occupations of life. Agriculture is one of many arts, all of which, so far as they relate to their professors, have the same governing laws. The planter must be prepared by a continual study of the plant itself; he must first learn the nature of the soil which it loves; the temperature which delights it; the degree of shadow or sunlight which it needs, or can endure; and adapt the soil to the plant, and both, as well as he may, to the fluctuations of the seasons. Virgil teaches this doctrine in more elevated language:

> "Ere virgin earth first feels th' invading share,
> The genius of the place demands thy care;
> The culture, clime, the winds and changeful skies,
> And what each region bears and what denies."

How little of this knowledge can one obtain from his neighbors. How much by a patient and dutiful attention to his own fields, and by a constant exercise of his thoughts upon the result of his observations. This course alone can teach him what it is necessary for him to know. No man ever yet became a good planter, or a good anything, from asking questions; for, indeed, such a person, like Pontius Pilate, though he asks for the truth, is seldom willing to wait for the answer. Our oracle must arise from the earth, like all other oracles; and let no man fear, if he knocks with a strong arm, and with proper courage, at the door of that ancient temple, that he will knock vainly, and without profit. The answer will be such, we warrant him, as will amply satisfy any reasonable mortal. Pass me those waffles, if you please.

BONHOMMIE.—Father, we have a bushel of fine oysters, which Truesdell, hearing of your arrival, has sent over with his compliments. Shall we have a few of them roasted?

ABBOT.—No, I pray you; so far as I am concerned, let them be kept for dinner. Our brethren must answer for themselves.

OMNES.—For dinner, surely.

ABBOT.—You have celery, Brother Bonhommie, in your garden?

BONHOMMIE.—An abundance, Father.

ABBOT.—Good! Celery seems the natural adjunct of the oyster. I fancy, if he could choose his vegetable, he would decide on that. By the way, speaking of oysters, Brother Bonhommie, is any use made of those great banks which rise out of the water between the extremity of Haddrell's and your Island? They seem as regularly ranged, as if laid down by art—the moles apparently of some ancient bridge, and on the side of Haddrell's there seems an artificial causeway, as if meant to facilitate a communication from shore to shore.

BONHOMMIE.—You are right, Father; that line of oaks which seems striding down from Haddrell's to the sea, indicates the line of causeway. The tradition is, that it was raised by Gen. Gadsden, who built a bridge across, during the time of the Revolution, in order to facilitate the escape of the garrison from Fort Moultrie, should it so happen that they were overpowered by the British. I have no doubt that the bridge did exist; for, on this side, we have a wharf to correspond with the causeway opposite; but my faith in the other part of the tradition is somewhat shaken. I have not the histories at hand, but I believe, that, in the fight of the 28th of June, the bridge provided for the escape of the garrison, was one entirely of boats.

Abbot.—So I think also. But the tradition may be reconciled with the history, if you will remember that the Fort sustained *two* actions. I have no doubt that the bridge was really built, as you describe it, to meet the exigencies of the second assault in 1780. But was it not General Pinckney, rather than General Gadsden, who built the bridge?

Bonhommie.—No, Sir; it was Gadsden: and there is still extant, a lively letter of Col. Barry, the British wit, in regard to, and ridiculing it. I have also in my possession the extract of a letter to Hon. George Bryan, of Pennsylvania, dated 14th March 1778, which confirms it. The writer says, "This harbour is well fortified, and *their bridge from Sullivan's Island is an amazing work—nöthing like it on the continent. It is called Gadsden' bridge, from General Gadsden, who had the direction of it.*"

Abbot.—That should be conclusive. It is greatly to be regretted, that we have not a bridge there now. It would increase the securities of the settlement, and afford the means for some delightful drives at Haddrell's, giving variety to the amusements of those who find time hang heavily on their hands at all watering places. Let us hope when the new Hotel is built, and the Island thronged with the wealthy and elite of our middle and mountain country, that the old connection between the two places will be re-established. The work would neither be unsafe nor expensive. The distance is not great, and the water is comparatively shallow, almost too shallow for steamboats.—But let us not forget the oysters. They belong, on those banks, to the raccoon tribe, a small long pointed oyster, growing in immense clusters, and sticking together with all their heads upwards, like a close knit family of ancient Hunkers.

Beauclerk.—I am told, Father, that the raccoon has an appetite for them, and goes out oytering for himself, and hence their name. It is said that he has the cunning to provide himself with a number of dry sticks, which he slyly slips into each open mouth, and the oyster perishes; the sun bursts its valves, and the raccoon feeds at his pleasure. They say also, that the oyster knows his enemy; and sometimes, while the raccoon is busy thrusting his stick into the jaws of one of the family, another pair will open, and take in his foot or tail. He will then be kept fast until the tide rises and drowns him, or the sharks snatch him away.

Abbot.—Invention has been bnsy for our benefit in these stories. What does Brother Bonhommie have to say?

Bonhommie.—I have heard these stories and many others. One of them occurs in connection with the question of the holy Father, touching the *uses* of the raccoon oyster. Until a comparatively recent period, they were as much eaten as any other in our harbor. Half that were sold in our market belonged to this family. They were gathered chiefly by old negro women, who fished for them in *dug-outs*. But since the Yankees took up the business, they have driven Sally, and Sukey, and Mimy, and Ba'sheba, pretty much out of sight. But a succession of mighty bad scares, contributed something towards directing the old ladies to a safer occupation. On one occasion, a devil-fish received the anchor, or grapnel, of one of the boats, within the capricious vortex of his antennæ, and made off with it. It was the first time that any of the African race had seen iron swim. But a more serious fright was in reserve for an old negro wench belonging to a widow lady of Charleston. It appears that she landed at low water on one of these oyster banks, and soon filled her dug-out. Finding the interval short and shallow between that and another bank, she fastened her boat, as she thought, securely, and waded across the intervening space. She loitered from one to the other; at length fell asleep upon one of them, and was only awakened by hearing the murmur of the waters, and feeling the surf break over her. The space between her and the point where she had left the dug-out, was widened to a chasm quite impassable to one who could not swim. The bank itself was covered; and soon the fastening of the boat became unloosed, and it was seen floating high up into the marsh. The poor wretch was in despair. The tide was still rising. The spot of bare rock which she occupied was soon reduced to a smple ring, which her person nearly covered; and in a little while, the waters were over her ancles. They continued to rise some six inches higher; and there she stood, momently expecting the billows to sweep and carry her off.—They did not, however; but a new horror, as she told it herself, shortly assailed her. Looking forth she discovered, steadily approaching, the dorsal fin of a shark. The voracious beast himself, was soon visible through the water. He had seen or scented his prey, and she watched him with all the agonies that predict a most terrible death, as he quietly encircled her narrow territory. She could see his gigantic form gleaming through the waters; and she imagined she beheld his fiery eye, gazing with all a serpent's power of fascination, directly into her own. She could neither scream nor speak, nor indeed would the effort have saved her. She could only follow his movement, wheeling as upon a pivot, as he circled the bank. The water was too shallow where she stood to suffer him to approach her in that manner which alone enables him to seize his prey. But, desperate with inflamed appetite, he dashed at her with a fearful plunge, which brought his head quite out of the water, and within a foot of her person.—Then she screamed, and, in receding from his jaws, had nearly fallen backwards into the deep. But she recovered herself; and, shivering with dread, continued to confront him. Again did he slowly move about her narrow eminence—twice, thrice—with his terrible eye watching hers.—Again, desperate as before, did he rush upwards almost to her person, his great head quite out of the water, and his long, double range of sharp white teeth, broadly opening to snatch her into his jaws. But he failed a second time, and drew off, without making a third attempt, as if he had suffered some hurts, probably from scraping upon the sharp oyster-beds, in those which he had made already, But he did not abandon the spot. Still, round and round the bank, did he perform his constant evolutions, until the poor negro was almost ready to resign herself to fate, and fling herself into his jaws in despair. But, at this juncture, some oyster hunters, like herself, discovered her predicament, and came to her relief. I have heard that she gave, in a single sentence, the whole terrible agony of that fearful trisl: "God a'massy, I bin dead tousand times dat day!"

Editor.—When did this happen?

Bonhommie.—Oh! it was long ago! I forget when I heard it.

Abbot.—Quite a scene, my son; and, I think, in all probability true. The shark has been known to rush clean out of the water, assailing a man in a boat. It is curious he prefers white to black meat. He will pass a negro in the water to get at a white man. This might be in consequence of his *seeing* the white skin more readily than the black. It is one of the admirable advantages of Sullivan's Island, that bathing here is so easily rendered safe. The power of the surf itself, secures you from his assaults; and the surf line gives you security against the retiring floods. On the back beach you have no surf;—but, higher up,—here, where you abide, my son—the marsh tracts interpose for your safety, and these creeks are at once noble and secure bathing places. Where do you propose to plant your oysters?

Bonhommie.—In the basin, Father, from which you see the carts now hauling. I shall make ample provision, in future, for the reception of the brotherhood. In another year, I hope to be the father of a thriving family, which, in comeliness of outline, plumpness of form, and sweetness of flavor, shall equal those of Truesdell. But come, Father, if you have finished. I will conduct you through the myrtles, where we find a shady horseback ride to the end of the island.

Abbot.—A moment, my son, while give thanks and invoke a blessing.

XI.

Bonhommie.—Our horses are ready, Father, for the canter.

Abbot.—Boots and saddles! I am ready also. Let us mount.

Bonhommie.—We commence our ascent here, at the foot of Prospect Hill. We have a pleasant ride from this point, all the way to the eastern end of the Island, through a grove of myrtles, which affords us shade, and through which, with a little grading and trimming up, we might have a pathway for a carriage The ascents are easy—the undulations, though frequent, are slight, and the breezes of the sea gratefully fan us throughout the progress.

Abbot.—These *are* hills. Your foreign tourist might smile at such a designation for them; but all things are relative; and, once familiar with the general dead level of the Island, but little above the sea, the eye acknowledges the dignity and importance of these sandy hammocks. What a curious spectacle do they present! Here, on one hand, the south and southeast lie spread out, a vast stretch of sand and sea. The plain of earth, I suppose, extends for nearly half a mile, before it touches the billows. Of this stretch, more than a hundred yards at low water, is the firm and sounding beach. Beyond that is the great blue ocean, spreading away into the infinite distance, beguiling the imagination into unknown realms and regions. In all the space of sandy tract, on this hand, there is not a shrub large enough to make a toothpick. But, on the left, north and northeast, the woods almost accumulate to a forest. The myrtle and oak, hidden from the sea by this line of hills, flourish in unsuspected size and numbers, and accordingly, in security. What a deep dell is immediately beneath our feet, in this region! How thick the growth, how grateful is the shade! Some of these great oaks were here long before the battle of Fort Moultrie; coeval, probably, with the first European knowledge of the Island. Here the Pirates may have frequently harbored—here they may have buried their treasure in secret. You are aware in what manner they usually guarded their buried treasure, and to what terrible superstitions they appealed to make it safe?

Bonhommie.—I cannot say that I am, Father.

ABBOT.—They led some wretched captive to the spot in the depths of midnight. They chose the place of safe-keeping by the gloomy light of glaring torches. The hole was dug, not only large enough for their treasure, but for the captive. The treasure was deposited; and the sudden shot or axe, or sabre stroke, slew the victim upon it. If they had no captive, some one of their own number—some incompetent, timid, or offensive member—was butchered in his place. The victim was sometimes an unsuspecting boy—a youth, eager to win their favor, and totally ignorant of the bloody treacheries which distinguished the infernal brotherhood. The question was put in vague language: "Who is willing to stay and watch the treasure?" When the poor simpleton replied by a profession of readiness to do so, the answer was immediately accompanied with the sudden stab or shot: "Stay then, till we call for it, and see that you watch it well!" He was tumbled into the receptacle, and his sleepless ghost became the keeper of the treasure. It was the presence of this watchful spectre, that, in all the attempts of which we read, to recover the buried treasure of the Pirates, opposed his supernatural authority to the labors of the seeker; and defeated his operations, seemingly, in the very moment when he was about to obtain his wishes. His oath bound him to yield to nobody but tee Pirate crew; not even to suffer a single one of their number, without the concurrence of the rest, to pluck it from his custody.

BONHOMMIE.—What a terrible superstition!

Abbot.—It was, indeed. And the whole coast of the Atlantic, from Passamaquody to Pensacola, is full of legends derived from such superstitions, and from the character of these deadly wretches. Kidd, Teach, or Blackbeard, Steed Bonnet, and a thousand others, have left their fearful memories impressed upon these shores in every form of crime, and every character of blood. But let us descend one of these gorges into into the burial place among the myrtles. I have heard of the place, but have never beheld it. Even here, it seems, death has found his victims—here, where salubrity speaks in the ever murmuring breezes, and in the incessant rolling of these surges on the shores.

Bonhommie.—The graves are not numerous, Father, and most of them are of very ancient date, probably even beyond the revolution.

Abbot.—The place is very still and solemn!—How well chosen! How peaceful is the hush which prevails above the scene! How much does that line of hills conceal from the passing world without. The billows break not here.—Their loudest murmurs subside here into faint, sad harmonies that suit the quiet purposes of death. Here are some noble oaks sheltering the repose of unknown inmates. The names, none of them appeal to my memory. How lightly, in such cases, do we pass over such memorials—as if man recognized no kindred, no sympathy, at least, with any of the race, his own family or his own associates excepted. Yet these sleepers had friends and kindred. They were nursed by dear affections.

They inspired hopes of the future—vague, beautiful, perhaps magnificent hopes—in the bosom of fond and generous parents. What if we could follow each of them, from the beginning to the close of his career ? It is, perhaps, a mercy that we may not. The shroud of death is a mantle also. We should be grateful for what it conceals, satisfied that the judgments of Heaven, tempered by the mercies of a common Father, can never be more severe than those of man. Doubtless, most of these sleepers were poor, struggling daily for the bitter bread of labor, too frequently prosecuted without any adequate reward. Their friends were likely to have been of the same class. Yet, a true affection has gleaned from its little means, to rear the headboard of stone or wood, to the object of its sympathy. Here and there, an unintelligible initial appears. To us, its says nothing; but there were some from whose eyes it compelled instant overflow. Others are obliterated quite; and here are the outlines of the grave upon the earth, without any other memorial. No doubt, the inmate slheps quite as soundly, as those for whom an ostentatious memory would raise the temple. What an absurdity, it seems, that we should fondly desire to enjoy the memories of those we leave behind us; since they so soon must follow also. How much more grateful, could we be sure of the fond sympathies of those who have gone before; could we be sure that our faults and offences have all been sweetly forgiven, by those whom we are sure to meet, and who are equally sure to know the full extent of our offences! Oh, brother, what a living monitor is the grave! How it speaks to pride; to vanity; to the oppressor and his victim; with what terrible threatening to the one; with what consoling promise to the other! And how much more impressive seems its voice, here, by the side of the great ocean, sounding forever in one's ears, as if an awful chaunt of eternity itself. It seems ever more to cry aloud—that dirge of winds and waters—"thus still shall our voices prevail at last over all others!" Brother, those billows will continue to speak to myriads of ages and generations, long after we, and those whom we love, are wrapt in a silence deep as that of these sleepers at our feet! Let us ride, my brother.

Bonhommie.—Pursuing this grove for a while, we shall reach the foot of another gorge, by which to ascend the hills. Here, Father, you perceive, we may enjoy all the seclusion of a forest, without its interminable depths. Here is shade, quiet, and the whispering silence of the woods. Here are spots which the sun's rays never penetrate. Here one may sit and meditate over favorite hopes and studies. Here love may bring his favorite to enjoy the transport and security, of which Campbell sings so sweetly in his Gertrude. And this region is here at our feet on the one hand, while on the other is the sandy desert and the great blue ocean sea.

Abbot.—Some of these gorges should be deepened, conducting, by an easy carriage ride, from the sandy tract of the southern side of the Island, to the woody ranges opposite. A brick or stone work, with a broad solid arch passing through these hills, would afford a picturesque and cavernous opening to the interior. Groves might be trimmed up among these woods, and a grotto might be established for supplying refreshments and rest to the rambler.

Bonhommie.—You now catch glimpses, Father, of the farmstead of Truesdell. From that point he is monarch of all he surveys. There lie his corn, potato, peas and oyster beds. A noble creek, which, elsewhere, would be called a river, passes before his door with a free and joyous rush. You see his oyster flood-gates yonder, distinguished by the brick abutments? Do you see a group of negroes emerging from the boat, their baskets full of fish? They never cast their nets in vain. They have only to throw out the line, and they draw in whiting, cavalli, yellow tail, trout, crocus, and blackfish, in never ceasing abundance.

Abbot.—What glorious and endless sport, all this, to our friends from the interior. Here, with fine boats, well covered from the sun, with ample bays, broad reserves, friths, great arms of the sea, and beautiful creeks, winding through broad green meadows, they might consume a summer in delights, conscious never of the flight of time. How gloriously comes up the breezes of the ocean. The tide is now pouring in; and, almost with the same glance, we behold the sea in all its wild and imperious life, in front, and the sweet repose which pervades the sheltered tracts of meadow, and wood, and water, in the rear.

Bonhommie.—Hold up, Father. We are now at the eastern extremity of the Island. We can go no further, except to descend upon the beach.

Abbot.—Let us stop here, to look about us!—here, amidst this little clump of myrtles. What a wild and beautiful prospect. What a tract of tumultuous billows grow up before the sight! How the breakers roll up, and roar upon the shore!—How they bound, and rush, and curl over each others back, scattering themselves abroad in foam. See, they come on, like a charging host, a thousand wild steeds of the sea, champing their bits, breaking through all restraints, and dashing headlong over the shoals, as if resolute to trample them down forever. Is it an islet that rises up between us and Long-Island? It seems so, from this point of view.

Bonhommie.—I frankly confess, I cannot answer your question. It certainly has the appearance. Yet I was always of the impression, that Long-Island was the next shore to the east.

Abbot.—It should be explored. If we had a boat now! Yet there would be no easy crossing that breach. How the seas boil there, as if in a whirlpool. At low water it would not be so hazardous, and I should love to explore all these places—to paddle from islet to islet—to climb the sandy heights and ascertain their hollows; and to drowse away the hours with the sound of those tumbling billows always in mine ears. One might realise the charms of Robinson Crusoe, in perfection, along these solitudes. These islands and islets, which skirt our Southern shores, all along the Atlantic, from North-Carolina to the Bay of Pascagoula, are among the most curious and lovely features of our country. To sail among them of a rich moonlight evening, affords you continual prospects of fairy lands. They rise out of the ocean like little gems; and, with a smooth sea, the charm is rare and inexpressible—the harmony of relation between the object —the peace and beauty of the scene—the billows slightly curling upon the white sands, as if in homage, rather than hostility! The inland navigation which is thus afforded, is a singular advantage, particularly in seasons of war, to the interests of commerce.

Bonhommie.—And when art and industry have converted these grey sands into green and golden gardens, such as Edisto Island, for example, how much lovelier becomes the scene.

Abbot.—Our children, brother, will see a progress in this respect which has not blessed our eyes. The green spots of cultivation will be made pleasingly to alternate with these barren, but lovely wastes. Do you know any thing of the occupation and uses of Long Island?

Bonhommie.—Nothing, Father.

Abbot.—How pleasant would its exploration be by occasional trips from Sullivan's in midsummer. One might fish along the coasts, and spread the sail for different points with each returning day. You are aware that Clinton occupied Long-Island with his troops, when Sir Peter Parker attacked the Fort with his fleet. The attack was designed to be a combined one by land and water.

That frith was to be crossed by Clinton with the land forces; but we can see that the passage was no easy one, particularly at a flood tide, which was probably the period chosen for the fleet to arrange itself before Fort Moultrie. It would have been difficult for boats to have made their way through that gulph of waters, and still more difficult to have effected a landing under the fire of the Riflemen by whom this part of the Island was defended. Here Col. Thompson, of St. Matthew's, was posted with seven hundred men. He was provided with an eighteen-pounder and a field piece, which probably occupied the headland upon which we stand. His force consisted of the third South-Carolina Regiment, all superb sharp-shooters. Clinton must certainly have attempted the passage, but the effort was not a serious one. If it had been made his boats must have been swamped. His men could not have waded it without being swept away. We are told, they got entangled among the shoals. That entangleness saved them. Had they forced their way through the surges, under the mouths of the cannon, their landing must have been effected under such a terrible fire from our people, as would have doubled to the British the disasters of that sanguinary day.—The question is, had Thompson any battery, any bulwarks at all, except those afforded by nature? Another question—can this Island be held to be properly defended, unless there be a fortress at this point? Steam affords facilities now for conquest which were then unknown. It would require, no doubt, but a small fortress and a moderate garrison; since the wild force of the sea in this quarter, certainly at high water, would always contribute greatly to the strength of the place. It is probable that the Island here was once connected with Long-Island. The waves have cut for themselves an avenue. With what fury do they plunge through the gorge. Whether Sullivan's Island was not once connected with the main—whether the tract of creek, bayou and ledge, lying between Haddrell's and this strip was not once solid ground, is a question. It appears to me that such must have been the case. May we not suppose that the range of heights upon which we stand, once indicated the general elevation of the Island, reduced by the constant assaults of the sea, front and rear, until, as we know, the ocean at length, in some fearful tempest, the waters of the Gulph pouring in upon us, made a clean sweep over the whole western half of the Island. I cannot persuade myself that these heights are structures reared by the sands and soil of descending rivers, or the heaped up tributes of the sea. And how reasonable to suppose that the clearing the Island partly of its timber, as Drayton tells us was the case, has been one of the causes of its depression and the subsequent encroachment of the seas. I have discovered the roots of large trees, laid perfectly bare, and lying upon the surface, along the outer margin of the southern beach.

Bonhomme.—The conjecture is certainly not an unreasonable one. It should be our policy to restore the foliage to the Island, with an equal eye to comfort and protection.

ABBOT.—Trees, the seeds of which are wind-sown, should be introduced for this purpose.—Such trees are generally of hardy and quick growth, requiring little soil, and spreading themselves about with amazing fecundity. They seem designed for these very situations. The Ailanthus or Tree of Heaven, is one, in particular, which might be recommended for introduction upon the Island.

BONHOMMIE.—I shall introduce it myself, Father.

ABBOT.—To the people of the interior, Sullivan's Island ought to be a spot of qute as much attraction and interest, as to the people of Charleston.—Hither may they come in midsumer, and remain till frost, in perfect security, and realizing that luxury—that of salting themselves, which is a regular habit with a large portion of the Northern people. They may come and refresh themselves upon shrimps, fish and oysters, bathe in Neptune's own bath, and enjoy a thousand sports at once novel and attractive. They could visit the city daily, and attend to business; and should the city be unhealthy, could retire, in half an hour, to a scene of equal salubrity and sweetness, nor would they be without frequent spectacles of rare interest and grandeur. The broad ocean spread out before them with all his billows, ever more rolling, and ever more pouring forth a wild chaunt, whose harmonies appeal more deeply than to the ear of man—which sink deeply into the soul, and stir up the sublimer thoughts and more spiritual fancies, —is, alone, a spectacle which forever feeds the mind with pleasure. Here may the idler behold the porpoise, in vast schools, rolling and plunging with an obvious joy and luxury; and sometimes he may chance to see the mighty liviathan of our seas, the Devil Fish, famous in Beaufort annals, flinging out his gigantic but slender flippers, above the billows, as if he would embrace the passing ships. At our feet lies a proof of powers in the great ocean, the display of which, to the man accustomed only to the forest and the mountain, would be such a spectacle as his thought would brood upon for long seasons after. Here, safe, himself, might he behold the storm-spirit rioting in his native element, and the great ship, cowering and stifled in his wild embrace, lifted up, as an infant in the grasp of a giant, and flung scornfully upon the shores, as if to mock the builder and the owner, with the folly and the feebleness of his creation. It is a sloop which lies below us, half buried in the sand?

Bonhommie.—A sloop, I reckon.

Abbot.—Mast and spar were torn out of her in the fearful struggle, when she rushed headlong on the shores! What did mast, and spar, and bolt, and cable, avail against such an enemy? She had some fair feminine name, perhaps—a tribute of admiration to birth or beauty. She was called the "Polly Whitesides," perhaps—the "Fanny Folsom," or "Lucy Laidler." But no invocation to the fair spirit, who presided at her christening could relieve her then. The skipper Hopkins—

Bonhomme.—I think, Father, it was not Hopkins.

Abbot.—Jenkins, then, or Thompson, it matters not. He felt the gale coming on, and he knew the qualities of his clinker built clipper. He had his little son with him, Tom, I think, but we may call him Dick, or Peter, and the tender years of the boy made him thoughtful of the mother. She scarcely knew the child was out. The skipper knew she looked for them at home that night to supper, and that she felt anxious enough at the approach of the gale. Thompson had no reason to doubt the anxieties of his wife, and he was man enough to respect them. "Tom," says he, "there's old Harry getting up, there in the southeast. Up hellum, my lad, and push for home." Tom looked out, having never seen old Harry before. But the power of which they spoke in phrase so familiar, seemed not disposed to give them any chance; and the doubt arose, which to peril, old Thompson and his son Tom, or the fair beauties of the "Polly Whitesides." It was a long struggle. But necessity and the storm prevailed. It was God's blessing, Thompson's working, and perhaps Tom's peculiar destiny, that enabled the father and son, to beach her here, and make their escape to the myrtles. They laid the aching ribs of "Polly Whitesides," high and dry, upon the beach, and here she lies. But how little like the beautiful thing she was. She reminds us, Brother Bonhomme, of the cruel wreck of other beauties. But you weep.—The remembrance is a painful one, I see. Let us depart.

XII.

Bonhommie.—We are safe at home, again, Father; and see, the Brotherhood are descending from the piazza, to give us welcome.

Abbot.—Something has happened. They wear faces of unwonted pleasure. They have been made happy by some peculiar event. Let us see; we have been long enough absent for a variety of events. I can conjecture the occasion. Well! my children, you seem in great spirits?

Editor.—We have been honored, Father, in your absence, and chiefly on your account. The honorable Council of the Island, have been to wait upon you and us. They came in state, as is their custom, when waiting upon distinguished strangers; in a splendid barge. They have bestowed upon us the freedom of the island, and compelled us to accompany them on a fishing expedition, in which we have had a great time and caught multitudes of fish; more than seven hundred among the party, trout and whiting, sheephead and cavalli, in the space of three hours. We have enjoyed a glorious swim in the public Gondola, a glorious repast among the Island Fathers, and as much wit and humor as might suffice an ordinary brain during the summer solstice.

Abbot. My children you have been blessed and honored. I do not regret that I was not with you, for I have been sufficiently refreshed and gratified in my canter through the myrtles. But I can fancy your satisfaction; such distinctions do not wait upon ordinary men. I have heard of the wit and humor of the Council. I am told that these, along with wisdom, are among the requisites of office on the Island.

Beauclerk.—Beauty also, Father. It is understood that no man becomes a candidate whose pretensions to personal beauty are not considerable. The ladies vote here, and they insist upon this quality. They assume that gentlemen of great personal attractions, are never willing to hide their light under the bushel; and take for granted that an administration of handsome men, will give them numerous balls throughout the season. They are seldom disappointed.

Abbot.—Pshaw! Get thee behind me, Sathanas! Am I fit subject for thy quizzing, and at this time of day?

Beauclerk.—Nay, Father, believe as much of it as you please. It might as well be true as not. It is certain that the Council of the Island has always been remarkable for the beauty of face and person among them; for their wit and wisdom; and for the number of balls which they give during the season. They reason justly, after the manner of the Government of France, and take public amusements under the patronage of Government.

Editor.—We have certainly had a most delightful time of it. As a stranger, Father, you would have found yourself in the full enjoyment of the degree of love and attention which you deserve.

Abbot.—As a stranger, perhaps. But say no

more of it, my son. Of course, the funds of the Island justify these liberal expenditures.

Beauclerk.—The receipts are not more than half a million, chiefly derived from imposts on the oyster and shrimp business. The licenses to fish in these waters are in great demand; and since the Yankees have taken to manufacture sardines out of silver fish, a new and prolific source of income has arisen from this commodity. Shrimps, too, are now put up for export to California and Patagonia, in oil, after the manner of the sardines; and there is a trembling anxiety to increase the revenue, from the anticipated uses, in the same way, of the forests of young crabs and fiddlers, which literally swarm in these diggins. It is calculated, that, from fiddlers alone, should they be found to answer expectation, the revenues will be increased to a million. The Council have it in contemplation to memorialise Congress in behalf the utter abolition of the duty on foreign oils, and, failing in this, to offer bounties to those who shall first make a profitable business of expressing the oil from the *bene* plant, the sunflower, and the cotton seed. The intelligence, the vigor, the liberality, with which the Government of the Island pursues its course of public policy, shows that wisdom is very far from being inconsistent with personal beauty, and the freest exercise of wit; as some grey beards were pleased, in former times, to imagine.

Abbot.—Beware, son, lest thine own humors do not find thee a place in the new Calaboose, (which is to be a Penitentiary also,) which, it is said, is to be established on the Island. Here, perchance, you may find employment in preparing sardines, shrimps, and fidlers for the markets of California.

EDITOR.—The Council did us the honor, Father, to invite us to a public dinner, which they propose to give in compliment to us to-morrow. Here is a written invitation, under the broad seal of the Island, to yourself. We excused ourselves from any immediate answer, inasmuch as we knew not what might be your purpose in respect to the future proceedings of the fraternity.

ABBOT.—Your caution was a proper one, my son. It will not be in our power to accept. We must decline, though we shall do so with proper respect and regret. Our time expires to-morrow. We must return to the city in the first morning boat.

BONHOMMIE.—Alas! Father, how shall I survive your departure?

ABBOT.—By the consoling hope that you will live till our return, my son—that you will then be properly prepared to welcome us, by reason of the wonderful improvements which you shall have made upon your farm—in the introduction of new vegetables and fruits, and in your improvements upon the old. Your oyster reserves will then be crowded with sleek citizens, eager to open their bosoms to your friends; and your juvenile poultry will then have assumed that degree of maturity which will enable them to assist in entertaining us. We shall have more satisfaction, Brother Bonhommie, when partaking of the luxuries and comforts of your household, in knowing that they are all the products of your own ground and genius.

BONHOMME.—You overwhelm me, Father.— You are too good. I have a motive to live for, if it be only to deserve your praises. Shall we sit in the piazza, Father?

ABBOT.—It is a sweet air, and the prospect of the sea never stales upon my sight. It is a moral prospect. It appeals to all a man's energies. It is a spectacle to stimulate courage, enterprize, progress; to brace the thought, as well as the bosom; to chasten and purify, as well as freshen and excite. There is an analogy of a very striking sort, between mountain life, and life beside the sea. In both cases, the objects of contemplation lead to elevation of thought and purpose. The natural aspects presented to the eye, are those which at once lift and depress the soul. We are raised in the contemplation of vastness; a world of distance; sublime and towering forms; vast heights that seem to stretch away to the cloud and sun; vast tracts which seem to bury cloud and sun within their bosom! The same prospects depress and humble, because they awe. They tell us at every breath, of our inferiority and insignificance. They rebuke the pertness of self-conceit, and compel the respect of vanity. And these lessons lead to reverence; to acknowledgments, which, as they teach us of a Superior, moderate our own assumptions, and force us to a recognition of the Divine Master of worlds, suns and systems. The social advantages of veneration are also incomputable. Perhaps it may be safely asserted that no man, without this quality, can ever have a proper respect for genius, art, virtue, or any great human endowment; any, and can never have any just respect for humanity itself!

Editor.—You were remarking, some nights ago, Father, upon the growing deficiency of this virtue among us, when you were interrupted by that grinning and chattering mime, Chiffinch.

Abbot.—The beast! I think if I were a potentate, I should make an express edict against your professional jokers—poor inflated devils, who fancy that it is a sort of duty with them to be funny. Now, nobody likes a good jest better than myself; but the first requisite of a good jest is, that it should be in season. It should be accommodated to the moods of the hearer, and not conflict with the necessities of the occasion. The jest, no less than the sermon, requires propriety for its *accoucheur*. Now, this is what that foolish fellow, Chiffinch, cannot understand. He thrust himself in among a knot of us the other day, when the occasion was one of deep gravity to all, and of great sorrow to one of the company;—a serious and ruinous involvement of his affairs, which might beggar a large and lovely family. We were discussing this necessity, when Chiffinch approached. Had he possessed the slightest capacity *to look out from himself*, he would have seen, from our faces, that we had a cause of anxiety among us which left us incapable of fun. But, espying us at a distance, he began instantly to prepare his joke,—such as it was;—and with him to conceive, implies as, a matter of course, the necessity for being delivered. He was inflated with a straw, and would have burst with it, could he have found no hearers. So he kept us for half an hour, while he drew out his slender circumstances of humour. On another occasion, he stopped a gentleman, who had just buried an only daughter, with a story of a goat and a pumpkin, and I have heard that a sack of sour meal, kept his wit sweet through the dog-days. He is a man to die of croup, in a state of second infancy.

Editor.—And yet, Father, Chiffinch is, at times, exceedingly funny.

Abbot.—So is Mumbo Jumbo, the African monkey, when he has his red breeches on, a feather in his hat, and has not yet danced that day. But Mumbo Jumbo, *always*, is a poor devil. Chiffinch needs only to know his time to be a very clever companion. If he would believe more in Solomon, and less in himself, we might almost fancy him a Solomon. Certainly, Shakspeare's counsel, properly valued, might enable wit frequently to pass for wisdom.

> "A jest's prosperity lies in the ear
> Of him that hears it; never in the tongue
> Of him that makes it."

But this brings us back to the subject of veneration. Veneration is necessary to wit, if the claims of the latter are to be respected. Wit, in proper hands, is the sharp and always polished rapier of wisdom. Its purpose is never wantonness. It is never drawn unadvisedly, and never works injustice. It does no wrong to a gentle and innocent nature. It assails no becoming sentiment or affection. It is legitimate only in such hands as need every sort of instrument to punish brutality, presumption and offence. In other hands, it is the sharp razor which the monkey shaves with; a weapon that most commonly cuts the shaver's throat. Veneration and wit should always harmonize; and must, for their mutual safety. The legitimacy of wit depends upon its willingness to be the subordinate. Some things are every where sacred. An earnest purpose, an honest though erring faith, and above all a manly enthusiasm! Enthusiasm, perhaps, is one of the most sovereign of the virtues. It is essential to the perfection of all the rest. It stimulates the others to performance; it sustains them during the trial and the struggle; and it soothes and cheers them in defeat. Without this virtue, socity languishes everywhere; the energies lie prostrate; the more generous tendencies of the race suffer neglect and scorn; the community lacks courage; trade and commerce wither; industry is at an end; the arts abandon the soil in loathing, or bury themselves from sight in dread and silence; while cold-blooded and soulless self-conceit sniggers and sneers at every appeal to patriotism, and every sentiment which seeks to encourage the resurrection of the nobler virtues. We have been laboring under this very curse in Charleston for twenty years. Enthusiasm has been crushed out of us by frivolity. Life was a mere drowse in the lap of vanity. Men had no high purposes, or they were frowned upon; society degenerated into a miserable pageant, in which the only struggle was, which could show himself most conspicuously in the front ranks, and with the greatest amount of tinsel. If a man rose up and spoke of a new hope, with zeal and earnestness, he was set upon as a common enemy, whose very nature was at hostility with that stagnation of social energy, which was foolishly mistaken for calm and peace. "They made a solitude and called it peace!" They had no faith in any enterprise which rebuked their incapacity; which seemed to insinuate a doubt that all was not perfect in their condition. And this condition, how joyless, how soulless, how unperforming! Society was not without its refinements, but these were of a sort that rendered it feeble and effeminate. Our polish was gained at the expense of our energies and there was no heart in it. When I was a boy, the custom was, with the close of the day's employment, to seek some friendly fireside. Here, the young of both sexes met each other. The sweetness and grace of the damsel, subdued and refined the rough vigor of the youth; the manly energy and performing thought of the youth, stimulated the mental activity, and compelled the studies of the damsel. They acted upon each other, and the result of this attrition was a calm, strong, dignified intellect on the part of both; accommodated, in each, to the proper characteristics of the sex. It is all altered now. We have become fashionable and foolish. We have the smoking and the swearing boy, the flashy and the giggling girl. You no longer drop in, at evening, at the friendly fireside. You call in the afternoon, when you know that all are out, and leave your card; and, during the season, the cards thus left, bring you an invitation to a grand ball, and you dance and sup, and there an end. And this is society! We have exchanged a thing of simplicity and heart, for a thing of affectation, which is utterly without feeling. In the language of Wordsworth—

> "Altar, sword and pen,
> Fireside, the heroic wealth of hall and bower,
> Have forfeited their ancient English dower,
> Of inward happiness. We are selfish men."

And again:

> "I am opprest,
> To think that now our life is only drest
> For show: mean handiwork of craftsman, cook,
> Or groom! We must run glittering, like a brook
> In the open sunshine, or we are unblest;
> The wealthiest man among us is the best:
> No grandeur now, in nature, or in book,
> Delights us. Rapine, avarice, expense—
> This is idolatry—and these we adore.
> Plain living and high thinking are no more;
> The homely beauty of the good old cause,
> Is gone: our peace our fearful innocence,
> And pure religion, breathing household laws."

These are the evils that have got too much sway among us, and we must amend them.

Editor.—We are beginning to amend them, Father.

Abbot.—Not too soon, or too actively. We are doing something, I believe. But much is yet to be done. We must bring back to society its very noblest element—the one which perfects all the rest—without which all the rest is insecure—I mean veneration. There were, perhaps, but three States of the old thirteen—and these have been the chief maternal States of the Union, that ever impressed their characteristics deeply upon the character of the nation. These were Virginia, Massachusetts and Carolina. Their power lay in one great virtue, veneration. They had each of them a living and a working faith. They were earnest in their purposes. They were not to be deluded by vanities. They had pride, such as the Englishman possesses—and this led them to achievement. Their pride and faith, joined with earnestness and enthusiasm, made that great virtue which constitutes the social religion. Home was in their faith, and this conviction led them to do justice to all the constituents of the sectional character. They might be emulous of one another, but they always *believed* in one another. Envy did not blind them to the merits of a brother; nor vanity delude them in respect to their own. And thus they wrought honestly, to a common end, and made their country famous. Who among us is likely now to make our country famous? Honest zeal is rebuked by a sneer the moment it rises. Generous enthusiasm feels ever the curb of sceptical and denying society. Your wits, who claim to be your wise men also, are those who put their fingers to their noses, and cry "ha! ha!" whenever they behold an unselfish virtue that says: "Brethren, let us work, together for the common cause." They say to themselves, first: "What office are we to have?" Would you speak of serious topics, such as belong to the common necessity, lo you;—Senator Smirk appears, or Counsellor Quiz. They have been laboring all the morning at a joke; they have toiled all day and manufactured a pun, and they thrust themselves upon you with all your enthusiasm working in your soul—deep in your project for a common good, or to meet a threatening emergency; and, with a snigger—for a drowsy self-esteem seldom laughs quite out—they lay the little, wriggling, wormy thing before you, in the hope to make you snigger also. And this when your City is struggling to sustain position; when your great men are perishing from among you, when open and secret enemies are busy to destroy your liberties and securities! Verily, are not these, on a small scale, the Neroes that fiddled when Rome was burning?

Editor.—Father, this is very terrible!

Abbot.—Son, is it not very true! If it be a truth, however terrible, it is the only hope for us that there be some who will speak, and others who will see the truth. Were the disease incurable, incurable, my son, it would be only folly so to speak, or so to see. But, thank God, I see in my eye daily, troops of goodly and generous youth rising into the ranks of performance; full of soul and energy; loving their country, and anxious to achieve something in its behalf. We shall soon need all their strengh and enthusiasm; and now is the time, if ever, to cast down the false idols of society, and to show the true Gods.

Now is the time to set up in high places, as models, *Labor* and *Thought*, as the only true sources of manhood and character; to teach simplicity of manners, earnestness of purpose, and that hearty courage which grapples with difficulty as with a mistress; with a love for the wrestle, and proportioned to the vigor of each youthful Sampson. My Sons, my appeal is to Young Carolina! To the veneration and the will, linked with enthusiasm, which made old Carolina famous!

OMNES.—They will answer to the call. Three cheers for young Carolina!

ABBOT.—What a grateful augury, my children! Behold, even as you shout, that noble ship heaving in sight, and, with every sail set, pressing forward to her port. Let her be your emblem. See how she flings and scatters from her bows, the assailing billows. She how she cuts her way through the yawning deep. She compels the service of the winds. She loses no time in her progress. She puts on all her energies, and is winged for the attainment of her goal. Only fancy some of our mountain friends, here, at this moment;—men who have never beheld the ocean, nor seen those great swans of commerce, speeding over the waves with the grace and dignity of Queens. They would feel, as should we, beholding a mountain for the first time, and upon it the great world Behemoth, about to realize the Indian tradition, and leap from pinnacle to pinnacle, onward and downward, until, at last, he buries his mighty and smoking flanks in the waters of the sea.—But where is our Poet?

Poet.—Here, Father.

Abbot.—You improvised the other day, my son, on seeing just such a goodly vessel. I am not sure that the moral of your verse was not somewhat tinged with an unwise cynicism. I did not feel the justice of your sarcasms on Love and Friendship, for I believe in both. It is a faith that wrong and folly shall never beat out of me. Man is a better animal than we think him, and few are utterly without some redeeming virtues. You Poets are apt to mistake weaknesses for vices, and to be terrible when you should be tolerant. Nevertheless, let us have your verses. Let our brothers hear them. The picture of the ship, if I recollect rightly, exactly suits that which stretches away before our eyes.

Poet.—*(Recites.)*

How proudly o'er these swelling seas,
  Yon gallant vessel holds her way,
Borne on the bosom of the breeze,
  With maiden-grace and Queenly sway;
The sunlight basks upon her sails,
  The billows bear her gladly on,
And meekly fond, the obedient gales,
  Attend her till her port is won.

Thus, in the hour of man's success,
  The cringing slave becomes the tool,
And Pride will stoop, though not to bless,
  And cringes where he still would rule;
Yet let the sun but cease to glow,
  And falser still than wind or wave,
The servile friend becomes the foe,
  And Pride the tyrant, late the slave!

The sycophant who bow'd of yore,
And lick'd the foot, nor felt the shame,
Polutes the shrine he sought before,
And speaks, instead of praise, in blame.
Nor is it Friendship that, alone.
Thus false to every faith can prove;
The guilt assails a nobler one,
And men have said the same of Love!

ABBOT.—Some truth, no doubt; but the conclusions are false, if they go to justify our want of confidence in the race; of worldly goods we may save something by our scepticism; but not to confide is to lose ourselves. Faith is the great secret for society. Believe in the family if you would prosper. You may be defrauded freqently; but it is a greater misfortune, by your own doubts, to defraud yourself of human sympathy.

BONHOMMIE.—Pardon me, Father, but "roast beef waits for no man."

ABBOT.—It seldom has need, my Son. Let us begin with Truesdell's oysters by way of appetizer.

XIII.

ABBOT.—Brother Bonhommie, the lofty but, deserted dwelling house in front, reminds me of a duty. Fill your glasses, my children:—We will drink—"the Pinckney's—the noble and courteous gentlemen,—the fearless and honored statesmen, —the pure, polished and incorruptible citizens."

Omnes.—Standing!

Bonhommie.—There is another dwelling in sight, Holy Father, which counsels me to a similar duty :—that of Bond I'on. Father, with your permission, we will drink,—"the fine old gentleman of a better day and school: the good and benevolent man; one who has served his country faithfully, and who still serves society gratefully."

Abbot.—We drink with pleasure, my children pleased to perceive that we still possess the power of discriminating and appreciating those virtues which are not sufficiently esteemed as models.—And now, my son, let us rise. That is the true temperance which knows how to employ God's blessings without profligacy or wantonness. Let us adjourn to the piazza. It is the Wilmington steamer that goes out, I think, and there is another that comes in—see, our ship has nearly reached the city; a brig and a schooner are also in motion, and so are our Island steamers. These are the human adjuncts and agents, that animate the scene. What a picture of life is in that sea, that sunshine, those sweeping swanlike creatures, the gay and glittering hamlet of the Island, and the illuminated spires of the distant city. But the sea itself suffices me.

Editor.—It would be a noble study to most persons but for its annoyances.

Abbot.—These are greatly exaggerated; and are felt chiefly during the first three days of a voyage. Our coasting navigation, which seldom now keeps you out three days, does not suffice for experiment. In that period you can have only the *desagremens* of the sea, without its excitements.—It requires a longer time to recover the tone equally of the body and the mind, and to acquire that sort of "sea change," of which we are told in the "Tempest," which alone can possibly make you at home as a voyager. Then your thoughts and stomach come back to you together. Then you see the wonders of the great deep and rejoice with the rejoicing elements.

EDITOR.—I am afraid, Father, that the sea soon loses its freshness to all but the poetical temperament. I have frequently remarked, with surprise, how little there is visible, in the progress over the great deep, to those who go down frequently in the ships upon the waters.

ABBOT.—It was ever thus, my son, with this class of people, even when they made their very first voyage. They never did conceive the wonders and beauties of the sea. It requires the creative and endowing faculty—the imagination for this. But the ordinary traveller does not possess much of this faculty. He fancies neither marvels nor mysteries, and solves none, unless they be those of trade. His philosophies seldom go deeper than his appetite, and if he loves the sea at all, it is because of the potent influence which it possesses in sharpening the desires of the abdomen. It is quite a study to watch this class of persons on board ship. You will find them always, either peering into the larder, or dreaming about it. The Steward, (whom they always call *stewart*—the vulgarians!) and cook, aboard-ship, are the persons whose acquaintance they are first to make.

These they contrive to bribe with shillings and civilities. You will scarcely open your eyes, in the morning, ere you will see these "hail fellows," with toast and tankard in their clutches. A bowl of coffee and a cracker is the initial appetizer, with probably a toss of brandy in the puple beverage, as a lacer. Then you see them hanging about the breakfast table, where they take care to plant themselves in the near neighborhood of certain of the choicest dishes. All their little arrangements are made before you can get to the table, and there will be a clever accumulation of good things about their plates, in the shape of roll and egg, etc., which would seem destined to remind the proprietor, in the language of warning, which was spoken daily (though with a far different object) to the monarch of the Medes and Persians—"Remember, thou art mortal." This is a fact which our veterans of the high seas never forget. They carry within them a sufficient monitor which ever cries in their ears, like the daughter of the horse-leech, "Give, Give!" They have no qualms of conscience or of bowels; and it seems to do them rare good to behold the qualms of others. It would appear that they rejoiced in these exhibitions, simply as embodying the assurance that the larder was destined to no premature invasion, on the part of the sufferers. I have often looked upon this class of travellers—not with envy—Heaven forefend!—though it would have rejoiced me frequently, at sea, to have possessed some of their immunities—that rare insensibility, for example, in the regions of diaphragm and abdomen, which, if unexercised for appetite, might at least suffer other sensibilities to be free for exercise. But it has provoked my wonder, if not my admiration, at that inflexible stolidity of nature, which enabled the mere mortal so entirely to obtain the ascendancy over the spiritual man. He sees no ocean waste around him—follows no tumbling billows with his eye—watches not with straining eagerness, where the clouds and the waters, descend and rise, as it were in an embrace of passion.—Sunrise only tells him of his coffee and cracker—noon of lunch,—sunset of his tea,—and the rarely sublimed fires of the moonlight, gleaming from a thousand waves, suggest only a period of repose, in which digestion goes on without any consciousness of that great engine which he has all day been packing with fuel. Tell him of porpoise and shark, and his prayer is that they may be taken. He has no scruples to try a steak from the ribs of the shark, though it may have swallowed his own grandmother. Of the porpoise he has heard, as the sea-hog, and the idea of a roast of it, is quite sufficient to justify the pains-taking with which he urges upon the foremast man to take his place at the prow, in waiting, with his harpoon. Nay, let a school of dolphins be seen beneath the bows, darting along with graceful and playful sweep, in gold and purple,—glancing through the billows, like so many rainbows of the deep,—he thinks of them only as a *fry*—an apology for whiting and cavalli, for which he sighs with the tenderest recollections. Such is very apt to be the character of your veteran voyager; and, with him, let me assure you, the novelties of the sea never had a charm. In losing its sense of freshness, he never lost a single fancy.

EDITOR.--Steam has robbed the sea pretty equally of its terrors and its charms—I mean to the great mass of persons, Father. To a certain class of persons—"a thing of beauty is a joy forever."—You now scarcely make the acquaintance of the deep before you leave it; you are not sufficiently long upon the waves to feel the caprices of the winds; you are hardly ever out of sight of land. Even when crossing the "great pond," you travel in such mighty vessels, and carry with you such a various community, that you scarcely feel conscious of any change, restraint, or inconvenience.—You have society in abundance, books, sports, balls, and dinner parties, to say nothing of *tableaux vivants*, and ocean theatricals. In our short voyages along the coast, from town to town, upon the sea—as in the route from Charleston to Wilmington—you are out but a single night, and have seen nothing. You fling yourself into your birth in the one city, to awaken in the other. Few persons care to look abroad in this interval. Few care to traverse the ship's deck in the face of smoke and steam, to catch glimpses of mysterious forms, wrapped up, but not concealed, in the billows rolling by—that recall to you as they pass, strange but sweet reminiscences of friends left, or friends lost; friends whom you are about to visit, and friends whom you are never more to see. You see now-a-days nothing of the wonders of the deep. You hearken to none of its voices. The spell has been taken from its fountains—the trident is broken in the grasp of its Triton. The old fables have been driven away by that inveterate smoker which the world has agreed to call by the name of Steam! Mighty word, before which—

> "The sea—
> Its deep green mansions, and it sparry caves,
> Its shells, its naiads, and its warring waves;
> Its stirring dangers, its great terrible things,
> Monstrous and savage, that, from secret springs
> Course in pursuit of prey——"

are puffed away, as by a breath—disarmed of all but its tributary and subservient attributes, and rendered as patient as the wild horse under the lasso—subdued, from a condition more wild than his, to the will and domination of man.

Beauclerk.—How happy was that prediction of Darwin with regard to the future uses of steam.

Abbot.—Repeat, my son. The poets are the only prophets.

Beauclerk.—

> "Soon shall thy arm, unconquered steam, afar
> Drag the slow barge, or drive the rapid car;
> Or on wide waving wings expanded bear
> The flying chariot through the fields of air.
> Fair crews triumphant, leaning from above,
> Shall wave their fluttering 'kerchiefs as they move;
> Or warrior bands alarm the gaping crowd,
> And armies shrink beneath the shadow cloud."

Abbot.—Darwin wrote—I speak from memory—about 1790. The railroad and steamboat have realised his predictions in regard to them. It remains that the balloon shall come into general use for the purposes of war and travel. I see, recently, that it was gravely proposed to employ balloons in the bombardment of Venice. Certainly, the idea must be a terrible one to a city: that of having paixhan shot tumbled in upon them from the clouds! By the way, are you aware, my children, that the Spaniards have put in a claim, on behalf of one of their mariners, as the first inventor of steamboats? It precedes all others—Fitch, Fulton—Scotchman, Englishman, American. It depends upon the authenticity of the documents which have been brought to establish the claim. The allegations and dates would seem to be conclusive.

EDITOR.—You have been a great reader, Father.

ABBOT.—And not always a profitable one. My memory begins to fail me, from the simple fact that it never received good training. I was desultory as a reader. But that was not an error or a misfortune. It is a vulgar mistake to object to desultory reading. The more desultory the better. This has been the sort of reading which has distinguished most great men. It is, perhaps, the very reading to bring the individual judgment into full play. Read but one order of writings, and you are very apt to imbibe your opinions tacitly—to accept them—and without investigation. But reading variously, by compelling you to decide between adverse authorities, brings your own thoughts into exercise. You are required then to think as you read, not gulph and swallow merely. Read everything, my children. But, mark you, I do not counsel desultory *studies*—*study* the one thing, which is your peculiar vocation, and you may read every thing besides. It is my misfortune that my youthful habits were not studious. I confess my boyhood to have been a truant one. Grammar was my abomination, and I know nothing about it now; Arithmetic, a terrible torture that kept me sleepless, unless I skulked it, which I was very apt to do. Certainly, I thought that no Christian soul could reproach me for endeavoring to escape such cruel persecutions. What I might have been, or become, with proper training, is scarcely proper for discussion. It suffices that, though I do a great deal of what the world calls "work," I regard myself as really but an idler.—The habits of my boyhood were the fruits of a neglect which, considering the present happy indolence of my life, it would not become me to deplore. My irregularities in youth brought me no punishment. I had no parents to be troubled at my absence, or to chide and chasten me at my return. My guardian was very much a person after my own heart. He partook largely of my nature, and craved nothing more earnestly than repose. So that I trespassed not upon his leisure, I might do as I pleased with my own. My school-master was one of those trading professors who come from abroad, for no better purpose than money-making. He was not only dishonest, but incompetent; and I now look back with absolute surprise to the fact, that, with so slender a capital of sense and acquirement, he should have been suffered so long to defraud the community, and defeat the purposes of nature in the sixty children committed to his care.

He knew nothing of the minds or of the temperaments of his pupils. He taught us very much as a drill sergeant would have done, but without his rigor. The boys were ranged in classes according to their sizes. The tallest formed his upper, the smallest, his lower classes. Certain tasks in memory were set them, which they acquired or not, at pleasure. He did not punish, for that would have irritated all parties—the children, the parents and himself. The former were pleased with him, as they were neither tasked nor punished; the parents were content, since their sons were so, and since they always received an admirable account of their progress from the master; and he was satisfied, as he grew wealthy upon a rare repose.

Editor.—Here were the seeds then planted of all your Epicureanism, Father. I do not use the word, of course, in its vulgar sense.

Abbot.—Truly; I understand you. My philosophy, which has commended me to my present dignities, was a simple one. It had its seeds sown, as you say, under that scoundrelly schoolmaster. To economize and cherish the pleasant associations of life, and fly from those which are humiliating and painful, was my school boy instinct, long before my reason taught me to adopt it as a philosphy. It was the instinct, probably that made the philosophy reasonable. It came in admirable conflict with the duties of the school boy. Accordingly, the sixth day in the week did not prove sufficient for my necessities. I made a holiday of sundry more. Monday frequently found me upon the highways, and Tuesday upon the sea-shore; Wednesday was a famous day in our almanac of plasure, and Saint Thor, as we all know, confers special privileges on the succeeding day, upon every young Goth who remembers his Teuton original. Friday we are apt to surrender as an act of grace to the pedagogue and birch. And one day in the week seemed to give ample penance for all sins of the rest. It is surprising how easy it was in those days to repent. We had no long rebukes of conscience to contend with. A sin was forgotten in its successors, almost as soon as committed, and accumulated offences did not seem to add materially to the burdens of conscience. Happy days of childhood, which really know nothing of the nakednesss which a whole life after is consumed in the endeavor to hide from other eyes.

Beauclerk.—You are not half so indulgent, Father, to your flock, as you have been to yourself.

Abbot.—My son, we learn the right way, because we have once stumbled into the wrong one. It were sorry wisdom, with me, having seen the error of my own ways, to wink at yours. I am too faithfully the father of my flock to suffer you to run wild in your indulgencies. My policy is to economize your passions, by their seasonable restraint. This checks their excessive growth, which would only be to their own cost and peril, and your suffering. I thus keep your minds and modes in perfect balance, and, by due restraint of the animal tendencies—and all boyish tendencies are animal, when they are very decided—

maintain the superiority of the moral and intellectual nature. On this subject but too little is understood among us. Our affections, our sympathies and passions, receive too little training. We address ourselves wholly to the instruction of the head. The mind, the mind, the mind—receives all our care. We give too little to the heart—too little to the moods, the impulses, and those more exquisite sensibilities with which we are originally endowed, which are so many antennæ of the soul—delicate feelers of love, and reverence, and faith—without the due employment of which, we neither preserve our own better affections, nor give heed to those of our neighbor. There was much more in the old conventual custom of penance than we are apt to acknowledge. The mortification of the flesh is a prime requisite for maintaining a spiritual ascendancy and control over the more humiliating tendencies of the animal. I would not recommend the rod, the laceration of the limbs, the cruel self-torture of cord and steel. But simplicity of food, the total absence of stimulating drinks, the cold and solitary chamber, and temporary privation of books, music and conversation, are admirable means for subduing self-discord, for elevating and feeding thought, for schooling irregular and evil impulses, for framing the mind to devotional and better moods. In the training of children, let no worthy parent apprehend, through excess of tenderness, that privation will prove hurtful. It is surprising how litle nature craves. Satisfy the absolute wants of life—see that health suffers nothing—

L

and the food cannot well be too poor, the clothing too thin, the indulgencies too few, the tasks too many. There must be a time for rest and for sport: but work and denial are perhaps more necessary to strength, health, happiness and virtue, in the case of childhood, than all your gifts. Wonderful, indeed, to see how a proper degree of privation and toil expands the frame, enlarges the limbs, elevates the soul, informs the mind. Our error is, that nothing of this kind is now permitted. Our sons have no training. They are neither worked nor whipped, and without the burdens of the one, and the chastenings of the other, they are not likely to arrive at perfect manhood.

Editor.—You do not seem, Father to confide much to moral suasion

Abbot.—Moral fiddlestick! If you could confine the pupil to one exclusive community, which was not only pure in its morals, but perfect in its wisdom,—moral suasion would be a thing of course. But do not undersand me as arguing in behalf of harsh treatment and violence, as absolutely necessary in subduing a stubborn nature. I prefer privation; the denial of those things upon which the boy has set his heart. I insist upon seclusion, cold food, sparingly given, cold water,—and if the urchin be very fat, a hair shirt. But I contend that he must be made *to obey.* That is the inevitable necessity, and if the privation, and the starvation, and the hair shirt, will not bring him to his senses, then clothe him with birch as with a garment.

BEAUCLERK.—You were certainly born for your office, Father. You were born to be a disciplinarian—a monk of the Ascetic School—a——

ABBOT.—Avaunt thee, pagan! This is the gratitude for all my indulgence. For this have I suffered thee to take champagne with me upon the beach, to the great consternation of the rigidly righteous.

BEAUCLERK.—But a single bottle, Father!

ABBOT.—The allowance was small, I grant ye, but in full proportion to your merits. Still, you are half right. with all your impertinence. I have often fancied that the mode of life pursued by those old Monks would be the very sort of life for me;—the life of contemplation rather than of action. I envy the luxuries of their long life repose, in the embrace of a thought that never lacked its ideal. I frequently catch myself thinking and dreaming of the pleasant in their lives—their secluded cells—their brooding devotions—their sublime and spiritualizing fancies. I imagine to myself the venerable abbey on the hill-side, or in the hollow, or over-grown with ivy, the drowsy porter at the gates, and the aged sacristian among the tombs, spelling out the inscription, the self-chidden man prostrate before the altar, with muttered '*miserere*' deprecating the wrath of Heaven by humbling himself in the face of Earth. I seem to drink of the dim, religious light which streams through the groined and painted window, like some spiritual effusion rather than like ordinary sunlight; and crouching beside the gigantic column, whose capital is lost in the various tracery of the lofty roof, I feel myself annihilated in the immense space which there seems pregnant with Deity. The very idea of such security, expands the soul. The exclusion of daily cares, of crowding man, of ordinary hopes and yearnings, brings us visibly and momentarily nigher to Heaven. In proportion as we shut out the struggles of our fellows, and their communion, the soul feels the necessity of turning to some influence by which its solitude can be peopled. And thought peoples the solitude always with the spiritual. To the good man confident in virtue, the forms which gather about the hermit, are fresh from the crystal hills of Paradise; the murmurs which musically fill his ears, are echoes from the thousand stringed harp that sounds ever at the portals of Heaven; and how subdued become his passions, and how sweet his fancies, and how full of strength and richness are his thoughts. If he trembles or falls—if he is hurt or apprehensive—it is because his struggle is like that of Jacob in the valley of Penuel—a struggle with an angel in which he prevails at last—in the very failure of which he is endowed with the strength of Princes. The great benefit of solitude is in the self-communion which it brings. God is always a party where man communes with himself. Whispers salute the mortal ear which mortal tongue offends not. High counsels informs the spirit in its solitude. Self studies alone unveil the strength as well as the weaknesses of the inquirer. Man can only know himself in this fashion, through this medium, under the sacred influences of solitude. It is the error and the misfortune of our world and day, that we all of us live too much abroad. We have no homes. There are no places sacred to the thought and self-communion. We deliver ourselves to the multitude. We ask them to examine us. We dwell out of doors. Our thoughts are uttered for the press; our virtues for show. "The world is too much with us;" and, in its communion, we utterly forget our own. No man knows what an empire he has—how well peopled—how rich in all sort of possessions—all in his own soul. What pregnant fancies that are never let to fly; what abundant resources which are never put to interest; what ingenuity that is never made to spin or weave; what art that is never suffered to build or to create. And, thus endowed, we travel to the mart, and in the monotonous under song of our neighbor, we grow blind and deaf to the exquisite musical keys which lie open and yearning for the appointed pressure of our own fingers. We lack courage for our own world, and rely too much upon that over which we can seldom acquire any, or only a very brief control.

Editor.—And singing for one's neighbor, one is constantly called upon to stoop, to make concessions which mock the truth of the soul, and all the pride of the sensibilities.

Abbot.—As Byron said of the Laureate's song of homage—"which dare not aught prolong," save the "Eulogy" of his sovereign. The servile desire to please simply, is as little consistent with the vocation of the Poet, as with that of the Prophet or the Priest. His mission is a nobler one. He is himself a Prophet. He is decreed to be a leader—a guide—a discoverer. He does not, and must not, confine himself to the language of the pesent, since his special duty is the future. He cannot hope for the love of his generation, since he is sent only for that succeeding. The genius that lowers his standard to the time, cannot survive his time, for the sufficient reason that the time itself is not stationary. The age hurries on with sensible rapidity. We are daily making new blazes in new forests. The old land-marks are abandoned—swept away in the fast rushing floods of an enlarging civilization. To plant his banner in advance of this mighty coming—to hew out the first path-way—to say, "in this route shalt thou travel, and upon mountains and oceans yet unseen, but which, from my eminence, are visible to me, shalt thou fix thy future eyes"—this has always been the business of the prophetic genius—the master spirit of the time.

Editor.—Could we be persuaded of the truth of this, Father, and enter the solitude, in search of thought, at the frequent and needful season!

Abbot.—We are not quite ripe for it, my son. We are in the enjoyment of the first gush, of an unexpected power. The great mass is rushing on, eager in acquisitions which another age will abandon as worthless. Some master spirits may behold this even now—may see the coming discoveries—may look out upon the Canaan which their own footsteps may never tread. In the literature of the age, we may possibly even now, read dim prophecies of this future. No age is left utterly unattended to by its seers. They share the usual fate of those who tell imperfect or unwelcome truths. Like her Troy, "blasted by Phœbus with prophetic fire," they win no faith from those upon whom they bestow the very secrets of the deity. Vainly they cry from their solitudes. The voice is lost in the storming of the billows, that rock to and fro in the struggle of the highway, wave succeeding wave, and crest after crest swept forward in the continual flow of the capricious waters. Happy he who goes aside from this multitude--who can detach himself from the mass, and, in the independence of the forest, appeal to his own individual nature and bring the internal man out of the depths and retreats of his own heart. Less happy, but far happier he, than the million whom he leaves. He will gather none of their spoils but he will grow richer in the knowledge of his own. He will not flourish in their eyes, but he will be conscious of himself—which they are not. He will live. Every emotion will have its proper utterance—the hope its fruition, the fancy its flowers, the imagination its wing—the man will know his God feel himself made after his glorious image.

EDITOR.—Alas, Father! the great difficulty seems to be in determining one's *status*. What is our rank; what is our trust; the duty specially confided to our hands?

ABBOT.—It is the study of a life, my son; and the end of it may leave us still in doubt whether we have pursued the true vocation. But there can be no doubt that the search is still decreed. Know thyself! Ascertain thy use, and work according to what thou knowest, and according to the strength that is in thy sinews. We may work as thoroughly in repose as in action. Some men are made for action, others take a humbler place in the business of human performance. But they work together, though they work apart. Here is a new truth—the world has got possession of it—no matter how. It prefers not to ask who discovered it, least its gratitude may be taxed. It would be easy, perhaps, to show whence, by whose researches, and how long it lay imploring man to behold, before he deigned to set his eyes upon it. But, once found, and seen, the truth is set in motion. It is to perform. It has a working destiny before it; for every new truth is God's agent, for a time, or for all times, in the proper training of the race. It is delivered to us only when the race is prepared for its reception. For its transmission certain fiery spirits are employed, who carry it aloft above the crowd, but in their sight, as one carries a torch, which, thus lifted high, the winds cannot extinguish. These men go by various names. In one land they are called Moseses, in another Mahomets, in a third, Luthers, and so on—every land being in some degree provided with its working spirit according to its progress and its necessity. Glorious they are and great, and needful—but, behind these, and quite out of sight, are the greater but more shadowy forms, by whom the torch was first enkindled—the sacred fire preserved in secret places—and finally given into the hands of these fiery-working spirits. These were the men who wrought in solitude—who communed with God in the wilderness—who went up to the struggle, in the solitary mountains, while the million strove together with loud cries below, and wasted life in vain tumults, whether of danger or delight.

The world is thus made up. There are many classes, it is true, but these need not all be considered. Two of them stand apart, which are the true mental leaders. The one finds the truth, the other carries it forward. The one sees the present deity, the other lifts his image before the multitude. Contemplation is the life of the one—action of the other. Of these, the last is the true offspring of the first. No child was ever born more legitimate. But they frequently come in conflict—sire and offspring. The genius which conceives the truth passes on to other discoveries. The true worker never rests. The seeker is never satisfied with the found,—for the forms of truth are infinite, and the tasks of search are strictly set for each succeeding generation. It happens that, while the discoverer toils in new developments, he comes in conflict with the zealot whom he has himself employed to carry forward the preceding. A blind worker is the latter, if a strong. It is perhaps well that he should be so, else where would he procure his courage—where find that confidence in his mission which makes him hurry in its prosecution, though he sees and feels that his goal must be the stake. It is this faith in the light that he carries before men's eyes that makes him war against other lights. Error, he knows, has its lights also —shining and burning lights for a season—comet-like effulgences that show a glorious train which satisfies myriads of gazers who ask not after the body from which it is supposed to flow. Natural it is that the should war with every light but his own. Thus comes the conflict even between the professors of truth itself. They do not see that all human truth is partial—that it is the divine truth alone which is perfect. They cannot be taught that the several fragments which they bear are capable of union—that they are parts of each other, and all parts of the perfect form after which the successive races are destined to struggle. It is only in the new revelations that they give up their issues upon the old. It is only in the broader blaze of a yet more perfect light, which absorbs all the scattered gleams which have preceded it, that they discover how frequently, in their zeal for the truth, they have labored in deadly hostility against the true.

Bonhommie.—Your segar is out, Father.

Abbot.—No more. I am for a *siesta.* Pray, brother, waken me when I have slept *seven* minutes. The siesta never sheuld exceed *ten.* We take supper on Prospect Hill to-night.

XIV.

Beauclerk.—You have heard, boys. We have but seven minutes. The old man will probably take ten for his *siesta*. We have no time to lose. I am for the other bottle.

Bonhommie.—The motion is a good one. Is it the Champagne or the Perry that you prefer?—There is a bottle of each upon the table.

Beauclerk.—The Perry is good, brother, but it has not the virtue of the Champagne. We will keep it in reserve, until our tastes become less nice. Allow me, and you shall see how I shall persuade that cork out of coventry. Ha! smack!—With what a burst of delight it bounds for the ceiling, like a noisy boy just let out from school. Let it play. It shall never again be put in bonds by us. A good creature is Champagne.—Ha! my Bard of the Isles—you do not drink! What's the matter?

Poet.—I am troubled. Our venerable Father seems sad.

Beauclerk.—Pshaw! only sleepy! He took too many of the oysters.

Poet.—No! He was sad before dinner. Something touches him. His conversations, of late, seem to me to lack their customary buoyancy.—They sound in my ears like melancholy notes of warning.

Beauclerk.—Pooh! pooh! That's because he preaches so much. He will neither be happy himself, nor suffer us to be so, In the language of Mose: "He won't give the b'hoys a chance!" I confess, I'm restive under his asceticism, and I am not the only one of the fraternity. The truth is, the Abbot gets old apace. He is on the decline, and the sooner we let him know that we have found a proper successor the better.

BONHOMMIE.—Brother Beauclerk, how can you dream of such a thing?

POET.—Monstrous! Talk of decline; talk of deposing our venerable Father; talk of his asceticism; his severity; his restraints; when we all feel them to be our best securities. We enjoy, now, Brother Beauclerk, the right sort of freedom—that which, while it encourages pleasantry and happiness, is not inconsistent with propriety. It is the curse of most clubs that their freedom soon degenerates into mere license. This is not the case with us; yet we are permitted all social enjoyments.

BEAUCLERK.—He has forbidden brag, vingt'un, poker, and other games, which I like.

PICTOR.—Those only which derive their chief interest from the gains which they yield. Games of mere chance are forbidden. He encourages whist, chess, billiards, backgammon, and many others.

BEAUCLERK.—Yes, but only as moral exercises!

POET.—You know his philosophy on that subject. He approves of games, which exercise the thoughts of the mind, or the muscles of the body; which promote intellect and memory; agility, strength and grace. He only discountenances those which provoke dangerous appetites, and exercise selfishness and cunning. Talk of his age and asceticism, when it was only a week ago that he beat us all at goff.

BEAUCLERK.—He has a sort of good humor, but it don't suit me exactly, and as for keeping us leashed as it were, denied to engage in the sports we desire, and forcing upon us those only which he approves, I frankly tell you, I don't relish it at all. The Abbot's a good man enough, but he's quite too much a puritan for me; and I tell you that's the opinion of more than half the fraternity.

PICTOR.—I don't believe a word of it.

BEAUCLERK.—You'll see! He will have to give place to another.

POET.—Who! indeed! I'd like to see the brother of the fraternity bold enough to take the seat which he abdicates. His own consciousness of presumption will sink him through the chair. No! no! brother Beauclerk, these are damnable heresies which you utter, for which no penance can be too severe.

BEAUCLERK.—You will find that I shall be absolved. He will walk, you'll see! I wouldn't give the old man pain, and we shall vote him a service of plate when he retires; but his day's done: he's *passée*. Your health, Bonhommie.

PICTOR, *(aside)*—'Tis the wine that speaks.

POET, *(aside)*—Not altogether. *In vino veritas!* Where there's so much smoke, there's some fire. Something's wrong. Beauclerk's got into bad company. He has been a little surly for some time past. But say nothing to the Abbot. Let our brother have time to feel his follies, by privately meditating them.

BEAUCLERK.—What do you whisper? Come! glass all round. Brethren, don't suppose me hostile to the holy Father Abbot. I love the old cock: 'pon my soul I do! But I would spare his age the trouble of keeping in check such troublesome sparks as myself.

BONHOMMIE.—What say you, my brothers for a *siesta* all round? I confess to a certain sort of drowsiness.

BEAUCLERK.—Not a bit of it—not certainly till we finish the bottle. I'm for a song my boys.

" 'Twas a monkey that danc'd on the top,"——

Eh! the Abbot!

Enter Father Abbot.

ABBOT.—Continue your song, my son.

BEAUCLERK.—Beshrew me, Father, if I can! Your sudden appearance has exorcised the spirit of song within me. Have you enjoyed your siesta?

ABBOT.—My seven minutes are eleven.

POET.—But you have not slept, Father?

ABBOT.—Yes, slept and dreamed; and such a dream! I dreampt my children that, all at once, all the teeth dropt out of my head.

BEAUCLERK.—Hem! an omen!

POET.—In former days superstition had declared such a dream to be of the most fatal character; but now——

ABBOT.—Dreams are simply thoughts, my son; the exercises of an imagination without its usual restraints. I can account for this of mine. It is the result of a previous train of thinking, upon which, hitherto, I have said nothing to any of you. The loss of my teeth signifies the loss of my children.

OMNES.—How, Father?

ABBOT.—It signifies that we are to separate. That the teeth fell out all at once, shows that the act which separates me from *one*, separates me from *all*. This can be only in two ways—by my death or withdrawal from the fraternity. But as the teeth fell out without let or hindrance, it is clear that the separation is my voluntary act. Now, as I certainly shall never commit suicide, it follows that I must leave you. This, my children, was the secret determination to which I had already come.

POET.—Impossible, Father! You surely will not leave us. Our shepherd—

BEAUCLERK.—You have been our Father so long.

ABBOT.—Precisely! It is for this, among other reasons, that I feel bound to abdicate. There is a grace and propriety, my children, in not lingering unnecessarily upon the stage. Old men should learn to retire, and give way to their sons, before they become *too* old. We thus save ourselves from sneer and censure; we thus escape the exercise of one of the most ungracious sorts of tyranny. It is the misfortune that old men, accustomed to office, never know when to retire. They never reflect upon the hopes of youthful ambition, in whose way they stand. They are as little considerate of society, whose affairs they can no longer conduct with energy and skill, and seem not aware that they are kept in place rather by a deference which cannot forget the past, than in consequence of their admitted capacity to do the business of the present. I shall endeavor not to fall into this error, my children, and my determination was made only the week before we came to the Island, to make the conclusion of our visit here, the close of my administration. My dream forced the utterance of my secret from me. You will have to appoint my successor in your next regular chapter. In the interim, hearken to the disposition which will be made of your time. From the Island, we visit Cooper river for a day. The planters are now harvesting their crops, and the scene will be a grateful one. After that we proceed to a tour among the mountains of Georgia and our own State, the scheme of which will be submitted you to-morrow. You have heard my children.

Beauclerk.—Eheu!

Abbot.—Be not sad, my children. You tremble, my Bard! Dear young son of Apollo, wherefore should you tremble?

Poet.—Alas, Father!

"Cosi stupisce, e cade
Pallido, e smorto in viso
Al fulmine improvviso
L'attonito pastor."*

Abbot.—Ah, my son, you have your answer in the remaining verse of the same passage:

* Thus stunn'd, and stupified, and deadly pale,
Falls to the earth the Shepherd, as he hears,
The sudden burst of thunder o'er his head.

"Ma quando por s'avvede
Del vano suo spavento,
Sorge, respira e riede
A numerar l'armento
Disperso dal tumor."†

We always exaggerate our losses in the moment when they occur. With time, we feel the idleness of our fears. The scattered flock is soon recovered by a new Pastor. God never leaves any community without the Shepherd who can lead them to safe and pleasant pastures; always assuming that the sheep are not of that perverse breed which is properly decreed to the butcher. You will not miss your present father, my children, so much as he misses you; and, believe me, it is high time that you should make provision for the future. The fraternity has numerous brothers, most of whom are quite as well fitted as myself to serve you. They have seen my system. It is generally approved of. They will carry out my plans. You will enjoy society without formalities; leisure and luxury even, without license; sports and pleasure without excess; labor without exhaustation; and the flow of a various conversation, without dispute or controversy. We have studiously excluded from our order, all that class of spirits who lie in wait for disputation; who cavil at words; who are forever on the look out for flaws in your grammer or your

† But, as he finds how idle were his fears,
He rises from the earth—he breathes once more,
And seeks and numbers his fear-scattered flock.

argument; not so much with the view to correct your error, as to exercise their polemics. You will continue to exclude all such people from your haunts: all peevish, captious spirits; all triflers who never rise to the dignity of an earnest intelligence; who never respect the moods of a neighbor; and who find an excuse in the emission of a bad pun, for interrupting a fine philosophy. You will enjoy the creature comforts with like caution and moderation; assured of this, that excess always brings its own penalties, and that the pleasures of life, of whatever kind, are like sweetmeats, comfits, &c.—very good things in their way, and at the proper season, but the worst things in the world upon which to make a meal; not only hurtful to the health, but to the appetite itself. But a truce to this, my children. These texts have been too often preached from before, to render necessary their repetition, even at the moment of parting. If, hereafter, you remember me, you will not easily forget my lessons. Let us now to other matters. I could wish, my dear Pictor, that you would seize upon that evening landscape. The view from this point, in the direction of the City, would make a lovely one on canvass. You look through a delicious avenue, the long stretch of shore, Haddrell and Mount Pleasant on the right, and the western extremity of the Island on the left, forming, as it were, a framework for the picture. The evening sun sheds a glorious halo over the City that seems to loom upwards to its embrace. Its darker features turned towards us, with the sunlight in the back ground, affords all the effect of an exquisite and noble contrast; while those richly dyed and fantastic clouds, with edges of crimson and orange, hanging over it as the ample curtain of some imperial couch, render wholly unnecessary the relief which flat scenery so commonly seems to need in the absence of lofty wood crowned elevations. Here, in the foreground, the village of Moultrie comes out boldly and beautifully: a city seemingly itself, and seeming, indeed, at its western extremity, to unite with the more distant City. It is only by the bold outline and lively clearness of the one, and the faint, subdued and dimly shining aspects of the other, that you are led to suspect the interval that lies between them. The two steamers now sweeping over the space between, give you all that is needed for the *vitality* of the picture; which, beheld as we behold it now, and from this point of view, is as lovely a landscape as ever charmed the eye. It is not, indeed, the common painter who can do such a subject well. Bold outlines may be hit off by a very ordinary hand; but the delicacy, the sweetness, the soft tenderness and grace of this picture, require the nicest circumspection, the sweetest fancy, and the most elaborate finish. Such a subject would honor the pencil of Fraser.

Pictor.—I have been sketching the very scene already, Father. I have seen it very much with your eyes. If permitted it shall appear in the gallery of the Abbey, at the next regular chapter.

Abbot.—Ah! my son! This is what I love! The art which *works*, rather than *talks*—which performs rather than promises;—this is what is most needful among our social virtues. We are beginning to bestir ourselves my children. I feel that a new era has dawned upon our people. We can all of us report progress. Charleston has hitherto consisted, really of *two* communities, and these have been in deadly conflict for twenty years or more. The one community consisted of a people coerced by the necessities of life, devoted to toil and business, and bringing to their work the capital of fresh energies, eager hopes and sleepless enterprise. Their deficiencies chiefly lay in the respects of social tone. They had no acknowledged place in a society, which, peculiar at first, and forming one of the oldest communities in the country, had acquired a certain permanence of position;—was fixed and recognised;—and had, in various ways, reached a very high distinction. This distinction formed the capital of the other portion of the City. Its people could boast of *a past.* They could look back with pride to their ancestry, many of whom occupied an acknowledged and high place in our annals. They had been accustomed to wealth,—had all the advantages of social training and education, and could assert those graces of manner which require leisure and society as well as education and wealth. It is difficult to realize the charm and extent of these accomplishments, and we are thus too frequently led to over-rate their value. Certainly, there is nothing so grateful in society as exquisite manners—that nice delicacy of deportment, which never outrages a sensibility, which tempers earnestness with grace, and seasons an attic wit with a politeness that takes all venom from the point. Now, to attain these graces of society, we are required to make *some* sacrifices; but our old community had made too many. The danger is always that, in the perfection of our tastes, we lose some of our necessary energies. The secret is to refine our manners without forfeiting our strength. This might always be effected, if a miserable vanity did not interpose equally to thwart natural events, and a just philosophy. The man of manners and refinements, is apt to make them especial objects of pride; and in doing so, emasculates his mental energies. He perpetually contrasts his quiet, graceful manner, with the rude hurry of the working man; and in proportion as the rough energy of the other offends his tastes, will he turn away equally disgusted with, or unobservant of, the vigor and power which are coupled with the roughness which offends him. In rejecting what is evil, or inferior, in the manners, he makes the mistake of rejecting also the virtues of that manhood which is the secret of safety in all communities. He learns to dispise labor and art, which are the two great conquering agencies of society and man; and, in the over appreciation of his own graces, he loses utterly the great virtues of his neighbor. The other, in turn, too often revenges himself on the society which rejects him, by disparaging the accomplishments which he had not allowed himself the leisure to acquire. He rushes to the other extreme of behaviour. He adopts a rude bearing and an abrupt manner. He studiously roughens his tone, and strips his deportment, as far as he may, of the exterior graces which convention has established as the means of softening the necessary attritions of society and business. You will have perceived, you who can remember, what a contrast in the behaviour of too many of our youth to what it was only twenty years ago. In the school which furnished our models, at that period, we were studiously taught to give way to age, to infancy, to woman, whether white or black. The concession was made to feebleness no less than dignity and distinction. We never hustled the crowd for place or position. If we entered the lobby of the theatre there was no struggle. Did we go to the post-office for letters, we waited our turn. It was no justification for thrusting our elbows into the ribs of our neighbor, that we were in a hurry. My neighhor's corns still demanded my respect, though I had business elsewhere. The truth was not then wholly forgotten, that the world was not made simply on our account. I see a great and melancholy change in this respect, which change I charge, in some degree, upon the recklessness of trade, and its too little regard for the requisitions of society. This demeanor is the more reprehensible, inasmuch as trade should especially cultivate the graces and needs not violate a single social propriety in order to success. Its energies need not be impaired, in any degree, by a careful regard to the *suavitor in modo.* Trade, which is the tributary of commerce, has only to take its character from its superior. Commerce is, perhaps, the greatest of civilizers. It subdues war; it reconciles hostile nations; it appeals to art, and nourishes it with veneration; its representative have been the most noble of the princes of the earth. There could be no better teacher of what is at once manly in social energies, and lovely in social refinement. Denied social position, at the beginning of his career, the working man has only to wait patiently, and prosecute his toils, modestly and earnestly, with his proper lights and guides before him. Society demands an apprenticeship, as well as arts and sciences. At all events, no man must seek to revenge himself upon society for its seeming neglects, by abandoning his soul to Mammon. This is to sacrifice the substance for the shadow; the soul for the purse. Too many are apt to make this mistake, and to set up Plutus as the only true idol in society. The faith is a common one enough, but a false one. That society which mere money can command, is seldom worth having. The wise and the good must equally despise it. Yet a bad passion helps this vulgar faith, too frequently, into a strange activity. The disappointed and vain aspirant after position, feels that money brings him power; that, with money he can master men; that, in process of time, he will buy the homestead of the haughty aristocrat, who has too much scorned his pretensions; that he will become the master of those fair fields that have hitherto mocked his eyes at a distance; and that the sons, or grandsons, of his social rival, will yet be compelled to throng about the doors of his counting room, soliciting the patronage and employment of the very person whom their sires could despise. This has been a common history among us. What with exclusiveness, and the enjoyment of the *dolce far niente*, the honored names of a past generation are greatly reduced in dignity and fortune. They thrive no longer; but the good omen is to be found in the fact that so many of their descendants are showing themselves willing to work. I have in my eye at this moment several noble youth, who are grappling with their duties with that hearty zeal and courage, which make the only true manhood—not dipping a little into business as a timid boy goes into the water, as if he dreadfully feared to wet his feet;—but plunging, head-foremost, fearless, as the bold swimmer who is resolved on wrestling fortune from the waves. When this shall become general in our community;—when society shall recognize the necessity of coupling manhood always with its refinements; not suffering taste to degenerate into fastidiousness, or good manners into feeblenees;—but honoring these only as they are tributary to manly performance;—and when, on the other hand, the performing and the business men, shall recognize the just claims of a social organization;—shall recognize what is due to good taste, social refinement, delicacy and propriety of manners; and all those arts which tutor the sensibilities, and civilize the rude humanity,—then shall the two branches of our society work together as they have not done before in my recollection.—Hitherto, there has been no communion between them. They have not only not worked together, but one portion has opposed to the other *vis inertiæ*, —denying itself almost wholly to a cause that was common to them both,—the maintenance and progress of the community. Now, we have a grateful prospect of better things. We are fast getting rid of our absurdities. We are beginning to see life in its just attributes. Necessity is doing its work, and vanity and pretention no longer fold their robes about them, looking with contempt upon that energy which impels the engine,—which drives the barge, and harnesses the very lightning to the cars of commerce and society. True manhood, now, is everywhere regarded as to be found *only in performance;* and the youth now-a-days, who is not willing to work cheerfully in his vocation, and according to his endowments, should be shorn of his beard, dressed up in petticoats,and set to brood with foolscap and bells to the en d of his baby destiny.

Editor.—The exclusiveness, Father, of which you have spoken on the part of a portion of our community, was, perhaps, in no respect more injurious than in the frequent family intermarriages.

Abbot.—You are right, my son. Nothing so much tends to destroy the moral and the physical virtues of a race as a habit like this. The breeds must be crossed. It is surprising that, with the general conviction, so common among us, of this necessity in the case of animals, we should have disdained to acknowledge the importance of the rule in respect to man. In this connexion men are to be considered as animals also. No man should marry his cousin, of any remove; and it would be well if men always sought their wives in other Districts, or in other States. Insular and small communities, in particular, should always send their young men abroad to wive. Failing in this, their children must necessarily be of a puny and inferior physique, will be of inferior intellectual endowment; in repeated cases, will become idiots, and finally will cease to breed at all. Family intermarriages in our country, are too frequently devised for the maintenance of that exclusiveness which family pride too much regards as its only security. It is thus that we seek to supply the guaranties of distinctions which, in aristocratic governments, are afforded by titles of nobility. The better specimens of the European nobility, are almost invariably the fruit of a cross; the nobleman seeking alliance with the commoner. The *motive* with the British nobility for such alliances, is that wealth which the heir to a great house requires to sustain his dignity. The *result* is the perfection of physical manhood. The British aristocracy are probably the finest looking set of men in the world; exhibiting an organization of form and feature which has never been surpassed. The effect upon their *character* has been equally admirable. You would be surprised to see the number of these young scions of nobility who traverse the world in all sorts of exploring enterprises. Now you find them in the East, on the back of a dromedary, coasting the desert, and sleeping in tents, among the most lawless tribes of the country. You remember the exquisite picture painted by Lord Byron, in his "Dream;"

"He lay—
Reposing from the noontide sultriness,
Crouch'd among fallen columns, &c."

The picture is common to the English nobleman. Anon, you find them, ranging over the plains and prairies of our Northwest, pursuing the buffalo and the grisly bear. No hardships discourage, no dangers affright them; and they combine admirably the virtues of a bold, impulsive manhood, with the best breeding of a social aristocracy. We must protect *our* family dignities by other virtues than those of exclusiveness, my children—by *performance*, by achievement, by deeds, by enterprise, energy, perseverance—the very virtues which originally conferred distinction upon, and planted pride within the bosom of the founder of the family. Many, if not most of the leading names in Carolina were merchants, tradesmen and mechanics. There are few, however haughty, who, travelling backward a few generations, would not stumble over the family heir-loom in the shape of an axe, an anvil, a jack plane, or an anchor. Let us teach the true pride to our sons which should make them honor forever, and prize, with a sort of reverence, the implements by which their fathers acquired fortunes for their children, who have not always preserved, or prized properly, the tools by which they did so. He who feels shame to be reminded of the craft of his ancestor, deserves none of the profits which followed from its exercise. What I should like to teach in particular is—that nobility lies wholly in noble performance; that without performance, there is no manhood, and that, while occupations differ in degree, quality or profit, he is to be esteemed as a man, and he only, who, having ascertained what he is good for, goes to his task; not merely beneath the goad of necessity, for that betrays the base nature of the slave; but as one eager for the duty which is assigned him, and anxious to make himself distinguished in his vocation: and every vocation may have its distinctions, if those only attempt it who are equal to its tasks.

EDITOR.—Were these the common principles—the general sentiments, Father, what a glorious community we should have. What a splendid spectacle is that of a great city, all parties working together in the common cause; all eager, hopeful, cheerful, industrious—proud only in emulation, and thoughtful chiefly of the means of multiplying the common resources and the common securities.

ABBOT.—Do you remember Milton's picture, my son, in the "Areopagitica?" "Behold now this vast city; a city of refuge, the mansion-house of liberty, encompassed and surrounded with his protection. The shop of war hath not there more anvils and hammers waking, to fashion out the plates and instruments of armed justice in defence of beleaguered truth, than there be pens and heads there, sitting at their studious lamps, musing, searching, revolving new notions and ideas wherewith to present, as with their homage and their fealty, the approaching reformation. Others as fast reading, trying all things, assenting to the force of reason and convincement. What could a man require more from a nation so pliant and so prone to seek after knowledge? What wants there to such a towardly and pregnant soil, but wise and faithful laborers, to make a knowing people a nation of prophets, of sages, and of worthies? We reckon more than five months yet to harvest; *there need not be five weeks, had we but eyes to lift up. The fields are white already.*" There is another passage of this noble sort of eloquence near this, in the same treatise.

Editor.—I remember. "Methinks, I see in mind a noble and puissant nation, rousing herself like a strong man after sleep and shaking her invincible locks, &c."

Abbot.—Let us now stroll upon the beach, and gazing upon the distant city in the evening sunlight, our Poet shall declaim for us Milton's description of Athens.

Editor.—The motion is a good one. The evening speaks to us very seductively, and Brother Bonhommie talks of a *late* supper—an intimation with a significance quite as great as that of Lucullus, when he ordered his supper in the Apollo chamber.

Beauclerk—*(aside to Pictor)*—I am afraid the old man heard me. I am monstrously ashamed.

Pictor—*(aside to B.)*—No! I think not. I am sure not.

Beauclerk.—Yet he spoke of the very subject.

Pictor.—Which he would *not* have done had he heard you. Be at ease, and repent of your error with what speed you may.

XV.

Editor.—You were interrupted, Father, while speaking of the projected Hotel upon the Island. You spoke of your *prevision* in regard to it. We are now upon the western edge of the Curlew Ground, where it seems to me, the best site could be found for such an establishment.

Abbot.—It is the very spot that has been chosen, my son—that *will be* chosen, I should say.—I am speaking now of that which is yet in the womb of the future. Eight acres have been selected at this point, which are ample for this purpose; and I rejoice to say, that the subscriptions made already, realize the estimated amount of the expenditure for such an establishment. Our men of substance have come out manfully, and more than twenty-two thousand dollars have been raised for the purpose. Doubtless, ten thousand more could be easily procured, but the proprietors will content themselves with five thousand.

Editor.—With such an amount we should have a very splendid building.

Abbot.—I have already seen the design, my son, and it will suit in all respects the object. It will constitute an imposing and beautiful edifice, rising gracefully upon the spectator coming in from the sea. The style of the fabric will be at once simple and showy, somewhat after the style of architecture at Oran. You shall have a sketch of it here upon the sand. * * * * *

You see what a noble colonnade is before you, covering both stories of the building, from roof to basement, and extending the extreme length of the structure, which is full three hundred and fifty feet. The projection in the centre will be nearly, perhaps quite, an hundred feet. It will thus relieve the uniformity of a range so extensive. The dome-like elevation from the roof, corresponding happily with the general style of the building, contributes also to the general relief, and constitutes one of the most grateful features in the plan. Here my son, is a glorious promenade, from which you may drink in the breezes from all quarters of the compass, range with unimpeded vision from East to West, from North to South, and shift the scene at pleasure, from sea to land, from shore to forest, from bright, flashing and rolling breaker, to the harmonious tints of green umbrageous wood, and bright, and flower-garnished thicket. With the aid of glasses of sufficient power, you will be allowed to look upon the bathers at Cape May, and, by a twist of the same instrument, you may see the toilsome workers after the picturesque, as they shout from the top of the Stone Mountain to the fair damsels who are content to look up from below. I hold it, my son, not impossible to realize all these prospects from our Island Belfry, always assuming the powers of the telescope, and the imagination of the gazer, to be equal to so magnificent a survey. For persons of moderate fancy, a view of the harbor will be sufficiently compensative.

I need scarcely call your attention to the scene immediately before us. Its exquisite grace and beauty are unquestionable. I see that Sir Charles Lyell has recently been pleased to acknowledge it. He is a man of taste and decency, as well as a Geologist. Certainly, so far as nature is concerned, no son of Carolina need go out of Charleston harbor for a noble ocean prospect. In regard to the *coup d'œil,* she ranks very near New-York,—lacking, it is admitted, the immense vivacity, which results to the latter, from the crowding cities and villas, which, upon the two great rivers at Manhattan, sit picturequely placed in equal beauty and animation. But, the Bay of Charleston, almost immediately upon the sea,—the waters of the great deep rolling into the doors of her habitations—she springing, sudden, like another Venice, from their embrace—her broad and graceful rivers Ashley and Cooper (Keawah and Etiwan) clasping her, with murmurs of affection, in their arms, ere they pass away to the gulf in which they are swallowed up and lost—the green stripes of shore that stretch away on either hand, and, sloping off to the sea, contrast exquisitely with the silver of its glancing billows—the grey islets that lie between these and the ocean,—the fortresses that crown the whole with imposing moral associations—the queenly city in the midst,—the deep, dark, foliage in the back ground,—these are all, in such beautiful relationship,—in themselves how beautiful—that it needs nothing but a becoming faith in themselves, and in the material possessed by our native artists, to furnish them with a thousand scenes of loveliness and grace, such as Doughty has made to live for ever upon the canvass.

Editor.—You are quite right, Father, in the appreciation of the prospect. I feel that I have undervalued it until now.

Abbot.—So have we all, my son. I contend that our entire Low Country, resourceless as it hath hitherto appeared to the vulgar sightseeker, up to the first *steppes* of the mountain region, is abundantly provided with characteristics, peculiar to itself, of grace, animation and beauty, without the advantage of a single mountain. But it is for the painter of *detail*, rather than of *outline*, to distinguish and relieve it from the cumbrous masses of the forest, and the unimposing uniformity of place. In other words, it must be the *student* of scenery, and not the mere *sightseeker*, to delineate such portraits. We have had, we have now, living artists, to whom the discovery of these beauties would be easy. Let me not forget in this connection, the happy talent of one who is no longer with us. Trouche was the very painter for such scenes. The swamp and forest scenery of the lower country, had infused itself into his very nature. He dreamed it, and he painted accordingly. He has left too many pictures unpainted: called away too soon, himself young, and young in all the impulse of his art. Had Touche found a patron, twenty years ago, in some liberal man of fortune, had he been put to a stern apprenticeship of taste and genius, how would he have honored his patron—how done honor to his country! He was undoubtedly a man of genius, whom we did not sufficiently honor.

Editor.—Do you know, Father, that there is

still extant a small collection of cabinet sketches by Coram—Views on Ashley and Cooper Rivers, most of them mere outlines—studies for future use, rather than pictures, which prove the susceptibilities of these views?

Abbot.—I have seen them. In the hands of a painter of talent these sketches, even now, might be elaborated with the most admirable effect. I wish that we could persuade Fraser to address his pencil to materials so easy of access, so grateful to the genius *loci*, and so worthy of his grace and exquisite finish. By the way, my son, you should see two beautiful things, recently from his easel, entitled "Still" and "Running Water." They are the sweetest things I have seen for many a day. I confess to lusting after them. When I think of them I violate the commandment. But let us descend from our imaginary perch to the ground floor of our Hotel. Having past through the front colonnade the building opens in the centre into an ample hall. This, in turn, opens upon a ball-room on either side, the dimensions of each of which are *one hundred and ten* by *thirty* feet. These ball rooms may be united with the hall, making the grandest of all saloons for state occasions—the arrival of emigrant Princes, Ex-Presidents, or a visit from the entire order of the "Monks of the Moon." I have great pleasure in informing you that I am already in receipt of a communication from the proprietors of the Hotel, which advises me that an apartment shall always be held in reserve for the fraternity, and that the freedom of the establishment shall be accorded to the Father Abbot, the only condition annexed to his privileges being the performance, at proper seasons, of the duty of the Chaplain. After this, I need not pass any eulogies upon the taste, the good sense, or the liberality of these excellent gentlemen. They have an eye to merit; they know what is due to literature and the fine arts. They feel, with a proper sense, that they have in hand a work which appeals to the higher graces of society; that they are providing, in fact, for the *elite* of the South—its wealth, beauty, fashion and intellect. In this connection, I may add, that a very civil request has been made, through me, to our brethren, that they will prepare a series of studies, from Southern History and tradition, for original *tableaux vivants.* They are properly sick of the stale repetitions of Dukes and Marquisses; Macbeths and Hamlets; Queens and Shepherdesses; Turks and Banditti. I have already considered the subject, and have designed more than one hundred studies, from Carolina history alone, each of which, in a dramatic representation, would bring down all the thunders of the house. In this Hotel, the *tableaux* can be arranged, privately, in either of the ball rooms, the spectators occupying the hall.

Editor.—Verily, Father, our proprietors design the thing handsomely. They have wondrously risen in my esteem.

Abbot.—And with reason. But to proceed. Back of the hall is the *office* of the Hotel, occupying a recess which opens upon the piazza in the rear, and which, on three sides, is surrounded by a spacious court. On the extreme right of the front, is a spacious *parlor* for the ladies, in the rear of which, occupying *one hundred*, by *thirty-eight* or *forty* feet of the eastern wing of the building, is the *Dining Saloon*—a hall large enough for a hecatomb. I have not before told you of these *wings;* which are spacious buildings in themselves. They stretch from either end of the main building, one hundred and twenty feet, the colonnade covering them in like manner with the front, and connected with it. In the rear of the dining room is a *pantry*, to which the fraternity is to have a pass key. The inner area of the building is sheltered by its piazzas extending its entire surface. The *chambers* number *one hundred and five*, and are no miserable little closets, such as serve painfully to remind a man of the narrow limits of that last chamber which he needs; but are such as the climate requires—ample, cool, well ventilated and sheltered by be colonnade from the direct entrance of the sun. The beds are all on springs, elastic always, and, therefore, cool; and West Indian Hammocks, of strongly plaited cane, it is suggested will still afford to the sleeper the choice of swinging, or simply rolling himself into the embrace of Morpheus. A *grand passage* divides the double ranges of rooms, by passing through the centre of the building its entire length. From the Eastern wing of the building extends a covered way which conducts you to the *Bathing Hall*. This is designed to be sufficiently large to accommodate Diana and all her Nymphs. Here, *Douches* and *Shower Baths*, ropes pendant, swings, and other agencies, borrowed from the Gymnasium, are to be furnished, enabling the virgin beauty to frolic through Summer hour, in the two-fold embraces of sea and air. Hither, no miserable Actæon can penetrate; no Arcadian Damon pop into sight, unadvisedly, to apostrophize his, unconscious mistress on the scantiness of her wardrobe. Here, all is to be lulling security and sweetness; a delicious retreat and shelter, soft and dreamy, as any furnished by Thompson, in the castle and domain of Indolence.

Editor.—'Pon my soul, Father the prospect is a delicious one.

Abbot.—You may well say so; but this is not all. Our excellent proprietors know well, how much the virtues of society depend upon its amusements. They know, that where we fail to provide the young with innocent amusements, the devil will take precious good care to see that they have others of his own choosing. They know that nature craves and will have amusement, whether as a relief from labor, a physical exercise, or the satisfaction of mental curiosity. They have, accordingly, allotted apartments in this same neighborhood, to a Bowling Saloon, and Billiards. Here, then when the lady has had her *cue*, and exercised herself as much as she desires,—she disappears amid the placid waters, and is nerved and strengthened for new trials of skill, by their refreshing embraces. Here, pleasure ministers to proper exercise; to purification, purification to repose; repose to health; and a joyous re-appearance with the morrow's sunshine, on the part of the damsel, brings the moral and the physical world together in the happiest unison. As Chaucer writes it—showing the coincidence between Light and Beauty—

> "Uprose the sun, and uprose Emily."

Editor.—Our conference, Father, was interrupted on a previous occasion, when we were discussing the proper name to be given to such a Hotel. In your absence, the Brethren continued the subject. Beauclerk proposed, "The Island House;" Bonhommie, the "Rutledge House;" Benison, the "Summer Retreat;" Beauregard, the "Marion" or "Moultrie," "Gadsden" or "Pinckney."

Abbot.—And you?

Editor.—I was divided between Rutledge and Moultrie, but remembering what you had said, on the subject of the inappropriateness of the names, I forbore.

Abbot.—And, our Poet?

Editor.—He said nothing.

Abbot.—Ah! he could feel this unfitness. His veneration never allows him to vulgarise, by too much frequency, the thing he honors. I am afraid that our opinions will have but little avail, since it is whispered that the child is already christened "Moultrie." I confess that I am sorry for this. It is our infirmity here, that we ring the changes quite too frequently upon a favourite name. Here, now, is Fort Moultrie, the Village is Moultrie, and the Hotel is to be called "Moultrie." Nobody honors Moultrie's worth and public services more than I do; but I cannot see the propriety of these iterations. Moultrie's great distinction was the defence of the Fortress which properly bears his name. I should have been content with this. Certainly, however, when the village received the same name, it should have been enough. If the defence of the Fort still demanded such expressions of gratitude, something surely was due to Rutledge, by whose orders, by whose determined will, the Fort was defended, even in spite of the commanding general, Charles Lee, who insisted that it should be given up. "I will cut off my right arm," said Rutledge, "before I will write such an order!" But we scarcely honor a great man, by christening a hotel after him. If hotels are to be named after persons, I should prefer to honor thus, some individual who had distinguished himself in the *cuisine*. The inventor of a famous sauce might thus be honored. Monsieur Ude, for example, or Hannah Glass, would be proper claimants for selection. Certainly, the *objects of the house*, should be considered in its designation—Moultrie, Marion, Sumter—are all good names for ships of war and fortresses. Let us keep them for these higher purposes. Let us not degrade them by making them unnecessarily frequent. You remember the peasant, who gave as a reason for voting Aristides into banishment, that he was tired of continually being reminded of the justice of that citizen. We, of the low country, have been offending our interior by continually insisting upon our favorites. They are the capital of which we boast to others, however much we may neglect their claims at home. It has grown to be a proverb in the interior—"It is only a Charleston affair." Let us not offend any prejudices, unless, by so doing, we can cure them; but this was never recognized as the proper process. Now, regarding the objects of the Hotel—its situation, the peculiarities of the scene, and the latent purposes had in view by the proprietors, I should have studiously rejected the names of persons in this choice. Here is an establishment beside the sea—it is the only great ocean summering place from Cape May to the Mississippi; it is really the great ocean refuge of the South, a central point from the Chesapeake to the Gulf, as healthy as any place in the world; very beautiful to the eye; very grateful to the physique; a point easy of approach, by railroad and steamer, from every quarter in the South—the ocean point, *par excellence*, along a thousand miles of coast! This is the idea to keep in view while naming the Hotel. Thousands of the people of the interior who will naturally seek such a retreat in summer, have never beheld the ocean.—The idea of its vast wilderness of wave is to them as vague and imposing as to a low countryman the idea of a mountain country. They seek it as *an ocean retreat*, and so I would have named the Hotel. Our Poet, in his poem, descriptive of the scene, speaking of the village, seems to me to have hit upon a phrase which would have better suited than any other, at once novel, euphonious and highly significant—the "Ocean Hamlet; or "Ocean House," or "Ocean Retreat," should have been the name; and names are things. They fall upon the ear with a force to which we do not yield sufficient credit. The ear will tire of a too frequent name; while the force of an appropriate and grateful name will be suggestive of fancies which work upon the mind with all the strength of an affection. But enough. I would have had it otherwise.

Editor.—It is evident, Father, that you attach considerable importance to this establishment.—You regard it for its effects, apart from its obvious uses?

Abbot.—It is something gained. It is one more step to our emancipation. It is a gain upon our former condition. It will do something towards curing us of that self-disparaging weakness, that of *absenteeism.* It is the infirmity of a provincial people that they have no faith in home. Let us prove that even the follies and fancies of home, can have their charm quite as well as those of other people. But the Hotel proves something more. You remember what is said of that Saint, I forget which, who, when his head was off, walked with it for half a mile under his arm. To prove that he only took the first three steps, in this condition, is sufficient for my faith. I require you to prove nothing more. Now, when you show me Carolina going into her own manufactures, sending her own ships upon the sea, and providing for her own people home places for refuge, you show me the first three steps taken towards an indefinite progress; and I care nothing then whether she carries her head under her arm or upon her shoulders. I feel that she must go *ahead*, at all events. The progress is begun. The apathy is at an end. There is no more stagnation; and even a thunder storm may be considered grateful, as it relieves the atmosphere, and shows the presence of a real and active principle of life. Our ships now move daily over the waters. Our harbors resound with the volumes of escaping steam. Never was there more competition for our trade. And our steam shuttles begin to make such a music, as guarantees us against "a little more folding of the hands to slumber." Be sure that other sounds and signs will follow, significant equally of pleasure and business. This little bridge uniting Haddrell and the Island must be built. Our country friends from Columbia, Camden, Augusta and Greenville, will demand it. You have no ideas of the beauties of the country to which it will conduct—leading you to the banks of the Wando, and affording a thousand pleasant rambles and retreats to the summer idler. You will probably have a railway from this very Hotel to Mount Pleasant, where it looks down from its yellow hills upon the City, and where I hope soon to see more than one Cotton Factory in full blast. All these points and headlands, these islets and promontories, will become, as I have said before, gay and lovely hamlets adorning the harbor. We will pass from point to point—from river to river, and I feel sure that you will see among other improvements, a noble bridge spanning the broad Ashley itself, and uniting the Neck to St. Andrew's Parish—the very region which should be covered with smiling farms and marked by the most productive tillage.

Editor.—A bridge across the Ashley, Father?

Abbot.—And why not?

Editor.—One would suppose, Father, that the unsatisfactory result of the first, and most expensive experiment, would suffice to discourage all further enterprises of this sort.

Abbot.—Really, I see not why it should. A bridge was built, and blown away, in one of the most destructive gales that was ever witnessed.—Should that discourage from future efforts? We know that ships, by the hundreds, are annually lost at sea, in squall and tempest. But who acknowledges this as a sufficient reason to forego the future building of merchantmen and men of war? Hurricanes and tornadoes have swept the very bed of Ashley river and the harbor to the bottom. One of peculiar terror and power is recorded by our early historians. It laid the ocean bare to its secret gulfs, and many noble ships were torn from their anchorage, and scattered in wreck and fragment along the shores. But what merchant ever dreams of avoiding the usually safe harborage of the bay of Charleston? There is nothing in the objection to a new bridge over the Ashley, because of the destruction of the old one. But the old bridge deserves no mention for another reason. It was a miserable trap-stick affair, badly conceived and badly built. I have it from old inhabitants, that it swayed perceptibly with the waves, even before it was torn up by the tempest. The piles were never driven below the mud. Modern science, and improved experience, would not be content with such an apology for a bridge. We should now drive our piles, shod with iron for the purpose, deep down into the marl itself, which forms the rocky and fast bed of the river. You have seen, the newly invented machine for driving piles, worked by steam, which is even now employed upon the causeway of the bridge, in repairing it? The ranging timber, sticks forty feet in length, and of corresponding thickness, are grasped by the iron antennæ of the instrument, are whirled aloft, without effort, and are driven down by a relentless stroke from a mall weighing eighteen hundred pounds. The shaft *must* go down—*must* bury itself in the marl—or must be shivered into splinters. It cannot help but take steadfast root in the rocky basin, and the tempest that tears it up must tear up the very bed of the river.

EDITOR.—But such a bridge, Father, must be very expensive. Where is the money to come from?

ABBOT.—Not so expensive as you may imagine. I understand that there are enterprising and ingenius architects prepared already to undertake the work: prepared to contract for its full performance, at a cost not exceeding *sixty thousand dollars.*

EDITOR.—Can this be possible?

ABBOT.—It is true! You will scarcely ask where such a sum is to be found. I can tell you, my son, that the money is ready for the work, and can be forthwith coming, in three weeks, if necessary. It needs but the movement; nothing more than the first step made in the business, and the performance follows. And it should have been done long ago. The old bridge, if am rightly instructed, worthless as it was, cost at least *one hundred and twenty thousand dollars*, raised almost in the infancy of our commerce. What ought we to do now, when our harbor is crowded with new and splendid sea steamers from every great port in the Union. When an immense line of railways, brings us to the trade of a measureless interior; and when a noble enterprise is already planning that which is necessary to the full success of our efforts—a direct steam intercourse with the great maritime cities of Europe? My son, the City of Charleston should link herself directly with every neighborhood, which can be made tributary to the farmer and the grazier. This country, south of us in particular, is admirably endowed with rich soils and a most fructifying climate, for the purposes of tillage. It is the natural tributary of the City. The whole of it, in process of time, those portions only excepted which are specially adapted to the culture of rice and the finer cottons—will be converted into farms; the production of which will not only render us independent of our Northern and Western neighbors, as respects grain, forage, vegetables, butter and cattle, but will be able to supply the earlier productions of the spring and summer, through the means of daily steamboats, to the cities of the North. We know how large, comparatively speaking, is the business already done in this respect. But the increase will be absolutely immeasurable and incomputable, when improved facilities to market shall have persuaded our planters along the Ashley and the Stono, to embark in the more lucrative business. What must be the effect of this, but the increased value of lands in these quarters, and a denser population? With a denser population, comes drainage; and, with improved agriculture, the use and absorption, into manures, of all refuse vegetable matter. Here we behold the the secret of salubrity in soil and climate; and all St. Andrew's may be made quite as healthy as Charleston and the Neck. What farther follows, from the introduction of this new system? Why, that the City builds up its back country population at its own doors; and the State keeps within its own limits, diffused among its own people, the hundreds of thousands,—nay millions,—which we annually send abroad for commodities, all of which ought to be raised at home. The money which you send North and West, for grain, forage, butter, potatoes horses, mules and cattle, never knows returning ebb. Not a dollar ever comes back to us. But, if we can create a population at our own back doors, which shall supply these commodities, all this money finds its way necessarily to the City, which can never fear a competitor as the domestic market of the State. Convert the lower districts into a farming region, with a tolerably dense population, and you save two millions annually to the State, which we now send out never to return. The Bridge over Ashley will contribute largely to this result. It is one of the most important steps in the career of local improvement. It supersedes a most tedious and expensive mode of travel. It invites and opens the way to travel; and other improvements hereafter, to continue from this, may even bring you a large and valuable wagon trade, from the middle counties of Georgia along the Savannah River.

Editor.—Certainly, the present mode of ferriage, its expensiveness and frequent and vexatious delays, have led to the temporary abandonment, by the people of the interior, of one of the most delightful and eligible roads conducting to the City.

Abbot.—No doubt of it. The complaints are endless in respect to the present system. Suppose you confine your view to the simple andvantages of *a drive* across the river and into the country? You may visit the Stono; you may stroll through the venerable precincts of St. Andrew's Church; you may take your dinner at Rantoule's, catch your own fish, and be back in the City in season for an early supper. And this over one of the finest roads in our low country—through most splendid natural avenues, in sight of lovely farmsteads, with the fruits of the season inviting you at every step, the song of birds to welcome you with music, and the gayest wild flowers to regale your eyes with beauty, and your nostrils with perfume. Only make the passage of the Ashley certain, at all hours, and make it cheap, and all the neighboring country becomes a garden; the farms become subdivided, cultivation becomes thorough, and the soil, under a good manuring system, is made to develope resources such as will surpass all expectation. The materials for vegetable manures are enormous through all this region. The miserable error, of which our people have been guilty, in all times past, has been that they destroyed the value of their works—their luxuries and necessaries alike, by the excessive prices which they put upon their enjoyment and use. They charged as if they were determined always to make the consumer feel that they were luxuries; overlooking the fact that no man, not even the wealthiest, lives habitually on luxuries. The proper process was to make the luxuries necessaries. This could only be done by making them cheap. When the "New Bridge" was opened, a natural curiosity led the carriage of the citizen, once or twice, across its arches, at a cost of a couple of dollars the trip! How often, at such a price, could he indulge in such a pleasure? Cupidity, like ambition, thus too frequently defeats its own objects. While one citizen made the journey at this expense, a hundred who would have relished it also, were compelled to turn up their noses, and cry "sour grapes." But what would be the effect, think you, in regard to the uses of such a bridge across the Ashley, if the four-wheel carriage paid twenty-five cents, and the two-wheel half that price; the horseman a fourth; and the foot passenger, but three cents; leaving the heavy wagon to pay fifty cents, and the loaded cart twenty-five? Why, the whole City would throng into St. Andrew's. Each would have his turn and come often. As a drive, and as a walk, it would become equally fashionable; and there is no pleasure so grateful to man as that which he enjoys under the reflection that his indulgence trenches upon no resources which can be illy spared from his necessities. I would guarantee the stock, the bridge costing not more than $60,000, as the very best in the country.

EDITOR.—Ah! Father, shall we, indeed, realize these glowing predictions?

ABBOT.—Why not? I tell you, my son, the ball is in motion. Our people have shaken off their slumbers, and it is one of the inevitable characteristics of a popular progress, that, once fairly begun, it goes through its cycle of performance, for fifty years at least, before it sleeps again. The truth is, a great moral amalgam has taken place in our society, the affinities of which enforce progress. You will live to see the promise realized. You will behold the City, and all its tributary islets, and shores, and waters, and fountains, linked together by indissoluble bands of iron. You will see this goodly city, seated by the sea, sending forth her messengers, winged by steam and sail, to the remote and mighty cities of the old world! You will see the internal resources of our vast interior finding their way to profitable exchanges, through this medium. You will see our people, instead of gaping at foreign towns and crowded cities of the East, listless, and without hope or occupation, concentrating all their energies, whether for business or pleasure, in and about the sacred precincts of home. There shall they discover, not only that they have a business to execute, a profitable labor and a duty which love delights in, but pleasures to enjoy, more exquisite, and more legitimate, than any that could be found abroad. We have discoursed in vain upon these subjects, my son, if it is needful that I should recapitulate our frequent conversations. But my words are so many prophecies. The work is fairly begun, and our people are rapidly discovering "the Home Secret"—the secret of true worth, true wealth, true pleasure, and true virtue. Let us return.—Our Brother Bonhommie signals us from Prospect Hill.

XVI.

The night was one of eminent beauty. The winds were light but lively. The moon, unembarrassed by a clond, was making her smiling way through the heavens; and the broad expanse of ocean, smooth as a lawn of silver, lay basking in her beams. The gay sands were glistening with a thousand pleasant fires. The village of Moultrie stretched away towards the West, showing like a fairy hamlet; while a solitary light revealed the distant City, sleeping serenely beneath the guardian watch of her ascending steeples. Immediately in the rear of Prospect Hill, a green and grateful stretch of forest lay in shadow, but not gloomily, touched, as were the tops of its oaks and myrtles, with the hallowing wand of moonlight. Such was the scene to which we were summoned by our considerate host and Brother, Bonhommie. He had spread his table for supper on the little white eminence of Prospect Hill, its brows partially encircled by a little coronet of myrtles. We shall not describe the supper, which was served in the best style of a taste that knew admirably how to mingle the delicate and the persuasive in his feasts. Coffee and tea were the essential spirits, and the venerable maid, Estifania, who keeps the keys at our Brother's farmstead, had shown herself singularly ambitious of securing the favor of the fraternity, being particularly desirous of the patriarchal blessing at the hands of our Holy Father Abbot. Her beverages were unexceptionable, and the accompanying cakes and cates, won the general approbation. Our Father was sad, however, and did not dilate with his usual fervor. It is probable that he has felt disquieted at the prospect of soon departing from a scene which we had all enjoyed with a pleasure having no qualifications. The same sentiment prevailed somewhat with the rest of the brotherhood. Beauclerk, in especial, was evidently humbled by remorse, at the unnatural feeling which had possessed him, though for a moment

o2

only, in regard to the Father Abbot. He was, no doubt, troubled by an anxious apprehension, lest the Father should have heard his language after dinner, in which he showed himself restive under that paternal authority which had kept his wild impulses in check. But there was no gloom in the assembly, as there was no asceticism in the speech of the Holy Father. The supper was gratefully discussed, and Brother Bonhommie was the happiest of men, at the tribute paid to his taste and hospitality. He absolutely wept when he heard the Father remind the brotherhood that the next morning was the time appointed for their departure from the Island. It is impossible to describe his satisfaction, however, the moment after, when one of the brethren reminded the Father that the next day was the Sabbath.

Abbot.—Then we shall remain another day, my children; and, with brother Bonhommie's permission, we shall discourse to the fraternity in the sacred groves which lie east of his dwelling.

Bonhommie.—Every thing shall be prepared, Father, for the occasion. At an early hour, chairs shall be carried out for the purpose. There is a peculiar sweetness and solemnity in hearkening to the words of truth and soberness in the deep silence of sheltering woods.

Poet.—The groves, we are told, were God's first temples.

Abbot.—Thou hast a hymn, dear son, descriptive of the Forest Worship. It shall be chaunted on the occasion. It is one particularly suited to the purpose; and as all discourse should be appropriate, not only to the spiritual, but to the human condition of man, adapted not only to his particular nature, but to the circumstances and necessities of his life, so will I endeavor to encourage our Brother Bonhommie in the career which he has so lately taken up, by dilating upon the characteristics and essential attributes of "The Good Farmer."

BEAUCLERK.—Don't you think, Father, that brother Bonhommie might establish here a successful vineyard? Don't you think that the vine ought to flourish here on the side of the sandy hillocks?

ABBOT.—Undoubtedly: and the suggestion is worthy of consideration. There is one law which should encourage frequent experiment in agriculture. It is found in the fact that *it is in the soul of man*, rather than the soil in which he works, that his fruits must first flourish. And it is difficult to say what climate or situation could prove itself inaccessible to the determined energies of the human intellect. The mind is remarkable in no respect more than by its so readily accommodating itself to the most adverse scenes and situations. Received directly from Divinity, designed, in however remote a degree, to resemble the nature of the Deity himself, it is of that commanding and conquering quality, as to subject all soils and all circumstances to its imperial progress. It adapts the man to all climates, and may in like manner, adapt the fruits of all climates to the particular situation in which his lot has been cast.—The earth and all its creatures were decreed to obey his will. No skies can repel or discourage, no condition always baffle, or entirely defeat, the man of equal thought and energy. Unite these, and it is wonderful how much the individual may achieve to his own astonishment.

POET.—The history of the vine itself, Father, will abundantly illustrate this truth.

ABBOT.—Yes, indeed! If any sceptic among us shall apprehend that cold and capricious seasons here, will discourage the vegetation, and defeat the growth, of the rich and delicate fruits born under the blue skies and generous suns of of Italy and France, let him hear the account of these same fruits from the eloquent pen of Gibbon. He tells us that "it would be almost impossible to enumerate all the articles, either of the animal or vegetable region, which were successfully imported into Europe from Asia and Egypt. Almost all the flowers, the herbs and the fruits, that grow in the European garden, are of foreign extraction. The apple was a native of Italy, and when the Romans had tasted of the rich flavor of the apricot, the peach, the pomegranate, the citron and the orange, they contented themselves with applying to all these new fruits the common denomination of apple, discriminating them from each other by the additional epithet of the country. In the time of Homer, the vine grew wild in the Island of Sicily, and most probably, in the adjacent continent, but it was not improved by the skill, nor did it afford a liquor grateful to the taste, of the savage inhabitants. A thousand years afterwards, Italy could boast that of the fourscore most generous and celebrated wines, more than two-thirds were produced from her soil. The blessing was soon communicated to the Narbonnese province of Gaul; but so intense was the cold to the north of the Cevennes, that, in the time of Strabo, it was thought impossible to ripen the grapes in those parts of Gaul. This difficulty, however, was gradually vanquished; and there is some reason to believe, that the vineyards of Burgundy are as old as the age of the Antonines. The olive in the western world followed the progress of peace, of which it was the symbol. Two centuries after the foundation of Rome, both Italy and Africa were strangers to that useful plant. It was naturalized in those countries, and at length carried into the heart of Spain and Gaul. The timid errors of the ancients, that it required a certain degree of heat, and could only flourish in the neighborhood of the sea, were insensibly exploded by industry and experience. The cultivation of flax was transported from Egypt to Gaul, and enriched the whole country, however it might impoverish the particular lands on which it was sown. The use of artificial grasses became familiar to the farmers both of Italy and the Provinces, particularly the Lucerne, which derived its name and origin from Medea. The assured supply of wholesome and plentiful food for the cattle during winter, multiplied the number of the flocks and herds, which, in their turn, contributed to the fertility of the soil"—and so forth.

Bonhommie.—Is it impossible! How encouraging, all this, dear Father, to a young beginner!

Beauclerk.—Brother Bonhommie has now a motive and a duty, at once before him. What a glorious triumph, if he shall succeed in covering those sand hills with the Scuppernong and the Isabella grapes. And why should he not? The whole southern slope of this range, might be made to flourish with the vine, which, springing up in the soil in the opposite side, would readily clamber over to this.

Bonhommie.—I shall certainly try it.

Beauclerk.—I have seen the Malaga, Father, produce fruit in our interior in four years after the planting of the seed.

Bonhommie.—I shall try them all.

Abbot.—And you will do well. The duty of the good farmer is frequent experiment—experiment so urged as not to interfere with his regular operations, yet so fairly urged as to leave him in no doubt as to the soundness of his conclusions.—The whole chapter which Gibbon devotes to this department of Roman economy, will well reward perusal. There is much even in this brief passage which deserves our consideration. If we do not suffer those "*timid errors*" of which he speaks, to keep us in perpetual bondage to the circumscribed condition of our present agriculture, we shall probably discover that our soil and climate are quite as congenial to the introduction of foreign products as those of any portion of the ancient world. We have, indeed, every variety of soil and surface.—The aspects of our country, in the three grand divisions of the State, are sufficiently diversified for every form of cultivation—and we are already rich in native and exotic productions, which only need that art should do her duty, in compliance with the suggestions of nature, to make them equal to any like objects of culture, in any other portion of the world. But we must beware of that "timid ignorance" which does nothing, under the convenient belief, which is always the argument of the slothful, that nothing can be done. Nothing is done, and nothing can be done, by those who doubt the ability of man—man, the appointed agent of God on earth—to do all things that God has ever yet permitted man to do. The earth is ours by the Eternal Bounty—but she does not yield up her treasures to the timid or the base. She has no fruits for the slothful. We must grapple her to our arms with a manly vigor, and compel the surrender of her virgin treasures.

Poet.—What says the Roman Poet—the agricultural moralist of Rome in the Augustan period?

"Not to dull ignorance, or transient toil,
Great Jove vouchsafed the conquest of the soil;
He bade sharp care make keen the heart, nor deigned
That sloth should linger where his God had reigned."

Abbot.—Appropriately quoted, my son. Let us not forget, in referring to the passage taken from Gibbon, that the regions of France and Spain which were considered so unfriendly to the grape and the olive, are those very regions from which we now receive these fruits in the greatest perfection. The rich red wines of Burgundy, come from those very grapes which, it was feared, could not be ripened under the severely cold temperature of that region: and Spain and France are now ranked among the favorite and native gardens of the olive. Gibbon remarks that, in the time of Homer, the vine grew wild in Sicily, but that it was not improved by the skill, nor did it afford a liquor grateful to the tastes of the savage inhabitants.—Could the vine grow more luxuriously, could it twine itself anywhere more lasciviously around the forest trees, than in Carolina and Georgia—in greater abundance, or in more fruitful variety? Impossible! our swamp and forest margins are wondrous to behold, at the opening of spring, and in the maturing embraces of the summer, in their luscious and liberal exhibitions of every sort of wild grape. Let us not expose ourselves to the bitter sarcasm which Gibbon inflicts upon the Sicilians. How keenly would our children, of the seventh and tenth generation, feel the reproach of the Historian, who, a hundred years hence, might relate that, "in the time of President Taylor, under the local administrations of Governors Seabrook, of South-Carolina, and Towns, of Georgia, the vine grew wild in these and other States of the great American Confederacy, particularly in the Southern portions, but was not improved by the skill, nor did it afford a liquor grateful to the tastes of the savage inhabitants."

EDITOR.—He might add that, in more Northern latitudes, naturally less favorable to its growth, it was rendered more successful, nay, made to produce in abundance, under the working and restless energies of a people, who were compelled to supply, with constant industry, the deficiencies of a sterile soil and an unfriendly climate. The Scuppernong, a native of the South, receives its more successful culture in the North; while Ohio is already manufacturing more Champagne in one season, than France exports in a dozen.

Poet.—I am afraid, Father, that the wonderful developments of gold in California will materially serve to injure our agriculture.

Abbot.—I hope not. I think not. It is only the diseased appetite, that is drawn away from the homestead by such temptations; the feverish discontent, the hungering thirst, that would seldom have done any good at home; and most of these poor adventurers will be wrecked and ruined in their search. It will require wonderful energies, and still more wonderful capacities of endurance, to succeed in the mines of California; and success itself is destined, with the greater number, to produce the bitterest fruits, like those fabulous apples of Sodom, lovely and luscious to the eye, but full of dust and ashes within. What a delusion is this search!

Poet.—An age of Gold?

Abbot.—Iron, rather, my son! We must not confound a figure with a fact. In the imaginative world, gold serves the purpose of a noble illustration. In the actual, it only degrades the imagination.

Beauclerk.—Was there ever a period which could properly deserve the name of the age of Gold?

Abbot.—I think so! Yes! The period fancifully denominated the "age of gold," was not one of simple fiction. It had its date and existence, without doubt, in the progress of every primitive nation. It was unquestionably that period when the great majority of mankind was engaged in agriculture—when there was no strife of commercial enterprise—when the jealousies of trade provoked not to war, and its attractions seduced none from the paths of industry—before cunning had sapped the strength from manhood, and baseness had corrupted the soul of magnanimity! Agriculture, being expressly a divine institution, had the natural effect of subduing the passions of men, of regulating their appetites, promoting gentleness, harmony, and universal peace among them. The earth was enriched by judicious cultivation, and the population of the world was necessarily and proportionately increased as Cowper writes:

> "Their harvests over swell
> The sower's hopes: their trees o'erladen, scarce
> Their fruit sustain; no sickness thins the folds:
> The finny swarms of ocean crowd the shores,
> And all are rich and happy."

The principles of agriculture were simple, exceedingly. That they might be made so, God, himself, was the great first planter.* He wrote its laws, visibly, in the brightest, and loveliest, and most intelligible characters, everywhere, upon

* Milton—"The Sovran Planter."

the broad bosom of the liberal earth; in greenest leaves, in delicate fruits, in beguiling and balmy flowers! But he does not content himself with this alone. He bestows the heritage along with the example. He prepares the garden and the home, before he creates the being who is to possess them. He fills them with all those objects of sense and sentiment which are to supply his moral and physical necessities. Birds sing in the boughs above him, odors blossom in the air, and fruits and flowers cover the earth with a glory, to which that of Solomon in all his magnificence, was vain and valueless. To His hand we owe these fair groves, these tall ranks of majestic trees these deep forests, these broad plains covered with verdure, and these mighty arteries of flood and river, which wind among them, beautifying them with the loveliest inequalities, and irrigating them with seasonable fertilization. Thus did the Almighty Planter dedicate the great plantation to the uses of that various and wondrous family which was to follow. His home prepared—supplied with all resources, adorned with every variety of fruit and flower, and checkered with abundance, man is conducted within its pleasant limits, and ordained its cultivator under the very eye and sanction of Heaven. The angels of Heaven descend upon its hills; God, himself appears within its vallies at noonday—its groves are instinct with life and purity, and the blessed stars rise at night above the celestial mountains, to keep watch over its consecrated interests. Its gorgeous forests, its broad savannahs, its levels of flood and prairie, are surrendered into the hands of the wondrously favored, the new created heir of Heaven! The bird and the beast are made his tributaries, and taught to obey him. The fowl summons him at morning to his labors, and the evening chaunt of the night bird warns him to repose. The ox submits his neck to the yoke; the horse moves at his bidding in the plough; and the toils of all are rendered sacred and successful by the gentle showers and the genial sunshine which descend from Heaven, to ripen the grain in its season, and to make earth pleasant with its fruits.

Poet.—Verily, that was a golden period, indeed!

Beauclerk.—Gold, itself, unknown! This is a still more encouraging picture, brother Bonhommie. Remember the grapes! *(aside.)*

Abbot.—The origin of agriculture being thus dignified, the art was pursued by the Grey Fathers of the infant earth! Its kings and princes drove the harrow, and dropped the grain, and danced, with songs of thanksgiving, around the harvest. Their exercises continued to ennoble it; and, for ages, the destinies of the world were happily committed to the hands of men, whose chief distinction lay in their superior use of the sickle and the ploughshare. These were patriarchal ages. Toil, then, if a duty, was no less an unadulterated blessing. Nothing can exceed the sweetness which and felicity with the poets expatiate upon this happy period. They sang, in its praises, without qualification, that it gave health to the body, strength to the frame, energy to the will, and nobleness to the purpose—that it conducted temperance, pure desires, devout thought, and becoming patriotism—that it inspired happy feelings among the people, brought the young together in fruitful marriage, and blessed the eyes of the patriarchal fathers with glimpses of a third and fourth generation. These were the very days of Astræa—the days of peace, and sunshine, and innocent myrth; of a long life of youth, unembittered by disease—health to the last; and when death drew nigh, his approach was gentle and kind, like that of some friendly attendant, who lets down the curtains around us, and soothes us to repose. The toils of the day in this happy period, were begun and closed in music. The shepherds led their flocks over the mountains, to the delicious strains of flute and flageolet—drew them together by the same process when they wandered, and, with a like summons, compelled them to follow homeward at the approach of evening.

Poet.—Will California ever realize such a picture! Portions of it must have done so—the great valley of the Sacramento—portions of it without doubt, but for this terrible discovery of metallic wealth. Proceed, Father.

Abbot.—Such, no doubt, was the golden age of every primitive people. Unhappily, it was of short duration only. Man seems to possess an inherent quality of discontent, which perhaps, is one of the strong proofs, apart from revelation, of the immortality of the soul. His flute, with which the shepherd led his flocks to pasture, became, in the process of time, the agent of a sterner influence.

That which had been the chosen voice of love, now spoke in louder language at the requisition of hate! The herdsmen and shepherds, when they became warriors, went into battle,

> "In perfect phalanx to the Dorian mood,
> Of flutes and soft recorders."

Hence the origin of martial music. The plaintive notes which had led the shepherds and their kine, and responded to their doubts and hopes, in melodious murmurs which betokened gentleness and peace, were now exchanged for those of angry warfare, wild passions, and insatiate ambition.

> "So violence
> Proceeded, and oppression and sword law,
> Through all the plain."

The application of an agent, once so innocent, whose only language, hitherto, had been that of love, to the purposes of strife and aggression, betrays, of itself, how large and how sudden was the change which had taken place in the minds and condition of the people. But this belongs, seemingly, to the usual, if not the natural order of events. The age of Iron had succeeded to that of Gold. Sterner feelings and passions overthrew the simplicities which had hitherto characterized the primitive races of the earth; even as the stronger appetites and desires of the man overgrow and absorb those, more gentle and limited, which prevail in the bosom of the child. Change naturally follows in the paths of prosperity, and the very accumulation of wealth occasions new desires, and suggests new necessities. When men had so far advanced in art as to be enabled to tame and gather within their folds the wild herds of the plain and prairie, a portion of their numbers was necessarily withdrawn from the cultivation of the earth and assigned the duties of herdsmen. These were required to contend with the yet unsubdued monsters of the wilderness, to grapple with the Asiatic tiger, the swarthy and fierce lion of the Numidian deserts, and to level their sharp arrows at the breast of the vulture of the Caucasus. The herdsman consequently became the hunter, and the use of arms brought with it a passion for their exercise. The world soon became filled with a class, of whom Nimrod, that mighty hunter before the Lord, is a sufficient sample. The transition was not difficult, from hunting the wild beast of the forest, to hunting MAN! and WAR became the next and natural employment of the hunter. It was not easy for men, who had been accustomed, for years, to rove at will, in pursuit of their prey, to fall back, after their final conquest of the common enemy, upon the peaceful and regular employments of agricultural life. The occupation was too tame, too wanting in those excitements, the desire for which had become habitual, in consequence of their employment; and they yearned for the licentious pleasures of their wild and warlike pastimes. They had tasted the sweets of power—they had acquired the appetite for blood—they felt their strength—knew the weakness of the peaceful and unsuspecting farmer, and they selected him as their victim. He was more profitable as a victim, and far less to be feared as an enemy, than the lion of Numidia. The grain was no sooner ripened than the warlike tribes descended from the mountains to the plains, and gathered their harvests with the sword. Vainly did the farmer strive to defend his possessions. The savage, inured to arms, and delighting in their exercise, was necessarily triumphant. Butchery followed, and the devasted fields grew fat in the blood of those who could till them no longer. Who shall predict or limit the penalties which flow from every departure from the imperious line of duty? These crimes, this fatality, were the inevitable result, accruing from the adoption, by the herdsman, as a trade and occupation, of one of the incidental necessities of his condition. The first ordinances of the Deity were forgotten. The decree of labor, pronounced by the Creator as a judgment, has ever been borne, except for the brief and blessed period described in the "Age of Gold," with discontent by the creature. The herdsman, too gladly becomes the hunter; the hunter, the warrior; the warrior, the robber; and the peaceful farmer, who feeds all, becomes the common victim. Hence, the desertion of fields, the depopulation of countries, the desecration of altars, the famine, the slaughter and unmitigated misery and devastation on every hand! In due proportion, as the pursuits of agriculture become insecure, the races of men decline. This is the unerring law of God's providence, and the unerring consequence of man's disobedience. It cannot well be otherwise; and with the decline of a population will be the equally certain decline of prosperity and happiness.

Poet.—We have an apt illustration from Goldsmith, Father—The Deserted Village.

"Ill fares the land to hastening ills the prey,
Where wealth accumulates and men decay;
Princes and Lords may flourish or may fade,
A breath can make them as a breath has made;
But a bold peasantry, their country's pride,
When once destroy'd can never be supplied."

Abbot.—It is through this process that most empires have been overthrown. The simplicity of the race has been lost, the more innocent appetites superseded by such as bring the worst passions into mastery. Such has been the common history. With the lapse of the patriarchal ages, Asia, the first and loveliest garden of the earth, became a desert, or something worse; Africa, a land of howling cannibals, which it must long continue; and when—

Beauclerk.—Do you note, Father, the recent discovery of men with tails in that country?

Abbot.—Yes, my son, but your suggestion would have kept until I had finished my sentence.

Beauclerk.—Hem!

Abbot.—And when, in the progress of pursuing centuries, Europe grew maddened with the perpetual and exhausting strifes between the spoiler, and the Providence of God vouchsafed America as a new land of promise, and of refuge to the fugitive, what was then the melancholy history? Did the story undergo a change? The colonists had glimpses there of a golden period of peace, but it was golden no longer. The iron age had succeeded to that of gold with the Peruvian and the Aztec, and the European colonists were not of a character to make any change from worse to better. In the region occupied by our immediate ancestors they found a wilderness, but it was not a peaceful one. Even here, the same bitter seeds had been sown, the same poisonous fruit eaten, and death was the consequence. The same inevitable fate had followed the same wilful disobedience of mankind. The departure from those holy laws which enjoined industry and blessed with abundance, had produced among the red men of the new world, the same profitless scenes of strife and carnage which had distinguished the career of the ancestral nations. It was the wretched boast of the American savage, that he was the conqueror of the country! that he had invaded a numerous and highly civilized people—that he had ravaged their fields; sacked and destroyed their walled places; and, having consumed the common enemy, had, at length, in the absence of all other victims turned the barbed edges of his thirsty tomahawk upon his own brother. But what was the history of the people thus destroyed? Were they wise—were they virtuous? For what unhappy sins had the Deity delivered them into the power of their wild invaders? Had they become inert in the accumulation of superfluous wealth? Did they disregard the wholesome laws of their creation? Did famine enfeeble their energies; or, in the sweet peacefulness of a golden age, that disarmed every domestic enemy, did they become heedless of those dangers which might follow the sudden presence of a foreign one? Perhaps, if we might trace the tale of their fortunes to its source, it would not be unlike that of all the rest! There was strife among themselves, which facilitated the progress of the invader, and sharpened his arrows. Faction strove with faction for the treasures of the commonwealth, or, which is the same, for its control. Then perished the public liberties. Then labor became a mercenary, and changed his ploughshare for the deadly brand of battle. Then industry and art were dispossessed of their fruits, and so, dishonored; and the city grew rank and ready for any pollution. When its suburban fields flourished no longer in smiling yellow, beneath the mellowing signs of the autumnal heavens, its golden age was gone—gone for ever! Then was it only fitting that the mountain robber should descend to the harvest that was ready to his hands. So long as he heard from its busy streets the clink of the morning hammer, and beheld the keen scythe throughout the long hours of the autumnal day, so long did he tremble to encounter the muscular hands which grasped them. But when these tokens of sure strength and manly virtue were withdrawn, then did he know that the age of Iron was begun. Toil had given place to cunning, and barriers of moral and physical defence were all swept away.

The story is everywhere the same. It admits

of no variation. The golden age is the age of agricultural pre-eminence. The nation whose sons shrink from the culture of its fields, will wither for long ages under the imperial sway of Iron. It may put on a face of brass, but its legs will be made of clay. It may hide its lean cheeks, and all external signs of its misery, under the harlotry of art; but the rottenness of death will be all the while revelling upon its vitals, and a poisonous breath will go forth from its decay, which will spread its loathsome taint along the shores of other and happier and unsuspecting nations!

BEAUCLERK, *(aside to Poet)*—He has positively given us a sermon.

BONHOMMIE.—Father, I have prepared a little display of fireworks.

ABBOT.—Fireworks! In the moonlight?

BONHOMMIE.—No, Father, we will descend to the deep shade of this thicket. Our rockets only shall be sent up from the hills. You will be surprised at the exquisite effect of such a display on the Island.

ABBOT.—I can conceive it, heightened by an unembarrassed plain of earth and sky, by the free flight of the breezes, by the broad expanse of ocean, to say nothing of its wild chaunt, by way of musical accompaniment. When the new Hotel is built, the Town Council will need to make an appropriation for a display of Pyrotechnics every fourth of July, and Twenty-Eighth of June. Lead the way, brother Bonhommie.

BONHOMMIE.—Take my arm, Father. We will descend this gorge, from the foot of which I have opened a private avenue to our little forest. I shall conduct you through the "myrtle labyrinth."

[*Ex. Father Abbot, &c.*

Manent, Beauclerk and Editor.

BEAUCLERK.—Hist, brother Editor. We have had rather a long siege of it—rather a dry discourse, and I need some consolation. Step with me into this hollow. See what a bower we have here among the myrtles.

EDITOR.—What are you after?

BEAUCLERK.—*(showing a bottle)*—Do you see what fruits these sand hills yield. Said I not that this was the region for the grape to flourish in.

EDITOR.—Champagne!

BEAUCLERK.—A single bottle, which we may discuss together while our Holy Father gropes his way through the thickets. He has all the passion of a school boy for fireworks, and will not miss us. And now—smack! It is one of the drawbacks to the luxury of Champagne that it will always make due report of its own excellences.

ABBOT.—*(suddenly reappearing)*—Only when the creature is good, my son! If vain of its excellence, it has grounds for being so—not always the case with those who consume it. Fill the glass for your Father, Beauclerk, and congratulate yourself that I do not fine you a basket for this pernicious habit of enjoying your pleasures selfishly. Take this counsel also, my son, and be always sure that the master is quite out of hearing, when you undo the wire.

BEAUCLERK.—*(aside)*—The Heathen Turk!

The event passed off good humoredly, and the fire-works brilliantly. We retired early and rose with the red-bird,—rather prematurely awakened I allow, by the screams of an enormous pea-fowl, which is one of the pets of Brother Bonhommie. From the dwelling to the sea was but a bound and plunge, and we were soon ready for the events of the day. Breakfast discussed, we adjourned to a thick copse beneath the sand hills, and there listened to a most refreshing discourse from Father Abbot, as he had promised, on the qualities and characteristics of the good farmer—a discourse fashioned in his peculiar way, and mingling equally the practical with the contemplative and spiritual. This discourse was followed by an admirable hymn, written by our Poet, descriptive and laudatory of forest worship. The day was spent in pleasant and serious conversation of a kind not unsuited to its equally grateful and sacred import. The next day witnessed our exodus. It was an event full of interest and excitement. The Town Council attended us to the steamer, and we could see that most of the windows were closed as we passed the houses, denoting the grief of the inmates. Brother Bonhommie was inconsolable, and found it impossible to restrain his tears. One incident must not be forgotten: as we were leaving the wharf, Truesdell made his appearance, followed by a heavy wagon laden with his largest oysters, which he forced upon the fraternity, modestly contenting himself with asking a blessing at the hands of the holy Father. This was bestowed with the grace natural to our reverend head; and the gratified recipient of the blessing went away with a grateful heart. The oysters thus provided served the brotherhood amply at their next solemn supper. Verily the scene was a solemen one, indeed. It witnessed the resignation of our excellent Father. He proceeded the next day, with a party of the brethren, on an excursion into the interior; and, at last advices, was meditating the sublime and beautiful along the glorious precipices of Tallulah. These chronicles have all been taken by the Recording Secretary, from the volume numbered 7, lettered the "Book of the Island," in the archives of the Monastery of the Moon.

THE END.

www.ingramcontent.com/pod-product-compliance
Lightning Source LLC
LaVergne TN
LVHW040756070826
844660LV00025B/1166

* 9 7 8 1 6 1 1 1 7 6 1 8 6 *